P9-DGL-845

DEAR OLD DAD

There was a sound at the window. It wasn't terrifying; it wasn't supernatural. Hell, it wasn't even scary. It was just a polite tap. One-two. Light and restrained. Your friend for the summer, your best pal at school . . . just passing by, you know? It was a rapping rich with familiarity and goodwill. Hey, buddy, whatcha up to?

So I looked up without alarm at the window that hung at the end of my bed. For a split second I forgot that I didn't have any friends since we moved. I didn't know anyone out here and no one lived close enough to be merely passing by.

Except family.

It hung outlined in the window by a scrubbed and shining lunar light. One hand was splayed on the glass with long thin fingers and skin as pale as the moon. A narrow, pointed face grinned at me with a thousand needle teeth and the predatory cheer of a fox in a henhouse. Slanted almond-shaped eyes glowed with sullen reds, scarlet as blood. Tapered ears pressed flat to the skull, and long hair as fine as milkweed shimmered in the air like a corona. The finger tapped again, the nail a metallic ticking against the glass, and a voice spoke. It was a serpent's hiss wrapped around the wet crunch of gargling glass. One word. Just one. It was enough.

"Mine . . ."

NIGHTLIFE

Rob Thurman

A ROC BOOK

ROC

Published by New American Library, a division of
Penguin Group (USA) Inc., 375 Hudson Street,
New York, New York 10014, USA
Penguin Group (Canada), 90 Eglinton Avenue East, Suite 700, Toronto,
Ontario M4P 2Y3, Canada (a division of Pearson Penguin Canada Inc.)
Penguin Books Ltd., 80 Strand, London WC2R 0RL, England
Penguin Ireland, 25 St. Stephen's Green, Dublin 2,
Ireland (a division of Penguin Books Ltd.)
Penguin Group (Australia), 250 Camberwell Road, Camberwell, Victoria 3124,
Australia (a division of Pearson Australia Group Pty. Ltd.)
Penguin Books India Pvt. Ltd., 11 Community Centre, Panchsheel Park,
New Delhi - 110 017, India
Penguin Group (NZ), cnr Airborne and Rosedale Roads, Albany,
Auckland 1310, New Zealand (a division of Pearson New Zealand Ltd.)
Penguin Books (South Africa) (Pty.) Ltd., 24 Sturdee Avenue,
Rosebank, Johannesburg 2196, South Africa

Penguin Books Ltd., Registered Offices:
80 Strand, London WC2R 0RL, England

First published by Roc, an imprint of New American Library,
a division of Penguin Group (USA) Inc.

First Printing, March 2006
10 9 8 7 6 5 4 3 2 1

Copyright © Robyn Thurman, 2006
All rights reserved

ROC REGISTERED TRADEMARK — MARCA REGISTRADA

Printed in the United States of America

Without limiting the rights under copyright reserved above, no part of this
publication may be reproduced, stored in or introduced into a retrieval system,
or transmitted, in any form, or by any means (electronic, mechanical, photo-
copying, recording, or otherwise), without the prior written permission of both
the copyright owner and the above publisher of this book.

PUBLISHER'S NOTE
This is a work of fiction. Names, characters, places, and incidents either are
the product of the author's imagination or are used fictitiously, and any
resemblance to actual persons, living or dead, business establishments, events, or
locales is entirely coincidental.
    The publisher does not have any control over and does not assume any
responsibility for author or third-party Web sites or their content.

If you purchased this book without a cover, you should be aware that this book
is stolen property. It was reported as "unsold and destroyed" to the publisher,
and neither the author nor the publisher has received any payment for this
"stripped book."

The scanning, uploading, and distribution of this book via the Internet or
via any other means without the permission of the publisher is illegal and
punishable by law. Please purchase only authorized electronic editions, and
do not participate in or encourage electronic piracy of copyrighted materials.
Your support of the author's rights is appreciated.

To my mom

ACKNOWLEDGMENTS

I would like to thank several people: first and foremost my amazing editor, Anne Sowards; my long-toiling agent, Wanda Cook; the brilliantly talented art and design team of Chris McGrath and Ray Lundgren; wonderful copyeditor Michèle Alpern; fellow author Mara; webmeisters Beth (also loyal MOTG) and Terry; good pals Mikey and Lynn; the evil twins Shannon and River; and last but not least—the Pack.

People . . . they do the craziest shit.

Yeah, I know. It's not the most elegant observation. But considering I was making it with a knife blade buried in my stomach, kudos to me. Although I had to say that it didn't hurt as much as I would've expected. In fact it didn't hurt at all. It just felt cold . . . cold and numb, like I had a bellyful of ice water.

It was the touch of a much warmer liquid on my fingers that let me know differently. It was blood. My blood. I tightened my hand over the one that held the knife handle. The blood covered both of our hands, his and mine. He had actually done it . . . stabbed me. Not that that was the crazy part. It wasn't, not by a long shot. No, the crazy part, the howling-at-the-moon madness bit was that he had tried so hard to avoid it. But wasn't that my brother all over? Honest, loyal, all but rolling in integrity. Too good for his own good. But, hell, in the end, too good for my good as well.

"Well," I said ruefully. "Look at that." Then my knees buckled and I dropped to them, sliding off the blade as easy as you please. There was the kiss of metal and then only gaping emptiness as I fell. Letting go of his hand,

I covered the wound in my abdomen. It was strange, how the blood was so warm while I felt all but frozen. I looked up into eyes the same color as mine, pale gray as a winter sky. Curling up the side of my mouth, I gave him a half smile. "My mistake. I guess you have the balls after all. Good for you, big brother."

The blade dropped from his hand to clatter on the floor with the metallic, ringing peal of a bell.

"What? No souvenir?" I asked curiously. The words came out slurred and thick, heavy and fading. Like me. Fading and fading fast. A morning mist dissipating in the rising sun. A broken bird plunging from the sky. A scuttling dark thing fleeing the light of day. Shit, I should've been writing some of this down. Dying really brought out the poet in me.

I heard the gate close, a thunderous and oddly final sound that threatened to bring the building down. The walls shook with a peculiar rippling effect that rose from floor to ceiling, and plaster and metal began dropping like rain. If you had to go, might as well go out with a bang. "Better run, Chicken Little. The sky's falling." Fairy-tale words with a predator bite. They weren't deep, not meaningful, but they had teeth. And like any good predator I wanted to go out with the sweet taste of blood in my mouth.

Naturally he didn't run. Heroes don't do that. And apparently neither do brothers. Hands gripped me and I was flung over a shoulder in a fireman's carry before I could even take a swing at him. Of course, that was making the assumption I had enough life left in me to make a fist. As assumptions went, they didn't come much bigger. Then he was running, jolting me up and down. Behind us I could see the monsters boiling in frustration, rushing at where the gate hung, impenetrable. This time it was closed for good and they knew it. To a one every narrow, pointed face turned in our direction, every molten-lava eye seething with bloodlust and a poisonous, black hatred. Like an ocean wave they came after us, a riptide of murderous intent. Monsters, they didn't handle disappointment well. I should know.

I was one.

1

Most kids don't believe in fairy tales very long. Once they hit six or seven they put away "Cinderella" and her shoe fetish, "The Three Little Pigs" with their violation of building codes, "Miss Muffet" and her well-shaped tuffet—all forgotten or discounted. And maybe that's the way it has to be. To survive in the world, you have to give up the fantasies, the make-believe. The only trouble is that it's not all make-believe. Some parts of the fairy tales are all too real, all too true. There might not be a Red Riding Hood, but there is a Big Bad Wolf. No Snow White, but definitely an Evil Queen. No obnoxiously cute blond tots, but a child-eating witch . . . yeah. Oh yeah.

There are monsters among us. There always have been and there always will be. I've known that ever since I can remember, just like I've always known I was one. Well, half of one anyway. And regardless of what inherited nastiness I might have on the inside, on the outside I was all human. In fact Niko had said, and pretty damn frequently, that I had more human qualities than I had good sense. He never hesitated to remind me that no matter how god-awful I thought my problems were, I was still his punk-ass kid brother. If I wanted to beat up on myself, I'd have to go through him first. Niko was such a Boy Scout—albeit one with a lethal turn and a Merit Badge in deadly weapons.

Niko, for all his fascination with sharp, pointy things, didn't have a drop of monster blood in him. Of course his father could barely be classified as human in my book, but technically the man met the definition. Worthless bastard. Niko had been two weeks old when his dear old dad had taken off. He'd seen him no more than three times in his entire life. There were some true parenting skills at work. Three times. Hell, I'd seen my father more than that.

Yeah, I'd seen mine at least once a month. It watched me. There were no father-and-son chats, no invites to see the monster cousins, no interaction of any sort. There was just a shadowed figure lurking in an alley as I passed. Or maybe a silhouette with lithe, sinuous lines and sharp, sharp teeth cast against my window at night. Of course, it wasn't like it was wearing a name tag that said "Dad" on it or leaving me birthday presents topped with a bow tied by unnaturally long, clawed fingers. I had no proof it was my demonic sperm donor, but come on. When your mother is quick to tell you you're a freak, an abomination that should've been aborted on cheap bathroom tile, you have to think . . . why else would this monster be stalking me? Funny, that monster had more interest in me than my mother ever had.

Over the years I got used to it, the shadowing. A couple of times I tried to approach it—out of curiosity, or a morbid death wish, who knew? But it always disappeared, melting into the darkness. Mostly I was relieved. It was one thing to be part monster, another

altogether to embrace that less-than-*Mayflower* heritage. Then when I was fourteen that all changed. After
that, I didn't look for monsters.

I ran from them.

Actually we ran from them, Niko and I. For four
years that felt more like forty, we ran. Ran until it was a
way of life. It wasn't the kind of life Niko deserved. But
did he listen to me when I told him so? Shit. Hardly. My
brother had made a career out of trying to protect me.
Talk about your minimum-wage, no-benefits occupa-
tions.

Sort of like the one I had now, I thought glumly.
Dumping the mop back in the battered bucket, I swirled
it around once in the gray foul-smelling water, then
flopped it back on the scarred wooden floor. You'd be
amazed at how much vomit a barful of drunks could
produce. I was, at first. Now I was just amazed at how
damn long it took to clean it up. It was rather ironic that
the fake ID that aged me up from nineteen to twenty-
one had me cleaning up alcoholic chunks rather than
spewing them myself.

"Cal, I'm heading out. Close up for me?"

I cast a jaundiced look over my shoulder. Good old
"Close up for me" Meredith. You could always put your
faith in her—that is, the faith that she would leave you
high and dry to duck out early. "Yeah. Yeah." I waved
her off. One day I'd tell her to bite me and stick around
to do her job, but I was guessing that day would come
when she was wearing a top that was a little less tight or
a shade less low-cut. "Want me to walk you out?"

"No, the boyfriend's outside." She tugged at my short
ponytail as she headed toward the door. "See you tomorrow." And then she was gone, her long cascading
red hair and curving figure lingering in the air to dazzle
the eye like a fluorescent afterimage. Meredith was all

about a look. She'd sculpted herself with the passion and precision of any artist. I doubt that even she had a clue what her original hair color was—or her original breast size, for that matter. She was a walking, talking advertisement for better living through plastic surgery.

And despite 99 percent of it being artificial, it was a damn good body. Fantasizing about it made the unpleasant chore of mopping up human bodily fluids pass a little faster. I actually didn't mind pulling "close up" duty at the bar. After bartending all night it was kind of nice to be surrounded by nothing but silence and empty space. I was beginning to think working at a bar was ruining my appreciation of a good party. Drunk people were starting to lose their charm; hell, they were even starting to lose their comedic ways. You can watch a wasted guy fall off a barstool and crack his head open only so many times before it's just not funny anymore. Well, not *as* funny anyway.

At the moment the bar was quiet. It was a comforting quiet, the kind that wrapped around you like the thickest of fleecy blankets sold at stores you couldn't even afford to walk through the front door of. It was nice . . . peaceful. It was also dangerous and Niko would kick my ass if ever I didn't recognize that. Being alone, being distracted, that all added up to being a walking, talking target. I was a fugitive, hunted, and not for one minute, one second, could I forget that. Other things I'd forgotten, in a big way, but never that. Putting away the mop, I finished locking up and ended up on the sidewalk about four thirty. Even at that late hour the streets of New York weren't totally empty, but they were sparser . . . for a few hours the road less traveled. With the chill of October already a vicious bite in the air, I zipped up the battered black leather jacket I'd picked up from a street vendor in Chinatown for twenty-five bucks. A knockoff of a knockoff, but all I cared about was that it let me blend in with the night.

Keeping my hand in my pocket and firmly gripping a deadly little present Niko had given me, I walked home. It wasn't too far, about five blocks over to Avenue D. It wasn't the best part of town by any means, but neither were we the best type of people. I kept my eyes open and my senses as sharp as those of any rabbit that smelled the wolf. Although to give myself some credit, I was a rabbit with teeth. Not to mention one helluva kick. This time, however, I made it back with no sign of anything with claws, molten eyes, or a hunger for my blood—a good night in my book. Niko and I lived in an older apartment building, pretty run-down but not a complete slum. Depending on your definition. The front door had been secure at some point in time, I suppose, but now it usually hung ajar by a few inches, the gap-toothed grin of a dirty old man. I took the stairs up, seven stories, grumbling and cursing under my breath. There wasn't an elevator; apparently our landlord considered housing laws not exactly a must-read. Not that it mattered. Even if there were one, it probably wouldn't work and if it did, an elevator was no place to be trapped. A metal box of guaranteed death for someone on the run, Niko had said on occasion. And as my brother had absolutely no talent or inclination for exaggeration, I tended to stay out of elevators. Picturing what might drop through the roof or burrow through the floor wasn't the kind of thought I liked to entertain. Making my way down the hall to our door, I slid the key into the lock and opened the door to a dark room. Finding the roughly aged plastic of the light switch with my fingers, I flipped it on.

Nothing happened.

The lightbulb could be burned out; that's what your average person would think. Not me. Instantly I shrugged out of my jacket; the rustle of the leather would do its best to give me away before I moved an inch. I let it slip to the floor as silently as possible and then slid along the wall, slow step by slow step. The plaster was cool even through my shirt, a light trace of ice against my spine as I listened and listened hard. There was no sound, not the brush of a foot against the floor, not the single sigh of an exhaled breath. But something was there. I didn't need to spend $2.99 a minute on Miss Cleo to know that. I crouched slightly and started a cautious pass with my arm through the pitch-black air before me. Not a good idea.

A grip as unbreakable as any bear trap snared my wrist. It pulled me away from the wall, virtually off my feet. Something hard hit me in the pit of my stomach and I flipped to land forcefully on my back, the air exploding painfully out of my lungs. An iron pressure was applied to my throat and a sibilant voice hissed, "Any last words, dead man?"

I coughed, sucked in a ragged breath, then drawled hoarsely, "You are such an asshole, Niko. You seriously need to invest in a hobby."

"Keeping you alive is my hobby. It certainly doesn't appear to be yours." There was a sharp clap and the lights flared on. Wonderful. We now had clap-on, clap-off technology in our midst. All the better to illuminate my humiliaton.

I scowled and batted in annoyance at the long blond braid that hung down in my face. "I already have the one side of my family out to put me in a box or worse. Is it too much to ask you stop playing Cato?"

"Yes, it is." With an automatic shrug he flipped the

braid back over his shoulder and stood. "And Inspector Clouseau would certainly be a better student than you." Holding out a hand to me, he asked pointedly, "And where exactly is that knife I gave you?"

I took the hand and let him pull me to my feet. "In my jacket pocket." Gray eyes shifted to the puddle of leather by the door, and pale eyebrows rose skyward in silent but potent disapproval. "Yeah, well, at least with it over there I'm not tempted to make like a Cuisinart all over your scrawny ass."

"Quite the threat," he said dryly. "I'm sure you are the terror of Girl Scouts everywhere." He brushed the dust from his black turtleneck and pants with a fastidious hand. "Lock the door, Cal. Let's not make it any easier for the Grendels than we have to."

Names were funny things. They meant things . . . no matter how much you might deny it, no matter how much you might want to believe they were chosen at a whim. Niko had come up with the name "Grendels." It wasn't enough he was a blond Bruce Lee, but he was smart as hell too. One reading of *Beowulf* in the sixth grade and he'd labeled my stalkers Grendels. I'd been only in the first grade myself, five years younger than Niko, so it hadn't meant much to me at the time. But Grendels they became; after all, monsters were monsters.

Of course now I was just three years younger than my butt-kicking big brother. Wasn't that a trick?

"Caliban" was a helluva name too. Nice label to put on a kid, right? Mom might have lived in a dark, cramped one-room apartment over a tattoo parlor. She might've told fortunes for a living, ripping off the naive, the desperate, the flat-out stupid. And she might have been as quick with a slap as she was to tilt a bottle of cheap wine. But one thing you could give her credit for, she knew her Shakespeare. *The Tempest*'s Caliban, born of a witch and a demon. Half monster . . . a slouching nightmare of a creature tainting everything he touched.

Gee, thanks, Mom. You really knew how to make a boy feel special.

I locked the door and headed toward our bathroom, saying with a grin, "What're you still doing up? You know all good little ninjas should be in bed, visions of homicidal sugarplums dancing in their heads."

With a grunt of resignation Niko retrieved my jacket from the floor. It hung from the point of one of his many, many blades until he draped it over the back of our battered sofa. "They're not *completely* homicidal." His lips twitched with amusement. He followed me down the tiny hall, leaned with casual grace against the wall, and folded his arms. "And I had a last-minute scheduling for bodyguard duty. An off-off-off-Broadway actress who imagines herself the target of a literal army of sex-crazed stalkers. It was exhausting."

"I'll bet." I gave him a mock leer as I leaned over the bathroom sink. As I pulled the rubber band free from my hair, the ruler-straight black strands fell forward against my face. Squeezing a generous dollop of tooth-paste on my brush, I went to work, scrubbing and spit-ting. Niko had a casual business relationship with an agency that provided bodyguards and security around the city. Actually, the agency was one guy with a lot of contacts, some of which were even almost legal. But it was fair money and the pay was strictly under-the-table. No taxes. No government. No trail for the Grendels. Not that I pictured a Grendel in a bow tie and spectacles climbing that corporate ladder or waiting on his retire-ment. Still, Grendels weren't above using humans, and most humans weren't above being used.

Niko watched me silently as I finished up, rinsing my mouth and then pulling off my shirt. I slid him a glance, a little worried. "Okay, what?" When you've known someone all your life you don't need a neon sign to know when something is wrong. A faint shadow in his eyes, a slight flattening of his mouth—something was bugging Niko.

He hesitated, then said quietly, "I saw one today."

Four words. That's all it took to have the ground disintegrating under my feet. Just four goddamn words. I wadded up my shirt with suddenly clumsy fingers. "Oh." Articulate as always. Flipping the lid down on the toilet, I sat, tossed the shirt into the sink, and started to untie my sneakers.

Niko moved closer, a solidly reassuring presence in the doorway. "It was in the park. I was doing my evening run."

"The park," I repeated emotionlessly. "Makes sense." Grendels, as far as we could tell, didn't much care for cities; they seemed to be more prevalent in rural areas, the woods, the creeks, the silent and sullen hills. But New York was one damn big place. Of all the cities we'd run to, this was the one where we were bound to come across the occasional monster, Grendel, vampire, ghoul, boggle . . . whatever. One Grendel in Central Park should not a crapfest in your pants make, right? Right? "So we stay or go?"

He knocked ruminatively on the sink. Once, twice. "I think that perhaps we should stay, at least unless we spot more. It's unlikely this one had anything to do with us."

"Had?" I dragged a hand through my hair and fixed him with a suspicious look. "I'm no English major, Nik, but that sounds like the past tense to me."

"It rather does, doesn't it?" he agreed mildly. Retrieving my shirt from the sink, he handed it to me. "Go to bed. I'll take first watch."

We were back to that, then. We'd done it almost religiously for the first year after I had come back from . . . wherever. But after a while we'd reverted to a more casual routine, and thank God for that. I'd been perpetually sleep deprived that entire year. And I loved to sleep. That's the definition of a teenager, isn't it? A coma with two legs and an endless appetite. Certainly being deprived of my God-given right to ten hours a night made me cranky.

I grimaced, then nodded. "Okay. Wake me in four." Hitting my mattress hard, I rolled up in the blanket and dropped off instantly, a skill I'd never had to learn. I could sleep anytime and anywhere. It was a good talent to have when you spent your life dodging monsters. Snatching minutes here and there was sometimes the best you could hope for.

On the other hand sleep meant dreams, and dreams meant nightmares. Or memories. As far as I could tell the two were interchangeable. I had some sheet rippers, no doubt, and I was betting Niko did too. Of course he would claim he didn't, that his disciplined mind was too well trained for such subconscious antics. Begone nasty boogeymen; I, Niko the Magnificent, have spoken. Nik did have a way of making even utter bullshit seem noble.

Yeah, I definitely took regular tours through nightmare city, and so far I hadn't figured a way to fool anyone about that . . . including myself. It was always the same, the dream. Maybe that should have given me some warning; even asleep I should've had a chance to prepare . . . to brace myself. Never happened. It started on the same note too, with the same feel, the same sweet taste of something bright and hopeful.

Wasn't that a bitch?

I woke up before my four hours were up. Catapulted

out of sleep with a pounding heart and a sweat that would've done a malaria victim proud, I swallowed the taste of bile and gripped handfuls of the blanket as if it were the only thing keeping me from plummeting into the abyss. Swinging my legs over the side of the bed, I grabbed at the lamp and found it with practiced ease. Light bloomed in the room, but some shadows remained. Right then even one was too many. I lurched to my feet and hit the wall switch. Every time we spotted a Grendel. Every goddamn time.

In the dream I was fourteen again. A punk-ass kid, but no worse than any other kid, I guess. I drank some. Shoplifted a few times. Skipped school once or twice. Usual shit. I didn't fight, though. Ever. You think you got it bad? Joe Junior whose daddy is an alcoholic? Well, screw your dependency gene. Try carrying a bucketful of monster DNA. While you were worried about having a tendency to have a beer glued to your hand, I was more concerned with pulling out the still-beating heart of the obnoxious asshole who sat in front of me in homeroom. It hadn't happened yet, but you never knew. *I* never knew. It was always there, the potential, whether I saw signs of it or not. I couldn't let myself doubt that. I wouldn't let myself doubt it.

That day was different, though. A good day. Hell, a great day. Niko had found a good job and a place of his own, and we were moving out. Moving on. Niko was in his first year of state college; he'd gotten a full scholarship. He could've done better, a lot better. But he'd wanted to stay close to home. Close to me, the demonic albatross around his neck. That was a thought I kept to myself. I liked my ass enough to want to keep it in one piece, and Niko would have been all too happy to put a boot up it if he even suspected what I was thinking. But, hell, it was only what Mom told me time and time again. And if anyone should know demons, it'd be her.

After all, she had screwed one.

She wouldn't be sorry to see me go, my mom, Sophia Leandros. She wasn't precisely overflowing with maternal instincts, even for her human son. It was like those TV specials about animals born and raised in captivity. The mothers had never seen babies born, had never had babies of their own, and had no idea what to do with them once they did. They'd give the mewling wet little creatures a disgusted sniff and a wary and disbelieving look, and off they'd go without a backward glance. Sometimes I imagine good old Mom made it to the bar across the street before the nurse even finished toweling the birth blood off me. The same went for Niko. She might have found him more acceptable, being human and all, but she didn't shower him with love and affection either . . . just a little less revulsion.

So, as they say, I was more than ready to shake the dust off my shoes. More than ready to get away from dark, dark hills and shadowy trees that could hide a thousand things. Grendels hadn't ever bothered us over the years; they'd just watched. But it was better in town; there you saw only a few once in a while. In fact it used to be only the one—Daddy dearest, I'd been betting— but over time that had changed. Dad had started bringing friends with him when he showed up to watch me. But out here in the country I saw Grendels almost every day. Sometimes, after the sun went down, there were as many rapt red eyes floating in the twilight as there were fireflies. It was . . . shit . . . creepy as hell. No matter that I'd seen them all my life. One or two were bad enough. More than you could count was enough to make the air freeze and fracture in your lungs.

Yeah, the city had been better, but Sophia had lost her lease after running off most of her regular clients through boozing. She'd also racked up a few debts that made a relocation to the country suddenly seem desirable. And off we went to live the good life, the good life being a battered, rusting metal trailer squatting on a piece of land far from the nearest neighbors. I didn't know who owned the land or the trailer. I'm not even sure Sophia knew. But she'd found it with a sixth sense honed by years of scrounging, conning, and outright stealing. We'd been in the tin Taj Mahal now for almost two months. I was lucky it was summer because I had no idea where the nearest high school was and even if I had known, there wasn't much chance a bus came out this way.

But today was the final day in the boonies. I was packing up the last of my shit in the best luggage garbage bag companies made when Niko shifted weight on my worn mattress and grimaced. "You can't want to bring that, Cal, honestly."

"Caliban," I corrected automatically. I'd decided recently that I didn't want to be called Cal anymore. "Caliban" meant monster, and that's what I was. I had no intention of forgetting that, not for one minute. Looking down at the sweatshirt wadded in my hand, I demanded, aggrieved, "Why not? It's my favorite one. I wear it all the time."

He let the name issue go for the moment. But I wasn't under any illusions that he'd give up. He'd give me some space and if that didn't bring me around, he'd jump on me when I least expected it. I was never going to be the poster child for mental health, but Niko wasn't about to accept that. Returning to the sweatshirt topic, he leaned over and poked a finger through a hole in the shoulder of the shirt. "Yes, I noticed that. It looks to have been almost favored to death. Not to mention the color."

"Purple? What have you got against purple?" I shoved the shirt into the bag and gave him a warning look. Love me, love my shirt.

"Only everything in the world, and that particular shade barely qualifies as a color. It's more a visual assault."

I grinned. "College boy with his big fancy words." I began to tie off the bag when the sound of shattering glass came from outside the tiny bedroom. "Mom's up," I said, matter-of-fact.

"I didn't think there was anything breakable left in this forsaken pit." A hand landed on my shoulder, a steady and comforting grip. For the first time in a while I didn't grumble or try to shake him off like any self-respecting, full-of-himself fourteen-year-old who knew he was too old to be treated like a baby. I simply soaked up the warmth that sank through my shirt.

"Probably just a plate. Breaking's easier than washing, right?" I pulled another garbage bag out of the box. The hand moved to my hair and mussed it without mercy.

"Considering the way you wash them, it's probably more sanitary at any rate." He stood and moved past me to the bedroom door. "Once more into the breach," he exhaled ruefully. "Keep packing. We'll be leaving in an hour or so."

And then we'd give the phrase "Don't look back" a run for its money. As I finished up with my things, I could hear Niko's quiet, calm voice and Sophia's slurred one coming from the kitchen. To be more exact, I heard every word spoken. Hell, the kitchen was barely twelve feet away; I didn't have much choice. "You two still here?" came the uninterested voice. Once it had been a smoky blue velvet; now it was a threadbare polyester, raveled around the edges and stained with cheap whiskey. I thought it had been one of the reasons she'd been such a successful fortune-teller. People paid not so much for what she said, but more for *how* she said it. Even the most stupid and inane "You'll meet a tall, dark stranger" sounded seductive and mysterious when Sophia Leandros said it. Or it had once upon a time.

I had her voice. I also had her inky black hair and slate gray eyes. No olive-tinted skin, though. I was pale, Grendel pale. Mom had looked at me once when I was younger, about eight. It was a strange look, one of repugnance mixed with a reluctant pride. "You're a monster, but you're a beautiful one," she had said. Great, I was an evil, squatting *thing* wrapped in shiny silver Christmas paper. Even at eight I hadn't thought that was much of a compliment.

As I gathered up a few musty, used paperbacks, Niko's voice drifted into the room. "We're leaving as soon as we get Cal's things loaded into the car. It shouldn't be long." There was a pause and then he added without any real enthusiasm, "Will you be all right?"

There was a humorless laugh and the clink of ice in a glass. "Without you and the demon spawn? Shit, sweetheart, things could only get better."

And just like that, before I even knew it, I was standing in the narrow doorway, my eyes on my mother . . . a fine upstanding woman whose reproductive system should've been removed at birth. She sat at the lopsided rickety table with her hand curled around a glass. Black hair untouched by silver spilled past her shoulders and onto a red silk robe that had seen better days, better years even. Eyes as polished and cold as steel studied Niko as she half emptied the glass in two swallows. "Where's my money?"

I watched as Niko silently pulled a wad of bills out of his pocket and laid it on the table. He'd been giving money to Sophia since his first job at fourteen. I'd have been expected to do the same, but out here there were no jobs and since I was too young to drive, there was no way to get to them if there had been any. She scooped up the cash and counted it with nimble fingers. "Keep it coming, puss, or our nosy little monster comes back home with me. We all clear on that?" Her gaze pinned me in the doorway for a moment, and then I melted back into the gloom of the bedroom.

I'd wondered why Niko hadn't stopped giving her most of his paycheck when he'd moved off to college and the dorm. But it was as I'd suspected. Sophia had us both over a barrel. I was only fourteen. She didn't have to let me go live with my brother, and the law would see it the same way. How the hell Niko would manage to pay for an apartment while giving her practically all his money, I didn't have a clue. Even with me getting a job there and helping out, it'd be tight. Real tight. But the dorm room . . . it had been part and parcel of the scholarship. No rent there. No younger brothers either.

Sitting on the bed, the mattress bowing beneath me, I took a good look at my pile of "luggage." Suddenly every bag looked like a chain, a heavy one made exclusively to drag my brother down. He'd end up quitting school to get a second job. He'd have to. He was smart as friggin' hell but there were only so many hours in the day.

Only so many chances in a lifetime.

I pulled the nearest bag to me and began to untie the knot at the top. A hand looped around my wrist and squeezed tight enough to make me turn loose of the plastic. "Don't even think about it or I'll put your things up front and stuff *you* in the trunk," came the unruffled voice.

Niko. And he was *pissed*. Niko kept his anger under rigid control and most people wouldn't have even known it was there, but I knew. I could smell it every time. And not once, in all my life, could I remember it ever being directed at me. Neither was it now.

"You are not staying here. Not for any reason." Eyes uncompromising on mine, he released me and retied the bag. "It will be all right, Cal. We'll do just fine. I promise you."

I wasn't too sure I bought that, but I did know one thing. Niko wasn't leaving me. For a year I'd made do with seeing him on the weekends, escaping Sophia only then. For a year we'd planned and saved. But the year was over and now, maybe, we would survive. Maybe it just took a little faith. And if I was short on that, it could be Niko might have enough for us both.

"Yeah?" I said with less skepticism than I was shooting for.

It didn't matter. Niko would've seen through it anyway. "Yeah," he repeated, the side of his mouth curling up faintly. "Of course, just fine means doing your homework, keeping our place clean and neat, helping little old ladies across the street, obeying my every sensible word . . ." There was more, but it was lost in the pillow I used to whack him in the face.

That was when the dream always took a turn for the worse.

It started with the car. It wouldn't start. Did that suck? Yes, it surely did. Was I surprised? Hell, no. That was life. You know that saying, right? "When life hands you lemons . . ." Well, when it does you might as well shove 'em where the sun doesn't shine, because you're sure as hell never going to see any lemonade.

Niko worked on the car for almost four hours before he finally got the cranky engine to turn over. Slamming the hood down, he motioned for me to switch the engine off. Walking back to the window, he wiped his hands on a rag that had once been an old shirt of mine. "I think we'd better spend the night and leave in the morning," he said reluctantly. "It's running, but I would hate to break down halfway there at midnight. A long walk doesn't begin to cover it."

I scowled and thumped the steering wheel with the heel of my hand. "Piece of crap," I muttered, sliding down in the seat a few inches.

"Yes, well, two hundred and fifty dollars doesn't buy what it used to," Niko commented wryly. "I should've driven the Jag instead."

So we were biding our time until the morning. It shouldn't have mattered; after all it was just one more night. But getting out of Niko's beat-up car and walking back into the trailer . . . it wasn't the best moment I'd ever had. It was like drowning and then being pulled onto the boat only to get booted off the other side. In other words, it sucked.

Still, I tried to keep it in perspective. One night, just one out of my entire life, it didn't amount to much. I tried repeating that to myself a few times while I was brushing my teeth in the tiny, cramped bathroom. I left the lights off. Our electricity had been cut off so many times, I'd gotten used to doing most things in the dark. As I bent down to rinse my mouth with water from my cupped hand, I thought I saw something in the mirror. Something behind me, a shadow against the shadows. "Nik?" I turned, but there was nothing but a wadded towel hanging over the rack. The wrath of the evil terry cloth . . . boogety, boogety. I snorted at myself and headed to bed. I lay on the field of lumps masquerading mattress and tried to doze off without success. prise. Eventually, too wired at the prospect

I rolled over, pounded the pillow a few times, and gave up on sleep for a while. I could hear Niko's slow, even breathing from the next room, where he was asleep on the couch. Laid-back to the point of coma—that was my brother. I was giving serious thought to getting a bowl of warm water and seeing if the legends were true, when another legend reared its ugly head. A darker legend, one that had shadowed me all my life.

It looked like its shadowing days were over.

There was a sound at the window. It wasn't terrifying; it wasn't supernatural. Hell, it wasn't even scary. It was just a polite tap. One-two. Light and restrained. Your friend for the summer, your best pal from school . . . just passing by, you know? Maybe you wanted to sneak out and smoke a cigarette or watch the stars. It was a rapping rich with familiarity and goodwill. Hey, buddy, whatcha up to?

So I looked up without alarm at the window that hung at the head of my bed. For a split second I forgot that I didn't have any friends since we'd moved. I didn't know anyone out here and no one lived close enough to be merely passing by.

Nobody but family.

The Grendel hung outlined in the window by a scrubbed and shining lunar light. One hand was splayed on the glass with long thin fingers and skin as pale as the moon. A narrow, pointed face grinned at me with a thousand needle teeth and the predatory cheer of a fox in a he   e. Slanted almond-shaped eyes glowed with
                  arlet as blood. Tapered ears pressed flat to
                  long hair as fine as milkweed shimmered
                  corona. The finger tapped again, the nail
                  g against the glass, and a voice spoke. It
                  iss wrapped around the wet crunch of
                  word. Just one. It was enough.

"Mine."

The roiling-lava eyes looked down at me with more pride than I'd ever seen in my mother's. Or maybe it wasn't pride so much as rabid avarice. I'd seen Grendels before, more times than I could count, but never like this. Never so close I could see the naked greed in the eyes, the poreless texture of the skin, hear the utterly alien whisper.

Jesus Christ, my mom had fucked that?

I tried to swallow, but the saliva pooled in my mouth as all my muscles gave up the ghost and turned instantly to overcooked spaghetti. My eyes were locked to the ones staring at me through the window as air stuttered in and out of my lungs. Breathing was pretty much all I was up for and even that was shaky. The Grendel tilted its head and rasped again, "Mine." Gloating and complacent.

And still I couldn't move. This thing, this monster, was claiming me as its own and I couldn't move a muscle, not a goddamn finger. That is, not until a pallid hand burst through the glass and wrapped around my neck. Sharp nails sank into my flesh, fastening tight like barbed hooks. That was when I rediscovered movement in a big way. Yelling bloody murder, I threw myself back desperately. Flowing like water over the jagged broken glass in the window frame, the Grendel followed suit. It landed hard on my chest with a weight that belied its slender frame. It easily weighed as much as I did. Tiny slits flared a bare inch from my face as it inhaled deeply. It was sampling my scent, *smelling* me.

"Blood of my blood. Flesh of my flesh. Breath of my breath." I felt the warm trickle of liquid on my neck as the shredding smile moved to my ear and murmured, "Time to go home."

I didn't yell this time. I screamed. It was with pure,

wordless terror as I tore at the hand at my throat and raised my knee up to push the Grendel away. I didn't budge it, not an inch. In fact its other hand snared my leg, and it felt like a bear trap. Suddenly, I was lifted into the air and then I was flying through it. I went through what was left of the window, glass and metal slashing at me. Hitting the ground hard, I felt the smothering sensation of the air being forced from my lungs by the blow. I gasped, trying to suck in a breath, as I managed to roll over on my back. The stars were out, dancing a duet with the brilliant moon. For a moment I lost myself in it, my thoughts slow and thick as molasses.

Then I heard Niko call my name. His normally calm voice had knotted into a barbwire ball of anguish and fury. That cut through the fuzziness like a knife, and I managed to get my hands under me to push up to a half-reclining position. The world spun lazily, but I could still see the trailer. Yeah, I could still see and I would've given anything at the moment to have been blind.

She stood in the doorway, Sophia . . . my mother. For one second, one moment outside time, she was as coldly beautiful as she'd always been. And then she was a bonfire. Her nightgown burned on her, a leaping red-and-yellow silk. Her flesh began to melt and blacken as her hair ignited in a glowing aurora. I think she was screaming or maybe I was. Then she disappeared, falling back into the raging inferno of the trailer. The screams remained; they must have been mine. Sophia was gone, but Niko . . . Niko, I didn't see. I couldn't see him, and I couldn't hear him anymore.

I tore at the grass and dirt under me and managed to flip over onto my knees. I couldn't walk, but I could crawl. And I did. I'd gone barely a few feet when hands on my arms and legs and in my hair jerked me back. Grendels, they were everywhere, on me, loping away

from the burning trailer, ripping a hole in the velvety
night. I kicked and swung my fists at the ones holding
me back from the trailer; I yelled for Niko until my
voice cracked. Beside me two Grendels had done something to the air itself. It had split longways, a ribbon of
pulsating, corpse-gray light. It widened, stretched, and
elongated until the night itself had a ragged hole in it. I
was still screaming Niko's name as they dragged me
towards it. Screaming his name even though I knew he
was dead. Knew my brother, the only one who'd ever
loved me, ever gave a shit about me, was gone. He'd
died not only for me, but also *because* of me.

I gave up. There was no reason not to. I'd tried; I
couldn't fight them. I couldn't get away. And now . . .
now I didn't even want to. "My blood," came the crooning at my ear as I was pulled along. "My spawn. Mine."
Skin as cold as bone pressed against my cheek as nails
sank deeper into my arms. It wasn't a hole after all. It
was a door, a door to hell.

Daddy, true to his word, took me home through it.

It was a dream maybe, but not just a dream. It had
happened, all of it. Fortunately, or unfortunately, depending on your view, I didn't remember what had followed my being dragged through the gate. Niko had had
to fill me in later.

He hadn't died. That was a big one in my book, no
matter how he glossed over it. The biggest. He'd managed to get out a window in the back of the trailer. He'd
had some burns and some cuts from the glass, but he'd
survived. He'd come running around the blazing trailer
just in time to see me disappear in the midst of monsters. The rip had closed behind the Grendels and me,
leaving Niko alone. I was gone; Sophia was dead. It was
just Niko and what ended up as a smoldering pile of
melted plastic and metal. He didn't leave, though. Didn't

get in his car and drive away. Didn't cut his losses and realize there wasn't a damn thing he could do to help Mom or me. He stayed. God knows why. But he stayed, all alone. No firemen came, no police. I guess we'd lived so far out no one even spotted the fire.

Niko had sat on the grass where I'd vanished and he waited. For two days he watched and sat vigil. He didn't give up on me. He never had, not from day one. So I guess it was no surprise he waited.

The surprise was that I actually came back.

On the second night in the same place at almost the same time, I came spilling out of the darkness. Limp and naked, I fell onto the grass, a panting, snarling mess. I'd growled like a rabid wolf when Niko dropped to his knees beside me. I might've taken a chunk out of his arm if I hadn't struggled past layers of confusion and a smothering blanket of disorientation. But in the end I'd recognized him. It took me only seconds even as whacked-out as I was. Took Niko a while longer to return the favor. It'd been only two days for him.

For me it had been two years.

That'd been our best guess, of course. Wherever I'd been, wherever the Grendels had taken me, time was apparently out to lunch. I'd dropped back into the world obviously older. My hair, once short, had grown to my shoulders; I was taller by inches, my shoulders broader. I was even going to bat with a little more wood than before. So there was one nice side effect to taking a time-bending trip through amnesia hell.

But I didn't remember a single moment after having been shanghaied through the gate with the Grendels. Nothing. That time was a darkness so deep and vast that I was hard put to even *know* it was there. If I hadn't been so physically changed, I would've sworn

I hadn't been gone at all. It was a memory loss so pervasive that I could barely recognize its presence.

If I was having some problems, it was ten times worse for Niko. He'd lost his mother and brother in one fell swoop. Yeah, okay, Sophia hadn't been pulling down any mother-of-the-year awards. God knows, we'd been more than happy to move out and leave her far behind. But hoping you never saw someone again is a damn sight different from wishing them dead. There are easy ways and hard ways to go; burning to death is in a category all its own. Then I come back, an amnesiac, howling loony who has no idea he's been gone for any time, two days or two years. Not a fun time for my brother. But he'd bucked up, sucked it up, and gone on. He'd put me in some of his spare sweats that he'd had in the trunk of his car. None of my clothes, which had already been packed into the backseat, fit anymore. After I dressed with clumsy, shaking motions, he checked me over. Pushing up the sleeves on my borrowed sweatshirt, he'd looked at my arms with a fixed gaze.

"I saw blood," he had said quietly. "When they took you. I saw blood on your arms, your neck." With a finger he'd touched the scars on my arm and then the ones on my neck. The puncture wounds were ugly, but long healed. "Jesus, Cal, it really is you."

Pulled into a crushing hug, I'd corrected numbly, "Caliban." Even Niko couldn't deny I was a monster now, right?

"Cal, anything wrong?"

Wrong. Even after four years of running from Grendels, Niko had never once called me Caliban. Never once given in to my darkest interpretation of self. Damn Pollyanna. I stood in the doorway, stood in the welcome light, and watched as Niko materialized out of the darkness in the hall. "Four hours?" I shrugged. "Who could sleep that long? Go on to bed. I'm up for good." I punched him lightly in the arm and grinned wearily. "Keep the snoring to a minimum, Cyrano. Can't hear the bad guys if you drown them out."

Niko had the nose of a Roman general. His profile was classic and clean and women always had a spare look or three for my brother, but I wasn't about to ever admit that. Instead I came up with lots of interesting names for him ("Cyrano" being the least offensive), and he loved each and every one of them—if love could be expressed as a smack on the back of the head.

This time he let it go, and he let my obvious nighttime lie go too. He knew as well as I what prompted it. Heading for his quarter-bouncing, hospital-cornered, anal-retentively made bed, he stripped down and climbed under the covers. I didn't comment on the large knife he slid under the pillow. We all have our security blankets in this world. Some are just sharper than others.

2

When morning finally dragged its tired ass in, I was making breakfast. My watch had passed without incident. It'd been just me, an exceptionally bright apartment, and a lingering nightmare.

"I'll take soy waffles with fresh fruit." Niko, already dressed, stepped out of the hall as he pulled his hair back into a ponytail that hung nearly to his waist. "And some freshly squeezed orange juice, if you please."

"Scrambled eggs and beer it is," I said matter-of-factly. "I guess it's my turn to make a grocery run, huh?"

"You could say that." Niko set the table with two plates, forks, and glasses. He also retrieved the ketchup from the fridge for me. "In fact you could say that for every week for the past two months." He raised his eyebrows mockingly. "Not that I'm counting of course."

"Uh-huh," I commented skeptically. Moving over to the table, I ladled out the eggs between the two plates. Dumping the frying pan into the sink, I pulled a chair out, turned it backward, and straddled it. A nice healthy squirt of ketchup on the puffy yellow eggs and I was good to go. A glass of frothy white milk was placed firmly in front of me. Narrowing my eyes, I mumbled around a mouthful, "That doesn't look like a Bud, Nik."

"Just think of it as white beer from a bovine keg. Maybe that will help." Niko sat and began to eat his eggs and drink his own glass of cow juice. After swallowing, he clinked his fork lightly against the plate. "I was thinking that after we eat we might go to Central Park and talk with Boggle, ask him about the Grendel."

"Boggy?" I brightened and curled up the corner of my mouth with savage cheer. "Just talk? Couldn't we kick some muddy ass too? Doesn't hurt to stay in practice." I might not be the deadly, precision fighter that Niko was, but I could hold my own. Long gone were the days when I'd avoided fighting, afraid it would bring out the monster half of me. After the Grendels had taken me years ago I had finally figured it out. You can't bring out something that's already snarling in the forefront.

Niko gave me a faintly reproving look. "As long as he's still only eating muggers there's no need to complicate matters." As I groaned in disappointment, he added casually, "Unless, of course, he doesn't cooperate with us."

"Here's hoping." I saluted him with the glass of milk.

Yeah, monsters were everywhere. Considering the world we lived in, that wasn't all that surprising. But it was astounding that most people didn't have a frigging clue. The monsters were there for anyone who just opened his eyes and looked. But ignorance is bliss and there were billions of blissful people in this world. Regardless, it was mind-blowing to be on the street and see a ghoul slinking along in the shadows or a werewolf cheerfully ignoring the curb law and absolutely no one noticing. Once I saw a grinning lupine half again bigger than any wolf on Animal Planet trotting down the sidewalk and checking out the nightlife. And nobody thought

that was somewhat out of the ordinary? I even saw one
pudgy animal lover chasing after it to check it for an ID
tag. Maybe stupidity was a demon all its own.

In the park the chill of last night's air had mellowed
to a brisk autumn cool. Niko and I jogged along a path
for nearly twenty minutes before cutting through the
woods to a more secluded area—a grassy, marshy spot
where thick pale brown sludge coagulated into a mudhole only a pig could love. Or a boggle.

I leaned against a tree, folded my arms, and whistled
two notes. "Ding-dong, Boggy. You've got visitors. Rise
and shine." The mud remained placid and unmoving.
There was the sound of metal being unsheathed as Niko
wordlessly drew a short wide blade the length of his
forearm. He kept the sheath strapped between his shoulder blades under his clothing. "See, Boggy?" I drawled.
"You've made Niko cranky. That's not a nice thing to
do. Not especially smart either." Moving away from the
tree, I stepped to the edge of the slime and crouched
down, arms resting on my upper legs. "I know you're
there, Bog. I can *smell* you. I'm like my dad that way."

Two softball-sized yellow orange eyes blinked lazily
from the mud. A deep voice rumbled and gurgled
sluggishly. "You're an asshole that way too. Ain't that
a coincidence?"

I had no idea how long boggles lived, but I was betting it was a damn long time. This piece of land had been
Bog's home long before it'd been called Central Park. I
guess that's how he'd picked up his New Yawk accent—
from the various joggers, in-line skaters, and mugger
lunchables. Rocking back on my heels, I snorted. "No
genetics involved there. I'm an asshole in my own right.
Don't ever doubt that."

The mud boiled and cascaded off massive shoulders
as Boggle lurched upward. "Shit. When you bust my

balls every time I turn around? Not friggin' likely." Upright he stood over eight feet, a massive hulking figure covered in oozing brown liquid and encrusted with petrified mud. Neckless, his head melted into his shoulders. His lipless mouth was full of large serrated teeth that angled backward like that of a shark. Each platter-sized hand was equipped with two fingers, a thumb, and thick black claws that stabbed outward to the length of nearly ten inches. Quite the specimen, our Boggy. A delicate dewdrop. A hothouse flower. A giant litter box come to horrific, murderous life. "What the hell do you bums want now?"

"A little polite conversation." Niko tapped the blade against his knee. "You wouldn't have a problem indulging us in that, now, would you?"

Soulless eyes, as empty of anger as they were of empathy, considered the bright glitter of the steel in Niko's hand for a long moment. Then the sloping shoulders shrugged indifferently. "Shoot the breeze. Yeah, living for that. So, whatta you want to know?"

"A Grendel," I volunteered. "It was hanging around the park yesterday." Tossing a glance in Niko's direction, I amended, "For a while anyway. We're curious to know why."

"Maybe you should've asked it before you chopped off its head," Boggle grunted. "Might've been easier."

Niko's upper lip lifted a bare millimeter to reveal a microscopic slice of even white teeth. "Not quite as entertaining, however."

Yeah, Niko talked a good show. Tough as nails, cold as ice. But no matter the face Niko put on it, he'd done it for one reason and one only. No Grendel was getting near me ever again. Taking chances was not a big part of my brother's philosophy. "Did you really cut its head off?" I asked curiously.

Touching the pad of a thumb to the blade's razor edge, he shook his head. "And dull the artistry of this on bone? I think not." Without missing a beat, he went on. "What was it doing here, Boggle? Merely passing through or was it something more sinister?"

"Sinister." A rough, gargling laugh had flecks of mud flying through the air. "You got to be shitting me." Spitting a mouthful of slime, he rumbled on, "No matter what the little shit was up to, it's gonna be depraved and misbegotten. You oughta know that. That's just the way elves are."

We hadn't known what Grendels were, all those years. Even after they'd made off with me, we still hadn't known. To me they were just monsters, demons, and I really didn't care to know any more than that. Niko was different, of course. He had a tireless mind that never ceased looking for the whys and wherefores. All our lives he'd wanted to know. He'd gone to library after library, he'd studied mythology and demonology until it was coming out of his ears, but he'd never been able to pin them down. It wasn't until we ran into Boggle that we'd been "enlightened."

Elves. Grendels were elves. Maybe you thought elves had delicate features, long golden hair, mystical blue green eyes. Maybe you thought they glided along draped in filmy garments that sparkled with semiprecious gems, and rode on ethereal white horses. Could be you were more modern than that, though. Could be you pictured elves living urban lives. Dressing in leather, riding motorcycles, and hiding their pointed ears under helmets. That'd be just as good a fantasy, right? Because elves were good, well . . . not *all* elves. There was the occasional bad magical apple, to add drama. But as a rule elves were good, and elves were cool. Every D&D-playing geek drooling to be one would tell you so.

So how did history get elves from the red-eyed demons that had spawned me? Shit, who knew? How did sailors get mermaids from manatees? Manatees were great animals, sure, but alabaster breasts, sexy scaled tails, pouty lips? Not hardly.

I never changed my way of thinking with this new info. Grendels were Grendels—no need to muddy the waters. It was kind of hard to wrap my mind around thinking of my childhood monsters as mincing fashion plates called Shealendil or Beoric the Beauteous. Hell, Grendels didn't even wear clothes, much less enough silk and lace to keep Lady Marmalade styling for years.

"So, is 'depraved and misbegotten' just a generalization or actual solid knowledge?" Niko asked evenly as he moved closer, the grass under his shoes fading into bare dirt.

"Just talk. The lay of the land, that's all." Talons scratched idly at rough, scaling skin. "Ain't seen any elf. I got no idea what one would be doing around here. Not their territory. They're not urban like me. The little shit was probably just passing through."

He said it dismissively enough that I believed him. Bog was obviously bored, not trying to put anything over on us. He hadn't seen the Grendel, and had no idea one way or the other what it'd been up to. So Niko and I left him to his mud and mugger munching and finished up our run with me grumbling the entire way. Niko ignored my bitching and in fact picked up the pace. When you were on the run, you needed to be able to actually *run,* he was fond of saying.

We stopped for lunch, since we were seriously destitute of all the four food groups at home. I was for burgers. Niko was set on something healthy and utterly lacking in anything that might pass for flavor. So we compromised and hit a hole-in-the-wall pizza place and ordered the vegetarian special. It was still pizza and covered in cheese so I could choke it down, and Niko could graze on the rabbit food toppings to his heart's content. Sitting with his back securely to the wall, Niko kept an eye on mine. I, on the other hand, was keeping an eye on my glass. "I think there's a bug in my Coke."

Niko leaned forward for a look and nodded thoughtfully. "It does look that way." Settling back, he pointed out, "It is protein. Probably would be quite nutritional. You should give it a chance." Snorting, I wavered between fishing my new friend out with a spoon or sending the Coke back. Decisions. Decisions.

Unsympathetic to my dilemma, my brother went to work on the fresh-from-the-oven pizza on the table between us. Pushing my glass away, I decided to let nature take its course. Sink or swim. Survival of the fittest. Ladling a piece of pizza onto the thick white plate in front of me, I yelped and blew on singed fingers. Looking down his not inconsiderable nose, Niko handled his steaming piece with smug aplomb and commented, "It's a simple matter of discipline. Mind over matter."

"Yeah, and I bet you can break boards with your dick. You're a helluva man." I picked something green off the top of my slice and eyed it narrowly. Broccoli. "So, what do we do now? Hope the Grendel was sightseeing or dig into it further?"

"I'm not looking into membership in the Optimist Club these days, Cal. Are you?"

"That's what I thought." I checked my watch. "You teaching today?" When he wasn't pulling bodyguard duty, Niko supplemented our income by teaching at a tiny dojo. More money under the table for our running-like-little-girls fund.

"Later perhaps," he dismissed. "If we get this re-
solved. Now eat your broccoli before it gets cold."

I scowled but obeyed. "Scrub the floor, Cinderelly.
Eat your broccoli, Cinderelly," I grumbled around a
mouthful of cheese and bread.

By the way . . . the bug made it. Good for the bug.

3

Mom had been a fortune-teller in nearly every run-down carnival and one-horse town in the country, although she'd actually preferred the towns over traveling with other carnies. She didn't have to split her money when it was just her in some gloomy one-room apartment ladling out useless bits of crap and outright lies to the desperate. Yeah, the whole ball of wax was hers then. And Sophia had liked her money. Or rather, liked the things it could buy her, booze and drugs . . . the bright-and-shinies of her world. Safe to say that she had never kept money long and she would have done anything for it.

And I do mean anything.

That's how she'd ended up with me. For a while, when I was younger, I thought it could've been another way. She'd been a young woman, a girl really, beautiful in the way storms are . . . wild and free. Maybe so beautiful that a monster couldn't resist taking her and doing things to her that might twist her. Twist her, change her, make her care about no one but herself. Drive her to the kind of destructive behavior that tainted her and everyone around her. How could she not hate me considering

where I came from? How could she forget an act so horrifying, so hideous? And how could you not forgive
someone who had had that hell visited on them?

Of course it hadn't been that way. This was real life,
not a made-for-TV movie, chock-full of bland, over-
wrought nobility. But I'd been young and stupid and
looking for any way to . . . hell . . . *absolve* her. One of
Niko's fancy words, but it rang true. Because no matter
how tough you are, how jaded, every kid wants a mommy.
Every kid.

Like all things with Sophia, though, it had been about
money. No victim. No aggressor. Just a simple business
arrangement. And, she'd said, the worst one she'd ever
made. The money hadn't lasted any time, not to mention
the trouble it took to convert raw gold and silver to
cash. She had laughed harshly over an empty glass and
said, "But you're still here, Caliban. The money is gone
and you're still goddamn here." The laugh had smelled
of whiskey and truth. Guess I'd been lucky she'd waited
until I was ten to let that particular truth slip. Sophia
might have been a fortune-teller, but she saved all her
truths for me.

I guess you could say I didn't have a whole lot of
faith in fortune-tellers after being raised by one. Me or
Niko. But we'd both gotten a bit of a surprise when we'd
first wandered to New York two years ago. We'd met
George. George was a genuine talent, a seer. George was
truth and faith. George was hope and warmth. George
was belief when you had none.

George was also seventeen. So we had to wait until
school was out to talk. Holding court in an ancient ice-
cream parlor run by a wizened old man who turned a
blind eye to the constant stream of people who came in
and out, George always politely suggested the clients
buy a soda or milk shake before they left. It probably

kept the place open and in the black. We were waiting in a booth when George came in, spotted us, and with a gentle smile slid into the seat opposite us. Everything about George was gentle, and in a world where that quality is more myth than fact, I had learned to cherish every glimpse I could steal.

"Hey, Georgie Porgie." I grinned. "How's the freckle queen?"

I had a routine with George, a trick that I liked to think kept me on the straight and narrow. Kept me sane. I treated her like a little sister—a kid barely off her Big Wheel. Hell, she was petite enough to pass for one. I teased; I called her affectionate yet annoying nicknames. Rolled my eyes at her stories, tugged her curls, and all but patted her on the head. I did my damned best to make the two-year difference between us seem like ten. But despite all the production, all the arm waving—"Look over here; look over there. Just don't, whatever you do, look at me. Don't see me, and don't . . . *don't* see what I'm trying so hard not to think." Despite it all . . .

None of it did me a damn bit of good.

Georgina shook her head, dark red curls corkscrewing wildly about her delicate shoulders. "The boys in my class are more mature than you, Cal," she said with soft humor.

Niko elbowed me sharply without mercy. He was aware of why I behaved the way I did, and he did me the remarkable favor of never saying a word about it. Neither I nor my inner monster was ready for that particular subject, and he knew it. "Something I have been telling him for years, Georgina. He refuses to listen."

George gave him a sympathetic look from huge velvet brown eyes. "Kids." As always she turned the tables on me so neatly that I couldn't stop the faint flush that burned over my cheekbones. Rough, tough, and capable of kicking anyone or anything's ass . . . and this girl had me squirming in my seat.

While they sympathized with each other over my immature ways, I retreated to the counter and snagged us three ice-cream sodas. Pineapple for George, boring vanilla for Niko, and chocolate cherry for me. Ignoring the fact it was almost bigger than she was, George went to work on hers immediately. She never took money for her readings. Absolutely refused. But she would take ice cream. With as many people that came to her, it was a miracle she wasn't a four-hundred-pound psychic.

"How is your family, Georgina?" Niko asked gravely as he slowly swirled a straw through the vanilla soda. "Your father?"

She touched the back of her hand to her mouth, blushing slightly under faintly freckled, caramel skin, and reached for a napkin. "He's doing okay," she replied with equal gravity.

George's father was sick, so sick that okay was the best that could be hoped for. Full-blown AIDS. He hadn't been such a great father to George or her brothers and sisters when they were younger. But he'd shaped up, pulled himself out of the deepest pit of hell, and given up the drugs. It just turned out it was too late. George and her family had gotten him back only to be on the verge of losing him again, this time permanently. Still Georgie was Georgie and she saw things in a light most people were blind to their whole lives. At least that's what Niko said. I was one of the nearsighted. If there was a light, I hadn't seen it, not even one dancing mote of it. The light was the big picture, the whole enchilada, life's puzzle. And I had two, maybe three pieces, none of which fit together.

"I'm very glad to hear it." Niko, a solid corner piece if ever there was one, laid his hands flat on the table. "Georgina, we need a reading."

"I know," she said simply before giving him a cheeky grin. "I *am* psychic after all."

Niko curled up one side of his mouth in a rare smile. "So you are." He held out a hand. "Shall we begin?"

Wiping her hand carefully on the napkin, she then laid it on Niko's, palm to palm. Her small hand dwarfed by his, she closed her eyes and hummed softly under her breath. It was a familiar process, one I'd seen several times before . . . with other people. This was our first reading, a fact that hadn't seemed to surprise Georgie at all. I'd considered, God knew how many times, finding out if George could see where I'd been those two years I was missing from my life. But in the end two thoughts always stopped me. The first being, wherever I'd been, whatever had happened to me, I was damn sure it was nothing she should have to see. And the second, I wasn't sure I even wanted to know. Maybe the Grendels had made sure I wouldn't remember or maybe I had. Whatever my life had been in that missing time, you could bet your balls it hadn't been all wine and roses. If my mind was the one refusing to remember, there had to be a helluva good reason. A helluva good one or a thousand god-awful, mind-shredding ones.

"Misty, water-colored memories," my ass.

George's humming had drifted away to a still, vibrant silence. Then one word, a distant bell, dropped into that silence like a stone down a well. "Ask." Niko didn't waste any time. Succinctly he asked if we should leave the city, if our enemies had caught up with us. George wasn't quite as quick with a reply. Eyes still closed, she tilted her head as if in thought or as if she could hear

someone . . . someone just a little to the left, a little
back, a little ways off. Maybe that's what the future
was . . . a place just *off* from ours, just the tiniest bit
askew. After a long moment she straightened and shook
her head.

"No," came her light voice. "You are safe. The Grendels can't see you here. Too many people. Too much
noise and light. You're just one grain of sand on an endless beach, one leaf in a vast forest, one star in the distant sky." She opened her eyes and dimpled. "Literature
was sixth period."

"Very poetic," Niko complimented with dry amusement. He didn't comment on George's pulling the
Grendel name out of nowhere. Grendels they were to
us, so Grendels they were to her. I wondered if she
could see what they looked like in our minds or if they
were just a word she'd seen painted in our thoughts. I
also wondered, more than I should, if she looked at me
and saw something less than human. If she did, she
didn't say anything and the smile she gave me was just
as sweet and open as always.

Ah, Jesus.

We finished our sodas while George chatted about
girl things. Cute guys and clothes. Cute guys and her impossible brothers, not to mention hopelessly vain sisters.
Then finally back to cute guys again. And all the while
she would watch me with reassuring eyes. See? she
seemed to say. You don't have to worry. I'll be a child for
you. I'll be safe and distant in the normal soap opera
world of high school romance. You don't have to worry.
You don't have to be afraid.

And she *was* doing it for me—to ease my mind. I suspected it was an exaggeration at best. I'd yet to see a potential boyfriend around the soda shop. With someone
like George—a high school stud would crap his pants at

the thought of approaching her. She was . . . hell, she was a glory. It was the only way to put it. A glory.

Even with his so-called iron discipline, our glory had finally pushed Niko to the edge with her faux teenage chatter. My brother was beginning to look amusingly glassy-eyed by the time we managed to polish off the ice cream. He thanked George as politely and precisely as any British butler, while I gave her a casual wave and a "So long, Freckle Queen." She scowled cheerfully at me and waved back as we passed through the doors, the bell overhead giving a rusty tinkle. I felt better about the Grendel. When it came to news, good or bad, George was as reliable as they came, better than CNN any day. If she said we were safe, then we were. My belief in George was as firm as any I was capable of.

At least it was until I turned my head for one last look at the little seer. She wasn't smiling anymore. She was crying. Head pillowed on her arms, her shoulders shaking, she was crying in eerie silence behind the plate glass. Weeping as if she'd lost a friend or family or maybe even a piece of her soul.

Funny thing about faith . . . it goes a lot faster than it comes.

To tell Niko what I'd seen or not to tell—actually, Hamlet, that was not the question. It wasn't so much a matter of whether Nik would find out as a matter of when. He had X-ray vision, my brother. He'd know, sooner or later, that I was hiding something, and I was betting on sooner. So if I wanted a chance to brood darkly over the situation in true Heathcliff fashion, I was going to have to manufacture my own opportunity. And I was going to have to do it quick.

I fell back on a tried-and-true plan that had never failed. Ten seconds after we hit our apartment I was out like a light on the couch. It was the perfect plan because there wasn't an ounce of deceit in it. I was the next best thing to some sort of friggin' yogi, able to enter a coma at the drop of a hat. When I woke up hours later the front door was securely locked and Niko had gone to the dojo to teach. At least that's what his note said, along with a scathing reminder that dishes didn't wash themselves and the fungus in the bathroom was one day away from evolving into sentient life. I folded the note into an airplane and sailed it across the room. It ended up perched jauntily on top of the ancient television. It looked good there and I left it as a tribute to freedom-loving fungi everywhere.

Pulling a half-empty peanut butter jar from the cabinet, I sat at the kitchen table and went to work. Just me, a spoon, and some peanut butter long past its prime. You can always tell. . . . It's crunchy, but you bought smooth. Texture aside, it still tasted the same. More or less. Taking a bite, I let my eyes unfocus and thought about Georgina. I'd trusted her, almost as much as Niko. And that was huge in my book. Hell, in any book.

But she had lied to us. Lies were like acid, corrosive: They could dissolve trust in a heartbeat. And while I always had a wary eye out for betrayal, I wouldn't have thought to look in George's direction. I'd seen her help a lot of people, seen her bring so much hope into bleak, empty lives. I'd seen her deliver hard truths as well. They'd always been softened with George's calm words that told of the beautiful and vibrantly colored bigger picture. But she'd delivered the truth, softened or not. Always.

Until now.

And I had to wonder what had happened. Why would George turn her back on an integrity that was as much a part of her as that curly red hair? I took another bite and grimly ignored the thick sensation as it stuck in my throat. Maybe I should forget the why and focus on the what. She'd obviously lied, but what exactly was the lie? Were Grendels actually here and combing the city for me? Was it that neither Niko nor I was safe? Hell, maybe it was both. Pushing the jar away, I rested my chin in my hand, my elbow on the cheap plastic surface of the table. Shit. Whatever it was, it meant bailing and fast.

I closed my eyes and swore out loud this time. The why refused to be buried under thoughts of moving on again. You'd think I'd just chalk it up as nothing new and start packing my bags. But it was *George,* and her hands had a tight hold on me, much tighter than I ever should've allowed. Jesus, Georgie, what are you doing? I pushed the jar away and dropped the spoon with a clatter. From day one we'd met her, George had had a light around her. Corny as hell, but true. She'd been at the fish market on Pier 17, a well-worn dog collar clutched in her hands. An old man had been with her, his sparse white hair standing on end from the frantic combing of agitated fingers. With ratty bow tie and stooped shoulders he'd been saying, "She slipped her collar. She's never done that. Never. Venus is a good girl."

Niko and I had been down there looking for work when we'd noticed the quiet little drama of man loves dog; man loses dog. Nudging Niko's ribs with an elbow, I'd given him a grim snort as I watched the little girl work the old guy. I'd seen this a thousand times with Sophia. "I've lost my wife, my fortune, my mom, my dad, my child. Help me. Guide me. Save me." The goddamn heartbroken, they were everywhere. I had to say I'd never seen Sophia "search the spirit world" for a mutt, though. Not that she wouldn't have given her spiel if there'd been money involved. She'd have channeled a guinea pig for the right price.

This chick had her own moves down pat. Hands stroked the collar; dark eyes had looked inward. A small face all but glowed with a light so pure that it *had* to be faked. She'd give the old man a few lines, a practiced patter, take the money he'd slide into her greedy hand, and then she'd be gone. And the old man would still be alone. Nothing but an empty collar to keep him company.

Those were the breaks.

And least that's what I thought until I saw Venus come dashing out from behind some pallets, all dirty white fur, flying feet, and yapping bark. Niko touched his shoulder to mine and murmured, "Well, who would've thought?"

Not me, that's for damn sure. While the geezer and Venus exchanged wet, sloppy kisses, the little girl had come over to Nik and me. Tiny, so tiny, she looked to be all of twelve. Later we discovered that she was actually fifteen, and about fifteen lifetimes wiser than I was. She had stood in front of us with her red hair pulled into braids and said solemnly, "There aren't any jobs here right now. You should check back next week. They'll need a night watchman then." And then she'd smiled, innocent and curious. "Caliban. That's a funny name."

And that had been George.

Jars don't shatter too well when the glass is glued together with peanut butter. It's not so much a satisfying explosion as a disappointingly muddy crunch. I was on my knees cleaning up the mess when the thought hit me. Maybe George had done what she'd thought to be the kindest thing. She could've seen our future set in stone. Could've seen that no matter what we did, Niko and I didn't survive. It could be that whether we stayed or left, our ass was grass either way. And while she delivered hard truths, maybe that was one even George couldn't see a silver lining in.

God knew I wasn't one for self-deception. I'd gotten out of that practice early on, but right at this moment in time I was about to change my tune. I was going to deliver the bad news to Niko, we'd pack our bags to get the hell out of Dodge, and the entire time I was going to firmly hold to the belief that George had her reasons, good ones. And yeah, it was probably utter bullshit, but since we'd be long gone from her and the city, hopefully it'd be harmless bullshit. I would put away the fairy tales and impossible hopes the second we passed out of the city limits and go back to full-time cynicism. And next time I saw a little-girl psychic tracking down a yappy ankle biter, I'd run the other way, fast. It wasn't a great plan; in fact, it was right up there with "Let's wait for one more song from the *Titanic*'s house band before we hit the lifeboats." But crappy or not, it was the only plan I had. Like they say, you either play the hand you're dealt or walk away from the game.

Permanently.

4

Niko had been my protector all my life. He'd been at my back when I'd needed encouragement. He'd stood in front of me when I'd needed a buffer between Sophia and me. Hell, between the world and me. He was always on my side, always my unfailing support.

Right now he seemed to want to support my ass right over the moon with his foot.

"I said I was sorry," I grumbled, sliding down on the couch and throwing him a half-repentant, half-petulant glance.

"When?" Niko demanded bluntly. Standing in front of me, he folded his arms and fixed me with a look of laser-sharp annoyance. "Because I don't remember any apology. Was I in the bathroom? Or perhaps this was something you only imagined in what passes for the thought processes of your tiny mind?"

"Or maybe it was buried in smart-ass sarcasm and died an ugly death." I scratched my calf with a sock-covered toe. "You think?"

"No, Cal, I do not think. What I *do* think is that you did something stupid and don't want to admit it, much less apologize for it."

This little conversation didn't seem to be in danger of winding down anytime soon. "Not that this isn't fun," I exhaled with a grimace, and tapped my watch. "But I gotta be at work in twenty." Bending over, I scrounged with a hand under the couch for my sneakers.

A fast hand efficiently snatched the retrieved shoes from my hands and slammed them down on the coffee table. "My best guess is that you'll be late."

My best guess was that being late was the least of my problems. "Jesus, Nik, what would you have done if I had told you then, huh? She'd already lied to us once. She probably would've just lied again. It's not like you can Hong Kong Phooey the truth out of a seventeen-year-old girl."

"Obviously," Niko said impassively. "But I'm not as quick as you to believe that talking with her would've been futile. Georgina is our friend, Cal, and she's special, gifted. We should have at least tried to find out what was going through her mind. We may have found out her crying had nothing to do with us at all."

It could be that we should've talked to her; maybe I'd made a mistake there. But on one thing I'd made no mistake. Her tears had been about us, maybe even *for* us. But in some ways my brother was as stubborn as I was. It was something he'd have to see for himself to believe.

"Maybe you're right," I said, noncommittal. "Why don't you try talking to her while I'm at work? See what you can find out." I reached for a shoe and this time Niko made no move to stop me. Slipping it on my foot, I tied the laces in a sloppy double knot. Picking up the other one, I continued softly. "I am sorry, Nik. I should've told you. I just . . ." I shrugged as I let the words trail off and silently finished up with the other sneaker.

"You just didn't want to believe it," he filled in for me.

"Yeah." I put my hands on my knees and looked up at him ruefully. "Denial, not just a river in Greece." I managed a halfway sincere grin as Niko's eyes all but crossed on that one. "Take it easy, Cyrano. I'm just kidding. Damn, you'd have made a great junior high teacher. Prim, proper, and anal as hell."

Gray eyes narrowed. "Considering you seem permanently stuck at thirteen, a junior high teacher is just what you need." He held out a hand and heaved me up off the couch. "Be careful at work, Cal. Especially careful," he amended. "I'll meet you before closing, just to be on the safe side."

"You are your brother's keeper." I felt the smile slip from my face.

I was sorry about that too.

Work was work. Wall-to-wall soul-sucking boredom, at least until Meredith showed up sporting a new shirt. That is, if five sequins and a spiderweb of shiny threads could honestly be labeled as an article of clothing. Hey, I didn't know fashion, but I knew what I liked. And lots of silky bare skin was right up there on the list. Cherry red nails skimmed along my jaw and tucked a loose strand of hair behind my ear. "Is the big guy already in, Cal? I think I'm a little late."

"A little late" in Meredithspeak translated to an hour and a half in the real world. I continued wiping down the sticky countertop from behind the bar and raised my eyebrows. "What do you think, Merry, Merry?"

She groaned and blew long red bangs out of her eyes. "He's pissed, huh?" Without waiting for an answer, she pulled at her top, managing to reveal even more cleavage, and then fluffed her hair. "Time to kiss some withered old ass. Wish me luck."

"With double trouble there you don't need luck." I grinned.

She beamed with genuine pride at her double Ds. "They are brilliant, aren't they?" I'd seen women suffer through men's staring at their breasts countless times. Hell, I worked in a bar, after all. That was 99.9 percent of the men there. But Meredith was the first woman I'd seen stare at her *own* chest with a fascination equal to that of any random perv. With another subtle rearranging of the twins, she disappeared into the back to work her wiles on the owner, Mr. Talley. Or, as he was inevitably known, Tallywhacker. As mysterious and rarely seen as the Abominable Snowman or Bigfoot, he lurked in the back office counting his money and doing God knows what else. Once in a blue moon he'd pop out, leer with soulless eyes at some of the women, comb his five or six silvery strands of hair with nervous fingers, and then disappear again. He was a creepy guy who spent more money on porn mags and Kleenex than on beer for the bar.

Shrugging, I tossed the dirty rag into the sink. Everybody needed a hobby, even the freaks. If Meredith wanted to keep this job bad enough to shake her ass for the 'whacker, then that was her own lookout. And if I kept an ear out for a scream, then that just meant screams were bad for business. Bartenders lived off their tips, after all.

"Excuse me, buddy, could I get some help here?"

I turned my head, mentally kicking myself. Niko would not be happy with the thought that someone could waltz up right behind me while I was distracted. I knew I wasn't too damn thrilled about it. A man stood on the other side of the counter waiting for my answer. He was a big black guy with hair razored short to his skull and a close-cut goatee. The red-and-black tattoo of a horse encircled his wrist, peering out from the sleeve of a black leather jacket. Patient brown eyes measured me as white teeth flashed in a friendly grin. "Catch you at a bad time?"

Reaching for a glass, I filled it up with soda and placed it in front of him on the bar. "Sorry, pal. What can I do for you?"

He curled his hand around the glass, a faint puzzled line between his brows. "Thanks." Taking a sip, he put the glass back down and gave me a rueful twitch of his mouth. "Glad you didn't give me a beer. I don't drink anymore."

I knew he didn't drink. Alcohol tended to linger in the scent a lot longer than in the blood. If he'd had a beer even a month ago, I would've smelled it. "Yeah, you look the sober and serious type. So," I repeated, "what can I do for you again?"

His smile faded a bit at my brusque words. "I'm with the band. I need to start setting our equipment up." He pushed the glass back toward me. "I need you to open up the doors in the alley."

"Band?" I snorted. "You're kidding, right? Talley sprang for a band?"

He settled his weight on a stool and knocked on the surface of the bar once. "Hey, now, we'll bring class and prosperity to this hole-in-the-wall. Your boss recognizes an opportunity when he sees it."

"Funny. He never has before." I wiped off my hands, grabbed the keys off the hook on the wall, and came around the counter. "Hope you got your money up front."

"We're actually working for a cut of the take." He gave me a mildly sheepish look and held out a hand. "I'm Samuel, the guitarist."

"Cal." As hard as I'd stuck to my guns, Niko had still managed, years ago, to break me of my "Caliban" fixation. But labeled or not, I still knew where I came from.

I shook Samuel's hand, the calluses of a lifelong guitarist evident against my skin. "Well, Samuel the guitarist, I hope you can divide jack shit evenly between the band because that's what we usually pull in around here." Heading toward the back of the bar, I kept careful track of his footsteps behind me. No Grendel, but that didn't mean he wasn't here to rob the place. We'd had our share of robbers before. Pissed-off, disappointed robbers once they got a look at what was in the till. "I'll check it out with Talley, then unlock the back for you."

"No problem," he said evenly from behind me. "Maybe then you could help me unload the van. I'd pay you a couple of bucks."

"Yeah, sure." It wasn't like I had anything better to do. There wasn't customer one in the place yet except for a regular huddled in the corner watching the static-fragmented TV screen. Jerry wouldn't even notice I was gone until his bottle was empty, and he had at least an hour left on that.

While Tallywhacker confirmed he'd hired Samuel's band, Meredith made her escape from the office. The half-scornful, half-repulsed expression on her face melted to a brilliant smile she flashed Samuel's way. Merry's boyfriend didn't keep her from flirting shamelessly. Niko had learned that on more than one occasion. I was fairly sure Meredith's boyfriend would have been dropped in a hot second if Niko had given her the slight-est bit of encouragement, but Niko liked his women more like himself. Intense and sharply real. Meredith was neither.

Out in the alley, I watched as Samuel unlocked his van. It was an older model, dark red with black gothic lettering painted on the side, spelling out THE HORDE. I indicated the name and asked curiously, "As in the Mongols?"

He nodded and swung open the doors. "Our lead singer calls himself Genghis. How hokey is that?"

I wasn't exactly in the position to be throwing stones, but at least I hadn't voluntarily chosen my name. "Pretty hokey," I agreed. Within a half hour we had the van unloaded and I was back at the bar pouring Samuel another glass of bubbly and nonalcoholic. He gave a grateful nod and slid a ten and a five across the counter to me.

Shaking my head, I demurred, "Nah. Keep it. It's not like I was busy. Besides, it was entertaining." I gave him an amused grin. "A learning experience." Samuel was an easygoing guy, companionable, and had some stories that would curl hair. Bad-boy band antics, most of them, from drinking binges to the sexual escapades of the mighty Khan. The singer had apparently never met a groupie he didn't like or a booze he didn't love. Mixing both had led to the occasional arrest and a frequent-flyer card at the free clinic.

Samuel returned the grin and checked a heavy chrome watch. "You'll get to live the experience in about an hour. Just keep nine-one-one on speed dial. Last place we played, we had to call in the Jaws of Life to get Genghis out of his leather pants." Polishing off his soda, he retrieved the money and stuffed it in the tip jar. "You earned it. Thanks for the help, Cal. I've got the sound check to do. Catch you later." He gave an easy wave and moved across the bar, half disappearing in the gloom, a shade among the shadows.

"Mmmmm. Delish." Meredith appeared at my shoulder, her pointed tongue touching her upper lip. "All strong and confident. Smoldering. A big juicy stallion."

I snorted caustically. "Hell, Merry, you thought the UPS guy was a stallion too until you found out her name was Sherry."

"It was dark, okay?" Miffed at my lack of enthusiasm for her man watching, she flounced off to bus Jerry's empty bottle. While she was there she wiped up a lake of drool that was forming under Jerry's unconscious, slack-jawed face. There was nothing like a dedicated customer. I hoped he woke up in time for the band, because I was willing to bet he'd *be* the audience, the sole head-banging member. Leather-boy Genghis and his Horde were going to be some disappointed, not to mention destitute, rockers. Hey, wasn't like I hadn't warned Samuel.

Three hours later Samuel and his pals proved me wrong. I wouldn't say the place was wall-to-wall people, but it was as packed as I'd ever seen it. Niko said nearly the same when he drifted up beside me, phantom silent. "It appears someone has raised your bar from the dead. This may qualify as a miracle even in the eyes of the Vatican."

"Yeah," I said briefly as I leaned, arms folded on the table in one far corner. I gave the opposite chair a shove, pushing it into his hand. "All this time I thought this place would never amount to anything without some decent booze or basic hygiene. Turns out all we needed was a new band."

"Wouldn't you require an old band to qualify this one as a new one?" Not waiting for a smart-ass answer to an even more smart-ass rhetorical question, he flowed smoothly into the chair and promptly made the sign of the evil eye at my dinner. "Get thee behind me, Satan."

I ignored him and continued to give my heart a run for its money with the fried sampler platter from the restaurant next door. Fried cheese, fried peppers, fried potatoes, and the topper, fried potatoes *with* cheese and peppers. It was the lowest common denominator of all the food groups and I was enjoying every life-giving molecule of grease. "How went your chat with George?" I said around a mouthful. "No go, huh?" There was an unmistakable, to me anyway, tension around Niko's calm eyes. Luck sure didn't look to be a lady tonight, more like the bitch she always was.

"She wouldn't speak to me. Her mother wouldn't even open the door," he confirmed with a grim twist to his mouth.

"And you didn't kick it down? What the hell kind of ninja superhero are you anyway?" I waved to Meredith across the room and pointed to Niko. She nodded and headed for the juice in the fridge. Niko wasn't much on alcohol and considering our mom, that was understandable. About things like that, he'd always been smarter than I was.

"I suppose I'm the kind that doesn't terrify teenage girls and their mothers."

I curled up the corner of my mouth at his disgruntled tone. "Yeah, they'd take away your cape for that."

Meredith slithered up at that moment, probably saving me from retaliation in the form of either a brisk butt kicking or a more lackadaisical steel toe to the shin. She put a glass of cranberry juice in front of Niko and draped over his shoulder like a silicone-enhanced orange tabby. "Nikki," she purred, her breasts threatening to swallow his neck in a loving embrace. "I haven't seen you in weeks. I'll start to think you don't love and adore me."

My brother's eyes slid back toward her with all the resignation of a man on death row, then returned to me with a roiling wrath that would've dropped a charging boggle in its tracks. I took pity on him. "Hey, Mer, I'm almost done with my break. Watch the bar for me for a few more minutes?"

She gave a long-suffering sigh that had the mounds of her breasts rising to smothering proportions. Niko was a man caught in an erotic avalanche. Giving him a lingering kiss on his cheek, she disappeared into the milling crowd, calling out over her shoulder, "You owe me, Cal."

"Get in line," I murmured. Pursing my lips, I turned my attention back to Niko and gave a low whistle. "I almost lost you there, big brother. Nearly had to send in the Saint Bernards to dig you out."

"What I cannot fathom," he gritted between clenched teeth, "is why she doesn't feel the need to include you in her voracious affections."

"Probably senses my inner slimy monster," I grunted philosophically, wiping the grease from my supper on my bartender's apron.

"Senses your outer sarcastic imp is more likely." A knuckle knocked lightly on my forehead. "The only monster in there is laziness. It's more than voracious in its own right, however."

"Pick up your socks. It always comes back to that, doesn't it?" Scooping up the stained paper plate, I smothered a yawn. "Finish your juice, Grandpa. Then come help me at the bar. This is the first time I've had to actually work since I've had this job. It's killing me."

"And there's the monster," he said dryly, shaking his head.

For the next few hours he worked with me slinging booze and refilling the bowls with cheap, generic pretzels. He spent a lot of time dodging Meredith too, but I'd take that out of his tips. I was wrestling with a new keg when I heard a newly familiar voice. "The new help isn't quite as pretty as the redhead."

Looking up, I saw Niko raise his eyebrows at Samuel and say gravely, "My ego is shattered." The words were joking, but his gray eyes were cool and distant, a frozen layer of unconcern over a lake of mistrust. I might be running out far in front, but I didn't have the corner on suspicion. Niko was smart as hell and wary as shit, and that had kept us alive. Had kept me free.

But now would be the time, wouldn't it? This was the moment I would step up and say Samuel was okay. He wasn't a Grendel in the world's best human suit. Wasn't a crook. He was just your average Joe, a good guy, one I'd enjoyed talking to. So I should tell Nik that, right?

Shit. Not in this lifetime.

Yeah, Samuel seemed like he was all right, but realistically, I didn't know him from Adam. Snap judgments? I'd gotten over those about the time I was toilet trained. Swore off diapers and faith in the human experience all in one week. You had to admire my efficiency. "Niko, this is Samuel. He's with the band," I said neutrally before adding slyly, "Minion to the leather god."

Niko kept pouring pretzels into a bowl, precisely to the rim, no less, no more. The Zen of pretzel arranging— it's long been a lost art. "Ah. The singer that time forgot. To be more exact, that the eighties forgot. His hair spray bill must be staggering."

"You've got a lot of room to talk, Rapunzel," Samuel pointed out. "You're not exactly going for the brush cut look yourself."

I grinned and reached over to tug on Niko's braid. "He's got you there."

Samuel took a handful of pretzels, disturbing Niko's pristine sculpture of bread and salt. "You two brothers?"

Niko gave him a narrow-eyed look, then repaired the damage. "That obvious, is it?" he asked blandly.

"Oh yeah. You boys are just two sides to one coin." Samuel chewed with a marked lack of enthusiasm. "Man, where'd you get these? Dumpster? Sawdust factory?"

"How'd you know? You play the best joints; you get the best grub," I grunted. After serving some beers and a shot or two, I turned my attention back to Samuel. "You guys are pretty good. Retro, but harder than I'd have thought, Genghis's leather pants aside."

Niko gave an inaudible humph. Inaudible, but heavy in the air nonetheless. "Yeah, yeah, Nik. It's not the Beatles, I know. No 'Long and Winding Road.' " I raised my eyes toward the empty, sterile heavens. To Niko there had been one band in existence; the rest was just derivative noise. "You were born old, you know that?"

"Their work is timeless. It transcends the bubblegum pap that passes for music now. A Beatles song is a flawlessly executed kata. Anything else is simply wrestling in Jell-O," he returned with disdain.

I snorted, "You're only hurting your argument there. Jell-O wrestling is even better than the mud kind." Behind Samuel, who was following our discussion with interest, the crowd parted like the Red Sea and the leather god himself appeared.

A tousled mass of bleached blond hair was tossed à la Fabio over an overly muscled shoulder that had to owe something to steroids. A red silk, or its white-trash cousin polyester, shirt hung open to show a broad hairless chest with only one or two razor cuts. Manly sweat coated chiseled features as flame-hot blue eyes seared the air. Granted, the eyes were closer together than your average weasel found attractive, but otherwise Genghis knew how to take care of business. Business being fronting a band and keeping the horny little girls happy. A rough life, but someone had to lead it. The asshole.

A hand tanned a suspiciously orange color slapped the bar. "Who the hell do I have to screw to get a beer in this place?"

I considered and tilted my head toward Niko. "That," my brother commented coolly, "is almost as humorous as my fist inserted into your left nostril."

Giving up the taunting while I was still mobile, I fetched a brewski for leather boy. "There you go, Mr. Khan. No whoring of your body necessary."

Offset eyes gave me a disinterested once-over. After all, I wasn't a band babe. Hell, I wasn't even a woman. No record exec, no one who could advance his career in the slightest . . . just Joe Blow bartender, so far below the radar that I didn't even register.

His next beer I'd spit in.

He took a swig of the beer, wiping off the foam mustache with the back of his hand. "Friends of yours, Grainger? You're sure spending enough time over here. Thought we were going to do another sound check."

"We've done ten, Roy," Samuel said with only a glimmer of a strained quality to his patience. "The equipment's fine." Then he added under his breath, "It's your voice that's the problem."

It was the faintest whisper and passed by Genghis completely. Not by me, though. I had good ears too. Not pointed maybe, but sharper than ordinary. Not bothering to smother the sardonic quirk of my lips, I felt it widen into a full-fledged smirk when the singer hissed, "It's Genghis. Jesus Christ, Grainger." Finishing the beer in one long gulp, he slammed the mug down. "We're back on in five if you can tear yourself away."

I waved at his back as he disappeared into the crowd. "Nice guy. Salt of the earth. The stick up his ass is just a bonus."

"Let us not make light of the rectally challenged." Niko disposed of the mug with disdain, wiping his hand thoroughly on a towel afterward. "The condition is no doubt congenital. Completely beyond his control."

"You've got that right." Samuel stood and gave us a faintly apologetic grimace. "A born asshole. But it's his band, his van, and my cross to bear until a better gig comes along." Ramming hands into the pockets of his jeans, he aimed a jaundiced look at the makeshift stage where Genghis was waving an imperious hand. Turning back to Niko and me, he gave us a companionable nod. "See you guys Friday."

"Back for another show? Damn, seriously?" I couldn't keep a sliver of disbelief from my voice. They had packed the place, but still . . . make playing this hole-in-the-wall a regular thing? What the hell for?

A philosophical smile lightened Samuel's dark features. "It's a dump, no doubt. But the competition is fierce out there. Sometimes you take what you can get until something better comes along."

True. True words. But truer ones might be that sometimes you got out while the getting was good. But that was my motto and I didn't share it with Samuel. And I didn't tell him that by Friday Niko and I would be long gone. We'd be a soon forgotten memory, the same as we were to so many people already. Just ghosts. Because in a world of monsters, you had to be a ghost to survive.

5

The next morning I was dressed and out before Niko. As events went, unprecedented wasn't the word. Desperate situations . . . I didn't have any illusions that my brother had slept soundly through my leaving. I wouldn't have even wanted him to, not with the threat of the Grendels looming. As it was, I simply skipped out on the last fifteen minutes of my watch duty. I knew Niko would wake up the moment I opened the front door, and more than that, he would know exactly where I had gone, and why. A note wasn't needed. But I didn't understand why my feet carried me there.

Or maybe I didn't want to.

It was too early for the soda shop to be open. I knew that. I also knew it would be open anyway. And I knew George would be waiting for me. How I knew, I couldn't say, and the headache that analyzing it would cause wasn't something I aspired to. So, as with so many things in my life, I let it go. I let it go and walked on.

When I reached the shop the security gate was already up and George was standing at the door. In a slim sweater of jumbled golds, reds, and browns and the silky sweep of a dark bronze skirt, she watched my approach with her arms wrapped around her waist. She looked older. Such a short time had passed since she'd been giggling and drinking her pineapple shake, yet it could've been years, from the haunted quality of her eyes. Through the glass, the bright copper of her hair was muted, the gold of her skin tarnished . . . a shadow of the Georgina I knew.

I stood and looked at her, just looked. It was easy to picture my hand rising to grasp the handle and pull the door open. I could see it so clearly, yet my hand didn't move from my side. Maybe it knew what part of me didn't want to admit. The door was locked. If I tried to open it, it wouldn't budge. I knew that in the same way I knew George would be here.

She didn't say anything, my girl. Not a word. She only watched me in return with a smile so wistful and fleeting that I might have imagined it. Then she leaned a few inches closer and her lips grazed the glass to frost it with her breath. In the fog her finger traced a few curving lines, simple and spare. And then she was gone. Disappearing into the gloom of the lightless shop, she was the autumn glitter of dying leaves and then she was nothing. Nothing to hold in your hand, nothing to catch the eye. Nothing at all.

Her breath the only thing left behind, my finger followed the same path hers had taken. I frowned. A car. She'd drawn a car. What the hell? As the glass warmed, even that vanished, the same as its maker. Knowing how it would end, I tried the door anyway. I'd been right.

Locked.

By the time I made it home Niko was up and packing. It was a ritual for him, done in just the same way every time. As for me . . . we'd been on the run for so long, Niko and me, that I'd stopped putting our personal touches on the places we stayed. Because in the end, that's all they were . . . places. They weren't homes, just disposable living space. Forget that and one day you might slow down; you might take the time to regret your loss. And if that happened, if you took one second to mourn what you were leaving behind, well, your ass was grass. Devil takes the hindmost, but Grendels went one better. They took the middlemost and even the front-runners if there was the smallest misstep.

All this bleak and impersonal existence might scar the soul, but hey, it was a nice bonus if you were a chronically lazy bastard like myself. Packing usually consisted of shoving my dirty laundry in a garbage bag and putting on my shoes. Sixty seconds max. The ex-cruciatingly efficient Niko tended to take longer. That might've been surprising had he not had so many sharp pointy things to gather up. We didn't quite need a U-Haul for all his weapons, but it was a near thing.

Walking into his room, I leaned around him to ex-tend a finger and run it along the smooth, silver satin of an elegant dagger. "The acid of skin is detrimental to the metal," Niko said mildly as he rolled another blade in a length of dark green felt. He didn't mention my absence and I was grateful for the restraint.

"And all the blood is like mother's milk," I snorted, raising a different and more eloquent finger for his perusal.

"Actually . . ." He curved his lips in a contemplative shadow of a smile. "Never mind."

I lowered my finger before he took the notion to treat it like a wishbone. "So when do we pull out, Mas-ter? In the morning?"

"Patience, Grasshopper." Rapping me reprovingly across the knuckles with the swaddled weapon, he went on. "He who makes haste risks falling from the path of enlightenment."

And suddenly George's good-bye to me made sense. Swearing, I fell back against the wall, the mattress creaking and complaining beneath me. "It's your car again, isn't it? Your goddamn hunk-of-junk car." The same hunk of junk I spent more than my fair share of time moving from one side of the street to the other to save it from the wrath of the boot.

I would never see Niko looking sheepish. It simply wasn't in him. But he did shift minutely, almost a whole millimeter, and his nose somehow or another became more hawkish. "She runs reliably nearly seventy-five percent of the time. For the money that's more than acceptable."

Seventy-five percent of the time wasn't so great when you were on the run *all* of the time. And wasn't this a blast from the past? The last time we'd had this conversation, I'd taken a walk on the Grendel side. Here was hoping we didn't have a rerun of that little experience. Still, I had no real desire to bring up that nugget of ancient history, so I kept my mouth shut for once and quietly watched as Niko continued to pack.

Not fooled for a moment by my silence, Niko zipped up the long duffel bag and set it easily on the floor. "I honestly don't believe there is any desperate hurry, Cal. Boggle has his muddy ear to the ground. If he's not heard anything, chances are, that Grendel was a lone anomaly." His eyes narrowed. "A lone ex-anomaly, if you will. In any event I believe we comfortably have a few days to get things in order." Clearing his throat, he added offhandedly, "Perhaps buy a new car."

"You think?" I drawled sarcastically.

Niko was as deadly with a headlock as he was with a sword. He had me in one before I could blink. With his mouth close to my ear, he warned mildly, "Be careful, little brother. Any further comments from the peanut gallery and I may just purchase a motorcycle. Perhaps strap you to the handlebars when we leave town."

"Couldn't be any worse than that death trap we're rattling around in now." I feinted an elbow at his gut and then simultaneously hooked a foot around his ankle and bit him on the arm. Niko went down and I landed on top of him hard. Rolling off, I bounced to my feet and aimed a one-two punch at the air. "Put 'em up. Put 'em up. I'll take ya with one paw tied behind my back." It was faked, the humor, but Niko went along regardless. He wasn't one to let me stew.

Niko snorted through his long nose, sitting up with ease. "The lion? Hardly. Toto maybe. A member of the Lollipop Guild on your very best day."

Triumph over Nik wasn't something to be wasted, no matter how black my mood, and I gave him a faint grin. "Sore loser." Reaching down a hand, I heaved him to his feet. I was under no illusion that I'd actually taken Niko down. It was a simple move he himself had taught me and one he was more than prepared against. Every day in every way, my brother was testing me, teaching me. I rubbed my thumb over the faint bite impressions in the skin of his arm. "Maybe we should put some barbecue sauce on that."

This time I was the one who went down. And it damn sure wasn't a legal move. After all, how often is a Grendel going to give me an atomic wedgie?

An hour later we hit the streets in search of a good used car. We started in Brooklyn but kept New Jersey open as an option. A scary last-ditch option. Grendels had nothing on a Jersey car salesman. Emerging from the womblike darkness of the subway and a heavy nap full of copper and glass dreams, I blinked at the bright sunlight that spilled out of a piercingly blue October sky.

Grumbling incoherently, I fished in my jacket pocket for sunglasses.

"Fear not, night dweller," Niko said with mocking gravity. "It is merely the sun, something you would see more often if you would roll out of bed before late afternoon."

I would never know if my morning sluggishness was inherited (the Grendels had obvious nocturnal preferences), or just sheer human laziness on my part. Either way Niko was damn hard to take this early. Rolling my shoulders, I snarled silently and kept trudging down the sidewalk, brightening only when I spotted a hot dog stand a block down. Five minutes later I was happily buried face-first in a chili cheese dog heaped with onions and relish. Everything but the kitchen sink—just the way I liked it. It really was the simple things in life that kept you going.

Niko kept his distance, claiming the fumes were making his eyes water. Big baby. He wouldn't touch anything that was even remotely in the mystery meat family. "Do you have even the vaguest idea what is in that thing?" He eyed the dripping dog with distaste.

"Nope." I took another bite. "I've carefully avoided that knowledge my entire life just so I could enjoy this one moment. You mind?"

He folded his arms and gave me an exasperated look I was more than familiar with. "It does no good to survive the Grendels if you lodge a mass of shredded rat and chicken lips in your heart. Not to mention dissolving your intestines altogether."

There was more of the same, but I tuned it out and savored the bliss that only a New York hot dog can give. By the time we reached the tiny car lot I was licking the last of the orange chili off my fingers. While I might have been able to ignore my brother, he was incapable of ignoring me when I was at my Miss Manners best. Hissing between clenched teeth, he fished a clean napkin out of his own pocket and pressed it into my hands. "Do me the favor of rising from the preschool hygiene level." The gray eyes narrowed. "In fact you'd also be doing yourself a favor." Niko was good at threats, very good. I'd never seen anyone or anything not at least hesitate in the face of one of his chilling smiles or predatory stares.

Me, I just burped and tossed him back the now soiled napkin. "Come on, Grandma. Let's buy a car."

We wandered the lot with a slowly increasing sense of pessimism. It might have been a small one, but the cars were mostly new or older, immaculately expensive models. Quite a few convertibles were available for the consumer on the go who liked inhaling big chunks of pollution while idling in never-ending traffic. Good for building up your tolerance to carbon monoxide. Still, I couldn't deny my hand swept across the clean lines of a classic Mustang before I shoved it back in my pocket. "I think the only thing we could afford here is a pair of skates," I grunted.

"You might be right." Niko still had the napkin in his hand. Frowning in annoyance, he was looking around for a garbage can when we were nailed. A flashing charismatic smile, a pricey suit, sunglasses that cost more than Nik and I had to spend on a car—it all was aimed in our direction like a heat-seeking missile.

"Oh, damn," I groaned wholeheartedly.

"It's an unfortunate fact of life," Niko said with grimly amused resignation. "Where there are graveyards, there are flesh-eating revenants. Where there are cars, there are car salesmen."

"I'll take the flesh eaters any day. At least they leave you your soul." The guy was getting closer. "How about we make a run for it?"

His hand snagged my jacket before I could move, and he reproved smoothly in a line straight out of our childhood cartoons, "Honestly, Cal, are you a man or a mouse?"

"Neither, remember?" I grumbled under my breath. What a waste of time. There was nothing here we could remotely afford. It was bad enough to suffer through this crap when you actually got a car in the end. To do it for no other reason than to not look like a coward as you sprinted for safety—that just sucked.

And then it was too late. Mr. Glad-hand Luke was on us like shark on chum. "Gentlemen, beautiful day, isn't it? Rob Fellows, at your service. What can I put you in today?" Cards were slipped in our hands with the quick-silver finesse of a Vegas magician. "Sports car? SUV? Maybe something thrifty with the gas? Foreign and domestic, we've got it all." He waved a hand. "You leaning toward a color? Red is popular, naturally, but you two . . ." He leaned back an inch and framed us with his hands. "I'm thinking simple black. Good color. Can't be beat. I have a brand-new Camaro over in the far corner. A jewel it is, a veritable glory. And, here we go. This way. Watch your step."

Okay, here was a man for whom caffeine wasn't an occasional indulgence; it was the actual fluid pulsing through his veins. He was a veritable whirlwind and it was distracting as hell, almost distracting enough.

But not quite.

He smelled weird. Different. Not human. He looked human, though, thoroughly. In his early thirties, he had short curly chestnut hair and revealed the cheerfully

amoral green gaze of a fox when he pulled off his sunglasses to indicate a gleaming black car two rows over.
His smiling, wide mouth was constantly in motion. He
was the grown-up frat boy next door who'd conducted
the panty raids, set up the keg, and knew everyone's
name. Ex-BMOC. But in this case it stood for "Big
Monster on Campus," because there wasn't a drop of
human blood in him. The pungency of his scent was
completely alien, oddly earthy, and like nothing I'd ever
smelled before.

It didn't take much to tip off Niko, just the briefest of
glances and a minute shift of my stance. He narrowed his
eyes a millimeter in acknowledgment, and almost before
Fellows could make his pitch, Niko and I were ready to
sign the papers. He seemed pleased, not suspicious in the
slightest, smugly secure in his position as salesmonster of
the year. There was probably even a plaque on his wall.

Actually there were nearly twenty. I whistled lightly
at the sight of them and settled into the chair on the
other side of his desk as Niko drifted around the room.
"Aren't you a regular Willy Loman?"

That ever-present blinding smile became pained. "I
like to think I'm more successful than that, Mr. . . .
er . . ." He leaned across the desk to extend his hand.
"I'm sorry. I didn't get your name."

I took his hand, then wrist, in an iron grip and bared
my teeth in a wolfish grin. "Caliban. Nice to meet you,
Loman."

The smile had melted off his face even before Niko
ghosted up behind him, placing a knife at his throat.
"What the hell?" He started to struggle against my hold
but froze as a tiny thread of scarlet trickled down the
line of his neck.

"Sharp, isn't it?" I said sympathetically. "Niko does
like to take care of his toys."

"Not toys," Niko admonished, his blade as still and unmoving as stone. "They're more of a way of life. A philosophy." His mouth moved closer to Fellows's ear as he murmured serenely, "Perhaps even a religion."

That'd put the chills up anyone's spine. Hell, make those vertebrae get up and take a walk, for that matter. I tilted my head and suggested lightly, "Maybe we should have a chat, Loman, before Niko decides to baptize you. What do you say?"

I don't know what gave me away. He didn't smell the difference in me or he would've caught on much sooner. Maybe it was the way I quirked my head or my pale, pale skin? Could have been the near-murderous curve of my lips. Whatever it was, he knew. Somehow Fellows knew. The green eyes widened; the mobile face tightened. "Auphe. You're Auphe." There was wariness and a thread of sheer revulsion in his voice as the smooth cheer fractured into a hundred crystalline shards.

Elf. Auphe. Grendel. A rose by any other name would still draw blood if you didn't watch the thorns. Niko's tranquillity vanished in a heartbeat as he hissed coldly, "He is *not*." Lifting the blade away, he fisted his hand in Fellows's suit to yank him out of his chair and slam him up against the wall. "But he can kill you as quickly as one, and so can I."

Moving up shoulder to shoulder with my brother, I touched a fingertip to the small rivulet of blood on Fellows's skin and sniffed it. "Funny. It looks like human blood, but it sure as hell doesn't smell that way." I wiped it off on my jeans. "So, Loman, tell us . . . just what kind of monster are you? You eat children? Haunt graveyards? Drink blood and howl at the moon?" I shook my head before he could answer. "No. You don't smell like any of those things."

"Because I'm not any of those things." He put a

hand to his neck, wiped the blood away, and studied me with suddenly appraising eyes. "No more than you're Auphe. Not pure Auphe. I was wrong about that. But part, yes? Half?" An automatic grimace shimmered across his face. "I didn't know anything would breed with an Auphe. Even other Auphe are probably loath to do it. It would have to be a tale even the Grimm brothers would find too grim. Shakespeare would like it, though. But with a name like 'Caliban' I guess you already knew that."

Niko lifted a disbelieving eyebrow in my direction. "He never stops. A creature that suffocates his victims with an unceasing flow of words. I don't recall that in any of the mythology books."

"Horrible way to go." I hooked a hip on the edge of the desk and exhaled, threading both hands through my hair. "Loman, why don't you just shut up with all your goddamn questions and answer just one of ours, huh? How about it? If we like what you say, we can get on with our lives and maybe, just maybe, you can get on with yours."

At that moment the door to the office swung open six inches and a bespectacled, wizened face topped by a lavender-tinted Albert Einstein do peered through at us with curious eyes. "Mr. Fellows, you have Steven Phillips waiting on two." Thin lips painted with a thick coat of bubblegum pink pursed as the eyes moved to Niko's grip on the monster's shirt. "Oh. You're . . . oh. *Oh.*" She continued to blow bubbles like a confused goldfish until Fellows gave her a smooth, reassuring smile.

"Everything's fine, Dorothea," he said with a genial sangfroid. "Tell Steve I'll call him back and he better have that Lexus he promised me. And could you bring my guests some coffee and some of those cranberry muffins? That's my doll."

Dorothea gave him a flustered nod that had the glittering purple glass dangling from her earlobes ringing like wind chimes, and disappeared, closing the door behind her. And I had to wonder . . . when exactly did Niko and I lose control of the situation? Hell, did we ever even have it to begin with? I dropped my chin into my hand and groaned, "Ah, jeez."

Niko palmed his blade, sliding it back into concealment, and gave me a rueful look. "It is difficult to threaten someone who doesn't have the necessary attention span to register fear."

Fellows straightened his suit and ran a hand over his hair. "As if a pair of puppies like you could scare me," he snorted, but I noticed he gave Niko a wide berth as he moved back to his chair. Me . . . me, he kept in sight at all times, a combination of fascination and repulsion mixing in those cat eyes. Sitting, he placed his hands flat on the desk and made us an offer. The traditional one you can't refuse. "How about a deal, gentlemen? You tell me your story and I'll tell you mine."

"What the hell," I sighed. "Nik?"

He slowly nodded, and then gave Fellows an implacable order buried under a veneer of steel. "You first." Sketching a mockingly courteous bow, he added, "I insist."

"Fair enough." He gave us another smile. This one was genuine and somewhat sad. Pensive. Definitely not the high-powered ones he'd zinged our way earlier. "It's been a long time since I've been myself with humans. It's been a long time since a human has even believed in me, believed in my kind."

It was polite of him to include me in the human race, especially considering he still had half of me firmly chalked in the Auphe column. "Auphe," it suited better than "elf." It was a darkly acidic burst of taste on the back of your tongue ... the whisper of scales sliding through the grass. The musky smell of a corpse filling your nose, sucking away your breath as clawed hands caressed the skin of your neck. Swallowing thickly, I forced my attention back to Fellows and decided to stick with "Grendels." There's comfort in the old childhood ways when monsters, even the real ones, were defined by you.

Clearing my throat, I asked, "How long's long?"

His eyes went dark and distant. "Long enough that the sky was more amethyst than blue. The moon hung closer, easily as bright as the sun some nights. The water was sweet and pure with the hint of honeysuckle in every handful. Butterflies were as big as blackbirds. . . ." He paused, lost for a moment, then shook it off to finish slyly, "And there were more virgins than you could shake a stick at."

Niko folded his arms and snorted disdainfully. "I'm quite sure there were far less when you were through."

Fellows's smile moved into the scorching range. "You have no idea. Actually, however, I do remember a time when your kind was still picking fleas off one another for a nutritious bedtime snack. It was quite a while before the virgins were worth chasing. But I made up for lost time."

"Yeah, I'll bet you did." I was losing patience, not that I'd ever been long on that quality to begin with. "Enough with the trip down memory lane. Who the hell are you anyway?"

Leaning back in his chair, he linked hands behind his head and gave a good-natured smirk. "Robin Goodfellow at your service. Maybe you've heard of me? Shakespeare gave me lots of press. Mostly good, I have to give him that. But that was only one of my incarnations. Puck.

Pan. All one in the same. Different cultures, different times . . . still, it was always me. More and less than the legend."

Niko lifted both eyebrows at once; he was that surprised. "Honestly?" Cocking his blond head, he peered over the desk with a reluctantly curious gaze. "Aren't you supposed to have the legs of a goat? Even the most talented of tailors couldn't hide that."

His eyes rolled cheerfully. "Fur chaps. I try and make a fashion statement years before its time and this is the thanks I get."

Luckily, the fashion commentary was interrupted by the lovely Dorothea and her plump and juicy muffins. Now, there was a combination that you really did not want to picture. I waited until she left and idly dug a succulent cranberry from the surrounding cake. Popping it in my mouth, I chewed and swallowed before saying, "You're famous, then, huh?"

His shoulders squared as the vanity he wore like a cloak became a shade threadbare. "No," he admitted grudgingly. "Not just me. My entire kind has provided a template, I guess you'd call it, for the myth. We're all Robin. We're all Pan playing our pipes in the endless green wood."

"Even your women?" Niko had finally deigned to relax enough to sit in a chair, although his hands were, as always, within easy reach of any number of weapons.

Fellows shrugged dismissively and poured a cup of coffee. "We don't have any females of our own. Never have." Eyes gleaming brightly, he sipped the hot liquid. "And don't ask me how we make little pucks. You're not ready for that lesson in reproduction."

Now, *that* was a statement I was wholeheartedly behind if there ever was one. "So," I started slowly, "you've been around forever and a friggin' day, longer than Dick Clark even. I'm guessing it's safe to say you could tell us a lot about Auphes, am I right?"

"The Auphe," he corrected grimly. "Singular is plural. Just like the Book says, call them Legion, for they are many. Or were at one time. They've dwindled over the millennia and there isn't a creature out there that's not grateful for that." The serious expression retreated slightly as he leaned back in his chair. "Sure, I know about the Auphe, but I think you gentlemen owe me a story first. A deal is a deal, and I'm all about the art of the deal. So shoot. I'm all ears." He cupped both to show just how ready he was and gave us a winning smile.

Goddamn, but he was annoying as hell. Maybe that had something to do with our so-called deal and maybe it didn't. Either way I wasn't waiting around to figure it out. Propelling myself up out of the chair, I muttered, "Think I'll see if Miss Dorothea has any more muffins."

Ignoring the fact that four of them still rested on the desk, Niko nodded, comprehension a hidden warmth in his eyes. "I wouldn't mind some tea if it's available."

"No problem." I didn't slam the door behind me, but it was a near thing. Leaning against the wall, I sucked in a deep breath, then pushed off. Whatever was said behind that door, I didn't want to overhear any of it, not one single, solitary word.

There was tea, not that green grassy crap Niko drank, but still, in his eyes it would be better than coffee, I knew. By the time I carted that and more muffins back, blueberry this time, Niko was done talking. I knew he would've only sketched the bare bones of my life story, but that didn't stop Fellows from visiting a look of sheer heartfelt pity on me. I could've been generous, could've called it sympathy instead. But it didn't matter; I didn't want either one. Not from him, not from anyone.

"What're you looking at?" I asked sharply. "I'm still a half-breed Auphe monster, same as when I left."

Taking the tea from my hand, Niko said softly, "Cal." Just my name, nothing else. It was enough. I sat down without another word.

Fellows had buried his empathy deep out of sight and now regarded me with only inquisitiveness. "Well, well, aren't you something to write home about? I've never heard of an Auphe-human mix. And you have no idea why it even happened?" He shook his head in amazement. "Damn, if it's not a puzzle."

Nothing like having your whole life summed up as nothing more than an interesting riddle. "Yeah," I responded flatly. "It's a puzzle all right. Almost as big of one as why we're sitting here listening to you. If you can't tell us about the Auphe, then you're just one big fat waste of our time."

At the *f* word a hand automatically went to his trim waist and Fellows scowled. That type of glower shouldn't have sat well on a foxy, blithely cunning face. But it did, perfectly. While I didn't know one-tenth of the mythology my brother did, it seemed to me that maybe good old Puck Robin hadn't been all game playing, piping, and flirting with virgins. There was a temper there, one that could be spiteful at times. And considering how we'd roughed him up even before I began sniping at him, it could be a temper we deserved.

Sliding down a few inches, I rested my chin on my chest and gave a reluctant apology. "Sorry. I'm being a dick. I haven't exactly given you much of a chance to talk." The frown stayed in place, as did the hand on his abdomen. "Oh. And those are abs of steel if I've ever seen 'em," I added lightly. "You could bounce a quarter off those babies."

Fellows's scowl faded as Niko's hand came over to

tousle my hair. "That's a good boy," my brother said, amused.

"Gee, thanks, Wally." I reached for another muffin, not because I was hungry. I was about the furthest thing from it. I just needed something to do with my hands. Mutilating a pastry was going better than clenching my fists until my knuckles popped. Whatever we found out about the Grendels was bound to be less than a good time. "Okay, Fellows, *A* is for 'Auphe.' Clue us in."

He nodded, face still somber. "Call me Robin, would you?" he requested with a wistful note. "It's been a while since anyone has. I guess I rather miss it." He propped his feet on the desk, expensive shoes gleaming in the fluorescent light, and continued. "Gather around, children. It's time for a lesson in history. Ancient history."

Figured. I'd almost flunked my last history class. Hopefully this time I would do better. My life did seem to depend on it.

Robin did his best to talk well into the late afternoon. Not all of it was related to the Grendels. Occasionally he wandered off the subject to spin some tale about wine, women, and song. Sometimes it was about wine, men, and song. I had the feeling Robin was all about equal opportunity when it came to debauchery. I was just grateful he didn't stray into wine, *sheep,* and song.

I didn't really mind the change of subject once in a while even if it did revolve around him. It was a welcome break from the bottomless poisonous swamp of Auphe/Grendel history. You could swallow only so much murderous lust, freezing cold rage, and soulless torture before you began to choke.

It turned out that Grendels were more than mere monsters after all; they were part and parcel of a living nightmare. They seemed to live for only one purpose, one passion, one raison d'être: violence. Destruction. Mayhem. Working separately or together, they had considered the world their personal game preserve. They'd hunted and killed with gleeful abandon, mutilating, torturing, ravaging, living as wolves among the sheep. But wolves killed for food; Grendels killed for the pure love of the game. They killed for fun.

Around since the dawn of time, they'd been here before humans, even before Robin's people. There were no Grendel cities, though, not on the surface. They preferred living either underground in the feeble light of glowing cave fungi or in a place even colder and more barren. It was a place that existed side by side, in and of the earth, but distinct and separate. If you knew just where to look, you could find a doorway. And if you knew just how to walk, you could pass through.

Or could be dragged through as a screaming fourteen-year-old kid.

It was a place sterile of life except for the Grendels. At least so Robin had heard through the mythological grapevine. He'd never been there, actually paled at the thought. Tumulus, he called it. When Niko murmured that the word was Latin, Robin nodded in confirmation. "It seemed appropriate. It means grave. Tomb. Auphe hell. Whatever you want to call it. You'd be better off dead than there, trust me."

Now, there was some information to be filed in the "too little, too late" column. "Time runs differently there too, huh?" I said neutrally. It had for me anyway.

"That's what they say." He hesitated, then furrowed his brow and asked, "You don't remember anything at all? Two years for you and you don't recall even a moment?"

Ignoring the question, I silently dumped the abused muffin on the desktop and brushed the crumbs off my hands. He took the hint and commented briskly,

"Probably for the best. I doubt it'd ever rank with Club Med for vacation hot spots."

"*No.* You think?" I challenged acidly.

Niko was ever the peacemaker, whether with reason or the ultimate in last words, the sword. He interceded, "While their history is fascinating, in a bloody fashion, we are more concerned with why the Grendels have done what they have done. Why did they approach our mother? Why did they take Cal? What do they want? It seems all too intricate for mere random maliciousness."

"Especially since you seemed to have nearly every Auphe living keeping an eye on you then." Robin rubbed a finger along his upper lip, lost in thought.

"Every Gr—every Auphe?" Niko repeated. "I thought you said they were legion. We saw many, far too many, but they were hardly countless."

"I said they *were* countless. That changed long ago." Robin stood and walked restlessly around the room, straightening sales awards on the wall as he went. "Changed for us all. Man." He shrugged his shoulders diffidently. It made me realize he had some memories he probably would've as soon forgotten as thoroughly as I'd managed with mine. The green eyes flicked toward Niko, excepting me from humanity without thought. "You breed like rabbits on aphrodisiacs. One moment you were the occasional star in the early-evening sky and the next, a smothering blanket snatching ownership of the very air itself. None of us had a chance, not even the wretched Auphe."

"Ah," Niko acknowledged with a philosophical regret. "Unfortunately, it is basic biology. When one only lives a short time, reproduction is a built-in priority."

"Every nine months versus every ninety years or so. It makes a difference." Robin blinked, then shook off the past to check his watch. "Sorry, compadres, it's been nice rehashing old times with you, but I have an appointment. There's still a living to make. Takes money to wine and dine the virgins nowadays. Devastating good looks and a big dick just aren't enough anymore."

I quirked the side of my mouth in dark humor as Niko sympathized with mock gravity, "Yes, a tragedy of epic proportions. However, the vast importance of your social life aside, I don't believe we are finished here. Do you?"

His knife might have been out of sight, but Niko was more than capable of making his point without it. Straightening his tie, Robin gave us both a jaundiced look and a reluctant promise. "We'll meet tomorrow, all right? Come by about eight p.m. That'll give me time to think on the situation anyway. I don't have my finger on the Auphe pulse, but I might know someone else who possibly could."

We were almost out the door when I turned and asked one last question. "Loman. Sorry . . . Robin. You seen any Auphe in the city lately?"

His hand, still on his tie, tightened involuntarily like the hand of the condemned on the hangman's noose. "*Here?* Auphe here? *Katadikazo, no.* Never."

Too bad for Robin, too bad for us all, but *never* had just gotten a whole lot shorter.

6

Entertainers, with a capital *E,* are a whole different breed. They're about five steps below your local slime monster on the evolutionary ladder if you ask me, but they were a major portion of Niko's bread and butter. Unfortunately for us have-nots, big money did pave the way for a lot of self-centered, outrageous behavior. Of course with Niko that kind of crap simply rolled off his back, water to a particularly phlegmatic duck. When you could kill someone with a dirty tube sock, you couldn't afford a careless temper.

That didn't mean those nut jobs didn't succeed in bugging the living shit out of me. "Niko, come on," I wheedled like a whiny twelve-year-old, as opposed to the whiny adult I was. "Why do you have to drag me along to the freak show? It's my night off. I'm supposed to be lying on the couch, eating pizza and watching TV. It's the high point of my week. Hell, it's a God-given constitutional right."

"Thank you, John Hancock." He tossed me a pony-tail holder. "Put your hair up. Tonight you're a professional. A professional what, I wouldn't even want to wager a guess, but at least you'll be clean-cut. In any event, since our car-buying venture was unsuccessful, we should try to salvage what remains of the day. You lazing about corrupting your mind and body is not what I consider productive."

"And who died and made you boss?" But I knew a lost cause when I saw it and was already pulling my hair back with nimble fingers.

Niko slapped a shoulder holster against my chest. "No one. Like all truly great dictators, I seized that power myself. Now finish up. We leave in five minutes."

I slipped on the holster loaded with two knives. Niko had already tucked away his fifth blade and wasn't half done yet. "Who are we slaving for tonight?" It wasn't the first time I'd helped out Niko and I had a mental list of the prima donnas, drama queens, and jackasses that I was sincerely hoping to never suffer through again.

"I think I'll let you be surprised." Niko shrugged into his black suit jacket, forgoing a tie against the gray silk shirt. "It will make the walk over less trying."

"That bad? Damn." I pulled on my own blazer, a slightly more rumpled version of Niko's that I'd borrowed from him last time I'd helped him out. It was a given I wouldn't have spent good money on it myself. If the occasion called for more than jeans and a casual shirt, it was safe to say I had no interest in it. Tugging irritably at the collar of the also borrowed turtleneck didn't do anything to relieve the feeling of being choked by a pair of unrelenting polyester hands. "This Robin Goodbar, you believe his spiel?"

"I think you mean Robin Goodfellow." With an exasperated shake of his head, Niko went to the shelf against the far wall and removed a book about the size of the *Titanic*. He had entirely too many thick, esoteric volumes, all educational and all devoted to research on my behalf. When we moved they usually took up the whole backseat of the car. Mythology, ancient civilizations, five thousand ways to slice and dice your opponent—it was all represented.

Niko's library was a stark contrast to mine, if you could even call my books a library. I had a handful of ratty paperbacks to my name, fiction exclusively. There were Westerns with the half-naked saloon girls on the cover, sci-fi with the half-naked three-breasted alien women, and pulp detective fic with the half-naked femmes fatales, anything that caught my discerning eye. No fantasy, though, and no horror. That would've been nothing but a waste of good déjà vu.

"I know what I mean." I staggered under the weight as he dumped *War and Peace*'s big brother into my arms. "Okay, he's definitely not human, but it's still kind of hard to believe Studly McGee's been around since dinosaurs roamed the earth."

"Not all creatures evolve at the same rate, Cal. Be kind." He began to turn the pages with a fast thumb.

I had to snort at that one. "He's an arrogant SOB. Shallow as a parking-lot puddle, not to mention vain as hell." I suppressed a sneeze as the musty smell of a lonely, deserted library wafted up from the pages. More subdued, I added diffidently, "George told me we needed a car. Funny we should run into this guy looking for one."

"Did she?" Nik said without surprise. "Georgina is wiser than we'll ever comprehend. She may have known that Goodfellow could help us in some way." Sparing an exceedingly sore spot for me, he didn't push the subject any further. "In any event, Robin is certainly something of a peacock, I'll give you that. But considering how long he's survived, flourished even, perhaps he has some reason." A preemptory finger landed on the page in front of me. "You should try literature that contains words of more than two syllables, little brother. You might just learn something."

" 'Voluptuous' has more than two syllables." Turning the book right side up, I scanned the page. "So does 'nymphomaniac,' " I added, distracted by what was before me. It was Robin as Puck. No, it was Pan, his earlier incarnation. The caption read that the picture was from a temple painting discovered in the ruins of Pompeii. It wasn't exactly a Polaroid, but the artist had obviously known Robin. Not known *of* him, but been acquainted with him personally. The sly glint in green eyes, the wildly curling brown hair, the smugly lascivious grin, it was our Loman to a T.

"Yes, but 'trash' has only the one." Niko retrieved the book and closed it with a decisive snap. "And your five minutes are up. I suppose you'll be going without shoes?"

I had to put on my black sneakers, the closest thing I had to a dress shoe, one at a time as I hopped down the hall. It was that or go in my socked feet. Niko never had been one for idle threats. Five minutes was five minutes; he had an infallible inner clock . . . and no snooze button.

By the time we hit the street, I was more or less put together and still curious, in a morbidly apprehensive kind of way, who we were covering tonight. It was simpler to think about that than what we might find out from Robin the next day. They say not knowing is the worst and maybe that's true most of the time, but if anyone could prove that theory wrong, it would be me. Running from the Grendels was bad; losing two years of my life, worse. Being half of a *thing* so twisted and evil that it was feared even by other legendary creatures, that was the topper. Or was it? It could be that if we did find out why I came to be, did find out what the hell the

Grendels were playing at, it'd make our lives now seem like a walk in the park.

And the park was a good place. Green and full of trees, blue skies and Frisbees, hot dogs and Sno-Kones. Okay, sure, the occasional mugger with sharp claws, needle teeth, and maniacal red eyes. You dodged, you ran, you fought, and you went on. The park had its shadows, but it might be better than the alternative. The devil you know . . .

So contemplating what god-awful psychotic pseudo-celeb Niko was throwing our way was a distraction I wasn't about to turn down. I ran through my mental list, wincing with almost every entry. My brother's clients might've been short of true fame, but they were long on character, 99 percent of it bad. It was a regular mixed bag of the good, the bad, and the ugly. Or more realistically, the bad, the worse, and the plastic surgeon's Porsche payment. "It's not Glenda Glamstein, is it? Jesus, please tell me it's not her."

"It is not Ms. Glamstein," he responded obediently. "Though I'm sure she would be quite disappointed at your lack of enthusiasm if it were."

The sky was a sooty purple, at the cusp of twilight as the sun tumbled into its grave. There were more people on the sidewalks rushing home to dinner, their hobbies, their pets, their families. They all looked annoyed; it didn't say much about their home lives. I bumped my shoulder against Niko's. Most people didn't know how lucky they had it, and most didn't have a clue what family was all about. "Right, and you were so ready to go along with her uniform code."

"It would be tricky to hide very many weapons in a leather codpiece." He pursed his lips and looked down the length of his long nose. "For the less endowed among us certainly. I suppose I could've lent you a penknife." Before I could defend myself, not that Cal Junior needed it, Niko delivered the news early. "But have no fear, your virtue, such as it is, is perfectly safe. Your assets aren't liquid enough to draw the attention of Ms. Nottinger."

At the name I relaxed slightly. Tonight wouldn't be too bad after all. Promise Nottinger was one of the more well behaved of Niko's clients. Never mind that she was more commonly known as Promissory Note. As long as you were under the age of seventy and had less than fifty mil in your bank account, you weren't even a blip on the horizon. She might have been the human version of a succubus, but she was one with very specific tastes. As far as she was concerned, bodyguards were professionals there to do their job, nothing more or less, and she wasn't going to interfere with that. You can't really marry five doddering millionaires and their money without making an enemy or two. Keeping the bodyguard's mind on his business could only be in her best interest. There were plenty of disgruntled and disinherited family members out there just itching to have a go at Promise.

Not that she was a black widow from the "Late Late" movies. No, she didn't drop a subtle poison in hubby's warm milk or give him and his wheelchair a push down the stairs. As far as I knew, they had all died the natural death of the truly elderly. Then again there was more than one way to skin a cat. And if the majority of them had died in bed, shortly after their honeymoon or even while on it, who's to say they didn't get what they paid for? They probably died happy, happy men. To every husband, Promise kept her promise. But more importantly, to me anyway, she was quiet and restrained, and let us fade into the background. She didn't treat us like a circus act or a badge of fame and wealth. Promise was always a lady.

From the first wedding to the last funeral . . . always a lady.

We got on the 6 train and then made our way up to Sixtieth Street. Promise's place was on the Upper East Side, naturally, and thirty stories up in a building on Park. It wasn't the absolute best money could buy, but instead comfortably sandwiched between the obscenely wealthy and the disgustingly rich. There were shining wood floors, jewel-bright rugs, soft misty paintings, and plump grapes on wafer-thin crystal. Not a television or a bag of Cheetos in sight. Maybe the rich don't have everything after all. Niko liked it, though; I could tell. It wasn't necessarily his thing. Even if we'd been swimming in money, his ideal would be much more spartan, more utilitarian. Still, from the tilt of his blond head to the quicksilver flash in his eyes, I could see he appreciated its beauty, though it was entirely too elaborate for his taste.

Promise herself was much simpler than her apartment. Mink brown hair pulled back tightly from her face, pale skin, a full but unpainted mouth—she was saved from anonymity only by cheekbones that could cut glass and a pair of arresting purple eyes the color of blooming heather. In those eyes you could easily get lost, drowning in a field of summer wildflowers. It was easy to see how five rich men had fallen, and fallen hard.

We'd barely arrived at her place before we were leaving again. Always unfailingly prompt, she swept out the door, cloaked in silence as shimmering as her silk shawl. Promise wasn't much on the spoken word. If she had something especially pertinent to say, she would. If not, she let her eyes speak for her. And they did, in volumes that had even the most jaded, sneering maître d' scrambling frantically to smooth her path with verbal rose petals.

Me? I was lucky to get a grunt from the local pizza delivery girl. And *I* had nice eyes too, not to mention a killer ass. There truly was no justice in the world.

How did I know that? Aside from the ass thing, one clue was how our easy night went downhill as fast as a runaway sled. The first hour went well enough. Tedious enough to have my jaw aching with restrained yawns, but it was better than a kick in the head. Just barely.

I started out circulating throughout the reception at the Waldorf. Art for art's sake, save the starving ring-tailed dingoes, eliminate tennis elbow—it was for some charity or another. And if in reality it was just a social opportunity for the bored rich, I guess the money was spent all the same. I'd long given up on pulling on my collar for oxygen and now my hands hung loose and easy at my sides as I moved through the crowd. Niko and I swapped every twenty minutes. He'd cover the client and I'd run the room looking for possible threats and then if all was quiet, we'd switch out. It was the same routine I'd worked with Niko several times before and I had it down pat enough that half my mind was on the job while the other played a little what-if.

Watching all these people socializing, living their lives for the better part oblivious to the dark undercurrent that ran beneath all our feet, made me think. What would it have been like for Niko and me if I'd been normal, your average Harry Human? Okay, probably not like this. And Niko, who was smart as hell, could've achieved anything he turned his mind to. In the end, though, I had a feeling Niko had certain priorities, not to mention a certain edge, that would've led him in a particular direction. Considering his martial knack combined with a driven intellect, I imagined my brother kicking criminal butt on a federal level.

Either that or teaching college medieval history, dressed in tweed and waving around a broadsword. Swallowing a grin, I didn't dwell as much on what my life would've been like. Where Niko's might-have-been was painted in bright and vivid if whimsical strokes, mine was a canvas of murky shadows. It could be it was just harder to take yourself out of context. Or it could be the realization that if I were human, I wouldn't be me. Not even a through-a-glass-lightly version. A white-washed, demon-free Caliban was a concept I simply couldn't wrap my mind around, no matter the effort I put into it. College and frats, girlfriends and road trips, it was a make-believe landscape that flourished fine until I inserted myself into it. Then it just faded away. For better or worse I was Grendel-American, and that was one gene pool no lifeguard could pull you out of. My imagination knew that as well as I did.

So I tucked it and the fantasies back where they belonged and directed my attention, all of it, back to the job at hand. I did another circuit of the reception without incident. Since all seemed relatively quiet and assailant free, I decided on a quick pit stop. Unfortunately even bodyguards of steel had all-too-human bladders. After giving Niko the high sign from across the room, I drifted through the throng, snatching a crab-stuffed mushroom from a silver server as I went. By the time I walked into the bathroom the hors d'oeuvre was nothing but a mellow, smoky memory on the back of my tongue. The taste, rich and potent, matched my first glimpse of the bathroom.

Walls the color of ancient parchment met a marble floor shot through with gold and a rich toffee brown. A nearly full-sized chandelier hung from the ceiling, muted topaz gems glittering softly. The long countertop was one vast piece of lovingly polished wood embedded with several beaten-brass sinks. The mirror that hung above it all dominated the eye. Framed with a twisted line of copper and brass that blossomed into leaves at the four corners, it covered nearly the entire top half of the wall.

I doubted I'd ever pissed in a place so fancy.

Unimpressed, my bladder let me know there was no time like the present. Once I'd finished business and zipped up, I went over to a sink to wash my hands. Several folded towels, thick and fleecy, balancing on a stool showed someone else was on a break as well. Good for you, buddy, I thought. Helping myself to a chocolate-colored towel, I was drying off when I saw it.

Out of the corner of my eye, a dark slithering as subtle as a coyly beckoning finger. Like most things glimpsed in the periphery it had my heart slamming in a way something seen face-to-face wouldn't have. The towel dropped from my hand as my knife sprang into my grip practically of its own accord. I turned fast half crouched on the balls of my feet with my blade close to my body to face . . . nothing.

Nothing, that is, but my own reflection. It stared at me grimly as we both drew in lungfuls of air as suddenly thick and choking as river mud. "Damn," I muttered. I had not lost it over my own image in the mirror; that jumpy I wasn't. I refused to believe it.

As I quickly scanned the rest of the bathroom the lights overhead flickered once, the autumn gold disappearing into a velvety black. And in that moment, the barest slice of time, I thought I felt the air ripple against my skin, as if something had passed right before my face. Or maybe it was a breath, fetid and hot, as teeth aimed for my neck. I was already swinging blindly with a deadly slice when the light returned. And once again it was just me and my shadow. At least he looked as sheepish as I felt. I sighed, put away the knife, and knocked lightly on the bright surface of the mirror. "Alice, you in there?" There was no answer in Wonderland. If she was there, then she was perfectly happy behind the looking glass with no intentions of coming out.

1

By the time I'd navigated the crowd back to Niko's side my heart rate had dropped to normal and the cold sweat prickling the back of my neck had subsided. It was nice to know how quickly I could recover from the gibbering terror of a malfunctioning bathroom light. I gave Niko a nod and took my place discreetly behind Ms. Nottinger, who was a pale sun orbited by several planets long past their prime. She seemed more distantly amused than appreciative of the attention. Just went to show, there is a point where enough is enough ... money, that is. Promise had retired from business, although her would-be sugar daddies didn't seem to want to believe it. I wanted to tell the group of horny Methuselahs to give it up, but instead swallowed the impulse and watched as Niko melted into the milling crowd to disappear from sight. Literally. One second there, one second gone. Get the man a white tiger and a silver jumpsuit and he could play Vegas. I might be more or less than human, depending on your viewpoint, but it was my brother who had the abilities that were all but supernatural. "Later, Houdini," I murmured to empty air, and then moved to subtly discourage a gentleman whose wrinkled, palsied hands were too ambitious for his own good.

Promise didn't stay more than an hour or so, just long enough to do a few circuits, bemuse a gaggle of old men, and make her donation. She might have come by her money in a less-than-orthodox manner, but she played by the same rules of her adopted social class. After she bade her farewells to several disappointed suitors, we left the hotel for the crisp night air. Underneath a midnight sky reflected orange by a million lights, Promise raised her face and said softly, "I miss the stars."

I slid a curious glance toward Niko. That was the first personal comment I had ever heard the woman make. And granted, I'd only met her twice before, compared with Niko's dozens of times, but from the eyebrow he raised he seemed as surprised as I was by the remark. Noncommittal, he responded, "Too much ambient light, a pollution all its own." He indicated her car and driver at the curb. "Shall we go, Ms. Nottinger?"

"Too much light," she repeated. Then, her eyes still on the sky, she knotted her shawl briskly. "No, I think not. I'm in the mood for a walk. Tell Timothy he's dismissed for the night. Pity. He'll have to forgo his customary nap behind the wheel." I gave a silent wince at her arch tone, the needle-sharp point of a stiletto coated with warm honey. I had a feeling Timothy the driver was going to be in the unemployment line before too much longer.

After Niko knocked on the smoked-glass window of the car and delivered the news, Promise swept down the sidewalk to head north. I could say like a queen among the rabble, but it wasn't like that. It was more like a ghost among unbelievers. She made her way, a fantastic creature, unseen and unnoticed, suddenly as insubstantial as she had been brilliant at the reception. She was like Niko that way, a chameleon, visible only if she wanted to be. It was a rare skill that only the truly self-contained, the genuinely balanced, had. To know thyself, right?

No, thanks. Guess that was one ability I'd have to leave to the pros.

Niko moved on ahead of Promise, while I brought up the rear, my eyes open for the more mundane threats now. Pickpockets, perverts, general weirdos, the usual nightlife, it was all a possibility—although less so in this ritzy area. But the farther we walked, the more of a probability it became. And while the human threats might not have claws or fangs, some still had an insatiable need for blood that would rival that of any monster.

Promise's walk was beginning to lengthen into a genuine trek. The forty minutes stretched into an hour and the faint click of her heels became more noticeable as the people began to thin around us. Niko caught me checking my watch and sent me a look of stern disapproval. Subtle and fleeting, it still had me squaring my shoulders with an inner groan. Working the bar had made me lazy. Until Samuel and his friends had shown up, that place had been one long eight-hour snooze. This, on the other hand, this was work. And if our client didn't hurry up and pull a groin muscle or sprain an ankle, I might actually get winded. When she said she missed the stars, I had no idea she was going to try to *walk* to them.

She finally halted down a dark stretch of alley between two sketchy-looking buildings. She just stopped out of the blue, hands cupping her elbows, her distracted gaze on the glittering white lights slung carelessly on a fire escape. Someone had the Christmas spirit all year round, or was every bit the sloth I was.

"Not stars," she said pensively, and then smiled, soft and warm as a summer rain. "But still beautiful." Sighing, she tightened her arms around herself and tilted her head toward Niko. There was resignation in the classic line of her jaw. "We were followed, weren't we?"

"Yes," he responded calmly. "We were. It seems that is not a total surprise to you, Ms. Nottinger."

Maybe not to her, but it was something of one to me. I'd picked up on the guy a few blocks from the Waldorf, and Niko had probably picked him up from minute one. But that Promise had known all along someone might be lurking outside waiting for her, that I hadn't picked up on at all. She had been serene and self-possessed, apparently oblivious. I guess I'd forgotten that the acting skills needed by a professional succubus would be impressive. She had pulled the wool over my eyes, and by this point in my life I was not an easy person to fool by any stretch of the imagination.

"No, not a total one." Fingers lightly stroked the silken threads of her wrap. "I can explain, if you allow me."

"Perhaps you can. However, this is not the time to do it. Cal, you take the front. Ms. Nottinger and I will take the back." His hand firmly on Promise's arm, Niko ushered her to the end of the alley, where they both disappeared into a darkness as physical as a wall. I chose my own pool of shadows to submerge myself in and waited patiently, the bricks rough and suspiciously wet against my back. There'd been no rain, and I didn't even want to hazard a guess as to what was soaking through the material of my coat. That is, until I remembered it was Niko's jacket, and then I gleefully thought of a hundred noxious, disgusting fluids it could be.

My patience wasn't all it could be when it came to the day-to-day shit, but when it came to matters of survival, it was as still and cold as that of any cat waiting for an unlucky low-flying bird. And it wasn't too long before our feathered friend fluttered in. Sharp beak, darting black eyes—he really was rather birdlike with a black trench coat that even vaguely mimicked wings. He was a smaller man, a few inches shorter than me, with a slight build, but there was a glassy sheen in his eyes that gave as much pause as a muscle-bound body would have. He wasn't talking to himself or carrying any hand-made signs proclaiming the apocalypse was nigh, my brothers, but he had the same stark, white-eyed stare many of the street people had. Chaotic and intense as a laser beam without a guidance system.

He moved into the alley cautiously with quick short steps, askew gaze flitting back and forth. There was something in his hand, but it was hidden by the folds of his long coat. It had to be a weapon. Gun or knife, Taser maybe. And from his white-knuckle grip, it didn't look like he had any intentions of giving it up without a fight. I curved my lips in a silent, humorless grin. That was all right by me. I wasn't one to turn down pounding a de-serving head against the asphalt. Good stress relief. I watched as he passed my position without detecting me in the deep gloom. The twinkling Christmas lights gleamed off his high forehead and pale fawn hair like an eerie halo. It was a jaggedly bizarre contrast with his jit-tering eyes and ferocious intensity—a soulless and psy-chotic angel in desperate need of a Prozac-lithium cocktail. He was also an angel who was about to get his wings clipped.

I stepped away from the wall and moved in silently behind him. His bony shoulders were scarecrow thin and so tense it looked as if he'd shatter with one touch. Always being the curious sort, I gave it a try. Pulling a knife, I tapped him politely with the blade. "I think you took a wrong turn off the yellow brick road, pal. A *seriously* wrong turn."

They were words he took to heart, demonstrated by his next turn. He swiveled around with a slippery speed, his coat fanning out behind him and his hand thrusting with avalanche force toward my face. It happened with such speed and fury that it was like an act of God, inescapable. Not to mention uninsurable. I backpedaled, blocked the blow with my forearm, and aimed my knife for his abdomen. The metal cutting the air, I was just about to open him up like a piñata when I was able to make out what was flying toward my face. Not a knife, not a gun, not even a goddamn slingshot. It was a cross. It was a hugely ornate one, gleaming with a softly metallic sheen in the weak light. Still, as big as it was, it wasn't enough of a threat to justify slicing and dicing the guy. Not yet anyway. Hope springs eternal, though, right?

I pulled my blade up, and landed a hard elbow in his gut instead. He dropped like a rock, gasping for air, but stubbornly clinging to the cross. Squatting on my heels, I patted him down as he curled in a fetal position on the pavement. Out of his pockets I fished another smaller cross and a vial of colorless liquid. I opened it and was sniffing it cautiously when Niko appeared, empty-handed and apparently weaponless except for the wickedly amused twitch of his lips. "Embracing that old-time religion, are we?"

Grunting, I replaced the lid. It was just water. "Embracing it with my face, you mean. He nearly put a dent in my skull. Thanks for the help, by the way."

"If you couldn't handle one unarmed fanatic, Cal, then you are too frail for this world. Best to shuffle off that mortal coil before someone places you in a bubble for your own good." He reached down and took the small container from my hand. He didn't open it, merely held it up in the dim light and said simply, "Ah." Looking down at our mysterious lunatic, he tossed the vial from hand to hand. "Now, isn't this interesting?"

Annoyed, I puffed out air and grumbled, "Care to share with the class, Sherlock? Your leaps of logic tend to leave me motion sick."

An eyebrow rose. "Cal, it's obvious. A cross, what appears to be holy water. Our nutritionally challenged friend is after a . . ."

"Vampire," the man wheezed, his empty hand scrambling weakly at the alley floor. "She's a vampire." He coughed, sucked in a whistling breath. "A monster . . . a fiend from hell."

Well, how about that? Promise was a sister. "Is that a fact?" I commented neutrally, rising smoothly and planting a heavy foot in the small of the scarecrow's back to keep him down. "Did she happen to mention that when she hired you, Niko? That whole bloodsucking thing ever come up?"

"Mistress of the devil. Satan's scarlet whore," the voice rasped on from beneath my foot.

"Yeah, yeah, buddy," I said impatiently. "We got it. Zip it already."

"Queen of everlasting darkness . . ."

I sighed and delivered a short, sharp kick behind the nut job's ear. His head snapped forward and instantly he was out like a cheap lightbulb. He'd wake up with nothing more than a pounding headache, and I was betting it wouldn't be any worse than the one he'd given me. "You just can't reason with people these days. It's a goddamn shame."

Niko gave me a look of distinct exasperation. Was it disappointment for my silencing of the annoying fruit loop, my lack of the milk of human kindness for the overly mouthy of the world? Hardly. "Not quite as shameful as your sloppy footwork. An inch to the left will give you a much longer duration of unconsciousness. Did you even read that anatomy book I gave you, or are you using it as a coaster?"

"Actually it's propping up the kitchen table." Impatiently, I gave a nod to the shadows behind him. "Maybe your client could give us etiquette tips on that after she sucks out all our blood. What do you think?"

Raising his eyebrows, my brother gave an amused snort, then lowered his voice to a level for my ears only. "Do you actually believe that maniac, Cal? If she were one of the undead, don't you think I would have known, that you would have smelled her?"

I followed suit and answered with frustration, "I can't smell anything over her perfume. I'm half Grendel, not half dog."

"It is pleasant. Feminine and potent, yet fresh and clean," he mused. "Quite nice."

The voice of reason wasn't a hat I usually wore. "Niko, do you want to kill the monster or just date it?" I snapped with exasperation.

At that moment Promise stepped into view, a vision of tranquillity as her twilight-colored eyes lingered on the unconscious man. She shook her head, the silk around her shoulders shimmering from the movement. "Obviously a very disturbed individual, yes? A distant relative of my last husband. He has been following me for days saying the most bizarre things. Insane things."

"Then I suppose we should call the police and have him taken into custody." The sensible words hung in the air, but before Niko made a move to retrieve his cell phone, Promise held up a hand.

"Wait." She swallowed, a smooth motion under flawless pale skin. "Don't."

Niko's eyes darkened, the fascination with her perfume already a distant memory. He moved to her side, his face neutrally blank. Gravely apologetic, he said, "Ms. Nottinger, if you please." With the utmost care he cupped her chin and, using his thumb to delicately lift her upper lip, revealed exquisitely tiny pointed canine teeth.

I raised my hands and let them fall. "Jesus, Niko, are you the *only* human in this goddamn city?"

His old-world courtesy melting, Niko had already reached a hand into his coat to take out a long wooden stake. Knives, swords, stakes—he had it all and then some. It wouldn't surprise me if one day he pulled Jimmy Hoffa out of there. Keeping an eye on the deceitful Promise, I bent down and retrieved the cross from our stalker's slack fingers. I'd seen Niko handle any number of demonic creepy-crawlies over the years, so I didn't believe a petite 110-pound vampire would get the best of him. That is, unless her perfume overwhelmed him, I thought caustically. "Whatever you do, Nik, don't smell her," I drawled as I hefted the cross to shoulder height in my best traditional "Back, creature of the night" stance.

Before he could skewer me with a comeback or Promise with the stake, she touched his arm lightly. "It isn't like that, Niko," she said solemnly. "I swear to you. I may not be human, but neither am I a monster."

The point of the stake dimpled the skin over her breastbone. "Oddly enough that's what I imagine most monsters would say in your position," Niko countered without emotion, his hand holding steady. "Answer me this, then, Ms. Nottinger. Did all your husbands in fact die of natural causes or did they cut themselves shaving . . . perhaps with your teeth?"

I thought "natural causes" was covering a pretty broad

range, but since the FBI had yet to register sex as a deadly weapon there wasn't much I could say. Watching carefully, I saw Promise's mouth firm and her chin lift. "I don't drink human blood. Not all vampires do. Not the younger ones. There are better ways now."

"Really?" I snorted. "And what are those better ways? Pigs' blood? I'll bet you drink it from a crystal goblet, right?" There was no way I could picture that, her aristocratic lips swilling the blood of livestock as if it were wine.

"Hardly," she said with withering scorn. Her disdainful eyes returned to Niko and softened. "My purse, Niko. Look in my purse if you would." When he didn't move she added simply, "Please."

He considered for a moment with unblinking icy cool, then held out a hand for the tiny purse that dangled from her arm. His other hand didn't move a millimeter from its position on the stake. Promise stood as unmoving as a statue as her purse was deftly rifled through one-handed. It was barely a second before Niko fished out a pill bottle large enough that it must have filled the purse entirely, and held it up to squint at it in the low light. "Iron. Quite a high dose, I would say." Of course Niko would know the daily recommended dosage of any vitamin or mineral. He took that entire theory of your body being a temple seriously enough to quote it ad nauseam every time I even thought about having a cheeseburger.

"Yes, iron. So simple, and yet it was the answer to a disease that has plagued my kind for centuries beyond the telling." Placing her hand on the stake, she gently pushed it away and Niko, unbelievably, allowed it. "Every day for the duration of my life. It, along with certain other supplements, allows me to live without drinking blood."

Niko tapped his chin with the point of the stake thoughtfully. "So you are trying to tell us that basically vampirism is nothing more than an iron-deficiency anemia? I find that rather difficult to believe, Ms. Nottinger."

A shadow of a smile curved her lips. "It is slightly more complex than that. The pills don't fulfill the same need, the same *desire,* as blood does. They don't allow me to retain the strength and the powers of a truly fed vampire, but it does keep my blood cells from devouring one another in a cannibalistic frenzy. And it lets me maintain my existence without blind, voracious killing."

"Always a good thing," I commented sarcastically. "I'm sure butchering innocent people would play absolute hell with your social schedule." Still, whether or not I swallowed her story, Niko and I had never been superheroes, never defenders of the blissfully ignorant public. We were trying to survive, that's all. Keeping our own asses intact was more than job enough, and as long as Promise wasn't tearing out the throat of some golden-haired cherub right in front of us, I wasn't going to be losing any sleep over it.

"Yes, I suppose it would, but I could always make a onetime exception." From her pointed gaze I had no problem guessing just who that exception might be.

"Now, children," Niko said reprovingly. "Play nice. Ms. Nottinger, I am curious. How did this rather fanatical gentleman discover the truth about you?"

As it turned out Promise had been telling the truth there. He was the great-nephew and only living relative of her last husband. Whether or not he'd been disinherited in favor of his uncle's new wife was a point of contention. Regardless, in his mind it was true. He had done his level best to get something on Promise, anything at all. Yes, she had multiple late husbands, but among the wealthy, that wasn't necessarily that unusual a lifestyle choice. In the end all he could determine was that Promise had some peculiar habits, one of which was not going out in the daylight. Ever. That was still a big jump for your average person to make to creature of the darkness, but from what Promise's late husband had said disparagingly about his nephew, it seemed he'd already had bats in his belfry. It wouldn't be that much harder to turn them into vampire bats.

"He may turn into something of a problem for you, then." Niko tucked his stake away and handed Promise her pill bottle. "How will you handle him?"

"I really only see two choices in the matter." She replaced the pills in her purse and clicked it shut decisively. "The first would be to pay him off. I worked quite hard for that money and am loath to give up even part of it, but . . ." She shrugged philosophically.

"And if that doesn't work?" I asked.

Delicately pointed teeth peeked out from a pouty upper lip. "Diamonds aren't always a girl's best friend."

Well, the guy had a chance anyway. That was more than most people got in this life. I dropped the cross beside him and we left him in the alley, not too much worse for the wear. Forty minutes later we'd ushered Promise back to her building and watched her get into the elevator. But not before she'd put a finger on Niko's mouth as he'd called her Ms. Nottinger one last time. "I think after all we've been through, Niko, that I would like it if you called me Promise."

As the elevator doors closed, I shook my head despairingly at the bemused expression on Niko's face. "Are you certifiable? She's buried five husbands, not to mention she's the undead. A bloodsucking . . ." Okay, that wasn't strictly true. I amended, "An iron-pill-popping fiend from hell. She'd eat you alive."

"She would, would she?" Niko said dryly.

"Seriously, Nik, she's dangerous, a predator." This voice-of-reason shit, it had to stop. It was a strain on my resources.

His lip twitched. "And what, little brother, do you think I am?"

Damn. He had me there.

8

Locks.

They kept things in and they kept things out. In theory anyway. But in reality I had to wonder if there were enough locks in the world to keep the Grendels at bay. Whatever doubt I had, though, it wasn't enough to keep Nik from installing the best money could buy not even twenty minutes after we'd moved into the place two years ago.

I stripped off Niko's ruined jacket, wadded it into a ball, and tossed it into a corner. Outside the bedroom I could hear him checking the locks on the door. Never mind the things were so sophisticated they practically locked themselves; he still tested them. Every night. Even in the throes of a star-crossed vampire love, that wasn't going to change. Snorting to myself, I sat on my bed and toed off my shoes. My sister-in-law, Countess Dracula. It could've been funny. Hell, it should've been hilarious, but it wasn't. Yeah, hard to find the humor when you realize that thanks to you there might never be a sister-in-law, human or no.

Life on the run didn't lend itself to long-lasting relationships. And lying about your past, your present, your whole damn life, didn't much lend itself to relationships of any kind. I could count on one hand the people we considered even acquaintances ... and most of them didn't really come under the typical designation of "people." Boggle was one, although in actuality he was more of a restrained enemy. There was a witch in Louisiana that dabbled in everything from Wicca to voodoo, a Selkie that swam the Oregon coast, and the closest, a healer that lived on Staten Island. Rafferty was the first and only healer I'd ever met. I had no idea how prevalent a talent that was in humans, but Rafferty damn sure had a handle on it. It was a shame he was practicing under the radar in med school. But then again he didn't need med school. In minutes he could do what most doctors couldn't achieve with hours of work and years of education. Of the few people we'd actually taken the time to know over the years, he was the only one I regretted not being able to take the final step with from acquaintance to friendship. It couldn't happen, not without trust. And Nik and I had never been in the trust business. We couldn't afford to be.

Now that life, or lack of it, was going to cost Nik a rare opportunity. Without removing any more clothes, I fell back onto the mattress and studied the ceiling with sleepy eyes. Not that Niko blamed me; he wouldn't. We were family. Considering the way we'd grown up, if we didn't look after each other, it was a fact that no one else was going to step up to the plate to do it. No, he didn't blame me, but that didn't mean I couldn't blame myself. Rolling onto my stomach, I pounded the pillow and dropped my head onto it. Guilt, it got old sometimes.

So did the running.

So what if we saw one Grendel? It had been years since the last time they had caught up with us. As a matter of fact, that had been the event that had propelled our asses to the big city. We'd been lucky that time. No fire, no melting trailer, no mother going up like a Roman candle, just swords, knives, and the purple blood of monsters. But that had been nearly three years ago. At some point the Grendels had to give up, didn't they? At some point didn't they have to cut their losses and chalk me up as the one that got away? I had no idea what those bastards wanted with me, but whatever it was, there had to be a time when enough was enough. Even for the Grendels. Had to be.

Rolling out of bed, I shook off the thoughts and headed to the bathroom. As my hand went to the light switch, I hesitated and then left the bathroom in darkness. I wasn't still jumpy over the mirror incident at the Waldorf; I just didn't need the light. And if I avoided my shadowy reflection in the mirror, it was purely by accident. I didn't need to see myself to brush my teeth. Some things are best done unseen anyway.

Lying to yourself is one of them.

The next day didn't improve my mood any. And there was one big obnoxious reason for that. Robin friggin' Goodfellow. The guy was like a hangover without the actual alcohol. Too loud. Too bright. Too *everything*.

I'd spent the day grabbing an early shift at the bar while Niko did the same at the dojo. Then we had eaten a quick dinner before making our way to the meeting at the car lot. I was tired, sweaty from the unexpected October heat wave that had descended that day, and in no mood to hear this guy run his mouth. But I guess that was tough shit for me because run it he did. Continuously. Nonstop. Ad infinitum and any other fancy words for "would not shut the hell up."

There he sat in a position already becoming familiar, his feet crossed casually at the ankles and propped on his desk, while he ate noodles out of a cardboard box with chopsticks. "You sure you guys aren't hungry?" He waved a chopstick at the numerous boxes littering the office. "I got Moo Goo Gai Pan. Fried rice. Sweet-and-sour pork."

Niko shook his head. "No, thank you. We've already eaten." He cast a dubious eye at all the food. "You must have quite the appetite for Chinese."

Robin flashed an insatiable grin. "I've a lot of appetites, compadre, and not just for Chinese. Did I tell you about the time . . . ?"

Here we go, I thought with a groan. We'd learned fast yesterday that once those words came out of his mouth he'd be heading at a rapid gallop down memory lane. And most of his memories were as off-color as month-old bologna. "Save it for later, Sir Raunch-a-lot," I rapped. "We're here about the Auphe. 'Robin Does Rome' can wait until later."

He contemplated me for a moment, measuring me with eyes an intense, serious green. Then he pointed a chopstick at me and announced, "Kid, you need to get laid in the worst way."

Niko coughed abruptly, throat spasming over what I strongly suspected was swallowed laughter. The bastard. "Yeah?" I gritted between clenched teeth. "You wanna talk laid? How 'bout I lay you out like a rug? Then I kick your ass for the annoying son of a bitch you are?"

"Cranky. Cranky." Unperturbed, he took another bite of his noodles. "Just like an Auphe. No sense of humor."

I was coming up out of my chair with a growl when Niko snagged the back of my shirt and pulled me back down. "As entertaining as all this is, gentlemen," he said mildly, "we are here for a purpose. Let's pursue it, shall we?" He added as Robin put down the carton and swung his feet to the floor, "Also, Goodfellow, I would prefer that you not compare my brother to the Auphe again. Ever. Are we crystal clear regarding that particular subject?"

Robin cocked a sardonic eyebrow at me. "You feed him dictionaries for breakfast or what?"

I twisted my lips in reluctant acknowledgment. "Yeah, he's a regular alphabet soup dispenser." Leaning back in the chair, I stretched out my legs and inwardly accepted there was no rushing a puck. You might as well sit back, enjoy the ride, and pray your Dramamine kicked in. "So fill us in, Loman. You find out anything?"

The cocky expression melted off Robin's face as he speared the chopsticks into the box and dropped it onto the desk. "Not exactly," he hedged grimly. "But I was able to track down someone who might be able to help. A troll."

"A troll?" Niko echoed. "Are they especially knowledgeable about the Auphe?"

Robin's mouth thinned contemptuously. "Trolls are knowledgeable about quite a few things, all of them unpleasant. Whether or not it'll care to tell us anything is a different story." Then his expression lightened and he said slyly, "But you pups seem like you might be good at getting people to open up. Look what you did for me. Must be those friendly, honest faces."

"Yes, it must be." Niko's smile was like a sliver of ice in the heart.

"We're just sharing the love." I stood and slapped a hand on my leg. "So just where is this troll? Under the Brooklyn Bridge?"

Robin grinned like the Cheshire cat. "He shoots; he scores."

"Damn, really?" I guessed it wasn't such a wild supposition. The fairy tales couldn't all be wrong.

The fairy tales, however, hadn't said anything about the smell. In the shadow of the bridge with the river at my feet, I bent over, resting my hands on my knees, and concentrated on not hurling dinner all over my sneakers. The rank scent of troll was everywhere and choking in its intensity. Thick as molasses, it saturated every molecule with the putrid stench. "Jesus, how can you not smell that?" I gasped.

Niko's steadying hand rested on my back. "I don't smell anything except the East River, although that is fairly unpleasant in and of itself."

"The Auphe do have sensitive . . ." Robin let the words trail away as Niko's withering gaze hit him. Clearing his throat, he crouched in front of me. "You going to make it, kid?"

I glared at him through watering eyes. "I'll make it." Coughing twice, I pulled in air through my mouth instead of my nose. It didn't help much. Straightening, I rubbed a hand across my face. Breathing . . . who needed it? "Okay, let's do it."

Robin followed suit. Crossing his arms, he made a face as water lapped near his immaculate loafers. "Filthy river."

In black pants, shiny black shoes, and a forest green shirt I'd bet my last buck was 100 percent silk, Robin wasn't exactly dressed for roughing it. He was in stark contrast with Niko, wearing a long black coat despite the heat, and me in a navy blue T-shirt and worn charcoal gray sweatpants. "Don't you think you could've gone a little more casual?" I asked caustically.

Robin threw me a disbelieving look. "What are you talking about? These *are* my casual clothes."

"Why am I not surprised?" I made my way past him, the mud sucking at my shoes. "So where's your pal, huh? Where's the bane of Billy Goat Gruff?"

"He's most certainly not my friend. Don't for a minute go into this thinking that. He's not necessarily my enemy, but that's the best interpretation you can put on it. Trolls are like storms. They're a force of nature, deadly and completely without conscience. Forget that and you could be killed in a heartbeat." Goodfellow's voice was as serious as I'd ever heard it.

"That's if the smell doesn't get me first," I grunted, slogging on. The sun had long since disappeared, but the light from the bridge was more than enough to see by. Not that there was much to see besides muddy water and bleak concrete. "Where is he?" I repeated. "This is one damn big bridge to be hiding under."

"An accurate assessment, to say the least." Niko had moved up silently beside me, seemingly skating along the mud that was miring me down. "The troll could be anywhere."

Following behind us fastidiously, Robin shook his head. "Could be, maybe, but he isn't. Abbagor likes to roam the undercarriage of the bridge, but he needs a hidey-hole too. A place for his . . . leftovers. It's early yet. He'll be there." Picking up the pace, he moved in front of us and led the way around the nearest abutment to a rusted iron grate set flush into the concrete. It was just like the ones you were afraid to walk over as a kid because you knew, just *knew,* that if you did, you'd plunge to the center of the earth never to be heard from again.

"In there?" I groaned at his affirming nod. "Great. Just goddamn peachy." Aiming a solid kick at the metal, I rammed my foot against it, sending a shower of orange rust flakes into the air. "Yo, Avon calling."

"You are just the soul of finesse, aren't you?" Robin shook his head in disbelief and disapproval.

"It isn't precisely his strong suit." Niko pushed my foot aside and grasped the grate with both hands, yanking it free with a tortured screech of metal. "Who wishes to go first into the gaping maw of hell?"

Ignoring his mockingly dry tone, I crouched and then dropped feetfirst into the hole, the inky blackness swallowing me instantly. It wasn't as far as the earth's center, but it was far enough to send an unpleasant jolt through my legs as I landed. Pulling a small flashlight from the waistband of my pants, I switched it on. Partially shielding it with my fingers to let my eyes adjust, I called upward, "Come on in. The water's fine." Gagging for a moment, I muttered to myself in the rising waves of troll reek, "Smelly as hell, but fine."

Niko landed beside me as agilely as a cat. Robin followed immediately, nearly as light-footed as my brother. I guess you'd pick up a bit of dexterity over a few thousand years or so. He wasn't as silent as Nik, though. "Grimy. Filthy. Putrefying. Abbagor, you abominable beast, wallowing in filth like a pig. This is *silk*. It will never come clean."

As he rambled on, becoming more and more outraged as he went, I shot the beam of the flashlight around the artificial cavern. The concrete walls were liberally coated with a wash of green slime, doubtless either fungus or mold. What the floor was made of was a mystery, as we stood almost calf deep in bone-chilling mud. "Helluva bachelor pad your pal Abby's got going for him," I offered with a curl of my lip. "Wonder if it's rent-controlled?"

"It appears to be a long-forgotten maintenance area," Niko commented. Taking the light, he picked out a far corner with it. "Ah, a tunnel, and not man-made, I believe."

Not man-made? Just because the concrete looked to have been gouged and ripped away in chunks by claws that had left scoring over an inch wide? Hey, let's not jump to any wild and crazy conclusions. "That'd be the front door," Robin said matter-of-factly before heading toward it, the mud making every move an exaggerated giant step from that old kids' game of "Mother, May I?" "Let's get this over with so I can burn these clothes and take an hour-long shower." He glanced back over his shoulder with a lascivious grin. "It's a big shower. Anyone care to join me?"

"This little adventure just keeps getting better and better," I hissed, mud sluicing up my legs and threatening to pull off my shoes as I went. "Nik, you want to poke me in the eye with a sharp stick, top the whole night off?"

"As amusing as that sounds, perhaps later." Niko passed me with ease. I could see he'd discarded his shoes and moved on silent bare feet. It was a good idea and I stopped for a second to pry mine off and toss them aside. I wasn't as quiet as my brother with the mud squelching between my toes, but it was still an improvement.

The air in the chamber, while rancid with the essence of troll, was still the air of New York. Unaccountably warm and humid for the season, thick with pollution, but still the same old air you breathed day in and day out. That all changed when we passed through the homemade, troll-made doorway. Every ounce of warmth was leached away and every bit of movement died with it. It became an *atmosphere*, heavy as stone, cold as the metal drawer in a morgue, and lifeless as the corpse in it. It was like breathing ice cubes. Chunks of it passed painfully through your windpipe and sat in your lungs like lead. The smell even faded some. After all, there had to be some movement to carry a scent, right? And there was none here. Even the very molecules seemed frozen, nothing daring to move, nothing daring to attract attention.

A deadly attention.

"Abbagor!" I yelled, my voice promptly echoing into the distance as a distorted gibbering howl. I had no problem with attention. After all, that's what we were here for. And quite frankly, I would rather have Abbagor front and center where I could see him, no matter how pissed he was, than lurking unseen in the darkness contemplating us with empty, soulless eyes. How did I know they were soulless? Hell. I didn't have a clue. But I knew. And when Niko's hand floated out of the darkness to fasten on to my arm and pull me closer, I could see he knew too. Niko always looked out for me, but he also knew in most cases I could more than take care of myself. This . . . this did not have the smell of most cases.

"I can't see a damn thing," Robin said, his voice tense. Apparently, he hadn't been lying when he'd said the troll was no friend. "Abbagor, we don't have all night. We want to talk with you. And could you take pity on us lesser beings and shed some light on the situation?"

"Afraid of the dark, randy little goat?" A cold, cold voice drifted from above. "Be very sure the dark isn't afraid of you."

"Come on, Abbagor, old buddy, old pal," Robin wheedled, slipping smoothly into his sales persona without a hitch. "Help me out, for old times' sake, and we'll be out of your tendrils in no time. My word on it."

"Older times. Moldered times. In all times, Goodfellow, you are the same. A boil refusing to be lanced." The words were amused, but it was the humor of a fat spider curled in its web with all the patience in the world. "If only you would hold still, I could remedy that."

Despite the less-than-comradely words, it looked as if Robin's request was being carried out. Light was slowly creeping into the air around us. It was a leprous and sickly pale green glow that seemed to be cast by a

particularly repulsive mold sliming the walls with an infinite number of greedy fingers. It was just enough illumination to sketch a vision of a ceiling that arched
nearly three stories above our heads. We must have
passed into an area under one of the masonry towers.
Abbagor had hollowed himself out quite a roomy lair.
Shifting on frozen feet to sink a few inches deeper in the
muck, I searched the artificial cavern with wary eyes.
The troll was talkative enough, sure, but where the hell
was he?

"Abbagor, Abbagor," Robin clucked his facile tongue
with a practiced ease that would've been believable if
not for the skin stretched tight around his eyes. "You'll
make me think you haven't missed me these past, what,
fifty years now?"

"Missed." The word was shaped with contemplation.
"So many interpretations to be lavished there. Yes, I did
miss you. Perhaps this time I won't." There was movement in the deepest shadows high above us, coiling and
sinuous. "You may have slowed in your old age, little
goat. Be assured I have not."

And that's when Abbagor came knock-knocking on
our door.

I was wrong when I'd guessed the troll would have
the soulless gaze of Eden's resident serpent. For that he
would've needed eyes. He had none. But even without
them, I was convinced he could see every inch of us,
from the glistening sheen of our own eyes to the pulse
beating in our throats, in rich predatory detail. "Holy
shit." I wasn't sure if I said it aloud or not, but I stood by
the sentiment. Abbagor was holy shit and a whole lot
more.

He descended from on high like a skyborne plague.
Thick dark gray filaments kept him suspended nearly
ten feet above us. It wasn't far enough, not by a long

shot. I'd never seen a troll before—didn't really have a clue what one looked like—but this was nothing I would've pictured. Abbagor was vaguely man-shaped, with hulking shoulders, and massive arms and legs. All right. No problem, that was doable. No different from a hundred other monsters out there. What *was* different was that he looked to be made of a convolution of fleshy cords knotted and wrapped around themselves, a mass of twisted tendrils given shape and form. Shape, form, and a hideously twitching life.

"I don't remember *that* in your goddamn mythology book," I gritted in a low tone to Niko.

"That would be assuming you'd actually read it, little brother. A rather optimistic assumption at best." His hands still stood empty, his shoulders were relaxed, and there was no tension audible in his voice. You'd think the son of a bitch was stargazing at the planetarium, the way he looked up with calm curiosity. Oh, the Big Dipper, you say? How interesting. And if it weren't for the fact that somehow, without even seeming to move, he'd managed to ease a protective shoulder in front of me, it might even have been believable.

Robin sketched a salute upward with a broadly artificial smile. "Abbagor, you're looking good. You been working out? You seem . . ." He swallowed. "Bigger. Definitely bigger than I remember."

"Big" was not the word. If he'd been on the ground, he would've stood at least nine feet tall and would've been nearly as broad. But you know what they say. . . . Size isn't everything. Of course the people that say that are divided into two categories: dickless wonders and those not facing the troll that could've eaten New Jersey.

Okay. He was big. So was Boggle, and we kicked his ass on a regular basis, I told myself sharply. Get a grip, change your shorts, and move on to the task at hand.

"Yeah, he's huge." I elbowed Robin pointedly in the ribs. "Buff as hell. The Brothers Grimm on steroids. Can we get on with this?"

The large head crowned with the upswept ears of a vampire bat turned in my direction. "An infant Auphe." The tiny slit of a mouth suddenly unhinged, dropping open like that of a python preparing to swallow a pig whole. "A bad choice of pets, Goodfellow. They always bite the hand that feeds them." Abbagor dropped closer, the tendrils reeling him down for a better "look." "It seems to have lost its collar. What a bad, bad boy."

That was enough, more than enough. Next he'd be suggesting I be neutered for a better temperament. Robin seemed to realize how close to the edge we were and spoke up before I could say anything stupid or inflammatory. And it would have been both—there was not a friggin' doubt in my mind. The relationship between my brain and my mouth tended to be casual at best. "Caliban isn't Auphe," Goodfellow denied hastily. "Not so much anyway. But that is why we came. We were hoping you could tell us about the Auphe. You've been around much longer than I have. Almost as long as the Auphe. If anyone knows them, it would be you."

"Slippery flattery from a slippery tongue." Abbagor's feet hit the ground and despite the thick cushion of mud I still felt the impact. The remaining filaments that had held him up wrapped around his body, wriggling and twisting, until they became part of the whole. It was enough to guarantee I never ate spaghetti again. "Why do you care about the Auphe? They are nearly gone from this world, entertaining though they were."

True. There was nothing quite like rabid homicidal mania. Better than cable, even. "Yeah, them and the dodo. And won't they be missed?" I shifted until I was shoulder to shoulder with Niko. I ignored his narrow-eyed look of disapproval and went on. "That doesn't keep me from wondering why the hell they made me."

Because basically that's what it was. I had been made. I wasn't created out of love and fidelity. I wasn't the result of horny teenagers caught up in the passion of the moment, or even just a busted condom. I was an experiment, the result of some cold calculation. That, I couldn't change, but if I could find out the reason behind it, it might just help to keep Niko and me alive.

The massive head tilted in Robin's direction. "You taught it to speak. Impressive. Does it get a treat now?"

Goodfellow spread his hands placatingly, although I wasn't sure the gesture was aimed at Abbagor or me. "Abbagor, please," he coaxed. "We're somewhat pressed for time. As much as we enjoy being toyed with for your amusement, and it's quite the party, I assure you, could we move on to the subject at hand?"

Only with the puck could pleading come off as a sarcastic demand. Abbagor let it pass, though, surprisingly enough. Either tiring of Robin or of the game of bait-the-doggy, he filled the air with a sound like the last breath escaping a dead man. It took me a moment to realize that was a venomous version of a snake's wistful sigh. "Very well. The Auphe. Since the dawn of time, perhaps before it, they have abided here. As old as the sun in the sky, maybe even the sky itself. They ruled this world long before man infested the globe with his stink." Ebon-rimmed nostrils flared with distaste. Now, there was the pot calling the kettle black. "But as the ages passed, the Auphe's iron hand became a child's feeble grip. They grew complacent . . . smug . . . and by the time they woke up to bitter reality it was too late. They were too few. Man was too many. And even the most pure, the most glorious of maniacal violence can be quelled by dullards if their number is large enough."

I aimed a whisper from the corner of my mouth toward Niko. "Score one for the dullards." A nearly inaudible snort was his only reply. Robin's comment was much more to the point. His hand circled my upper arm and squeezed warningly. I began to shake him off when I noticed the moisture on his upper lip and his tightly clenched jaw. He'd already told me Abbagor wasn't one to be messed with, and he didn't appear to have changed his mind. I decided, reluctantly, it might be for the best if I tried to behave . . . even as Abbagor centered his attention on me.

"And now the last remnants of the world's first dynasty has made you." It was enough to make me wish he had eyes. To be so thoroughly examined, so completely dissected, by a blind gaze was unnerving as hell. As Abbagor continued to ruminate, something stirred on his abdomen. It was just a slight twitching, a minute slithering, but it was almost enough to make me miss his next words. "It *is* a curiosity."

Almost, but not quite. My best intentions to watch my mouth went flying out the window. " 'Curious' is a good word," I drawled. "If it wasn't so goddamn curious, we wouldn't be standing here smothering in your BO. So if you have anything actually worthwhile to contribute, Abby, now'd be the time."

Behind me Robin gave a low moan of frustrated despair. Abbagor, however, didn't seem to take offense. If anything, his grin, if you could call it that, widened. "Sullen, resentful, full of rage. The apple never falls far from the tree. It makes one nostalgic."

The nest of tendrils on his stomach continued to writhe, revealing flashes of a pale color between strands of gray. "The Auphe were big pals of yours, huh?" I said, eyes riveted to the patches of white. What the hell was that, anyway?

"No, they were not my friends. They were something far more amusing than that." It was a hand. Holy *shit*, it was a hand. And it was moving, fingers bending and flexing. I felt my stomach do a slow roll.

"More amusing?" Niko questioned. I knew he saw it; there was no way you could miss it. But from his mellow baritone you would never have guessed that he saw anything out of the ordinary. "Then I take it they were your enemy."

"What could be more amusing than that?" The hand began to stroke the slate-colored flesh. Abbagor didn't seem to notice any more than Niko did. "They weren't particularly intelligent, no, but they more than made up for it in sheer ravening fury. I cannot deny I enjoyed our battles. But those days are no more. There are too few now. They avoid me, deprive me of the auld lang syne. Utter selfishness."

I said something then, something smart-ass I'm sure, but whatever it was it didn't even register in my brain, much less my ears. Concentration was just a little beyond me in that particular moment in time, as I noticed the hand had a tattoo. It was just a small one, a miniature red rose on the webbing between the thumb and the forefinger. A red rose and the name "Lucy." It wasn't anything special. But it was enough to let me know it was a human hand, a living, moving human hand. What it was doing in Abbagor I didn't know. Truthfully, I didn't even *want* to know. If I did want anything, it was to have never seen it, to not have to wonder what kind of existence it was to be buried in the body of a troll. Enslaved in rancid flesh.

As the hand continued its grooming, Abbagor's head bent lower toward me. Whatever I'd blurted out apparently wasn't worth a response because his words were back to the subject at hand. "Whatever the Auphe have in mind, you can rest assured that it can only be a mechanism to regain the domination they once had. That could be their only thought, their only dream. And since they made you, Aupheling, you must be part of that dream." More hands, then arms erupted from his body, muscles bulging, fists clenching. Abbagor's grin widened so far his jaw threatened to dislocate. "I wonder what they would do if I *unmade* you."

Abby wanted to play with the Grendels again and it looked like I was about to become the engraved invitation to his tea party. RSVP on my entrails. Niko had already prepared his own response by drawing a sword from beneath his long coat. "I would rethink that scenario, troll. Rethink it quite thoroughly." There was the lazy swing of silver metal. "Or some pruning may be in order."

God knew there were enough limbs there to keep a tree surgeon in business for a month. I backed up a step, using the momentum to propel Goodfellow several feet behind us. "Run," I ordered flatly.

He didn't run. Instead he staggered from my push, nearly falling before catching himself to say with desperate determination, "Abbagor, wait. We came to you for help, with respect for your connection to history. This isn't a game."

"All of life is a game, little goat. Ancient history will never change that." A snarl of small tentacles shot out with lightning speed to snare my right arm. "And the best games are those that end in a shower of blood." As the last word was still echoing in the air, I was yanked off my feet and dragged at a furious rate through the mud. But I was abruptly freed when Niko swiveled and swung his blade at the long streamers of flesh in one fluid motion, parting them like cheap party streamers. The dark purple blood that spattered my skin burned like acid and I swore as I backpedaled away from the troll.

"All right, asshole," I snarled. "We're gonna finish what Billy Goat Gruff started." Surging to my feet, I pulled my own knife. It was shorter than Niko's sword but just as sharp. "Loman, this is your last chance to get your ass the hell out of here."

A bright flash I saw from the corner of my eye turned out to be Robin with his own sword. Where in the world he'd hidden it was a trick only Siegfried and Roy could've solved. "I've had fights that have lasted longer than your entire short life," he countered grimly, hefting the weapon. "Take care of your own ass, Caliban, because I can certainly take care of mine." Good to know, because in this battle it looked like the devil would take the hindmost, and I wasn't at all sure that the devil had anything on Abbagor.

"You could let us walk out of here, troll." Niko's poker face didn't shift an iota, but that didn't keep a carnivorous light from flashing in his eyes. "Not, mind you, that we wouldn't enjoy dicing you to a fine purple spray, but we are on a tight schedule. I'm sure you understand."

"Now, what kind of host would I be if I let you leave without providing some entertainment?" Abbagor bounded from the ground to adhere high to one concrete wall without any regard to gravity. Hanging with his head down, he twisted it to aim his python smile at us. "And mutilation can be so very entertaining." Then he was on top of us like a falling mountain.

And that's exactly what it felt like when he hit. I was the lucky one; he struck me with only a glancing blow—and that was more than enough to catapult me through the air and slam me into the far wall. I impacted on my left shoulder and hip and then landed hard on my stomach. Mud splattered up into my face and mouth as I gritted my teeth against a groan. My hip ached viciously and my shoulder felt on fire, maybe dislocated. Pushing up on one arm, I managed to slowly get the other one to follow suit. Not dislocated, then, just sprained or badly bruised. Either way, it didn't matter. What was going on in front of my eyes pretty much banished any pain to the back of my mind. *"Shit."*

Robin was half buried in mire, an enormous foot planted on his back and shoulders. His head was completely under the muck and I could see his arms flailing as his body twitched frantically for oxygen. Niko . . . Niko hung from Abbagor's own huge fist. Other hands, tattooed and not, grabbed blindly at my brother's body, restraining his legs as he kicked with desperate but controlled strength. His face was turning blue as his hands tore at the steely gray flesh around his neck. Abbagor must've landed directly on him, half crushing him, before hoisting him high in the air. It was the only way Niko would've lost his sword. And the only way he would be in danger of losing his life.

Knife still in my hand, I shot to my feet. My left leg nearly buckled under me, but it still managed to hold as I ran. It probably hurt like hell, and maybe later I'd have the luxury of noticing it. But not now. Not when my brother was having the life systematically choked out of him. After a few steps the leg stabilized and I sped up. Just before I reached Abbagor I dived toward the ground, rolled, and scooped up Niko's fallen sword. "Niko!" I tossed the blade up with the unshakable faith that he would catch it. Absolute, utter faith, but that didn't keep me from saying a silent prayer. The second I saw his hand close around the grip, I turned and slammed my knife in the troll's leg, the one that was currently entombing Goodfellow in a makeshift grave.

"Naughty. Naughty." The leg didn't move, not even a millimeter, as dark blood coursed down it. The knife hadn't fazed Abbagor in the slightest. However, when Niko's sword embedded itself in the pulsing gray throat, that became a different story. Abbagor reeled backward one step, and then another. As he did, Robin came up out of the filth, spitting mud and spitting mad. He swung his own sword, slicing Abbagor across the muscled thigh. Blood sprayed several feet as Niko fell from the troll's grip to land beside Robin. I grabbed a handful of his coat to steady him as he caught his breath. He coughed, the blue fading from his face.

"You okay?" I demanded sharply. A single strand of long blond hair hung free from his braid as he sucked in deep breaths. It was the most disheveled I'd seen him since Meredith had last trapped him in the storage room. "Niko?"

"I'm all right." He squared his shoulders and went on calmly, if hoarsely. "Annoyed, quite annoyed. But basically in one piece. You?"

I didn't have a chance to reply and play the stoic hero as Abbagor gave a gurgling roar and spit blood. "Red rover, red rover, who shall I dare over?" It wasn't a roar after all. It wasn't even a growl. It was a laugh. The son of a bitch was laughing. He was having fun. Hell, he was having the time of his life. Wiping at the blood pouring down his neck, he licked it from his fingers as if it were the finest wine.

In unwitting imitation, Robin wiped a hand across his grimacing face, making a muddy mess even worse. His disgust, however, turned instantly to anguish as he looked down to see what was left of his cherished shirt.

And although he'd been as cyanotic as Niko, the lack of air didn't keep him from snarling at Abbagor, "I've always hated you, you walking piece of rancid calamari. Did I ever tell you that? You make my flesh crawl, every homicidal, putrid inch of you. You make me want to vomit until my insides beg for mercy. The very sight of you fills me with a repugnance so strong that—"

Niko flicked Robin's ear and suggested firmly, "You may want to save your breath for fighting, Goodfellow. I believe you're going to need it."

"The wise words of a dead man." The troll executed a spectacular backward flip off the wall to land behind us. I wheeled about as fast as I could with the mud dragging me down. It was just in time for a monstrous hand to seize me by the shirt and shake me like a rag doll. My T-shirt tore almost immediately and I dropped back to my feet. Lunging to one side, I managed to avoid another swipe and plunged my knife to the hilt in Abbagor's arm. This time I lost it. Tendrils lashed around my wrist and it was all I could do to pull myself free. The knife was history.

Niko instantly moved between Abbagor and me, lopping off two of the imprisoned arms with one stroke. I knew they couldn't belong to people, not people as we knew them anyway, not anymore. But it still sent an atavistic shiver down my spine. With fingers curled over the palms, the naked hands lay on the ground, leaking blood that was a nauseating mix of human red and troll purple. Robin didn't spare them a glance as he broke right to come around to Abbagor's flank and aimed a blow at his back. He managed to slice away a large portion of slithering flesh and received a punishing swat that sent him flying for his trouble.

And Abbagor continued to laugh. It was a dark gloating sound that filled the cavern with the peal of satanic church bells. It was nice to know somebody was enjoying himself. I figured I might have a better time if I rearmed myself. Dropping to one knee, I pulled up the leg of my sweatpants. I felt metal under my fingers, but my hand froze as I saw Niko disappear before my eyes. One moment he was there, the next gone.

Just gone.

Hundreds, *thousands,* of gray filaments hit him, cocooned him, and pulled him into Abbagor's body in less time than it took me to blink. Then there was nothing left of my brother but a sword half swallowed by the swamp under our feet. My throat was scorched by rising bile as I felt everything around me fade away to insignificance, everything but the monster before me. "Nik?" It wasn't my voice. It couldn't have been. That strained shadow, harsh and desperate? No.

How I made my way to my feet I didn't remember. One moment I was crouched on one knee; the next I was shoving Robin out of my way. His hand was on my shoulder trying to push me back and he was shouting something. "He's gone," I think it was. I wasn't exactly hearing straight, but yeah, I'm pretty sure it was "He's gone." No shit, Sherlock. No fucking shit.

I snarled silently and decided that it was time Robin stepped up and took one for the team. Without another thought I took a fistful of his shirt and gave him a hard push directly at Abbagor. He still had his sword. It was possible he could hold out for a second or two, and that was all I needed. The troll was reaching out for Goodfellow with a long arm, lethal claws slicing the air, when I ran past him, the air burning in my lungs. When I came up behind Abbagor I leaped. No fancy somersaults for me. I simply vaulted onto his back and using the tentacles as handholds, I climbed to his neck. Over his shoulder I could see Robin trying to fend him off with a blade that was now broken to half its length. Still alive. He'd proved already that he was tougher than he looked. But that was just a background musing, white noise, Muzak. I had only one thought, one goal. The cool metal in my hand was going to take me one step closer to it.

Pressing the muzzle of the semiautomatic SIG Sauer P226 against the back of Abbagor's head, I rasped, "I'm not quite as old-school as my brother, Abby." Then I emptied the clip into his mammoth skull.

He exploded. Not literally, but it felt that way. As he convulsed wildly I was thrown off. Hitting the ground, I rolled and was back on my feet before the troll even fell. And fall he did, shaking the cavern like an earthquake. By the time I landed on his chest I'd jammed another clip into the gun. Nothing like progress, is there, Abbagor? I thought savagely. Ramming the gun under his chin, I held the trigger down until there was a smoking silence. And with that silence, Abbagor stopped moving. God bless Charlton Heston and the NRA.

Shoving the gun into the waistband of my sweats, I used both hands to tear at the now limp tendrils. Within seconds I found a familiar black coat and purple-stained head of blond hair. Sucking a painful breath into lungs that refused to work, I yanked with all my strength. Joined by Robin, I pulled Niko free. His face was transparently pale; his eyes were closed. The breath that had never been accepted by my lungs exhaled harshly on his name. "Nik?" My hand clenched of its own volition in his black shirt. "Niko?"

Slowly his eyes opened, bloodshot and more than a little irritated. "What . . . took . . . you so long?"

I dropped my forehead onto his shoulder. "You son of a bitch," I laughed shakily. At least I tried for a laugh. I wasn't at all sure I pulled it off. "You goddamn son of a bitch."

His ragged breaths hit my ear as he regained his wind. "Where's the troll?"

I straightened and eased hands under his arms to help sit him up. "You're lying on him."

Niko frowned as he looked down on the limp pile Abbagor had become. "He's dead?"

Robin spoke up, tone as brittle and cutting as glass. "Hardly. I would advise we get our well-shaped asses out of here while we have the chance."

"Not dead?" I snorted. "You've got to be—" Kidding? Nope, he wasn't. Abbagor chose that moment to twitch beneath us. "Okay," I said hastily. "The exit's in the rear. How about we use it?" Keeping a hand on Niko's arm, I jumped down and hit the ground running. I didn't have to support my brother for more than a few seconds before he steadied and kept up without difficulty. Goodfellow was hard on our heels before passing us without a backward glance. I didn't take it personally. In the scheme of things it wasn't nearly as amoral a consideration as that I'd shown him. For all Niko's denial that I was Grendel, Robin had just discovered I was more Auphe than Niko liked to let on.

Behind us I could hear a now familiar slithering and a voice choked with blood and brain matter. "Aupheling . . . little goat. Come baaaaaaack."

Needless to say, we didn't.

Standing on my shoulders Niko managed to clamber out of our reeking pit. Then tossing down a rope, he reeled Robin and me out. Where'd he get the rope? His coat, the same place he got his multiple blades, stakes, and the occasional throwing star. That coat had more concealed weaponry than the entire state of Texas.

And then we were on the streets, free and alive. Of course, I was shirtless, Niko was liberally coated with purple blood, and Robin was five steps below a street person in the category of personal hygiene. In addition, we all looked as if we'd been on the losing end of a mud-wrestling match. But none of that mattered. We were free.

Wincing at the movement, Niko straightened his coat as best as he could and shook his head. "Well, we didn't learn much, but the effort is appreciated, Goodfellow." Brown hair plastered to his skull, green eyes as opaque as stone, Robin ignored him and kept walking, pulling away from us. Niko's blond brows drew into a puzzled V. He turned a curious look on me.

"Let him go, Nik," I said quietly. Because, really, wasn't that the best thing for the puck? It wasn't every day you survived a troll *and* a Grendel. Best to consider yourself lucky and hit the road before anything else tried to kill you. The devil you knew and the devil you didn't—both were dangerous in this world. Robin was old enough to know that. And if he'd forgotten, I had just succeeded in reminding him damn thoroughly. Yeah, I was a regular humanitarian.

Considering I wasn't even human.

9

It was just a normal night at home. A Bud, an evening snack, lounging around in sweats and relaxing—it didn't get any better than that. The first aid, okay, that was a slight hiccup, but it wasn't the first time that had happened. Not for either of us. And one way or the other, it probably wouldn't be the last. Unfortunately, that was a positive thing. Considering our lifestyles, if there were no more injuries, it could mean only one thing: We were dead. I guess life was all about taking the bad with the good. This time Niko had taken the fall; next time it might be me. Hell, it probably would be me. To give myself credit where credit was due, I could kick ass with the best of them. But Niko, his reflexes were sharper, more honed, and his cool . . . well, at least he had a cool to keep. I thought cool was something to keep your beer frosty.

I took a swallow of said ice-cold beer as Niko, with one towel wrapped around his hips and another in his hands, finished gingerly drying off from his shower. The red areas on his shoulder, neck, and back were raw and looked painful as hell. The small welts on my arm stung viciously and they were nothing compared with what marred Niko's skin. "Did you get all the blood off?" I asked as I went to the sink and scrubbed my hands with an antiseptic soap.

He nodded, folded the towel, and placed it on one of the kitchen chairs. "Yes, I'm clean."

"You sure?" I persisted. "That stuff's like acid." The top of the tube of burn cream untwisted easily. I then flipped open a packet of sterile gloves, squirted the ointment onto the inner surface of the packaging paper, and pulled on the gloves, coating the fingers in the ointment in the process. Nice time-saver.

"Trust me, Cal. I was thorough, uncomfortable though it was." He settled in a chair, leaning forward as his arms rested on his legs. "Uncomfortable" happened to be Niko's euphemism for "excruciating," not that you would've known that from the way he sat tranquilly, his face impassive, and as unmoving as a statue.

Scooping some of the cream up in my gloved hand, I applied it to the chemical burn on his back. I used the lightest possible touch, but I could still feel him tense beneath my hand. Even so, his voice remained placid. "Did you dispose of my clothes?"

"Bagged them and tossed them into the incinerator," I confirmed. When Niko had been inside of Abbagor he must have been near a ruptured tendril or whatever passed as a blood vessel in the troll. The purple ichor had soaked through his coat and shirt, searing the skin beneath. And as agonizing as that must have been, I had to think it was probably not the worst part of being swallowed by Abbagor. But that was something that had to wait for the moment. We had to fix the outside before starting on the inside.

As I finished applying the cream to his back and then his shoulder and neck, I laid a light gauze bandage over the worst of the burns. "All done, Patches." I grinned faintly at the white dressings, stark against the olive tint of his skin. I might have the coloring of my father, but Niko was all Sophia. If it weren't for our eyes being the same, anyone would be hard-pressed to physically link us as brothers.

"Florence Nightingale had nothing on you, Cal, I'm sure." Niko straightened and that olive tone turned to white laced with green. He could school his face to the end of time, but even Niko wasn't master of his own complexion.

Stripping off the gloves and tossing them onto the table, I reached for a pill bottle I'd already retrieved from the cabinet. Shaking two into my hand, I held them out to him. "Take these. I'll get you some water."

He automatically balked. It wasn't anything that I hadn't expected. He was damn predictable in that respect. No alcohol, no drugs, nothing that would blunt the edge or dull the senses. Not even painkillers, no matter how much pain he might be in. "No problem," I said smoothly. "If the Grendels come tonight, you can just barf on them. Very ninja of you." I slapped the pills on the table in front of him. "Asshole. Suffer all you want."

Niko pursed his lips. "I'm not sure Nurse Nightingale had your bedside manner. But the point is taken." He picked up one pill and raised an eyebrow at me. "Compromise?"

Considering this was the hard stuff, definitely not over-the-counter, I knew enough to quit while I was ahead. "Compromise." I opened the refrigerator and handed him a bottle of water. Niko wouldn't touch tap water. I'd gotten rather used to the metallic taste myself. The delicate bouquet of chlorine and lead, what's not to like? "You had a tetanus shot about three years ago, right?"

He chased the pill with a swallow from the bottle. Aiming an assessing glance at me, he stated, "You're hovering, little brother." The gaze softened. "I *am* all right, Cal. I promise you."

I was hovering . . . some. There was no reason to. Niko was fine, in some pain, sure, but he wasn't going to be pushing up daisies anytime soon. Not from this, anyway. No, there was no reason to worry, no reason to consider this a grim reminder that without Niko I was alone in the world. There was no reason to dwell on the fact that without Niko there wasn't a single person alive that I could depend on. For that matter there wasn't a single one who even knew who I was, exactly *what* I was. Boggle knew and now Abbagor, but no one who had an untarnished soul. Except . . . except now there was Robin. But I'd managed to finish any trust there before it could even start.

"Of course you're okay," I said brusquely. "You're too damn pompous to die." Sweeping up the mess from the tabletop, I dumped it in the garbage. Grabbing my beer, I headed for the living room. "I'm going to watch the tube. Let me know if you need help dressing."

"If Goodfellow were here, I'm sure he would offer his help as well," Niko offered dryly as he eased himself to a standing position.

"I don't think that'll be a problem anytime in the near future." Turning on the TV with the remote, I surfed through several channels without actually registering them. Robin was as conceited as a male model, horny as a dog the day before it's neutered, and generally a pain in the ass, but he had tried to help us. And considering we had all but blackmailed him into it, it had to have been against his better judgment. Despite all of that, he'd stood his ground when Abbagor went on his homicidal rampage. At least he'd stood it until I gave him a nice big shove. Then he was just damn lucky not to end up buried in that same ground he'd made his stand on.

"I gathered that." Niko broke my train of thought and settled onto the couch beside me. He was careful to keep his back from resting against the threadbare cushion. The grooves bracketing his mouth said the pain medication hadn't even begun to kick in yet. "What happened while I was . . . unavailable? Did you tell him his shirt was so very last year?"

I snorted and gave a reluctant laugh. "That would've really gotten his goat, wouldn't it?" In my mind I could hear the faintest bubbling echo. . . . *Aupheling, little goat, come baaaaaaack.* It sobered me instantly. "Yeah," I said absently. "Insulted his shirt. That's exactly what I did." I clicked the remote again.

"The man takes his wardrobe very seriously." Niko reached over and slid the remote from my hand and clicked the MUTE button. "But in spite of that, I think there may be more to the story."

"Too bad," I grunted, folding my arms and slouching bonelessly. "Because I'm not in the mood to tell any stories. Try channel fifteen. I think *Charlie's Angels* is on. All the martial arts your heart desires."

"Only in your perverse little mind would any of that pass for martial arts." A finger flicked the side of my head with a thump that connected hard enough to sting. "Then again, perhaps more perverted than perverse."

I gave him a glare and rubbed the spot with a knuckle. "My perversions are all that keep me going sometimes."

"That and a facile knack for changing the subject." Niko tapped the remote on his knee thoughtfully. "I could guess if you wanted. I'm rather good at that."

As if I didn't know. He was hell on wheels when it came to anything involving intellectual muscle flexing.

When we were kids he was busy dragging Colonel Mustard off to jail while I was still trying to figure out what the hell a conservatory was. What I'd found necessary to do to Robin wouldn't take many guesses on Niko's part. He was too goddamn smart and he knew me too well. "I needed a distraction." I shrugged. The gesture wasn't quite as careless as I wanted it to be. "I didn't have much to choose from. You survived. He survived. All's well that ends well, right?"

He grasped in an instant what had happened. For that matter, he may have known all along. Placing the remote on the table, Niko commented neutrally, "He's a good fighter. You saw that, and you had to know on some level that he could hold his own for the few moments you needed."

"Could probably hold his own" would've been a more accurate way to put it. And even though he'd chosen his words judiciously, Niko was as aware of that as I was. "It didn't matter whether he could or not, Nik," I said with bald honesty. "You know that."

He nodded slowly, eyes serious and calm. "I do. I also know I have a brother who would do anything to save my life. Anything at all. And that, Cal, is not such a bad thing to know." He stood, one hand using my shoulder for leverage. "You mind taking first watch? We're both going to need our rest for tomorrow. We still have a car to locate and I'm sure you haven't even begun to shovel your belongings in a pile for packing."

I stared fixedly as actors mouthed silent words on the television screen. My own weren't much louder. "I think we should stay."

The fingers on my shoulder tightened almost painfully. It wasn't often I surprised Niko; this time I'd managed in spades. "Stay," he repeated. "Cal, considering what we learned from Abbagor, not to mention the Grendel in the park, I don't think staying is an idea that promotes our continued health."

I slid an emotionless look up at him. "And what exactly did we learn from Abby anyway? That I'm the result of some bizarre experiment? That while I might be less than human, I *am* the new frontier in genetic experimentation? That's nothing new, and it's nothing we haven't suspected for a long time."

"Maybe not." His hand dropped from my shoulder to rub at his forehead. "But if nothing else, the troll put it in perspective. The Grendels, the Auphe, whatever we call them . . . they once ruled this place, once ruled the entire world, and they'll do anything to regain that. No matter how far we go or how long we hide, little brother, they're not going to give up. If you are somehow the key, they are not going to let you go. We have to keep running. We may never lose them, but we can stay ahead of them. And we will."

And the ones we didn't stay ahead of, they would end up like the Grendel in the park, nothing but a distant and bloody memory of Niko's sword. That had been our life up until now; that had preserved *my* life until this moment. I knew that as well as I knew anything, but I also knew something else. . . . Enough was enough. "You're right, Nik. I'm the bright and shiny key to something, all right, and the Grendels are never going to give up on me. One day they'll catch us. What's the difference if it's here or halfway across the world?"

"The difference," Niko pointed out with grim patience, "could be a matter of thirty or forty years. The difference could be almost a lifetime."

"Some lifetime." I kicked the table hard enough that it slid several feet across the stained and scarred plank floor. "Wouldn't you like to have a real job instead of just a string of crap details? Wouldn't you like to have a home instead of some piece-of-shit apartment? Wouldn't you like to have a genuine relationship with someone like Promise instead of . . . shit . . . nothing but one-night stands?" I know I wanted it for him even if he tried to deny he might want it for himself. And I wanted other things. I wanted the hope of touching a springy red curl, of rubbing the pad of my thumb softly across amber skin. I wanted to count freckles and see if they really did number as stars in the sky. I wanted to sit across from Georgina and have her tell me why she lied, and I wanted the reason to be one I couldn't question. All fairy tales are impossible, but I wanted this one badly enough to stick around and risk the brutal slap of reality.

"Don't you want all that, Nik?" I repeated.

There was silence, not accusing, just thoughtful. When he finally spoke, the grimness was replaced by unshakable conviction. "I'd like those things, yes. But there is something I want more . . . my brother alive. And, Cal, if I have to knock you unconscious and drag you out of town to keep you that way, then that is exactly what I will do." And just like that, the conversation was over. I could keep talking, but it would be pointless. The set of his shoulders, the flattened line of his mouth—all indicated that Niko was not in the mood for negotiation. In spite of that, I might have pushed. I normally did. But not now, not when I could see the bedrock of his stubbornness was still iced over with pain.

"Go to bed, Nik." Leaning over, I pulled the table back into position. The remote had fallen to the floor, so I retrieved it. "Four hours, and then I kick your ass out of bed."

"Cal . . ."

"Nik," I mimicked softly before grinning faintly. "Your towel's slipping."

He took a grip on the wayward terry cloth and gave in. "Four hours. No more." Then he disappeared down the hallway, his step slower than usual.

Four hours he would get. Four hours and then, if I could pull it off, four more. I could stay awake for eight hours, no problem. Considering what I would see when I closed my eyes, insomnia was my friend anyway. I'd lived through Niko's being engulfed by Abbagor once already; I wasn't looking forward to any repeat showings.

Turning the television's sound back up to a soft murmur, I stood and went to double-check the lock on the door. There were no windows to check, not the sort that locked. We had only the one window, but it was a doozy, taking up most of the far wall of the living room. I had no idea what the building had been years and years ago, but our apartment definitely had an unfinished quality to it. The ceiling was high enough to have any real estate agent dancing in glee, but it was also full of exposed wiring and rusty pipes. The floor was directly out of some run-down warehouse off the river minus the fishy smell. The super had put in a bathroom and kitchenette; those were the only modern touches. It was a dump, no doubt, saved only by the window. At night a thousand city lights glittered through the glass. It was like having your own personal view of the Milky Way.

Flicking off the lights, I sat on the couch, ignoring the TV and watching the window instead. Promise wasn't the only one who missed the stars. But as with most things in life, sometimes you just had to make do.

I didn't doze off. Niko and life itself had trained me better than that. But I did let my eyes unfocus and my mind empty as my ears stayed alert for any suspicious sound. It was a state I'd gotten used to over the years. Restful but ready. So when I first heard it, I was off the couch and down the hall before my thoughts fully kicked in. My body automatically reacted, even though the sound wasn't suspicious, just out of place. Unfamiliar. Wrong. The rustle of sheets, the shifting on a creaking mattress, it was the sound of a restless sleeper. But I was the only one of those in the apartment—at least I had been until tonight.

In the doorway to the bedroom, I hesitated as Niko struggled for his life a second time that night. He wasn't like me. He didn't toss and turn, kicking the blankets to the floor. His throat wasn't tight as he choked back a shout. His reaction to the terror of a nightmare wasn't the same as mine, no, but that didn't make it any less disturbing or any less desperate. As I watched, he changed position again. It was just by a few inches, but it still set the mattress to a subdued singing. His lightly stubbled jaw tensed until the bone was silhouetted through skin like old ivory. A solitary hand released its fistful of sheet and slid under the pillow to grip something a bit more substantial and a whole lot more deadly than a handful of cloth.

I knew better than to try to shake Niko awake from the dream. He wouldn't gut me, half asleep or not, but it might still give us a nasty moment. Whenever possible, I was all about avoiding the nasty moments. Instead, I stepped closer and murmured, "It's okay, Cyrano. There's no one here but us chickens. Go to sleep." Whether it was my voice, the familiar nickname, or even my scent, it worked. Niko's face smoothed out, the taut set of his shoulders relaxed, and he slid deeper into a more restful sleep. My brother . . . humans in general . . . didn't have the developed sense of smell I did, but even so, they had a better one than they gave themselves credit for. I remembered reading once (a Niko-assigned book, of course) that memory was more intricately linked with smell than any other sense. It might be that

Niko could pick me up, at least on a subconscious level. I wondered what I would smell like to him. Hamburgers and chili dogs? T-shirts washed with dish detergent because I was too lazy to go to the Laundromat? If laziness itself had a smell, I was bound to reek of it.

Niko, on the other hand, smelled like home. It sounded trite as hell, but it was true. I wasn't saying he smelled like homemade cookies or baking bread. I hadn't had that kind of home—probably no one outside a Disney movie had. No, Niko didn't smell like an amateur bakery. He smelled like steel, sharp and deadly. He smelled like the oilcloth he used on his blades. And he smelled green. That must've been all the health food he ate. Unusual smells for the average person maybe, but they were all the things that had kept me safe, alive, and sane all these years. If that wasn't a definition of home, I didn't know what was.

"Night, Nik," I said under my breath, slipping back out of the room and pulling the door closed behind me. In the hallway, I leaned against the wall with my arms folded, and stared into darkness. I hadn't asked Niko what it was like to be trapped inside Abbagor. I wasn't sure he would tell me. Wouldn't it be a stupid question really? Kind of like asking someone how it felt to be in hell. Hey, just how hot is it down there, huh? Is it the heat or the humidity? And, hey, is that torture and disemboweling by demons *really* as bad as they say it is? Jesus. There's a sheer level of awfulness that's incapable of being put into words, a terror so intense it can't be expressed. But in the end, even if Niko couldn't tell me exactly what it was like, couldn't articulate the godawful horrific details, he could tell me one thing. He could tell me how he felt. Then and now.

I didn't know if it would help; I was no psychologist. But if it'd help me regain the crown of nightmare king,

I'd give it a try. Niko needed his sleep. It took a huge amount of energy to mercilessly nag me day in and day out. Mind settled for the moment, I pushed away from the wall. It was time for another sweep. The locks on the door were excellent, but nothing was foolproof—in locks or life.

10

Niko slept through until morning. It was proof positive he'd needed the rest more than I did. Being injured knocked a person down a peg or two no matter how much a superninja he fancied himself. My good turn didn't count for much, however, because when Superninja finally rolled out of bed he was *pissed*.

I looked up as an inarticulate growl rolled through the kitchen, and raised cheerful eyebrows. "Is somebody a cranky monkey?"

"You didn't wake me." He stood by the table, sweatpants slung low on his hips, bandages still mostly in place. The burn on his neck had darkened in color and looked less painful. "I told you four hours. Did you lose the ability to count sometime during the night? That is, assuming you ever had the skill to begin with."

"I lost my watch. You want some breakfast?" I rose from the chair and moved to the refrigerator. "We never did make it to the store, but I think there's a couple of eggs left."

A hand fastened on to my short ponytail and held me firmly in place. "The perfectly ticking watch on your wrist?" The silky smooth voice tightened, as did the hand on my hair. "Is that the one you're referring to?"

"Okay, you're not in the mood for eggs," I said mildly. "How about some cereal?"

His hand released my hair. "I could put your watch in a place it would be much harder to ignore, Cal. Do not push me." Turning, I watched as he dropped into a chair and rubbed a hand over his face before reluctantly admitting, "Cereal would be all right."

Searching the cabinets, I found a box that wasn't geared toward five-year-olds, and filled a bowl. "No marshmallows or cute little prizes. It's your lucky day." Placing it in front of him, I fetched the milk and poured it over the cereal. "There you go, Mikey. Dig in."

He took a spoonful, chewed, and swallowed without pleasure. "I hope I'm safe in presuming there was no trouble last night."

I sat down opposite him, slouched over the table, and rested my chin on folded arms. "Actually I beat off a horde of zombies, all by myself. Even had one hand tied behind my back. It was quite a show."

A disparaging snort was the only comment on my imaginary heroics. "At least tell me you've started packing. Throw me that crumb, if you please."

"No reason to pack. I'm not going anywhere," I remarked amiably, then added before he could get a word out, "Nik, about Abbagor . . ."

The spoon was slammed down on the table with force. "Absolutely not. You are not changing the subject just like that, little brother. We decided this last night. We are leaving as soon as we obtain transportation. Today or tomorrow, no later."

"*You* decided, Niko. There was no 'we' in that decision." Since he seemed to have given up on his cereal, I snaked a hand over, pulled the bowl close, and helped myself. "But forget about that for a second. I want to talk about what happened under the bridge."

"Forget?" Niko wasn't at a loss for words. How could he be, with that overgrown vocabulary? But he was as stymied as I'd ever seen him. "Forget?" he repeated incredulously. "Forget that you're all but throwing your life away? That should be quite the trick. Do you have any suggestions how I'd go about that?"

"You could talk to me about Abbagor. That might take your mind off it," I pointed out promptly, licking milk from the spoon.

His eyes took me in with disbelief before he shook his head and pushed his chair back. "I'm going to wash up. When I'm finished we'll discuss this in more detail . . . while we pack."

I stretched out a leg to hook the leg of his chair and hold it in place. "I don't think so."

"If you value that leg, Cal, I'd remove it." His tone was icy, sharp, and utterly serious.

"I can get around on just the one." I was just as serious and just as determined. "Troll. Talk. Now."

He stared at me for a long, silent moment before his chest expanded in a lengthy exhalation. "Fine. Abbagor is the subject on the table. What do you want to know? What is so important it simply can't wait?"

You, I thought to myself. Aloud, I said, "It's those hands." I didn't have to fake the repulsed curl of my lip. "I can't stop thinking about the people, you know? Were they still alive? How long were they trapped like that? Shit. Were they even still people at all?"

Unblinking, Niko replied neutrally, "There's no way of knowing."

I pushed the cereal bowl away. "Yeah, probably not.

But . . . shit . . . what the hell must those poor bastards have felt?" That was the question, and it was one only Niko could answer.

"Felt." He rolled the word around on his tongue and laid his hands flat on the table. No nervous twitches for my brother. "How they felt. I imagine they felt like Jonah in the belly of the whale—only Jonah had some breathing room. He wasn't smothered by crawling, pulsing flesh. He wasn't wrapped so tightly he couldn't move even an inch, couldn't breathe even if there'd been oxygen. There were no tentacles probing at his mouth, trying to get inside and pump him full of God knows what." This time he did blink, just once. "And I don't think Jonah heard a thousand voices telling him, 'Welcome, brother. Welcome home. Welcome to hell.'"

I'd been wrong. It could be put into words after all, words that almost made me wish I were deaf. "I guess Jonah was one lucky son of a bitch, huh?" I said numbly.

"I guess he was," he commented, as matter-of-factly as if he'd been talking about the weather.

What the hell could I possibly say that would make that better? Nothing. Nothing I could say could blunt the horror of what Niko had experienced—but maybe . . . maybe there was something I could do.

The soggy clump of shredded wheat flew from my spoon and hit Niko's cheek dead on. It clung there for a second before slowly sliding down, leaving a milk trail behind it. Then I scooped up another spoonful and ate it with relish, as if I hadn't a care in the world. Frozen as an ice sculpture, Niko stared at me silently, the color leaching into a face that was still a shade too pale. The wad of cereal dropped off his chin to hit the surface of the kitchen table with a splat. I raised my eyebrows innocently. "Problem?"

He didn't bother to get up and go around the table. Instead, he came over it. The bowl went flying, cereal and milk falling every which way. My chair and I also went flying, results of a tackle that would've done the NFL proud. I managed to get a knee in Niko's stomach and flip him off. Before I could move, his hand latched on to my ankle. Swiveling my hips, I turned, planted a foot in his abdomen, and pushed hard enough that he slid several feet on the cheap linoleum floor. Scrambling to my feet, I ran. Two steps later he caught up with me and I was tossed through the air like a child's Frisbee. Landing on the couch, I was struggling to sit up when the heel of a hand jammed under my chin with ruthless force. It was a good move, kept your opponent's head hyperextended. Could be painful if done wrong, could be lethal if done right.

I grinned up into narrowed, steel-colored eyes. "Feel better?"

The eyes narrowed even further to nothing more than molten slits. Niko lowered his face until it was a bare inch from mine. "There was one thing Jonah didn't have, however," he said with chilling calm, forcing my head back another half inch.

"What was that?" I croaked as the tension on my neck increased.

"The absolute knowledge that there was someone who would get him out." He released me and slapped my cheek lightly with a sigh. "I guess he wasn't quite as lucky as me after all."

I sat up and rubbed my chin with a wince. "Why is it I can never get that move to work on you?"

"Because you never practice, Grasshopper." Leaning back, he tilted his head toward me with a faintly rueful air. "Thanks for the distraction, Cal. I do believe I needed it."

Snorting, I jabbed my elbow into his ribs. "Go take your shower, Cyrano, before you make me cry like a little girl."

He gave my offending elbow a painful pinch to the nerve. Ignoring my yelp, he stood and stretched, careful of his burns. "All right, then, a shower." Pinning me with a demanding gaze, he went on, "And afterward we pack."

"Afterward, we pack," I lied with ease, and nodded. Let the man have a few minutes of relief before we started that argument up again. I wasn't sure if he believed me or not, but he gave in without further comment and disappeared into the bathroom. Within seconds I heard the door close and water running. Then I heard him call out.

"Cal, what in the world have you done to the mirror?"

Oh, shit. I'd forgotten about that.

It had been Alice again. I'd stuck with the name I'd given it at the Waldorf. It was a good one as any for something living through the looking glass. Of course, it wasn't the original Alice. I didn't think a little blond girl who was too nosy for her own good was really responsible for scaring the crap out of me—at least I hoped I wasn't that far gone. Then again, considering I hadn't actually seen anything in the mirror last night before I'd covered it up with a towel, maybe I was a few fries short of a Happy Meal after all.

I'd heard it a few hours after Niko had had his nightmare. Another unusual sound, but this one wasn't that of a restless sleeper. But neither was it dramatic or even that spooky, not really. It was a humming. Faint. Barely audible, but melodic. It wasn't ominous in the slightest until I realized where it was coming from. Then instantly it became eerie as hell. Tracking down the sound, I'd padded down the hall on silent feet. With one of

Niko's spare knives in hand, I stopped by the bathroom door. The humming had continued, and it was definitely the product of vocal cords, but not mine or Niko's. Even if I had somehow missed hearing Nik getting out of bed, I would've recognized his voice. What I was hearing wasn't it.

Feeling my stomach clench like a fist, I'd pushed open the bathroom door with careful fingers. The musical murmur lowered to the faintest whisper as I moved into the room. I didn't turn on the light. There was enough illumination from the single bulb in the kitchen drifting in to cut the edge on the velvety shadows. I could make out the tub, the toilet, the yellowing porcelain of the sink, and nothing else. Empty. I'd always heard about the alligators in the sewer, but I seriously doubted one was singing a ditty through the pipes. I switched the blade to my other hand as I scowled and wiped a moist hand on my sweats. I did not need this shit.

Swiveling on my heel, I listened hard. In an instant I pinpointed the source of the rhythm, even fainter now but still clear as the chiming of a bell. The mirror. It was coming from the mirror. God*damn* it. Not this, not again. I'd pretty much managed to convince myself the episode at the Waldorf had been a fluke, just a hiccup of my nervous system. But here was the hiccup again, only this time it was more tangible and a helluva lot harder to dismiss as just a fluke.

I raised my eyes to the mirror over the sink. It was harder to do than it sounded. What is it about mirrors anyway? In nearly every B movie, a mirror is gleefully waiting to spring a demonic reflection back at anyone who passes. Movies, books, episodes of those creepy half-hour TV shows—evil mirrors were a common theme in all of them. So when I looked into that mirror, it was with the dread of a twelve-year-old—never mind I'd seen and fought monsters all my life. A dark room, a haunted mirror, it was enough to make me feel like a knee-knocking kid, who wanted nothing better than to pull the covers over his head.

But in my world that wasn't an option. You might think it, but the second that you acted on it you were dead . . . or worse. Hell, what was it anyway? A singing mirror? Objectively, how scary was that? Movies and little-kid terrors aside, how did a mirror stack up against all the other things I'd faced in my life? Not very damn high. So I did my best to forget my cold sweat and my slamming heart, and I looked.

The crooning stopped, and once again I was staring at my own image. This time I looked less sheepish and more annoyed. A hard smile touched the corners of my mouth, and even in the gloom my eyes reflected brighter and colder, almost silver. "Alice," I said grimly. "You are really starting to piss me off." I flipped the knife in my grip with every intention of smashing the glass with the hilt. After all, what was seven years' bad luck compared with living with a possessed mirror? At the last moment, however, I stopped, the knife only tapping the surface. It wouldn't do any good. It wasn't just this mirror after all. I couldn't go through life breaking every mirror I saw. In the end I just covered it up with a towel, meticulously tucking the cloth under the edges. There you go, Alice, I thought with a healthy dose of self-derision. Let's see you get past that. Forget brick walls or steel; I had the best protection terry cloth had to offer.

The towel might have actually held Alice back the rest of the night, but it wasn't going to do a thing to stand between me and Niko now. When he got out of the shower, I'd have some serious 'splaining to do. I couldn't say why I was reluctant to tell him. It wasn't as if he'd doubt me. It would just be one more thing in a lifetime parade of creepy-crawlies, even if it gave me an odd feeling of déjà vu. We had so much going on right then, though, and that could've been what was bugging me. We were already swimming in so much crap, we didn't need a few more gallons of it dumped on our heads. And while I knew ignoring it wasn't going to make it go away, I wasn't sure I wanted to spend that much time dwelling on it either. I had a musical stalker, so what? As long as it only whistled at me, I could deal.

By the time there was a knock at the door, I'd almost decided to try to slide the whole thing under Niko's radar. I wasn't too optimistic about my chances, but I was going to give it a shot. That thought disappeared quickly as I stared, nonplussed, at the door. Who in the hell could that be? Granted the front door was busted and the buzzer pointless, but Niko and I had never told anyone where we lived. The more anonymous you were, the safer you were. Outside of the odd Girl Scout selling cookies or a Jehovah's Witness selling salvation (and I couldn't remember the last time either of those had braved our neighborhood), there shouldn't have been anyone knocking at our door. When I leaned against the wood and peered suspiciously through the peephole, I got an eyeful of waggling fingers waving in a careless hello. "Jesus Christ," I muttered in surprise.

"Not quite," the muffled comment came through the door. "I dated his cousin, though. Great gal. Had a set of yabbos like you would not believe."

Rolling my eyes, I unlocked and opened the door. "Goodfellow, what the hell are you doing here?" Before he could answer, I added, "And how did you know where we live?"

Robin walked into the room, folded his arms, and gave me a neutral green glance. "Niko called me about half an hour ago. Invited me over. Being that *he* didn't try to kill me, I didn't see why I shouldn't come."

"Yeah, there is that," I said blandly. It seemed Niko had been up to something before he made it into the kitchen. Sneaky bastard. Turning, I strode to the bathroom door and pounded on it, hard. "Nik, get your ass out here. You have a visitor." When I walked back into the living room, Robin was standing in front of our bookshelf with a bemused expression.

"Quite the diverse selection." He touched a finger to one of Niko's many occult volumes and then to another book on European history. "History, mythology, chemistry, mathematics. Someone is well-read."

"Niko," I replied briefly. "If it's worth knowing, he knows it. If it's not worth knowing, chances are he still knows it."

He cocked his head in my direction as I sat on the edge of the coffee table. "None are yours, then, O member of the ignorant masses?"

I grinned caustically. "That's me. Dumb as a box of rocks."

"Don't believe that for a second." Dressed in fresh clothes, Niko stood in the entrance of the hall braiding his wet hair with skillful fingers. "I homeschooled the brat for a few years. Stupidity is not something I would tolerate. Laziness, however, defeated me. Thank you for coming, Goodfellow. Can I offer you something to drink?"

"And you thought *I* wanted to kill you," I grunted. "He'll finish the job with carrot juice." I had a good idea what Niko was up to and I wanted no part of it. All I wanted to do was forget about yesterday—every moment of it.

"I never thought that you wanted to kill me, only that you tried." Robin looked away from me to nod at Niko. "Whatever you have will be fine, even"—he made a face—"carrot juice."

"Don't worry. We're all out of carrot juice." Walking into the kitchen, Niko returned with a glass of dark green liquid. "Luckily enough, we do have an entire bottle of wheatgrass juice."

"Your sense of humor isn't all that it could be, you know that?" Goodfellow took the glass and stared into it morosely. He took a sip and the green in the glass was transferred to his face. "Holy Bacchus," he sputtered. "That is against nature and all things divine."

"But it's good for you," I pointed out with dark cheer. I might not particularly enjoy Goodfellow's company, but I did get a kick out of seeing someone besides me suffer Niko's peculiar nutritional habits.

"No doubt. Otherwise it wouldn't taste like warm liquid cud." Running a finger around the rim of the glass, he then flicked a finger against it. The glassy ring filled the room with its echo. It was unsettlingly reminiscent of the mirror creature's impromptu concert last night. "So, Niko, I appreciate the invitation and fungus juice, but what exactly is it you want? Auphe Junior here wasn't precisely expecting me."

I didn't blink at the insult. It was getting more and more difficult to be insulted by the truth. Besides, Goodfellow was more than entitled to a few cheap shots. Niko seemed less inclined to agree. His jaw tightened, but he let it go that time, saying evenly, "We still need a car. We're leaving town and we're without transportation."

"Ah. Business. Goody." He gave us both a mockery of his killer salesman smile. "How soon do you need it?"

Niko's "Immediately" was simultaneous with my "No hurry." "Cal, do not even start," he admonished sharply.

I shrugged and sat on the couch. "Fine. Get a car. There's no guarantee you'll get me in it."

"I think you'll be amazed at how fast your idiotic ass is thrown into that car and at how little you'll have to say about it."

Robin put his glass down on the table and clucked his tongue. "Do I have to separate you two?"

"If only it were that easy," I grumbled. "Ask him what he has to trade, Goodfellow. You'll have to tow it in off the curb."

Oddly enough, the cutthroat businessman part of Robin seemed uninterested. "Why are you guys taking off anyway? It's not Abbagor, is it? He never leaves the bridge. You should be safe if you steer clear."

It hit me then. Goodfellow wanted us to hang around. Despite what I'd done, he wanted us to stay. He was lonely. Sure, there were monsters aplenty in the city, but Goodfellow wasn't a monster, not really. As we'd never run into any other pucks, I guessed they were few and far between. It had to be a solitary existence, surrounded by the monsters who cared nothing for him and by humans who could never even know him. It was a feeling I was more than familiar with. But for all my bitching, I was the lucky one. I had a brother. I had at least one person in the world, and that was one more than Robin seemed to have.

Now that I knew, I could see it in his eyes. Behind the slyness, past the pompous strutting and overgrown libido, in the shadows the color of a shaded green forest, I could see a loneliness that was only a short step away from madness. I couldn't imagine it. Thousands upon thousands upon thousands of years spent, for all intents and purposes, alone. Cut off from mortals and monsters alike because of what he was. So desperate to stop his descent into a living hell that he actually chose to be with those who could blackmail him, those that he thought would only use him.

He chose to be with us. God help the poor bastard.

"It's not Abbagor," I denied quietly. "It's the Auphe. Niko saw one in the park."

It was a good thing he'd put down the glass, because otherwise it would've shattered in the spasmodic clench of his fist. Face frozen, he pushed out words through stiff lips. "Auphe. An Auphe is here?"

"Was here," Niko corrected. "That is why we asked you if you'd seen Auphe in the city. We wanted to know if it was a solitary occurrence. But regardless if it was or not, we've decided we cannot take the chance."

"You killed it?" Robin pinched the bridge of his nose tightly. "Please tell me you killed it. If it's alive . . ." He shook his head and let the words trail away.

"It's not alive. All the king's horses and all the king's men . . ." A humorless smile touched the corners of Niko's mouth. "Well, I think you get the picture."

"It's a good picture. I like that picture." Goodfellow sat with a graceless thump on the coffee table and dropped his face into his hands. Then he threaded fingers through wavy brown hair and sat up with a harsh exhalation. "Abbagor's big and homicidal, but for sheer deviousness, you do not want to screw with the Auphe. They're psychotic, they hold a grudge, and they're mobile as the plague." He rubbed at his eyes. "I realize you know that better than anyone, but it bears repeating."

"I'm not so sure Abby doesn't give them a run for their money." I kicked a foot lightly against the corner of the table and went on awkwardly. "About the troll, Goodfellow, I want to say . . . shit . . . you know."

He turned his head to study me soberly. "All you had to do was ask, Caliban. I'm something of a coward, but I would have stood firm. You only had to ask."

Niko had moved up beside me to rest his hand on my shoulder. "We're not used to depending on anyone else," he offered to Robin while giving me a reassuring squeeze. "Either of us. It doesn't come easy. I know that's not much of a justification perhaps, but we are sorry."

He was apologizing, Niko, who'd done nothing wrong. He was apologizing for me because I was too stubborn and too chickenshit to get the words out myself. I felt even lower than I had before . . . until Niko's hand left my shoulder to thwap me in the back of the head. "Aren't we, Cal?" he prompted sternly.

The self-recrimination flowed out of me as fast as water. Who needed a conscience to keep me in line when I had my brother around to do it for me? "Yeah, sorry," I muttered with a sullen scowl for Niko and a slightly softer one for Robin.

The killer smile returned, showing more teeth than an Osmond family reunion. "Forgiven and forgotten," Robin said expansively. "How about I treat you gentlemen to lunch and we can discuss your transportation situation."

It struck me then that Goodfellow could turn out to be an ally. He wanted us to stay, and I wanted to stay; now all we had to do was convince Niko. That shouldn't be too hard—no more difficult than convincing the sun to rise in the west and set in the east. "Lunch sounds great," I responded with alacrity. "Let me grab my shoes." I could feel Niko's frown aimed at my back as I bent down to root under the couch for my sneakers.

"I'm not sure we have the time for this. In fact, I know we do not have time for this."

I jammed the shoes on my feet and bolted for the door. "It's only lunch, Nik. Forty minutes isn't gonna make or break us." That wasn't necessarily true. In the scheme of things, forty minutes could turn out to be a lifetime, but at the moment that wasn't something I wanted to contemplate.

Niko wasn't too happy about it, big surprise, but despite that, we did end up at the nearest Italian restaurant. I snorted as Niko studied the menu with obvious ill grace. "Don't pout, Cyrano. You're scaring the waiter."

"I do not pout," he hissed between clenched teeth as he closed the menu shut with a snap. "Children pout. Brainless runway models pout. *You* pout. I do not." Turning his attention to the waiter, he went on more calmly. "I'll have broiled fish, no herbs, no sauce, and salad. No dressing."

That was Nik, living life on the edge as always. What a wild man. I ordered lobster ravioli with a side order of chicken parmigiana. Hey, it was Goodfellow's dime. I'd probably load up on a dessert or three while I was at it. Robin ordered in rapid-fire Italian, handing his menu back with a smooth *"Grazie, grazie."*

"Exactly how many languages have you picked up over the years, Goodfellow?" Niko questioned curiously.

"All of them." He shook out his swan-shaped napkin with a smug flourish. "I'm a bit rusty on a few regional dialects of the African bush, but otherwise I get by. And of course when it comes to the language of love, I have no equal."

Buttering a chunk of bread as soft and fluffy as a cloud, I groaned. "Jeez. Oh, well, it was a whole twenty minutes of peace anyway. That has to be a record. You know, Loman, they have a twelve-step program with your name all over it. 'Hi, my name is Robin and I'm a sexaholic.' "

"I've said it before and I'll say it again." He raised his wineglass to me. "You absolutely have to get laid." It was a nice restaurant, nicer than most I'd been to. That didn't stop me from lobbing the buttered roll directly at Goodfellow. He caught it easily, took a bite, and washed it down with the wine. "Delicious. Thank you. Now, gentlemen, I've been thinking about your problem and I may have come up with something."

"Nothing too sporty," Niko cautioned. "We don't wish to be too noticeable."

"What? No, no, it's not about a car." He waved a dismissive hand and took another bite of my bread. "Actually I was thinking . . . if you could find out what had happened to Caliban while he was with the Auphe, perhaps you wouldn't have to run. If you knew what they planned, you would have more options. Knowledge is power, after all."

Sudden dread killed my appetite instantly. "I don't remember. I can't remember. I've tried." And I was pretty sure I didn't *want* to remember.

Placing his half-empty glass on the table, Robin made haste to say earnestly, "I'm sure you did try, but if the Auphe did muck about with your memory, it would be nearly impossible for you to recover what was lost."

"If it's impossible, then why are we having this conversation?" Niko asked with thinly veiled impatience. He'd come to accept the fact that I wasn't ever going to remember what had happened in that missing time. At first he'd prodded me to try to recall, but in the end he'd let it go. Between my frustration over my inability to remember and our joint suspicion that whatever had happened might be well worth blocking out, we'd both left my past in the past.

"I said it would be impossible for Caliban to remember on his own. But with my help . . . a completely different story." Goodfellow stabbed a fork into his salad, then waved it about with enthusiasm. Chunky blue-cheese dressing flew, landing in tiny mounds on the pristine crimson tablecloth. "I picked up hypnosis long before Svengali gave anyone the evil eye. Hell, I taught Freud. I'm more than proficient in the art, trust me."

Niko looked at him askance. "Recovering repressed memories isn't quite like convincing random women to cavort around naked while clucking like chickens. If the Auphe did indeed tie Cal's memories into a knot, I'm not at all confident you could unravel them. I'm not even sure that you should be trying."

"O ye of little faith." The lean, mobile face sobered, all zeal channeled into determination. "I asked you to trust me and you can. I've had more practice at this than the most celebrated psychiatrist or hypnotherapist. I promise you. You pick up more in a long life than just bad habits."

Exhaling, Niko shook his head dubiously. "I don't know, Goodfellow. It strikes me as somewhat risky. I'm not entirely sure that the information gained would be worth Cal remembering his time with the Auphe."

"If worse comes to worst and it's that unbearable, I'll leave the memories locked in his subconscious. He wouldn't remember a thing once he came out of it."

Nice conversation these two were having over me. It could be I had something to say about it if only I could get a word in edgewise. "Guys," I said quietly.

Niko held up a hand to stall me while he countered Robin. "It sounds easy enough in theory, but theorems and proofs are two distinctly different entities. I don't especially want my brother used as a guinea pig."

"It simply isn't as dangerous as you're making it out to be." Clearly frustrated, Robin pushed his plate aside. "Getting the memories out might be difficult. Leaving them hidden isn't. That's their natural state now, be it an Auphe construct or a Caliban one. If I don't want him to remember, he won't."

I tried again, this time slapping the palm of my hand hard on the table. "Guys!"

Both turned their startled attention to me, Niko with his pale eyebrows quirked in concern and Robin with the hopeful expression of a cat with one paw in the fishbowl.

"Believe it or not, I think this is my decision. Not yours, Niko, and definitely not yours, Goodfellow." I pinned them both with an annoyed gaze. "Got me?"

"And what have you decided?" Robin leaned back in his chair, going for casual. He failed miserably.

"I'm still thinking." The thought of remembering was not appealing, but neither was running for the rest of my life. Ignoring Niko's silent look of disquiet, I motioned toward our approaching food. "Let's eat. Hey, Loman, tell us. Just how freaky was Freud anyway? Were you the one who got him on that penis envy path? Or did you go to high school with Electra and Oedipus?"

Giving in for the moment, Robin eyed his plate of pasta with pleasure and then gave me a snort. "Forget Sophocles. Let's talk Homer. Now, there was a bastard who could hold his liquor, damn near drank me under the table. And Sappho? That chick could party like there was no tomorrow."

Niko studied his fish glumly. "I think I have lost my appetite."

Join the crowd, big brother.

11

I'd kept the sweatshirt, Jesus, how many years now? Three? No, four. It had been almost four years since I'd come home, naked and vulnerable. I ran a hand over the worn material, faded with bleach spots here and there. It was barely more than a rag, held together by prayer and a few stubborn threads that refused to give up the ghost. Niko had tossed it in the garbage on more occasions than I could count, but I fished it back out every time. I talked big about not clinging to things; material possessions only slowed you down when you were on the run. You had to be ready to leave it all behind at a moment's notice. You had to lead a disposable life, and for the most part I stuck to that rule. Why this one sweatshirt was such an exception wasn't easy to understand.

Maybe it was because it had been the first sign of normality in a suddenly strange and foreign world. While the greater part of me wasn't even aware I'd been gone, there'd been a tiny corner of my subconscious that had been all too in the know. It was the part that had me practically foaming at the mouth like a rabid dog when I'd reappeared. When Niko had gotten the clothes out of the trunk for me and helped me pull the sweatshirt on, it was like . . . like I was putting a human suit back on. It wasn't an exact fit, the shirt or the humanity, but I'd held on to both throughout the years with a desperately tight grip. The shirt reminded me—reminded me that I was home and reminded me there was at least a part of me that was human. Sometimes . . . hell, more often than not, I needed the reminder.

There was another thing it brought to mind as well. It was what I'd worn the day I'd started running. And to bring things full circle, it would be what I was wearing the day I stopped. Stripping off the gray sweater I was wearing, I put on the sweatshirt. It was still too big. Niko always had been taller than I was. It was just one more thing for him to lord over me in the manner of all evil older brothers. I gave myself a halfhearted grin, but didn't succeed in cheering myself much. They say those who don't learn from the past are doomed to repeat it. What they don't say is what happens when you forget it totally. What did the Grendels have planned when they made me? Had I escaped from them or had they let me go? And if they had, why were they chasing me now? Could it be they weren't so much chasing me as keeping track of my location?

A thousand questions and not one single goddamn answer. It got old, it really did. For every fear of what I would discover, there was an equally strong need to know, to finally know. Sucking in a deep breath, I blew it out and then stood. Leaving the bedroom, I joined Niko and Robin in our living room. "So, you ready to slap the whammy on me or what?" I asked with dark cheer.

"You've decided, then." It was a calm statement of fact. Niko had resigned himself to the idea that in this instance I was the master of my fate and captain of my soul. I was sincerely hoping the metaphorical ship didn't go down, dragging its captain with it.

"Yeah, I have." Crouching by the sofa where Niko sat, I let my hands dangle over my knees. "I feel pretty good about it, Cyrano. No worries, all right?" "Good" was an exaggeration, but I did feel determined.

"Easier said than done," Niko said dryly. "But I'll take it under consideration. Still, I do feel somewhat better about it. I've been discussing the hypnotic procedure with Goodfellow."

"Grilling me is more like it," Robin corrected with a wounded expression. "The Spanish Inquisition had nothing on your brother. Put him in a red smock and funny hat and he'd be employee of the month."

"Regardless," Niko said pointedly, "as it stands now, I'm more confident in your abilities. I don't believe you'll turn Cal's mind into pudding."

"Damning with faint praise. Is that only a motto to you or do you actually have it tattooed on your ass?" Resting his chin in his hand, he flashed a bright rapacious grin. "And if so, can I see?"

"Whoa, don't even," I cautioned, holding up my hands as Niko threw me a look of sheer malevolence. "You're the one who called him. You have no one to blame but yourself." Pausing, I cocked my head and added with mock sincerity, "Oh, and your hot little tush of course."

Niko shifted his attention back to Robin. "Exactly how long can you leave him under? Days, weeks, a decade or two?" Poor Nik, caught between the proverbial rock and a hard place. I was damn glad I hadn't given voice to that particular thought. God only knew what kind of wordplay Goodfellow could've twisted that into.

"Family, the gift that keeps on giving." Despite the

cynical inflection Robin gave the words, I had a feeling the sentiment was genuine.

"You don't have brothers?" I asked curiously. I remembered he said there were no female pucks, so there would be no sisters. "Lucky bastard." I elbowed Nik sharply.

"No." He shook his head. "The fashion in which we procreate . . . no. There are no siblings, ever. Lucky . . ." The twist to his lips was as rueful as the green of his eyes was melancholy. "I guess that's one way of looking at it." Abruptly, he straightened and clapped his hands sharply. "Let's get this show on the road." Climbing out of the beat-up recliner, he motioned me toward it. "Have a seat."

Taking my position cautiously, I was suddenly wary despite my best intentions. I caught Niko's gaze lingering on the faded sweatshirt. His lips parted, but in the end he said nothing about the shirt. What he did say was, "If you change your mind, Cal, at any time, simply speak up. Robin will stop immediately. Correct, Goodfellow?"

"Right away," he promised promptly. "Hand to Zeus. Or Baal, God, Buddha, Amon-Ra. Take your pick." Sitting on the arm of the chair, he captured my eyes. "We'll start with a relaxation technique, and then we'll work on deepening the state. All of this is totally painless and probably even boring for you, Caliban. So get comfortable."

"What? No shiny gold watch to swing in front of me?" I shifted nervously despite myself. Some big, bad monster killer I was.

"No." Robin smiled reassuringly. All the teasing, provocation, and gleeful determination to annoy was gone. Here was a Robin as professional and empathetic as any doctor. Goodfellow was proving to have layers upon layers. "No watch. No amulet. I may have you focus on something in the room, but that's it. Are you ready?"

My mouth went dry, but I nodded. "Nik, don't let him make me act like a chicken, okay?"

"I won't." Niko squeezed my arm lightly, then tugged at my ear. "Not this time anyway."

"Ready?" Robin repeated.

"Yeah," I exhaled. "Let's do it."

Robin leaned in closer. "Listen to my voice, Cal. That's all you have to do. Listen. It'll be the easiest, most simple thing you've ever done. Just listen."

I did. I listened and the world went away.

I woke up with a wall in front of me and the hardwood floor beneath me. It was as if no time had passed at all. One moment Robin was talking to me in a soothing, lulling voice while I sat in the chair, and the next I was . . . where was I? I blinked several times and my vision cleared. I was on the floor, curled up in the corner of the living room. On my knees, hands flat on the cool surface of the wall, I had my head jammed into the corner hard enough I felt the pressure like an ache. I sucked in a breath that burned my throat like acid. My throat was sore. Why was my throat sore?

"Cal?"

Niko's voice came from behind me. It was calm and controlled . . . on the surface. Underneath I heard something I hadn't heard in a long, long time, not since the night I'd come home: anguish. Nik . . . what was wrong with Nik? I managed to turn my head, my neck howling in protest. It was stiff, tight, locked into place like the rest of me. But I still managed to move enough that I could see Niko and Robin crouched behind me, several feet away. Both looked the worse for wear. Goodfellow had a bruise blooming on one cheekbone, a scrape on his chin, and his shirt half torn off. Niko had blood trickling down one side of his face from four parallel scratch marks, and several hanks of blond hair had been pulled from his braid to straggle loose. He had a hand outstretched toward me, patient and unmoving.

"Nik?" My voice came out hoarse and strained, all but gone.

Niko sagged a bit, but his face remained placid and mild. "I'm right here, little brother. Everything's all right. We're home. Everything is fine."

One hand dropped from the wall to land on the floor beside my leg. I watched it blankly, feeling numb, disconnected. "Fine? Oh. Okay." Even those few words had the pain flaring in my throat with the heat of a volcano. Ignoring that, I concentrated and managed to get my other hand down too. The fingers were blanched white from the grip they'd had on the wall. "My throat hurts." I looked up again at him and Robin. "Why does my throat hurt?"

Robin turned the color of milk. His eyes dark holes in his white face, he scrambled to his feet and ran. Moments later we heard him retching in the bathroom. I tried for a smile for Niko. My lips refused to cooperate, barely twitching. "Something I said?"

"I think he blames himself." Niko moved closer to me and, with hands fastened gently on to my shoulders, carefully eased me around. Then he pulled me into a hug so tight I felt my ribs creak. "He isn't alone."

Bewildered, I patted him awkwardly on the back. "Nik, what happened?" The colors were beginning to seep back into my surroundings; I was losing that peculiar distance. "How'd I get down here?"

Sitting up, Niko released me and swiped an absent hand across his face, smearing the blood. "Ah, damn." Carelessly pulling his shirtsleeve over the heel of his hand, he mopped the blood from his face. It was one of the most uncharacteristic things I'd ever seen my obsessively clean brother do.

The blood under my short fingernails caught my eye. Fresh. Red. And I had a pretty good guess whose blood it was. "What'd we learn?" I swallowed thickly. "From the hypnosis? What the hell did we learn?" *That was worth this,* I finished in my head.

"Nothing." He stood and reached down to grasp my wrist to help me to my feet. "It didn't work, Cal, simple as that."

Simple as that? Robin was in the bathroom praying to the porcelain god, both he and Niko looked like they'd had the shit beaten out of them, I'd been trying to burrow my way to China via a living room corner, and it was as simple as that? I didn't think so. "What'd I say?" I insisted, unsteady enough to grab a handful of Niko's shirt to stay on my feet. "When I was under, what did I say?"

"You didn't—" He stopped, tightened his lips, and then tried again. "You didn't say anything, Cal. Not a word, I promise you." Urging me toward the couch, he gave me a soft push down. "Sit down. I'll get you something for your throat."

My throat. If I hadn't been talking, why was it so sore? It struck me then, hard and dirty. Screaming. I must've been screaming. And from the ripped sensation of my throat, I must've been screaming my guts out. As Niko headed to the kitchen, I heard Robin beside me, voice soft and hesitant. "Caliban?" I turned to see him standing beside the sofa. His face was damp from where he'd splashed water on it, beads of moisture sparkling in his hair. "I'm sorry," he said, still pale. "I thought I could . . . I thought . . . I'm sorry."

"What happened?" I asked barely above a whisper. Niko wasn't going to tell me, but maybe Goodfellow would.

"You . . ." Robin shook his head. "What happened to you is best left forgotten. You weren't . . . coherent. Whatever they did far overshadows any ability I have of letting you reexperience it with any range of distance. I'm sorry I ever convinced you and Niko otherwise." He raked a hand through his hair. "And if I can't do it, Cal, it can't be done. Never . . . *never* let anyone else try. It was almost impossible to bring you back. Others might not be able to."

Before I could question him further, not that I had any idea what I would say, Niko descended on me with a cup of steaming tea. "Drink," he ordered. "It has honey, loquat syrup, and garlic. It should soothe your throat."

"Or put me in the grave." I wrinkled my nose but gave in and took a sip. When it came to Niko's herbal remedies, there was no escape. He'd picked up more than martial arts in the string of dojos he'd frequented over the years. Choking down another swallow, I stated flatly, "I hurt you guys, didn't I? What did I do?"

"Not a thing," Niko instantly denied. "We just got in your way. All you wanted to do was escape. You didn't intentionally raise a hand to us. Cal, you didn't even know who we were. You didn't know who you were either. You didn't know anything. None of it was on purpose."

"Yeah?" I studied the golden brown liquid in the cup and then finished it. Handing Niko the cup, I said lightly, "All better." My throat maybe, but everything else was far from all better. I think everyone in the room knew that.

Robin broke the long silence with a grim comment. "I need a drink."

"I think we all need a drink," Niko agreed. Yet another un-Niko-like turn of events. Niko have a beer? The world truly was coming to an end . . . or had done so only minutes ago. And Niko and Robin had been forced to watch it.

I was the lucky one; I'd slept through it.

12

It's strange how a familiar place can be so comforting, even if that place is a run-down bar. You would think that as much time as I spent in that hole-in-the-wall while working, it would be the last place I'd want to be in my off time. Yet here we were. The three of us, blank faces over roiling emotions, walked through the door and headed straight for the bar. The tables, parked in the corners of the room, seemed too shadowed. Too isolated. As little as I liked having my back to the entire room, I liked the thought of sitting immersed in darkness even less.

It was still early enough that we were among a very select group of hard-core alcoholics. I slapped a hand on the bar to get Meredith's attention. "Hey, Merry, hose us down, would ya?"

She finished stacking glasses and moved over in front of us to lean suggestively on the counter. Her skintight, baby-doll T-shirt had a neckline low enough to display the produce far and wide. "Cal, Niko, who's your new friend?"

I should've known. Merry had probably smelled Robin coming five blocks away. New meat. Ding-ding-ding. Of course, it could be interesting. Two predators coming together. We could lay bets on who would get gobbled up first. "Oh, sorry. Meredith, this is Robin . . . er . . . Rob Fellows," I introduced less than smoothly.

She leaned further, the twins teetering precariously inside their cotton prison. "Nice to meet you, Rob," she murmured with a throaty purr. "Very nice indeed."

Goodfellow gave her only a shadow of his usual leer, the glance at her overflowing breasts barely lustful. "Not as nice as it is to meet you, my fairy princess. Especially as there is so much of you to meet."

It was almost disturbing, his lack of enthusiasm. This was not the Goodfellow we'd come to know and vaguely tolerate. "Merry, this man needs a drink and fast," I ordered with dark cheer. "Before we lose him altogether."

"We certainly don't want that, do we?" With a practiced and flirtatious flip of her hair she took our choice of poison. She was so enamored of Robin that she didn't even blink at Niko ordering a beer. Granted, it was an imported one, but it was alcoholic and it still gave me a shock to see Niko taking a pull from the bottle.

"No glass?" I touched my bottle to his with a clink. "You barbarian."

"I have every expectation the bottle is cleaner than any glass here," he said with lofty disdain. I couldn't argue with that. I'd washed some of those glasses.

Robin didn't bother with warming up, but instead skipped right to the hard stuff: Scotch straight up. No rocks, no water, hell, barely even a glass. I swapped amused glances with Niko as we watched him go. He'd said Homer had almost drunk him under the table. I didn't believe that for a second. The man, to use the term loosely, could drink. Within an hour he had all but drained the bar dry and wore out Meredith trying to keep up with his demands for more drinks. More people

had started to trickle in and she was looking more fr-
azzled with each new customer and every wave of
Robin's hand followed by a caroled "Another round,
fairy princess!"

Goodfellow was waiting for his latest drink when he
finally started to list on his stool. His head ended up on
Niko's shoulder, his nose buried in the long blond fall of
my brother's hair. The braid was history, courtesy of my
freak-out. Robin inhaled and murmured, "Your hair
smells good, like warm summer sun."

Niko sighed patiently and shifted him back up onto
his stool. Not one to give up so easily, he immediately
listed to the other side and took a nosedive in some
woman's shoulder-length brown curls. "Your hair smells
good," he repeated happily. "Like warm summer sun."

"On that note." Niko stood and stretched. "It's your
turn to babysit." He moved off toward the back of the
bar and the bathrooms.

Robin used the opportunity to plop down on the deserted barstool. Pillowing his head on his arms, he studied me with half-lidded, sleepy eyes. "Hello," he said
solemnly.

The alcohol fumes from his breath alone would give
you a contact buzz. I snorted, "Hello yourself, Loman."

"You all right?" Robin's sly, sarcastic mouth was
turned down with no hint of its normal irreverent twist.

He was worried, sincerely worried and obviously
just as sincerely sorry for what had happened. I had a
feeling Goodfellow wasn't used to being wrong. What
had happened had really thrown him for a loop, even
more so than it had me. In some ways I was relieved it
hadn't worked. That probably made me one helluva
coward. We hadn't gotten the information we'd hoped
for. In fact we hadn't gotten anything except a sore
throat and a few bruises. Considering I'd based a lot of

hopes on what we'd find out, you'd think I'd be more disappointed. But in the end I think I'd been afraid what I would remember would change me for good and not necessarily for the better.

"I'm all right," I assured him. "I don't remember a thing. Which is about par for the course for me, huh?"

"I'm not so sure you don't have the right idea there." Exhaling, he closed his eyes. "Wish I could forget." Then he straightened, sat up, opened his eyes, and shed the self-pity instantly. "Do you think you'll leave, then? Since we didn't find out anything, I'm sure your brother will be determined to hie for the hills."

I shrugged and took a swallow of my second beer. "Nik's got my best interests at heart, the stubborn bastard. Still, I want to stay. I'm tired of running." Setting the bottle down, I added without much optimism, "I'll talk to him, but Nik is Nik."

"You're fortunate, you know. Having a brother." He ignored the new drink Meredith deposited in front of him. Definitely less enamored of him than she had been previously, his fairy princess gave him a pointed glare and steamed off.

"I know." Revealing genuine emotion to someone other than my brother didn't come easily to me, but this was one of the rare occasions that I let it color my words. "As long as I have Niko, I think I just might survive all this shit."

An expression shifted fleetingly across his foxlike face. I thought it might be sadness or pity, maybe even both. "You realize that you could live longer, much longer than your brother," he said with grave apology. "You could still be young while he's old or even . . ." He didn't finish; he didn't have to.

I took another sip of my beer before replying matter-of-factly, "No, I won't."

"But, you *could*. The Auphe are enormously long-lived, as much so as I am. You may have inherited that. You could conceivably live hundreds, even thousands of years."

He thought that I didn't understand, that I didn't grasp what he was telling me. But he was the one who didn't have a clue. There was no way I was living without Niko, no way I could survive without my only family. No way I even wanted to. I pushed his glass closer to him. "Drink your Scotch, Loman. We're all fairy-tale creatures here, remember? Everyone lives happily ever after."

I wasn't sure if he read between the lines or not, but the gulp he took of his drink emptied half the glass. A cheerful rumble came over my shoulder. "You might want to cut your buddy off before he passes out."

I turned my head to see a familiar face. It was Samuel, the guy from the band, still as pussyfooted as ever. "You wouldn't say that if you'd actually spent time with him," I countered with mock gloom. "What are you doing here? I thought you weren't playing until Friday."

He leaned against the bar, a grin splitting his face with a blinding flash. "What? This isn't the place to be? Can't a guy come out for a brew?"

"No, it's not the place to be and I think Fellows here already drank all the brew." After leading a wholly solitary life except for Niko, I suddenly felt like I was developing an entourage.

A comradely hand slapped me on the back. "Well, I've never been one to get between a man and his liquor. Actually I came to pick up our money from last weekend. Genghis is running short of leather-pants funds. Your boss in the back?"

"Tallywhacker? I've never seen him anywhere else," I grunted. "Good luck prying dough out of his sweaty hand."

"I have my ways." He waved and disappeared toward the back.

As I looked over my shoulder toward Goodfellow, Meredith caught my eye. She was checking her reflection in a small hand mirror, primping like she always did. It wasn't her but the sight of the mirror that made me take notice. Abruptly, I asked Robin, "Goodfellow, you know anything about haunted mirrors?"

He raised his eyebrows, fingers curled around a now empty glass. "Now, that is out of the blue." The words were only the slightest bit faded around the edges, not slurred, but not crystal edged either. "Haunted mirrors? As in ghosts?" He wiggled fingers in the air. "As in 'boo'?"

"Never mind," I said dismissively, signaling for another beer. "It's nothing."

"Caliban, wait. I didn't mean anything by it." He paused as I received my new brew, then continued as Meredith passed out of earshot. "Tell me about your mirror problem."

I shot a glance toward the men's room. Niko had just stepped out, but Samuel had stopped him and was talking to him. Good. "It's not exactly a problem. More like a nuisance. A little annoying, a little irritating. Kind of like you, in fact."

"And you actually want my help," he said sourly. "That's what makes it so amazing."

It was my turn to say I was sorry. It seemed like I was doing that a lot lately and I wasn't so sure I liked it. What had happened to the unapologetic son of a bitch I'd always been? "Sorry." Shrugging uncomfortably,

I went on. "Something's been sort of following me from mirror to mirror, bizarre as that sounds. And it's weird, but I have the feeling it's happened before now. I've never actually seen it, but I hear it. It sings. . . . Well, it hums anyway. Maybe it doesn't know the words."

"That's not much to go on." Robin furrowed his brow and scratched his chin. "Lots of creatures are musically inclined. Sirens, for one. That guy and his rats, for another."

"The Pied Piper? Damn, was there anyone you didn't know?" I held up a hand just in time. "Rhetorical question. And anyway, didn't you play the pipes?"

"Who do you think taught Rat Boy? The ungrateful bastard." He sighed, leaning a bit harder on the bar. "Ancient history. Point is, between sirens, ghosts of opera singers, and hundreds of others, it could be anything. The mirror, though, that's more esoteric. Let me think on it." A slightly sheepish smile curved his lips. "When my thoughts aren't quite so bogged down in Scotch . . ."

"Okay." Niko had finished talking to Samuel and was walking in our direction. "Don't mention it to Nik, would you? I think he has more than enough on his mind."

He clicked a tongue against his teeth and shook his head. "All right, but it's not my ass on the line. Don't forget that when he's kicking yours high unto heaven."

I gave him a silencing hiss and was drinking my beer with casual aplomb when Niko moved up beside us. "Your friend Samuel is quite friendly." That wasn't a compliment, coming from Nik, no matter how it sounded. I might not have gotten my cynicism from my brother, but every bit of suspicion, caution, and flat-out paranoia, I'd learned from him.

"Except when it comes to his singer," I pointed out. "No love lost there."

"I gathered that was a recurring theme for him." He frowned. "I may have let it slip that we were leaving town. He offered us money to help him unload his equipment Friday. When I said we would be unavailable, I might have hesitated too long."

"Shocking indiscretion," I drawled. "I've lost all respect for you, Cyrano. Though in all fairness I blame it on the one mouthful of beer you drank." Leaving town. As if it were a foregone conclusion. All my arguments to the contrary hadn't made a dent in Niko's determination. I could still argue and I would, but I didn't have much doubt who would come out on top. When it came down to sheer ruthlessness, damn if my brother didn't put me in the shade. He'd threatened to physically put me in the car. That threat could and would become an accomplished fact in a heartbeat if I dragged my feet for much longer.

Robin ran both hands through wavy hair and then scrubbed his face with them. It didn't make him look much more sober, but he was giving it his best shot. It was an oddly forlorn gesture. "Are you sure leaving's really necessary? Who's to say the Auphe situation wouldn't be worse elsewhere? You've only seen the one here, and it's no more."

"Better safe than sorry." The black humor in Niko's next words was softened with a hint of sympathy. "If I did have something inscribed on my ass, Goodfellow, that is what it would be."

In Robin's life people were bound to come and go; I'd seen the result of that in his eyes. Considering his long life span, it probably happened with a depressing regularity. If they didn't leave, he'd soon be forced to leave himself to avoid discovery. His life had to almost rival ours for rootlessness. Hell, if we were in a Western, it would be time for the image of a lost and lonely tumbleweed to go drifting across the screen. But no such luck. It was always so much easier in the movies. I didn't envy Robin his near immortality at all. Mortality was more than challenging enough.

"Cheer up, Loman." I punched his shoulder lightly. "We'll send you a dirty postcard."

"Really?" He squared his shoulders and gave us a smile, breezy, carefree, and nearly convincing. "I'll hold you to it. You going to finish that?" He didn't wait as he picked up my beer bottle and took several long drafts.

"I think this evening is winding to a close, festive though it was. Pay the bill, Cal." Niko carefully pried the bottle out of Robin's hand and set it out of reach. In some strange, convoluted way I think we both felt a responsibility for Goodfellow's condition. If we hadn't stumbled onto his place of business, there was a good chance Robin wouldn't be drowning his sorrows now. It's easier to be alone when you're used to it, when there's no other option. It was just Robin's bad luck we'd presented a fleeting alternative, and now we were pulling his unexpected life preserver away. The hypnosis's going south in a big way hadn't helped him much either. Spreading cheer and joy wherever I went, the story of my life.

I dug out a handful of cash from my pocket and scowled pessimistically at it. There was no way in hell I could cover what Robin had drunk with two tens and a five. Sliding off the stool, I gave Meredith a casual wave. "Merry, I'll settle up tomorrow." Ignoring her outraged call of my name, I jerked my head toward the door. "Let's get out of here before she takes it out of my hide."

"The attack of the vicious barmaid. Your fear is quite understandable." Niko gave a disdainful snort and heaved Robin to his feet. "Goodfellow, you can sleep on our couch tonight. In your condition, even a human mugger could give you a run for your money." That was the ultimate put-down in Nik's book, a mere human giving one trouble. Niko may have been all human, but he was anything but mere.

"The couch?" Robin swayed and yawned, sleepy green eyes nearly closed. "How 'bout—"

"Don't say it," Nik cut him off immediately. "For that matter do not even *think* it."

"Spoilsport," Goodfellow grumbled as he was efficiently ushered toward the door.

I took one long look behind me as I followed them. Chances were, tomorrow would be the last time I was at the bar. It would be the last time that I'd smell that unique scent of sawdust and vomit. The last time I stepped over a regular to get to the bathroom. And it would be the last time I watched the rise and fall of the best-built edifice around, Meredith's breasts. It was a lot to say good-bye to, both good and bad. But one way or another life went on.

Unfortunately, I was only half right.

13

The things you think in certain situations . . . the thoughts that run through your mind, they're never what you think they would be. Maybe never even what they *should* be. My thoughts should have been solely on what was before me, but instead they twisted into one barely coherent whole that was practically screaming into my brain, "Run!" Survival instinct is, after all, an ultimately selfish mechanism. It's also damn hard to ignore, but I gave it my best shot for a few moments and knelt on the scarlet floor.

Blood was a sight, even a smell, I was used to. Thickly cloying, the copper of it coated the back of my throat until I could all but taste it in the air. You could say I'd come across a lot of blood in my time, mostly monster, but some human too. But I'd never seen it quite like this before.

"Merry?"

It was my voice, cracked and empty as a broken eggshell. My voice and then my hand reaching up to touch a velvety cheek, still soft, still warm. It was my voice and my hand, though I couldn't recall speaking or even moving. I cupped her face. It was like cradling a peach warmed by the hot summer sun. Magical, until the sensation of blood staining my hand registered. And suddenly what had been a person, a beautiful and carefree woman, was gone. Shallow, yeah, she'd been shallow. So what? She'd also laughed, flirted, worked, and goofed off by turns, and had more boyfriends than I could keep count of. She'd carried a picture around of a mangy alley cat she'd rescued, and applied five pounds of makeup per square inch. She'd tried to sing, but was tone-deaf beyond redemption. She'd danced like a goddess, albeit a goddess with two left feet. She'd been annoying, spoiled, and even manipulative, but she hadn't deserved this. No one did. What had been a gorgeous, living creature was now nothing but a pile of meat.

Meredith lay sprawled in the back room of the bar. She was draped over Tallywhacker's desk, a sacrifice on an altar, her hair cascading over the side like a carmine waterfall, made even redder by the blood from her throat. It lay in a pool under her head and mixed with her hair like a kiss. The white skin of her neck was slashed in parallel rows, each deep enough to show muscle and cartilage, deep enough to open her trachea and let her drown in her own blood. Her clothes had been shredded, and then the skin underneath. Slender arms, long legs, breasts, and stomach, nothing had been spared. Her brown eyes, now as dull as muddy stones, stared blankly up at the ceiling. It looked as if she were seeing something beyond this place, but I knew that she wasn't seeing anything at all, and that she never would again.

I stood clumsily, the knees of my jeans wet with Meredith's blood. I was completely numb, my legs, my arms, even my face. My heart was pounding hard enough that I could hear the echo of it in my ears. "I'm sorry, Merry." Unfeeling lips could barely push out the words, but I had to. I had to say it, because I was sorry. Sorrier than hell. It was easy to be when I'd known instantly what had ended Merry's life by ripping out her throat. I recognized the method of it, the brutality of it.

Grendels.

Grendels had done this. And with her skin still warm, her blood still wet, it hadn't been very long ago. I'd left my gun at home. I usually did unless I knew I was coming up against something big and bad. The police tended to take a dim view if you were caught in a conceal and carry. A knife was easier to hide and easier to toss. But as my fingers closed around the hilt, I couldn't help wishing it were something a shade heavier and a damn sight more lethal. Although, if I was going to wish for lethal, I might as well go for the big guns and wish for Niko at my back.

But Niko was back at the apartment with Robin. We'd spent all day packing, wrapping up loose ends, and waiting for Goodfellow to come through with a car we could afford. By the time I'd made it to the bar to pick up my last paycheck and pay off the tab, it was already dusk with an early moon coin bright in the sky. The door had been locked, which was odd. The place should've been open. Our regulars were probably halfway to D.T.'s by then. Shoving at the door, I'd discovered it wasn't locked after all, but rather blocked.

Talley's body, his hairless white gut hanging out from beneath a T-shirt, had been crumpled against the bottom of the door. His throat was slashed, the confetti of a shredded porn magazine pasted to the floor around him by blood. At least he'd gone out with his one true love by his side. I should've run then, the moment I saw him. But I couldn't. I knew Meredith was supposed to be at work. I was hoping that she'd be late as usual. I was hoping her bad work habits would save her life.

I had hoped in vain.

I tore my eyes from Meredith's limp form and took a step backward as I searched the room with a desperately feral gaze. The only light was from a single dim bulb overhead and it left the corners of the office impenetrable and thick with shadows. The Grendel scent was heavy in the air. Not a reek like that of a troll, it wasn't even that unpleasant. It was the smell of wet leaves, damp earth, and the acrid sizzle of lightning-touched ozone. Maybe it was the smell of an autumn rain or maybe it was that of a long-overgrown graveyard. And maybe if I stopped sniffing the air, I could avoid my own grave for a little while longer.

Turning swiftly, I ran. Knife in my hand, heart in my throat, I ran without a backward look. My good-bye to Merry was already said. My apologies would take longer. I'd led the wolves to the sheep and the sheep to slaughter. I wasn't sure there were enough "sorry's" in the world for that, or enough time to make them. I found that out for sure at the front door.

It wasn't dear old Dad. I'd come back through the gate an incoherent mess with no idea where I'd been, barely an idea of who I even was, but deep down, there had been one thing I had known. The Grendel that had dragged me off would never take me anywhere again. And I knew something else as well. Somehow, I was responsible.

So, no, it wasn't Daddy dearest, but in the end there was no difference. It was still a Grendel, still an Auphe— still a nightmare of claws, needle teeth, and an endless appetite for death and destruction. And more importantly, it was still between me and the door. It crouched atop Talley's body, its claws doodling idly in the blood on the floor. The pointed face looked up at me with fiery eyes and teeth glittering in a rapacious grin. "Cal-i-ban." A black tongue flickered in the air. "No more running, wretched boy."

From behind me I heard a second hiss, "No more running." I turned my head just enough to see five more Grendels behind me, pale skin and paler hair a luminescent smear in the gloom. Every eye was fixed on me with a maniacal and almost coveting glee.

It was judgment day.

Niko had been right all along. He always was, even when I wished with every fiber of my being that for once, just once, he wouldn't be. I only wished he were there to rub it in my face. It would've improved the odds a whole helluva lot. Instead, I stood alone with six Grendels. Alone—it was no way to live and it was no way to die.

"No more running." "No more running." "No more running." Different voices, but all chanting with the same serpentine gloat.

They could chant all they wanted because I was moving like a bat out of hell. Running? Hell, I was flying. I slammed into the Grendel by the door and opened his belly up with the backward slash of my knife. Ropy, almost delicate strings of intestines spilled out as it screamed with the agony of a burning man. Which, fortunately for me, was not my problem. Throwing him aside, I hit the door and then I was out. Not free, not safe. There wasn't much chance of that, not really. But I was out and I was running. If they wanted my ass, they'd have to catch it first. You'd be amazed how fast you can run when you're scared shitless. It also helps when you're running covered with blood, as people tend to clear out of your way. And when it's not your blood, they move even faster.

I raced down the sidewalk, every breath burning in my lungs, every heartbeat threatening to rip open my chest. The knife and the blood were both visible in the harsh glow of the streetlights. It wouldn't be too long before someone called the police, but it didn't matter. By the time they got there, I'd have vanished one way or the other. Whether it was from the street or from this world, I couldn't say, but I'd be gone.

Staring faces, gaping mouths—I saw all of that in the corner of my eye as I ran. I saw people scattering before me until I ducked into an alley out of sight. It was dark, secluded, and a shortcut I rarely took. You never knew what creature feature might be lurking there in ambush, but whatever might be in the alley couldn't be any worse than what was on my tail. I hadn't seen them behind me as I'd fled down the street, but I knew they were back there. Slinking in the evening shadows or leaping from rooftop to rooftop, they were coming. It was inevitable. Neither death nor taxes had anything on the Grendels.

The alley turned out to be empty and silent except for the sound of my pounding feet and the drip of water down grubby worn bricks. Splashing through puddles left by an afternoon rain, I exited the narrow passage and dashed across the street. There was the blare of horns, the squeal of tires, and the curses of pissed-off drivers. I ignored it all, even the bumper that scraped my leg hard enough to stagger me. Managing to stay on my feet, I kept moving. Home and help were only a few more blocks. I could make it. I kept that a single-minded point of focus in my thoughts. I could make it. And despite the doubts snickering in the back of my head, I did.

I didn't slow at the security door. The lock was still broken and the door flew open when I hit it like a runaway train. With the screech of rusty hinges, the door slammed into the wall hard enough to embed the handle into plaster. Job security for the super, just in case cleaning up our dead bodies later didn't keep him busy enough. I hit the stairs, every second an agony of suspense as I waited for the scrape of claws behind me, for the whisper of *No more running, bad boy, no more running.* When I finally reached the top, the muscles in my legs were in knots and the stitch in my side felt like an ice pick sliding between my ribs. I didn't bother fumbling for my key. Instead, I leaned on the apartment door and hammered the wood with my fist. "Nik!" My voice was hoarse, almost unrecognizable, as I dragged air into starved lungs.

The door was jerked open and I lurched into my brother. Niko caught me by my arm with one hand. His other was wrapped firmly around the hilt of his sword. "Grendels?"

I hadn't had to say a word. Only one thing could be responsible for the desperation in my voice, and Niko was well aware of exactly what that was. "Right behind me," I confirmed, my chest still heaving for breath. "They were at the bar. Merry . . ." Stopping, I pressed my lips tight and then tried again. "Meredith is dead. They ripped her to shreds."

His hand tightened on my arm. "Bastards." The word was bleak with a frozen fury.

I heard Robin's voice, hushed, almost resigned. "The Auphe? They've come?"

Niko slammed the door behind me and locked it. "I have an extra sword in the long bag on my bed, Goodfellow. I would advise you to get it." He would've let Goodfellow run for it if there'd been enough time. I don't know if Robin would've taken the opportunity or not, but there simply wasn't a chance to find out.

"No, thanks. I've been carrying my own since I met you two," he said with grim humor. "Luckily, it's close to trench coat weather, or the fashion police would be on my ass as surely as the Auphe are on yours." Reaching beneath his coat, he armed himself with a wickedly sharp blade.

"I'll take the sword, then." A gun wasn't much use against Grendels, especially in the close quarters of an apartment. There were too many and they were too goddamn fast. It didn't stop me from retrieving one from my bedroom. I might not be able to use it on the Grendels, but if I survived, I might need it later. As I took off down the hall, I could hear Niko and Robin moving furniture. Blocking the door, no doubt. Our locks were the best, but if the entire door is destroyed, locks aren't much use. And then as I hurriedly unzipped Niko's bag and started to pull weapons free, I heard it. Yeah, I heard it all right and I was so not in the mood for this shit. Not now.

The humming was louder than it had been the other night. Louder, faster, and maybe even a bit more cheerful. That was fine by me. As far as I was concerned, it could hum until the sun went out, the moon turned to blood, the seas boiled, and the frigging cows came home. It was the least of my problems and I just didn't have the time. Helping myself to one of Niko's spare hundred or so swords, I returned to the hall. I had every intention of walking past the bathroom without a glance. I nearly made it too—until I heard a new sound. The humming had been replaced by a scraping noise. It was as irritating as the squeal of nails on a chalkboard or the scratch of a diamond against glass. Reluctantly, I stopped in front of the bathroom. While nothing could be more urgent than the current wolf at our door, it was also true that I didn't want an unknown flanking us at one damn inopportune time.

Turning, I went in with the sword held before me. Armed to face the john—this was my life. By turns terrifying and humiliating, it wasn't exactly the stuff of legends. Flicking on the light with my spare hand, I moved in front of the mirror. I'd been through this a few times now and I knew what I'd see: myself . . . staring back. I'd be pale, I imagined, with eyes dilated with anger and fear. The Grendels had come and I didn't think I'd look too happy about it. I was right. I didn't look happy. In fact, I didn't look anything at all. It wasn't me. For the first time I looked into the glass and saw my stalker. Shit, if the book hadn't gotten it wrong.

Alice was hideous.

Round eyes as silver as the moon blinked lazily at me. Black claws flexed on the other side of the mirror. Everything about the creature was black except the eyes. The skin was polished ebony, smooth with the moist skin of a salamander burrowing in the darkness. The head was a mixture of reptilian and humanoid, as tapered and predatory as that of a rattlesnake. About the size of a Grendel or slightly smaller, the creature exuded the same evil, the same poisonous nature. The tip of a forked tongue touched the invisible barrier between us with a silent caress. Delicately vicious fangs the same color as its skin curved back like hooks. It was grotesque and yet . . . somehow . . . it was also beautiful. It was a bizarre and unsettling combination, the ravenous scuttle of a spider crossed with the sinuous grace of a feline, alien and stomach churning all at once. Except for its voice. That was simple and pure, like low-throated wind chimes, the shifting beauty of a wolf's howl, or the sound of air sifting through an angel's wings. It was the voice of a messenger of God . . . wrapped in a less-than-holy package. Its words, though, were mundane, if nonsensical.

"You don't look like a treasure," came the molasses-coated purr. The head tilted curiously to one side as talons drummed casually on the glass. "Value is in the eye of the beholder, I suppose." An eye winked slyly. "Just like beauty."

Then it exploded through the mirror to land on my chest, slamming me against the tiled wall. Shattered shards of silvery glass stung my face before falling with a tinkle to the floor. Eyes just as silver stared into mine from bare millimeters away. "Remember me?" it asked conversationally before laving my skin with its tongue. "You look lonely in there. Mind if I join you?"

I had no idea what it meant by that, but I did know it didn't sound good. Waiting around to discuss it didn't seem like the smartest option. Grabbing it by the throat, I flung it away before lunging at it with the blade. I missed. Of all goddamn things, I *missed*. The evil little shit was quick, I had to give it that. It flipped over my head with blurring speed to land high where the wall and ceiling met. Gazing at me complacently from an upside-down position, it mocked in a singsong, "Little piggy, little piggy, let me in."

I narrowed my eyes and balanced loosely on the balls of my feet. "I've got something you can blow all right, big bad wolf. So come and get it." The splintering crash of the front door interrupted my bravado. An inarticulate shout from Goodfellow and the meaty thud of steel in flesh had me turning my back on Alice. I fully expected the burning pain of claws in my spine as I raced down the hall to the living room, but only its laughter followed me. I wish I could've been as carefree, but the sight that met me as I exited the hall fixed that fast enough.

Grendels were everywhere. There had to be at least twenty swarming through the apartment. They were unarmed except for the weapons of nature, but slashing claws and a myriad of shredding teeth were weapons enough. Robin had speared one Grendel in the stomach, but another had a pale sinewy arm wrapped around his neck, its teeth buried in his shoulder. Nik . . . Nik was already surrounded by bodies. Four of the dead lay scattered at his feet as he swung a blade to take off the head of a fifth. The dislike of dulling his blade on bone had apparently been forgotten. With my brother in full swing and surviving, I charged the Grendel on Goodfellow's back. Cutting its legs from beneath it, I grabbed a handful of oddly silky hair and jerked the monster off Robin before heaving it across the floor. Grunting a thanks, Robin plowed into two more, wielding his sword with a desperate and deadly skill.

Turning my back to his to protect our flanks, I prepared to fend off some monsters of my own. God knew there were plenty left. But strangely enough, they didn't seem to want to cooperate. Concentrating on Niko and Robin, they either ignored me or skipped out of my reach. After an entire lifetime of being watched and then pursued, now that I was actually caught the Grendels seemed oddly uninterested. Growling with frustration, I lunged at the nearest one, slicing it across the rib cage to spill blood. It hissed with pain and outrage and started to swing jagged claws at my throat. Bare inches away from my skin, it stopped, its hand hovering in the air with fingers flexing. Then it smiled and grated, "Not so easy for you, brother. Never so easy for you."

Not disinterested, then. They didn't want to hurt me, simple as that. After all, they had plans for me, didn't they? And whatever those involved, it was apparently better for them that I was in one piece. Better for them, but no way in hell it could be better for me. Being dead was an option; going back with the Grendels was not. If they wouldn't fight me, fine. I didn't have a problem taking the fight to them. I lunged at the bleeding one, intent on slicing the smug son of a bitch in half. Niko was still on his feet with one hand clutching the throat of a Grendel as he buried his sword in its belly. Robin was holding his own as well, although he had a streak of blood on his face and one on his neck. The odds were bad; shit, they were goddamn awful. Still, I wasn't about to give up. I would live here or I would die here, but with Nik and Goodfellow at my side, the odds might just take a beating. The Grendels were tough, a force to be reckoned with. So were we. We had a chance. It wasn't much of one, but I'd take any port in a storm, any straw I could grasp.

Then that straw slipped through my fingers as what I thought was the least of my problems suddenly turned out to be by far the worst. Alice came loping along the wall. It was on all fours and moving with the speed and intensity of a greyhound. The big bad wolf was done playing and ready to get down to business. It was just my bad luck that its business seemed to be me.

I did try to get away. I'd been in enough fights not to freeze and I'd seen shit a damn sight scarier-looking than Alice. The trouble was that even though my brain agreed with all that, every other part of me was screaming a warning. It made my attempt to dive to one side seem impossibly slow, as if I were a fly trapped in amber. I heard Nik shout my name and heard Robin say a word I didn't recognize, and all the letters crept snail slow into my ears.

Then Alice hit me and all wondering stopped.

"Little piggy." A tongue touched my jaw again as gently as that of a mother nuzzling her newborn.

The body slam had knocked me over our recliner. I lay stunned in its splintered ruins with Alice crouched on my chest. The sword had flown far from my hand as my breath had been knocked painfully from my lungs.

With pale eyes staring into mine, I struggled to breathe and I struggled to say one word. "No." I didn't even know what I was saying no to. But I did know Alice wasn't looking to do me any favors. The weight on my chest, the trail of saliva on my face, the eyes as hypnotic and consuming as a cobra's—it was all *wrong*. Wrong in the way murder is wrong, wrong in the way torture is wrong, wrong in every way there is to be wrong. "No," I repeated, my voice brittle as glass. "No, you son of a bitch. *No.*"

Talon-tipped fingers cupped my chin, holding my head still. "Don't worry, Caliban. You don't have to open the door," it soothed before giving me a smile brilliant with triumph and vicious with glee. "After all, no lock has ever kept me out."

Alice was right. My locks held less than a second before it helped itself and moved on in. I tried to fight. God, I fought like ever-living hell. Every inner touch, every one of its fingerprints on my brain, burned like acid. It shredded the walls of my soul like tissue paper, tore aside my willpower like the filmiest of curtains. As it clawed its way to my very center, I couldn't tell anymore where it began and I ended. It poured into me like a river into the sea, mixing, melding, until we were one. One. For better or worse.

Until death do us part.

Suddenly I saw the world in a whole new light . . . and it was goooood. Sitting up, I held my hands in front of my face and wiggled my fingers. Warm-blooded. It was a weird feeling, at once odd and familiar. Looking a little farther down, I took in the result of that warm blood mixed with adrenaline and grinned. "Humans. Gotta love the horny little bastards." Rising, I pulled at my sweatshirt, snorting in disgust at the faded material.

"You have *got* to be kidding." Well, there was time enough for that later. After all, world domination came with a schedule and if I didn't get my ass in gear, I'd throw the Auphe off before they even got started. Couldn't have that. The customer's always right and all that bullshit.

Niko was still yelling my name, although now he was held back by seven of the Auphe. Goodfellow stood alone. What he knew, what he saw before him, held him just as solidly as the Auphe held Nik. His blade hung slack in his grip, the point resting on the floor. His mouth shaped a silent word. It was the same word I hadn't recognized only moments ago, but now I knew it as well as my own name. Because, hell, it *was* my name.

"Darkling." This time he got some air behind it so that I actually heard it.

I waggled my fingers at him in a cheerful wave and gave him an acknowledging wink. "He shoots; he scores. Too bad 'Better late than never' doesn't apply here, eh, Goodfellow?" "Darkling" it was . . . or "banshee"—I went by both. Not that I got a lot of face time in any mythology book. The female banshees, whiny bitches that they are, were all over the place, but me? Their humble brother, one of the few male banshees in existence? Jack shit, that's what I got. I was robbed, I tell ya, robbed. For a creature of my talents to be toiling in relative anonymity, it was a crying shame.

"Caliban."

I turned to look at Niko. As the King would say, he was all shook up. I couldn't remember him ever calling me Caliban. He knew I linked the name with being a Grendel and that was an idea he wouldn't ever give validity to. Nik lived his life denying my heritage, denying that I was a monster. Now, there was a thought that

made me smile. Monster. When I thought of all the long
years that I'd moaned and wailed about being a monster . . . shit. Now I knew what a monster really was.
Now I knew what I'd been missing.

But . . . business before pleasure.

I sighed regretfully and reached for the gun stowed
in the waistband at the small of my back. "Sorry, big
brother. I'd love to stay and shoot the breeze, but I've
got places to go, worlds to destroy. Busy, busy, busy."

Niko's face hardened. "Give him back. Whatever you
are, give my brother back." His eyes, promising all sorts
of dire consequences, were locked on mine. I knew what
he was seeing, once-gray eyes now turned mirror bright.

"Back?" I raised my eyebrows and shook my head. "I
haven't even gone for a test drive yet. Besides you act as
if this is some sort of *Exorcist* rip-off. That you can
throw a few splashes of holy water on me and poof, all
gone. Sorry, Cyrano, it doesn't work that way." Abruptly,
I turned and fired the gun.

The panoramic window shattered. A fiercely frigid
wind whipped into the apartment. It tore at my hair,
scattered an evening paper, and whipped away drops of
blood from where the Auphe's claws had punched
through Niko's skin. Glass glittered like shards of ice
on the floor, and outside darkness beckoned. I could smell
the city, smell the freedom. It was a wonderful moment,
goddamn *great* in fact. Only one thing could possibly
make it better. Swiveling around, I placed the muzzle of
the thirty-eight lightly against my brother's chest. "Time
to go, Nik." I couldn't leave him alive. He would never
give up searching and that could put a bit of a crimp in
the plan. I couldn't have that. "For me and for you."

"You couldn't." He seemed very sure of that, jaw set.
Too bad he was wrong.

"You mean he couldn't, but *we* can." I curled up the corner of my mouth. "And we will." Pulling the trigger was easy, so damn easy.

Hitting the target, though, turned out to be more difficult. Where Niko had been, suddenly an Auphe was standing, whom I unfortunately ventilated. It wasn't the most respectful way to treat an employer. "Whoops. Sorry about that, boss," I apologized. "Totally my fault." It crumpled, the light fading from its eyes. There went any chance of a bonus.

Niko had managed to wrest himself free of some of the Auphe, but was still entangled in several rolling around on the floor. It was a vicious fight and I wished I had time to watch, but orders were orders. I couldn't get a clear shot at Nik, and Robin wasn't much of a threat. My reputation preceded me there and I fully expected Goodfellow to pack his bags to hop the nearest plane. He was out of here, no doubt, and although Niko would definitely still be a problem, there wasn't anything I could do about it now. Later, though . . . we'd see.

Turning, I ran. I heard the the clink of metal against wood as the gun hit the floor behind me. . . . It was like the peal of a bell. I kept running, took a deep breath, and dived. I don't know if Nik got away from the Auphe or whether they let him go to follow me. Either way, it didn't matter; I knew it was his fingers tugging at my shirt. I knew it was his fingers trying to hold me back, but I still slipped free.

And then I was soaring.

Through the window and into the night. Air rushed up past me as I fell. Lights dopplered as the street rose beneath me with dizzying speed. Behind and around me I could hear the Auphe, laughing as happily as a weasel in a nest of baby rabbits, their white hair streaming like the tail of a comet. We plummeted together, joined by a murderous purpose and the sheer joy of raising hell. Then the gate opened and we exited the world together. But we would be back, to remake that same world into a new image, or rather an old one . . . very, very old. For now, however, to this place we were no more.

Elvis had left the building.

14

There are a lot of truths in this world.

When it rains it pours. It's always darkest before the dawn. He who smelt it dealt it. There was no limit to the little homilies, the facile and easy words. If humanity was good at anything, it was shooting off its collective mouth. They had a saying for literally every situation under the sun. Although there was one in particular that had always stuck with me. Choose your friends wisely. It bore repeating. Choose your friends wisely.

That and everyone has their price. That was a good one too. Right up there.

Combine the two and that pretty much summed up my philosophy in life: Pick the right side and get paid to do it. Calling the Auphe my friends might have been an exaggeration. Still, they had once been a reigning force and the way things were shaping up they would be again. I could take care of myself—that was a given— but being on the Auphe's bad side was no way to start a millennium. Besides, as I said, I had my price and they were more than willing to pay it. It was just too damn bad the assignment had called for a stop in their summer home. Which led us to another truth.

Tumulus was no Vegas.

The warm-blooded half of me was more intimate with that fact than either one of us cared to be. And so was my cold-blooded self. We had both been in Tumulus at the same time years ago . . . for exactly the same reason. Working for the Auphe. There wouldn't be any other reason to grace that pit. The place hadn't improved an iota since then either. Vegas? Hardly.

No buffets, no babes, no gambling. Hell, there was barely air. An hour there refining the details of the Auphe scheme and I was more than ready to be on my way. Not that I wasn't having the time of my life yukking it up with the black sheep of the Fae, but the Auphe did tend to be pretty damn intense. I enjoyed a good slaughter, same as the next guy. Wasn't I doing dirty work for the Auphe? There weren't many that could claim that particular distinction, doing the evil deed for creatures who had practically invented the phrase. Yeah, I could hang with the baddest of the bad, but even I had my limits.

Nothing ruined a good hobby faster than talking it to death with a bunch of drooling fanatics. If the Auphe had a problem, in my book it would be that they were just too single-minded. There was nothing wrong with having more than one interest in life. Carnage could be a wonderful thing, but there were other fish to fry out there that were almost as tasty. I liked to think of myself as a Renaissance creature . . . as a Renaissance *man* now. The Auphe were not, and even if they had been, their shit hole was definitely not my idea of luxury accommodations.

By the time I stepped through the door to Central Park I was more than ready to bid a fond farewell to icy, screaming winds, sullen red skies, and the fetid stench reminiscent of a hundred thousand rotting bodies.

Corpses were nice to look at and fun as hell to make, but I could do without the smell. Bad for my sinuses.

Not that the air in New York smelled much better, but it was warmer . . . barely. The temperature had taken a major nosedive since I'd been gone. Time in this world and in Tumulus had no real correlation. Step from one place to the other and minutes could've passed or weeks, and it was never the same. The Auphe understood how it worked, but I damn sure didn't and barring a handheld Einstein and the most expensive calculator money could buy, I wasn't going to. Quite frankly, I wasn't too concerned over it. From the looks of things a week or two had passed, and that guess was good enough for me. Around me winter had started to gobble up fall. Folding my arms against the chill, I shook off the effect of the rip the Auphe had opened for me and started walking. Theoretically, I should be able to open up a doorway myself now. This body was genetically hardwired for it. And after all, that was what I'd been hired to do . . . open the mother of all gates.

But for now that was off-limits. The Auphe were clear on that. There couldn't be any mistakes. It had taken years beyond the telling to get a breeding to work. They didn't want to lose their one and only mutt if I screwed up and took an accidental trip to the bottom of the ocean or the center of a volcano. So no trips without supervision. That was all right. I could be a good boy . . . for a while. There were other ways to travel. In fact I'd be willing to bet that somewhere out there was a sports car with my name all over it.

No more mirrors, though. Just as I wasn't cold-blooded anymore, neither was I ephemeral enough for surfing the reflective waves of light. I didn't mind, though—it was more than a fair trade in my book. I'd never set up house in something alive before. I had a long, illustrious career doing this and that, sort of a jack-of-all-trades. Mostly I guarded things. You couldn't beat good pay for sitting on your ass. Have a treasure you want protected? No problem. A crumbling relic of a lost age that needs to be preserved at all costs? Can do. A castle full of smelly live squatters that you'd like turned into smelly dead ones? Where do I sign up? Hire me and I'd move into whatever you wanted for as long as you wanted. With me inhabiting your most cherished possessions, you could bet they were safe. But this time my guardian aspect wasn't the only reason the Auphe had pulled me in for this task. In fact, I'd known of Caliban long before I started shadowing him in mirrors, and I'd been doing that much longer that he had realized. I'd been on the Auphe payroll for this job even before he'd been born.

As a rule the work was good, the perks and pay even better, but now I had the feeling I wouldn't be returning to dwelling in the inanimate for a long, long time. All those years, I had no idea what I was missing. Although I could solidify to a certain extent, my natural state was more tenuous. Incorporeal. But a human body . . . I couldn't get over what an amazing high it was. No cool will-o'-the-wisp fluid gently sliding through corkscrew-twisted vessels that were barely more material than a thought. Humans had fiery hot blood that pumped with all the force and speed of a raging river. They had bubbling hormones that gave an unbelievable punch to every single emotion. And adrenaline, holy hell, why wasn't someone bottling that?

I liked this body. I liked it a whole helluva lot and if it survived the Auphe's scheme, I didn't think they'd mind me holding on to it for a while. If it didn't survive, it'd be a disappointment but not a genuine problem. I'd just hop to something else. My choices would be drastically reduced if things went as planned, but that was the breaks. I'd make do. I always did.

For now I had a few days to kick back and enjoy myself. The big bosses needed that time to prepare, pick a site, and pull their entire population together. Until then all I had to do was keep this body in one piece and have a good time. Oh, sure, there were some loose ends to tie up in a nice, pretty bow, but that would be a huge part of my good time. There was only so much reining in by the Auphe that even an easygoing guy like myself could tolerate. They hired me to do a job. How I did it was a matter of my discretion, not theirs. I was a professional. In other words, don't teach your grandma to suck eggs.

Was I smug? Maybe. I could blame it on the new body, but, hell, I'd always been full of myself. Conceit—that, I'd admit to—but stupid I was not. There were ways to take care of one potential problem without any personal involvement at all. It was all about subcontracting. Lesser problems called for lesser solutions. The big guns like myself I'd save for the thorniest challenge, and damn, if it wasn't going to be a bitch.

But that was half the fun.

I'd stayed in some run-down places through the ages. Believe it or not, Tumulus wasn't the worst of them either. There had been damp, pitch-black caves with only blind grubs and creeping fungi for company. There had been a chest containing the opal-encrusted bones of a queen that had lain at the bottom of a swamp for so many years I'd lost count. I'd even once lived in the petrified body of a basilisk. Long dead and turned to stone, but it still stank. Don't ask me how. And don't ask me why the client wanted that piece of yard sale crap protected, because I didn't have a clue.

But this . . . this made the bowels of a basilisk look like Graceland.

I sat with curled lip on the edge of the bed and tried to decide if the stain in the center of the spread looked more like William Shatner or the outline of a ravenous, bloated yeti. The carpet was shag (or had been at some point), and was the exact yellow green shade of bile. It should've clashed with the brand-spanking-new purple polyester curtains, but oddly enough it didn't. They were too far apart on the color spectrum to even meet that much. Apples and oranges. I leaned forward and touched a finger to the cloth. I'd had a sweatshirt that shade of purple years ago. Frowning, I fisted the cloth. Years and years ago. I'd packed it the night the Grendels had come to take me away.

I felt my frown deepen. What the hell was I thinking? That wasn't my past. It wasn't even our past, not anymore. We weren't two bickering halves, fighting for control. We were one. Whole. Not two separate creatures coexisting, but an entirely new one. Greater than the sum of our parts and superior in every way, just as the Auphe had said we would be.

Of course, being superior didn't mean I wasn't currently residing in the most god-awful room that existed this side of Jersey. The communal bathroom alone was scarier than the Auphe and me combined. What went on there wasn't going to up the already teeming human population any, and that was the best thing to be said about it. As for the room, I wasn't the only thing scuttling around in its confines. Five stars for the religious and brotherly attitude of the place, one for the roaches and bathroom orgies.

Regardless, it was all I could afford at the moment; the cash in my wallet hadn't gone far. I'd given serious thought to paying Promise a visit and staking her right there in her marble-floored foyer. Now, there would be some digs worth holing up in. Only one thing had given me pause, and it wasn't the fact that my brother was warm for her undead form. It was the security in her building. It was top-of-the-line. I could get in; that wasn't a problem. She'd have the front desk send me up, if Niko hadn't warned her. She might even if he had. It would make a good trap. But I doubted Promise could disappear for more than a day before some of the staff came inquiring, whether it be security or her cleaning lady. It was just too much a pain in the ass for what would probably amount to only one night of extravagance.

Pity.

I pulled off my jacket and tossed it on the wobbly table in the corner before stripping the comforter off the bed. The sheets beneath were clean and smelled strongly of industrial-strength bleach. I doubted it would keep me up; I was dead on my feet. Wadding up the mottled bedspread, I shoved it under the bed and dropped onto the mattress, resting my head on a pancake-flat pillow. I could've hit Boggle up for some dough before I left the park. He had to go through his weight in muggers every month. He was bound to have a pile of wallets and jewelry he had no use for. I really should've spared the time. If I had, I would be sleeping on Egyptian cotton now instead of what felt like woven cardboard.

Shoulda coulda woulda. The bottom line was, I'd simply been too tired. There were advantages to this body, but there were disadvantages too. No getting around that. It still needed rest, needed sleep, and denying those needs wouldn't accomplish anything except to put my ass in a sling. Niko was out there and he would take immediate and ruthless advantage of any weakness, no matter how slight. It was what I would do. It was what he had taught me. I grinned with sleepy pleasure at the blood-soaked fantasies featuring my brother that danced in my head. They sure as hell weren't sugarplums, but enjoyable all the same. Rolling over, I fell instantly into a dreamless sleep.

When life was so good, who needed dreams?

15

The next morning, I decided to drop in on Promise after all. I'd mulled it over and decided that while I couldn't kill her and shack up at her place, I could kill her and steal whatever wasn't nailed down. As plans went it was both practical and entertaining, and those who knew me would be the first to say I was nothing if not fun-loving.

In no particular hurry, I made my meandering way to the Upper East Side. There were sights to see, so damn many. They were all familiar in Cal's memories, but I saw them with new eyes. Colors were brighter and the smells of food, perfume, and unwashed bodies were a sharp-edged, musky rose to inhale. The streets were bright with sun and oblivious cheer, but the alleys were dark with rage, terror, and endless waves of pain. God*damn*, who couldn't love this city?

When I finally reached Promise's building I'd decided the best course of action was the tried-and-true "I've been here a thousand times so let me up already." Every New Yorker knows it and sometimes it even works. Caliban had been here several times with Nik to act as Promise's bodyguards. Never in the daytime of course, but here was hoping they rotated shifts enough at the security desk that I'd see someone I'd recognize. And better yet, someone who would recognize me.

I wasn't precisely dressed for duty, still wearing the sweatshirt and jeans Cal had been in when I'd taken him. Consequently, I left a businessman in one of those dark alleys that felt like home. He was minus his shirt, jacket, tie, and wallet, but he had his life—more or less. So no bitching allowed. The wallet was sadly depleted, but the suit jacket fit well. It was somewhat loose in the shoulders, but nothing too noticeable. The pants had been obviously too big and I hadn't bothered to strip them off his limp form. The tie turned out to be more of a problem. It seemed neither of us, despite my whole-hearted appreciation of nooses, had much experience tying one of those. In the end, I tossed it with disgust on the sidewalk and settled for buttoning the jacket. The jeans were still jeans, but it would pass. Cal hadn't ex-actly been a fashion plate before. I, on the other hand, rubbed fingers along the expensive material of the stolen clothes and purred low in my throat. Nice.

I still had a ponytail holder and pulled freshly dried hair back with a ruthless yank. With sunglasses firmly in place, I made my move. The doorman waved me through without question and I stopped at the security desk and patted the breast of my jacket. "I have tickets for Mrs. Nottinger." Naturally, this guy wouldn't know Promise was of the supernaturally parasitic persuasion, but he was bound to be aware she wasn't a day person. I didn't want to arouse suspicion by insinuating I was here to escort her somewhere this early. A delivery of some sorts seemed the perfect solution.

Luckily for me, I'd seen this guy on night duty before, and he had seen me. He was heavyset with snow-white hair cut bristle short and black horn-rimmed glasses that all said his cop days were long gone. He still had an air of authority, but he topped it off with a pear-shaped butt that doesn't come from slavish devotion to duty. Waving a hand, he dumped his paper-bag lunch out of sight and down behind the sweep of marble counter. Apparently I'd hit him at some kind of shift change. Goody for me, all the better for distraction. "You're that guy Niko's partner, aren't you?" he yawned. "Go on up."

Just like that. Don't you just love it?

In the elevator I hummed to myself. My humming wasn't quite like the human version and after a few floors passed in silent speed, an old woman with an armful of even more ancient dog said, "You have such a beautiful voice. I've never heard anything like it."

I tilted my head and gave her a smile that bubbled with good cheer. "It runs in the family."

Crumpled and decaying rose petals masquerading as lips smiled back at me. Wrapped in mink with the finest leather shoes and purse money could buy, she was dressed like a predator—in her victims. Yet she failed to spot a real one when she saw it. Fluffy saw it, though. Fluffy saw me. Tiny teeth, blunt and worn, were bared at me in a rictus of fear and outrage, and a squirt of warm yellow urine poured over the mink. It only proved that the Fluffys of the world were far smarter than the ones who led them around on shiny rhinestone leashes.

I exited on Promise's floor to snarls and snaps from the dog and yelps from its oblivious owner. If possible, it put me in an even better mood.

Until I saw the door begin to open at the end of the hall. Twenty-three stories up. Who takes the stairs twenty-three frigging flights? It wasn't Promise's personal trainer, that was for damn sure, and that left only one other person.

Niko.

Not that taking on my brother wouldn't be fun. Many, many bloody escapades to be had there and I looked forward to it. Just not right now. Things might not have gone as swimmingly as they could have before I sailed though a shattered window to freedom, but I was distracted at the time. Putting on a new body isn't exactly like grabbing a shirt off the rack. It takes time and finesse to get it to fit just right—to use it as it was meant to be used. I could take him all right; after all, he was only a human. But there was no harm in waiting for a more opportune time.

There was a supply closet to my left and I dived into it, shutting the door behind me. The inside was three times as big as the bug-infested room I had spent the night in. The cleaning supplies were in oak-faced cabinets, tucked neatly from sight. The door itself was an ornately latticed affair, straight out of a sultan's palace. I left the lights off and, standing to one side, peered through one of the minute openings. I kept the sunglasses on. They didn't impair my newly improved vision any and I didn't want a gleam of silver to give me away.

Niko came through the stairwell door. Unwinded by the climb, smug bastard, he moved down the hall. My, my . . . big brother wasn't looking too hot. It was subtle, and if you didn't know him, you might miss it completely. But I did know him. I knew him inside and out, and I saw every sign of strain on his face. Cheekbones were sharper, lips tighter, and the shadows of sleepless nights were under his eyes. But the best evidence was found in the eyes themselves. They were bleaker than a grave-yard gone to rot.

Good stuff. Damn good stuff.

Curiously, I watched him raise a fist to knock once on Promise's door. A single soft rap, but it still had the door

opening after just a few moments. Good ears on vampires. Then again there were lots of good things on
Promise, I leered to myself, and ears didn't make the top
ten. She stood in the doorway, obviously puzzled to see
Niko. She was wrapped in a dressing gown of violet silk,
and her unbound hair was a fall of rippling brown water
that nearly reached her waist. A necklace wreathed her
neck once, then fell between her breasts. Pearls, she
slept in pearls. There was something very erotic about
that and I felt an interesting twitch below.

"Niko?" She didn't grasp the edges of her robe to
pull them closer together. Either she didn't care or
didn't notice, or maybe it was a combination of the two.
"What are you doing here?" A pale hand reached out to
rest on Niko's chest. "What's wrong?"

Huh. I wasn't the only one who could read Niko today. His head inclined, not much . . . maybe a few millimeters at the most, but for him it was a bow to
unrelenting pressure. "I need your help," he said in a
voice I didn't recognize. Not as Cal, not as I was now.
"I've lost . . ." He stopped, then cleared this throat and
finished with robotic determination. "I've lost Cal."

"Lost," and not as in misplaced your favorite pair of
boxers. He said the word as if he really meant it. Lost as
a child who disappears on the way to school never to be
seen again. Lost as the wife whose hand slips from yours
as she's swallowed by raging floodwaters. Lost as a
brother whose silver eyes watch you as he plummets
downward through the night air until you can see him
no more.

Pretty goddamn lost.

Niko couldn't lose control. It was as much a part of
him as his blond hair and lethal blades. He couldn't lose
it, but it did sag a bit around the edges. As I watched, he
rested his forehead on the top of Promise's head. Other

than that, he didn't move, simply remained still to repeat with a tone of weary disbelief, "I lost him."

Promise moved then, wrapping her arms around his waist and holding him. It was touching as hell, and I almost felt a tear well up. I checked my watch. Things to do, people to kill, and this lovefest was only slowing me down. It was too bad I'd lost my gun before I'd tripped out to Tumulus. I could've shot Niko in the back as well as done some damage to the cheesy latticework of the door.

After a moment Niko straightened, probably regretting the weakness he'd allowed himself. "I have to get him back."

"Then you will." Promise took his arm and urged him into the apartment. As they passed through her door, I heard her voice drift back. "I'll help you, Niko. In any way I can."

Wonderful. Now I had a human, a puck, and a vampire sticking their noses in my business. Everyone was invariably out to ruin my good time. It never failed. Not only was Promise joining forces with Niko and Goodfellow, but I still didn't have any damn money. Still, the day wasn't over and there were other ways to finance my love of luxury. Boggle was looking more and more like my best option. I left the closet behind and went to hit him up.

I'd known Boggle back when he was an ankle-biting pollywog. Years had passed and times had changed, but there was one thing I could depend on to stay the same: Bog's bottomless pit of an appetite. It defined consistency back when consistency was barely a concept, much less a word. So when I came calling, it was with a present in hand. I released my grip on it, letting it slump to the ground, and raised my other hand for a bite of hot dog. Chili cheese with onions.

"Boggy," I said indistinctly around a mouthful of sheer heaven. "Up and at 'em, tiger. I brought you breakfast. You want yours sunny-side up or over easy?"

The mud stirred, giving a sluggish ripple, and then Boggle raised his head above the surface just enough to show his jack-o'-lantern orange eyes like a bizarrely prehistoric frog. "You again." The words bubbled up through the mud with annoyed resignation. The resignation quickly melted as the eyes focused more sharply on me and widened. "You." This time the tone was different and certainly less complacent.

"It's me." I flashed a grin as I pulled off the sunglasses I'd lifted earlier from a street vendor and revealed my gorgeous silver peepers. "But are you sure which me it is, Bog? Because I'm more than willing to take the time to talk it over, to really hash it out with you. For old times' sake."

Ignoring the invitation, he rose slowly from his mudhole, eyes fixed on me as his face peeled back to reveal his teeth. "You merged with it. A human. Disgusting. Perverse." If he'd had lips, he would've pursed them and spit to show his distaste.

"Aren't you the delicate lady?" I snorted. "And he was only half human. Now we're a whole lot less." I put my foot on the motionless body in front of me and gave it a shove. It rolled down the incline into the thick mud with a splat. Beefy frame, fairly young—he'd make a good meal for Boggle. He'd followed me with dogged determination into the depths of the park, never quite as surreptitious as he'd hoped. He'd had a knife, handcuffs, a homemade wire garrote, and a burning look of hunger in his eyes. I didn't know if he wanted money or something much less mundane, but it didn't matter to me and I knew it wouldn't to Boggle either. Robbers or rapists, they all taste the same, he'd say.

Like chicken.

Either way it was a stroke of fortune I'd been all too happy to take advantage of. It saved me the trouble of dragging a kicking and screaming jogger into the woods. "Eat up, big guy, and we'll get down to business," I prompted, taking a seat on the grassy bank to finish up my own breakfast hot dog. I'd never been a big fan of poultry myself.

Giving in, Boggle grumbled, "It's always bidness with you. Been a thousand years easy and first thing you want is a favor. Least this time you brought me takeout."

As my old buddy made his way through the most important meal of the day, I filled him in on my plan and what precisely it was that I needed from him. He wasn't too happy. I didn't take it personally. Boggles are never especially happy; it simply isn't in their makeup. But that was all right. I had enough good cheer for the both of us and then some.

"Quit your bitching," I ordered, wiping the mustard from my hands on the withered grass. "So what if you have to move. You're looking flaky anyway. A change of scenery will do you good."

"It's the pollution," he said glumly, tongue swiping over his bloody teeth. "Plays hell with my scales. I lose a bucketful every morning. Ain't no combing that over, ya know?"

"Yeah, it's a crying shame." Balancing my arms on my knees, I let my hands dangle and gave Boggle a narrow-eyed glance. "It's been a while for you, eh, Bog? Holed up in this all-you-can-eat buffet? Hell, the muggers fall in your playpen and you barely have to lift a claw. I have to wonder, big guy, if you're up for some genuine action." Leaning back, I replaced my sunglasses and repeated flatly, "I really have to wonder."

The orange eyes turned sullen. "You think I've gone soft. That what you're saying?"

"Doesn't matter what I say, Boggle." My tone was as soft as the flash of my teeth was hard. "What matters is what you do. I'm a good guy. I'm willing to give you the benefit of the doubt."

"What a pal," he said sourly. "And what am I getting out of this, huh? You want I should move. You want my souvenirs. You want me to risk my muddy ass. And for what? I'm helping you, but what the hell are you doing for me?"

"Besides the snack? Besides all the nostalgia?" I rose to my feet. "I'm not skinning you alive, Boggy. I'm not turning you into a throw rug for my swinging bachelor pad. How 'bout that? Is that good enough for you?"

Turned out, it was.

I got nearly eight thousand dollars and a pocketful of gold jewelry from Boggle. The jewelry, mainly thick chains and clunky rings, was tacky in a way only Mr. T could truly appreciate, but it should be worth a fair chunk of change. The clothes and empty wallets I let him keep. When I left he was sifting mournfully through his reduced pile of mementos with a jackknife claw and exhaling a bubbling sigh of regret. Boggles liked their toys. It was a fairly dull existence, just eating, cracking bones, and stewing in the slime. A few baubles livened up the ole mudhole. He'd turned the majority of them over to me all the same. Why? Maybe for old times' sake? For our long-enduring friendship? Or could it be he wasn't the first of his kind I'd peeled like a grape?

Bingo.

Boggles were big and they were fierce fighters, but you couldn't accuse them of being the smartest mud pies around. Tactics escaped them and their attention

span wasn't all it could be. They weren't exactly fish in a
barrel, but neither were they at the top rung in life's
pantheon of creepy-crawlies. With a shred of perseverance and just a bit of forethought, it wasn't that difficult
to get the better of them. With guidance from me,
though, my particular boggle would do in a pinch.

Pocketing the money, I hailed a cab to the nearest
pawnshop. The backseat was as smelly as Bog's pits and
not quite as hygienic. The driver was a *ghul.* I hadn't
seen one of those in a while. This one was masquerading
as a shriveled older woman with matted locks, John
Lennon glasses, and a mouth like a rat trap. Most *ghuls*
originally came sweeping out of the deserts of the
bedouin like a foul wind. They lived to bedevil and annoy travelers, to lead them off the beaten path and on
occasion eat them. What better disguise for that than a
taxi driver? And what could be more annoying than being eaten?

It rolled a bloodshot eye back in my direction and
decided it would just stick with overcharging me. I was
in such a good mood that I actually paid the fare. It was
the city. I loved it. The atmosphere was charged with the
energy of supernatural beasts in the thousands. In an
age where we had come to be few and far between,
there was a heady jolt to being among so many non-
humans. When I closed my eyes, the electricity was visible, crackling in blue and green bolts. It was like the old
days. I hadn't realized I'd missed it like I did. On the
other hand, I was also rolling in the biggest concentration of cattle on the East Coast. There was a time when
that would've been entertaining as hell. Unfortunately,
humans were not as fun as they'd once been. They were
softer and slower now. They had better weapons, it was
true, but as they no longer believed in us, it didn't do
them much good. The challenge there had been when

they were savages was gone, but soon enough, it would be back. The entire landscape would change, physically, culturally, and in every other way. Thanks to the Auphe, we had the technology; we could unbuild them.

The pawnshop guy was a human, but not as soft and slow as most. He peered at me with pebble eyes from behind rusting bars. "Yeah?" A shaved head gleamed faintly under dim fluorescent lights. Pocked skin was marked with the shadow of a heavy beard, and a black tattoo of barbed wire circled the thick neck. Here and there a drop of blood was shaded in crimson dripping tastefully from the barbs. It was sharply ugly and jaggedly brutal. I touched the pad of my thumb to the side of my throat and considered how one might look on me.

Dropping the jewelry into a metal tray, I watched as it was pulled with a jerk back through an opening through the bars. "Grandma left me some of her baubles," I said with a winning smile.

The guy held up one thick chain with an oversized gold pot leaf hanging from it. "I'll bet," he grunted as he continued to root through the tangle of precious metal.

"Hey, Granny was a progressive broad." Adjusting my sunglasses, I drawled, "So what will you give me for them?"

"Eight hundred," he responded with disinterest.

I rocked back on my heels and folded my arms. "Let me rephrase that. What's it *worth?*"

Yellowed teeth showed in the frozen grin of a rabid dog. "Nine, ten thousand. You, valuable customer, get eight hundred. You want it or not?"

I'd like to say I dickered with him, got the cheap bastard up to at least three thousand. Didn't happen. My persuasive powers, awesome though they were, bounced off this block of concrete without result. I could've shot

him, if I hadn't lost my gun and the bars weren't sandwiched between two layers of bulletproof glass. Just
yesterday I would've been able to slither through the
molecules and strip his flesh into yummy bite-sized bits.
But today, I was different. . . . We were different. So I
swallowed my pride, accepted the money, and started to
leave. Pausing, I asked him, "You have some matches,
smiley?"

Tossing a book into the tray, he pushed them out to
me with an oily gloat sheening his eyes. "The least I
could do for you, buddy."

Well . . . not the very least. I moved into the back alley beyond the shop, and as luck would have it, I found
a homeless guy curled up in a doorway with an almost
full bottle of vodka. I hummed happily. It saved me a
trip to the local liquor store. Within two minutes the
back of the building was in flames, the bum was scuttling
for safety, and hopefully Smiley was roasting like a pig
at a luau.

Hearing the wail of approaching sirens, I strolled after the bum. It was possible Smiley would make it out,
and it was a shame I couldn't hang around to make sure
that didn't happen. Even so, I was betting nine thousand
dollars' worth of my gold wasn't going to pay for the
skin grafts, much less rebuild the shop. As I passed a
plate glass window, I touched a finger to my temple and
gave my reflection a snappy salute. Now you're a monster, Caliban. Ain't it great?

Ain't it just friggin' great?

I used some of my newfound wealth to get a real hotel room, one with chocolates on the pillows instead of
drool stains. I also bought a cell phone. All work and no
play made Cal a dull boy. We wouldn't want that. I could
keep my eye on the prize and still indulge myself. A fine
line, but I had faith that I could walk it. But more than

that, more than the confidence I had in myself, I *wanted* to walk it. I wanted to live life as half of me always had . . . with reckless abandon. It was who I had been and who I still was to a large extent. Without risk the eons could get boring as hell. Humans had a natural adrenaline. Nonhumans . . . the majority of us had to manufacture our own.

On first guess you might think that it was safe to say that Niko would've abandoned the apartment after it was trashed by the Auphe. A logical conclusion, but a wrong one. Who had stuck like glue to the burned remnants of a cheap trailer, all that was left of a Grendel slaughter? Though it was years later, I knew the same would hold true now. After all, if he left, how would poor kidnapped Cal find him again? No, he'd be there. Part of the day anyway . . . the part he wasn't out scouring the city for me. Niko hadn't been able to follow me through the gate, but it wouldn't stop him from the grim hope that, like before, I'd make my way back. Smart boy. He was right.

But when I called he wasn't the one to answer the phone. That put a nasty crack in my polished conviction. It was that son of a bitch Goodfellow, who I'd had every expectation would've been halfway across the country by now, if not the world. Damn flashy peacock, who would've thought he had it in him? Just as he knew my reputation, I knew his—shallow and self-serving, with a *highly* developed survival instinct, not that there was anything wrong with that. Those were stellar qualities in my opinion, but he had no appreciation for the finer things in life, the same ones on which the Auphe and I saw eye to eye. He actually liked humans, believe it or not. Liked them a little too much. Goodfellow should've run when he had the chance. Too bad. For him, there wouldn't be another.

"Goodfellow," I said smoothly. "When did you get a backbone? Are they selling them on eBay now?"

I heard the sharp intake of breath on the other end and then his words, wrapped in glowing red wires of anger. "Darkling, what the hell are you doing? You cursed son of a bitch, what could you possibly have to gain from this?"

"Language, language." Bending down, I broke open the minibar and helped myself to a bottle of beer and a bag of pistachio nuts. After a long, cool swig, I continued. "I'm doing what I've always done. I'm looking out for number one and getting paid in the bargain. Isn't that what you do, Loman? Isn't that what *you've* always done?" I tossed a few nuts back and washed them down. Two tastes, both salty but wonderfully different, mixed on my tongue. "And that leads me to a curious question. Why are you changing your ways now?" I *tsk*ed sorrowfully. "Had enough of this life, have you? Don't they have medications for that sort of thing?"

"Loman," he came back after a moment of silence, tone subdued but still set. "You called me Loman."

"I'll call you Mary Margaret if I want to. Or Danny boy. That's more appropriate, don't you think?" I hummed a few bars of the legendary dirge before deciding I'd had enough of Goodfellow and his changing ways. New backbone, midlife crisis, whatever. All that mattered was the end result, and the result would be his end. "Nik around, old friend? I'd like a word."

"I'm not your friend," he countered vehemently in my ear. "I was never a friend to you or any of your kind. I can't believe I didn't recognize it when Cal told me. I can't believe I didn't guess it was you."

It wasn't really that hard to understand. The mirrors were a relatively new thing for me, as I'd picked that up only in the past five hundred years or so. The other male banshees had never pulled that trick and now that I was one of the last, they never would. So it wasn't all that surprising Goodfellow didn't know of it. It didn't keep me from twisting the knife, however. "Yeah, that's too bad, huh?" I offered genially. "You could've saved Mr. Morose. You probably could've gotten a few more years of whining out of him, at any rate. What a tragedy." I finished the beer in one last swallow. "You might have saved him, but you were drunk and you didn't. I'll bet Niko's really loving you on that one."

Silence. But sometimes silence can be as sweet as any melody.

Dropping the bottle into the wastebasket, I said briskly, "Nik's not home, is he? There's no way you'd still be holding the phone if he were. That's all right—I'll call back. Nice chatting with you, Goodfellow. It'll be interesting to see how much you have to say when I see you next." I added as a cheerful afterthought, "When I rip out your heart and shove it in your mouth." Turning off the cell phone, I tossed it over my shoulder onto the bed. I could've called Niko's own cell and had another chatfest, one probably even more entertaining, but right now there were other sensations to enjoy, other pleasures to seize. And the sharp cramping of the stomach was a good indicator of which I should choose. I reached for the room service menu. The nuts and the conversation with Goodfellow had only whetted my appetite and my taste for blood. It was time to see what this place had in the way of a steak . . . an extremely rare one.

As I waited for room service, I went to the bathroom and stood, Caliban's pride and joy in hand, watching with interest as urine splashed into the gleaming white bowl of the toilet. Humans, they were really the most amazingly primitive pieces of work. They had a brain that elevated them almost to reasoning organisms, but still had the plumbing of the most basic of animals.

"What are you doing, worthless creature?"

I gave a surprised yelp and whirled. Luckily the shock to my system froze the stream of urine and I managed to avoid decorating the bathroom in sunshine yellow. It also did something else curious. The pride and joy became the embarrassment and shame. Like a turtle it withdrew promptly, leaving me with a lot less in hand than I'd started with. "Hey," I protested automatically. "Where did it go?"

"Be grateful I don't relieve you of it altogether." Long nails split the shower curtain with lightning speed and an Auphe stepped through, throat working to spit out the human words. "It would make your stay here less pleasing, yes?"

Upper management—the bastards were never happy unless they were busting your balls . . . literally, in this case. "I'm just doing the job, boss." I zipped up with alacrity. Best not to let temptation hang out there. "Everything's going according to our plan."

The head cocked and molten eyes narrowed on me in murderous contemplation. "It is the Auphe plan, never the Darkling plan. You are to do as you're told. This"— he waved and arm and hissed—"this is not as you were told."

"This" would be the hotel room, Boggle, and all the rest, I was guessing. I hadn't expected the Auphe to keep that close an eye on me. They never had during the other jobs I'd pulled for them. I should've realized that this one would be different. This was the big enchilada and they were going to try to micromanage the hell out of me. Gating into my bathroom and giving me shit was actually the very least of what they might do if they thought I wasn't taking my work seriously.

"You are making ripples." He abandoned the human tongue and reverted to Auphe, which I understood. It sounded like cockroaches had crawled into your ear canal and started mating, but I understood it. "Ripples become waves. Waves attract attention we cannot afford." He leaned close enough that I could see my reflection in the metallic sheen of his teeth. I looked pretty damn good. "Waves drown those who make them."

"All right, all right. I can lie low if I have to. But there are some things that need doing. Caliban's brother, Goodfellow—they're going to make trouble," I pointed out with annoyance. "You have to see that."

"Not if they cannot find us or you. And if you keep your rapacious ego in rein, they will not." The pointed jaw worked with the effort to keep from burying those shiny teeth in my throat. "You will do as you've been told or the next thing you animate will be your own bloody bile."

The Auphe did not usually waste their time on threats. They simply killed and went on. A threat really wasn't part of their belief system. Promises, however, were. But it was a different story now . . . a different situation. Whatever I did, whomever I wasted—and even if I danced in the streets buck naked—the Auphe couldn't harm me. Without me they had no plan. Without me they had no options. So I took this all with a grain of salt, smothered a yawn, and solemnly promised to be a good boy from then on. With a satisfied growl, he pulled another gate from thin air and disappeared back to the Batcave or wherever; I didn't much care.

Trying to instruct me as if I were a child. Trying to tell me how to do my job as if I hadn't been doing it since time had blinked its first sleepy eye. Trying to rein me in. I felt a muscle in my jaw bunch. Forget that I wanted to kill Nik and Goodfellow just on general principles. Never mind that seeing their blood pour free would give me a chubby of enormous proportions. That wasn't the point. I was a professional, and I knew that if those two weren't taken care of, they would ruin things. Nik's relentless determination combined with Goodfellow's sneaky ways could very well throw a wrench in the works. The Auphe might not see that, but I did. And I would do what was needed to take care of the matter. If the bosses didn't like it, they could suck my dick. If it ever reappeared, that is.

Room service finally came nearly twenty minutes later. After I cleaned the plate, I went over to the climate control with a jaw-cracking yawn and comfortably full stomach. I cranked up the heat as high as it would go. I wasn't cold-blooded anymore, but I still had a lingering appreciation for warmth. Whether it was basking in the sun or a sweltering four-star hotel room, it was all good. I blinked torpid eyes and settled bonelessly on the bed. Sinfully decadent heating, it was another amenity to soon bite the dust. A spark of genuine mourning pierced my chest. All this luxury doomed to nothingness before I barely had a chance to enjoy it. It was enough to make you cry. Or take a nap. I picked the second option. There was time enough later to wreak havoc and foment chaos. All the time in the world.

Pun intended.

16

Dogfights—if you wanted one and looked hard enough, you'd find one eventually. If you were lucky, you'd lose only your money. If you were unlucky enough to stumble onto the wrong one, you could lose a whole lot more than that. Some fights had a very selective clientele. Those were the ones where the dogs usually bet on themselves. It made for interesting odds.

I had a word with the bitch at the door. She hovered halfway between wolf and woman, frozen into a mutated shape, not one or the other. A fiercely thick unibrow shadowed amber yellow eyes. Her jaw, while of human shape, was longer than usual with an underbite to make an orthodontist cringe. Her brown shaggy hair was pulled high into a bushy ponytail. It was the same color as the hair that showed in abundance from the neck and armholes of her sleeveless T-shirt. She had that European look nailed.

It was a myth that werewolves are made. They're not. They're born. But not all are born equal. Among a certain stratum of werewolf society, inbreeding was the norm. They felt it brought them closer to pure wolf with less of the contaminating human element. That was

their theory, anyway. A normal Were could switch from
human to animal at will, completely human to completely animal. For these that wasn't enough. Total wolf
at all times was the only acceptable goal. This lovely
lady was the less-than-ideal result. I chatted her up a bit
and she could smell the difference in me right away.
Good noses on the wolves, even better than those of the
Auphe. Her eyes practically crossed at her first whiff of
me. Not Auphe, not human, not Darkling. None of those
things, yet somehow all three. It must have been an
interesting scent. She snuffled my hair with splayed nostrils repeatedly as we talked, and rumbled happily deep
in her throat. As long as she didn't start humping my
leg. I'd caught the distinct jump of fleas in her hair out
of the corner of my eye. You knew you were in trouble
when you had to dump the condoms and go for a flea
collar instead.

I slipped her a fifty and she slipped me two names.
Passing her, I went down the stairs to a dark basement
filled with people, some furry and some not. The air was
thick with the coppery tang of blood and the smell of
wet dog. There was a circular cage roughly constructed
of chain link fence in the center of the room. Inside it
two wolves were going at it. More lupine than the female at the door, they were given away only by a missing tail on one and a pair of purely human blue eyes on
the other. Fur and blood flew as fast as the buzz saw
snarls, and I watched the fight for a moment. I was appreciative of the unleashed savagery and not a little en-
vious of the clean slash that ripped one throat to a red
ruin. Wishing I'd dropped a dime on baby blue eyes, I
headed through the crowd for the far corner. Two figures hunched around a small table, sharing a bottle of
cheap wine. The male could've passed for human if it
hadn't been for a mouthful of jagged ivory teeth and an

overabundance of facial hair. The female had a smooth face, round light brown eyes, and slightly pointed ears tufted with thick pale blond hair.

Stopping beside them, I smiled and said lightly, "Fido, Bowser, hear you're looking for a job."

The woman's blond ears twitched with annoyance. Ramming a thumb against his broad chest, the male growled. "It's Wolfgang and Fang." His broad nose sniffed the air with suspicion as he regarded me with either squinting myopia or intense stupidity. The two looks were remarkably similar. "Who the hell are you?"

"Oh yeah, that's less of a cliché," I snorted. "I'm the guy who has enough cash to keep you in chew toys for a long time. That good enough for you, Spot?"

Wolfgang, apparently not a fan of straight talk, cocked his head and narrowed his eyes to icy slits as the growl that slid up his throat from his chest vibrated the table itself. Blunt nails scored the wood as knuckles flexed with an obscenely painful popping sound.

"Okay, you're a canine of few words. I respect that. Look, I'm not here to bust your balls." I'd leave that to the vet of his choosing. Pulling up a chair, I dropped into it. Removing my dark glasses, I met belligerent eyes with serene silver ones. "But, buddy, you do not want to get into a pissing contest with me, I promise you that." I put a hand in a pocket to remove a thick wad of cash. Dumping it on the tabletop, I continued, my eyes still fixed on his. "You look like a good doggy. And a good doggy would take the money, shut his trap, and listen."

The growl transmuted into a bass roar, then faded to silence as slender fingers fanned the green in Wolfgang's face like a winning hand of poker. As with most couples, Fang had her grip firmly on the finances of the relationship. With a grumbling sigh and after pulling his head back turtle fashion between arching shoulder blades, Wolfgang snarled, "Okay, okay. So talk already. What do you want us to do?"

"What comes naturally. Snack." Hands behind my head, I tilted back in the chair and raised my eyebrows. "After all, isn't that what big bad wolves do? Eat up grandmas and little girls?"

It wasn't that I knew for a fact that Georgie Porgie was going to be trouble. In some ways she was in this deeper than perhaps even she was aware. That was the trouble with psychics—you never really could know for sure. Georgina might not go to Niko, but it was a dead certainty he would go to her. Grasping at any and every straw to locate me, Nik would get around to George sooner or later, if he hadn't already. She had certainly stonewalled him earlier when he went to talk to her about the soda shop incident, and she'd definitely known then more than she was saying. There was no telling what she'd do now. Maybe she'd continue to keep it zipped up, and maybe she wouldn't. Maybe she actually knew something, and maybe she didn't. Either way I couldn't take the chance. Besides, an adorably wise little red-haired psychic? Please. She was simply too cute to live. I was doing the world a favor.

I was just that kind of guy.

Sometimes you have to stop and smell the roses. I still needed to check in again with the Auphe and see how things were progressing before they got antsy and paid me another visit—or, worse yet, started spying on me again. I'd kept a careful eye open this time and hadn't seen any sign of them. Hopefully, it would stay that way. As for the roses, I had managed to divvy up some of my work. Things were getting accomplished on schedule and I didn't see any reason I couldn't enjoy myself for a bit. In this city there were a thousand and one entertaining things to do and amazingly enough no all of them were violence related. It was time I played tourist and took advantage of the place while it was still around.

I watched the fights for a while, hit on Fang much to Wolfie's displeasure, and had a few drinks. When I surfaced on the streets again, evening was a dusky tint in the sky, and the twilight chill was cool fingers sliding along my skin into my hair. I inhaled the cold air with a scowl and a strong desire for my warm hotel bed with its scorching hot electric blanket. Deciding not to let the weather spoil my good time, I headed down the block listening for one of my favorite things, music. It was a given I was a fan. Had to be with my banshee sisters. Male banshees sang too, just for different reasons. No lurking on a castle turret bemoaning the approaching death of its lord or lady, not for us. No, thanks. Bringing death was one thing. Just sitting around and waiting for it, that was another. I mean, shit, how passive-aggressive can you be?

Yeah, I liked music. All music. It all had something to offer in one respect or another. It was the one thing in which humans had no equal. They might not have their own innate magic, but when it came to music, they *made* magic. Rock was the best, but I wasn't choosy. Over the years I'd managed to find something to appreciate in all the genres. If it had a beat, if it got my blood pumping, and if I could kill to it, it met all my requirements. It was while on the hunt for all three that I ran into something that distracted me. It was something that I'd thought about earlier but had forgotten until I saw it staring me in the face.

The Painted Lady was a tattoo parlor, wonderfully grungy and chock-full of bad, bad boys. Not as bad as me, of course, but then again, who was? There were more muscles, chains, and leather than you could shake a dick at. At least that was what Goodfellow would think. That soured my good mood almost instantly. I still wasn't at all thrilled about the puck's change of behavior. I thought I'd had him figured. The fact that I was wrong didn't sit well with me at all. And it wasn't just ego, although I had to admit that was a big part of it. No, the real problem was Goodfellow throwing one big anomalous monkey wrench in what I'd thought to be a perfectly running plan. If I couldn't depend on him to perform according to his reputation, what else couldn't I depend on? More specifically, who couldn't I depend on?

Or was that "whom"?

Either way, the answer was the Auphe. They were a lot like me, that was true. And that was also the problem. Know thyself. . . . It was a good philosophy. It often kept thyself from biting the big one. I did want to be on the winning side, but just how long the Auphe would want me there might be a different matter altogether. There's no honor among thieves or monsters. But if I did have faith in anything, it was in my ability to come out on top. Still, life could abruptly get more interesting as things went along, no doubt about it.

Shrugging it off, I concentrated on the matter at hand. Picking out my tattoo. There was plenty to choose from, all artful in their own right. Snakes, skulls, skulls vomiting snakes—which was meant to be an ironic twist, I suppose—and hundreds of other macabre gems. I was as torn as a kid in a candy store, but in the end I chose one of the classics. It was a word. Just one word surrounded by a candy red heart, the letters as black as what passed for my soul.

MOM.

"You should honor your mother, Cal," I murmured to myself as the needle stitched its happy way along my flesh. "If it weren't for her, we wouldn't be here. Neither of us." The design was about an inch and a half high on my bicep, cheerfully stark against my pale skin. It was worth every sting of the needle, every smear of blood on the rough textured gauze. It was enough to make me wish that for a moment we weren't one simply so I could see the look on his face. I touched a finger to a pinpoint of blood and then tasted it. My blood now, but the taste was deliciously strange and new.

The tattoo artist gave a minute shake of his head as he finished up the last letter, but remained silent. In this place he'd probably seen more bizarre behavior by far than some self-sampling. From around me as I reclined in the chair, a few rough looks were shot my way. It didn't go any further than that, though. Too bad. Menacing expressions didn't provide much in the way of entertainment, not enough to bring me up out of the chair. I was feeling nicely lazy, a lion content to let the gazelle pass by.

When the masterpiece was complete, I admired it in a mirror that hung crookedly on the wall. It certainly wasn't a mirror I would've been caught dead in, fly-specked and murky, but it cast an adequate enough reflection. I traced the letters ruminatively on my skin and then the surface of the glass. I couldn't help the sly self-satisfied grin that split my face. It may have contained something more than satisfaction if you went by the sideways twitch the guy gave as I paid him. The sheep tended to startle so easily.

When I hit the streets it wasn't with a new purpose, but with a reaffirmed definition, you might say. Next stop would be Auphe central. See what was up on the Grendel side of things. They most likely wouldn't be ready for a few more days yet, but best to touch base. It didn't pay to make the clients any crankier than they already were. And since I'd already pissed them off, not to mention shooting one of them, it was definitely time for my best behavior. Such as it was.

As I headed for the subway to catch the R train, I considered the Auphe. They'd really thought they had it all planned out and in most ways they'd done a bang-up job. There'd been the breeding program, of which Caliban had been the only viable result. You had to give them points for that. I would never have thought it was feasible—if they could even find a human who'd cooperate. Not that cooperation was strictly necessary, but in this day and age of technological beginnings and endings, cooperation was often more fruitful. So after a few decades or so of trying they had their hybrid Auphe-human. But although his mother had been the very spirit of helpfulness, the son was not. The Auphe had every expectation they'd be able to "convince" him to go along with their grand plan. You couldn't blame them. That was one bet I'd have guessed to be surefire myself.

However, they had been wrong about Caliban. He'd made a break from his indoctrination in Tumulus and they'd seen nothing but his heels since. And without Caliban the only thing grand would be the size of their failure. Big and stinking didn't even begin to touch it.

But while it would've been nice had the stubborn Cal cooperated, it had never been strictly necessary. It simply would've made things easier, especially in keeping track of him while he physically matured and his talent matured along with him. Yeah, it would have made things easier, but that didn't matter now that there wasn't a Cal, not anymore. Possession is nine-tenths of the law. You didn't need to be a lawyer to see that. Once again, thanks to me, the Auphe were in business. All they had to do was iron out the other minor details and they were home free. As the real estate vultures said, it was all about location, location, location.

The Auphe had Cal, they had me, but they also needed a massive influx of energy. This wasn't just any gate they wanted to open. A couple of double-A batteries wasn't going to cut it. They needed a major power source. Crossed ley lines might do it. An abandoned place of worship would be even better. They tended to store up a huge amount of energy over time if the faith was genuine. I was interested to see what the bosses had come up with.

The address I'd been given was in Sunset Park, Brooklyn. In a block that had seen better days, the large warehouse was a hulking, dilapidated brute squatting between two other deserted buildings. Brooding, sooty brick, gaping, shattered windows, and sullen atmosphere—I wasn't hearing church bells ring from this place. No, the sounds emanating from there would be more along the lines of bloodcurdling screams and sobbing pleas for help. That would be more welcome to my ears than any bell and it gave the condemned pit a whole lot of grace in my eyes. It wasn't an E ticket ride yet, but it would be. It would be the biggest, the best, and the very last ride the world took. That I was going to be in the driver's seat made it even more of rush.

Inside, the Auphe were milling about purposefully, clearing the enormous space of what looked to be a decade of debris. There were close to a hundred of them, their long hands pulling and pushing with an unnatural strength. A hundred, that must be just about every Auphe left in this world. Tumulus itself might stand empty as they gathered here. That's the breaks of having your own spot on the endangered-species list. "Hey, boss," I called to the nearest one. "What's up with the spring cleaning?" Transforming the very face of existence took some doing, but I didn't think absolute cleanliness was a prerequisite.

There was no mention of the visit paid to me earlier. The Auphe weren't used to disobedience. They were most likely assuming I was now walking the straight and narrow and saluting the almighty Auphe as I went. Dream on. I was a mercenary, not a whore.

In answer to my question, the Auphe's spidery finger pointed downward. It could've been China he was indicating, but I didn't think so. Jade, pagodas, and stir-fried noodles were nice, but not particularly helpful in our situation. Crouching, I laid a hand on the small area of floor that had been cleared. The concrete was cold to the touch, much colder than the air around us. Much colder than it should have been. It tried to leach the warmth from my flesh as it whispered black, poisonous things in my ear. Evil, horrible things that could turn a soul inside out and turn every shred of light into the darkest of despair. Nifty. "Ah," I hummed with approval. "Nothing warms my heart like a good slaughter."

That was another thing that would raise some serious power. Violent death, and lots of it. Many people had died in this spot and what was left of them was cradled deep in the earth beneath us. It had happened long ago by human standards, but it had poisoned this place so thoroughly that it was still tainted hundreds of years later. Here it had waited . . . waited for us, waited for just this moment. Kismet, huh? Brought a tear to the eye, it did.

It could have been Native Americans massacring the wannabes or it could've been vice versa. It may even have been before a white man ever touched this soil. Whatever it had been, it was human on human. It was peculiar how humans would kill at the drop of a hat—but they always had a justification . . . a *reason*. Defense, rebellion, justice, revenge, insanity—there were always excuses. The few that admitted the truth, that they did it just for the fun of it, those they locked up. Or they killed them, for the good of society . . . ironic, eh?

Heard the phrase "fuck up a wet dream"? That was humans all over. They could take a concept like killing, something so pure and pristine, and wrap it up in a mess of psychobabble, denial, and chains of ridiculous ritual. They did their best to ruin the simple joy, the magnificent beauty of it. And yet they managed to accomplish it on a grander scale than we ever had. I had to admire that.

I patted the concrete and felt the rage, the hatred, and the horror of life abruptly snuffed out. It tickled my palm like the silky hair of a mink. Sweet. "Hang in there," I said soothingly. "Won't be long." No, not long at all before we sucked them dry. There would be no more uneasy death echoing through the years, no more unheard screams for vengeance. There would be only nonexistence. Okay, it wasn't heaven, but neither was it hell. They should be counting their blessings. They were going to be luckier than most whose paths I crossed. I gave one last pat and stood. "You can thank me later."

As for that grand murderous scale humans laid claim to . . . we were about to give them a run for their money. Unmaking isn't the same as destroying, not at all, but the end result was. Since our planned result was the literal undoing of the vast majority of the human race, I had to think that end was plenty good enough. The Auphe had truly been inspired to come up with this scheme, I didn't mind admitting. Since the dawn of time the Auphe had been near the top of the food chain. I wouldn't give them the very top rung, but there was no denying that they thought they occupied it. But then the humans came. They weren't much of a threat. Hell, on the contrary, they provided entertainment. Fun to play with, cunning in their own brutish way, and they didn't break too easily. There's nothing worse than a flimsy toy.

The downside was, our toys bred. In one breath there were thousands, in the next millions. And even a million grunting, dirty pigs could take out one single farmer, no matter how clever he was. Yeah, one moment the Auphe were swimming along, happy as clams; the next a tidal wave of humanity swept them out to sea. Swept over us all. They were too many and we were too few, and that's just the way it was.

Now.

So, the Auphe reasoned, why not open a gate to then? And that's why they had needed me. No Auphe could open a gate to the past. The energy needed for that was phenomenal; they simply didn't have it. And channeling energy was not a talent the Auphe possessed. It was, however, one I did. I had quite a bit of natural energy of my own, and when I channeled a huge power source in addition to that, the end result was little short of a nuclear explosion. In a perfect world I could've inhabited an Auphe, channeled, and opened the gate. It would have been a piece of cake, theoretically. But naturally, it wasn't. We tried that before the breeding program began. Our best effort had resulted in several exploded Auphe. Turns out Auphe and I weren't a compatible merging. So, several experiments later, the Auphe settled on a human as the most likely option. I could possess one of those, we discovered, and with some tinkering a human's genetics could be manipulated enough to crossbreed. The finished product would be human enough for me to take over and Auphe enough to open a gate. It was easier said than done, but eventually it'd been accomplished—"eventually" being the key word here.

We'd thought we had the whole thing wrapped up with the half-breed. But Caliban had thrown a kink in it and good, the little shit. I grinned and patted my own chest with affection. My little shit now. He'd proved stubborn, both mentally and physically. Cooperation wasn't top on his list when he was still sane; it didn't shoot up any higher when he hopped aboard the loony-mobile. Not that that would've stopped the Auphe. But where that wouldn't, his physical failings did. He couldn't open a gate. His nervous system, inner battery . . . what-the-hell-ever . . . it just couldn't flip that switch. It was not mature enough, not sufficiently developed, to make that jump. The Auphe's only option was to wait, and wait they did . . . right up to the moment baby Cal opened his first real gate and took off. Now that . . . *that* had been hilarious. Too bad he didn't remember any of it. Killing his father and escaping under the nose of the Auphe, good times. Good times.

But it was four years later and Cal's run was over. Now it was simply a matter of opening that gate to the past. It was too late now for the Auphe to prevail against the bubbling mass of mankind, but before, when humans were few and far between, they'd be fish in a barrel. The in-the-know future Auphe would join the blissfully clueless past Auphe and that would be all she wrote for Harry Human. The Auphe wouldn't have to wipe them all out—95 percent would probably be enough. They *were* damn good playthings. No reason to throw out the baby with the bathwater, right?

Then life for the rest of us would become as it had been in the beginning. The humans would be huddled in huts or caves. Once again they would dread every rattle at their door, knowing that it could be the wind or . . . it could be us. Heady stuff, fear. It was the appetite teaser that sharpened the taste of violence and blood.

I would kiss the electric blankets good-bye, sad to say, but sometimes you had to suck it up and take the bad with the good. It was going to be a piece of cake. Smooth sailing.

Yeah, smooth sailing. Was I wrong to think they probably had that embossed on the *Titanic*'s cocktail napkins?

Turned out that, as usual, I was not wrong. When things go well, you should be suspicious. When things go *exceptionally* well, start sniffing for the dog crap on the bottom of your shoe. Or in this case the dog crap at your front door.

I'd given the fur balls my hotel address for a report on Little Red Riding Hood and the next morning I was eagerly awaiting word. That is, if "eagerly" could be defined as laid up in the Jacuzzi, drinking wine and smoking the richest tobacco that room service had to offer. Hearing the less-than-discreet scratch of claws at the door, I blew a plume of cigar smoke at the arched ceiling and called out, "Come on in. The water's fine." I heard the measured tread of two feet slowly approach the bathroom. Seconds later Wolfgang was in the doorway, blood and bruises barely hidden by a long, ratty coat. When he winced and spat red phlegm on the floor, I could see several teeth shattered to splinters. Fang was conspicuously absent. This was not good.

"Well, well, look who's back, tail between his legs." I dumped the cigar in the wineglass and went straight to the bottle. "Looks like someone got his furry ass kicked," I said coldly. Propping a foot on the edge of the tub, I took a long swig of grape to fortify myself against the mindless incompetence. "Spill it, Rover. How'd you screw up?"

"No girl." Absently, the werewolf lapped at the ragged slash on the back of his hand. "There was no girl there," he repeated defensively, licking his wounds both literally and figuratively. "Only men with swords. Many men."

There was a lie in there, maybe two. I could smell it. Cal would've been able to, and thus so could I. "No girl, you say." That, I was guessing, was the first lie. She'd been there all right. No reason for Niko to be standing guard if she hadn't been. Ruminatively, I tapped the mouth of the bottle against my chin. Now, as for the second lie. "A whole slew of sword-wielding, bloodthirsty men, all to defeat your worthless ass. Don't you rate? Where's the girlfriend?"

"Dead." There was a brief spark in his eyes. Fury, sorrow, loss. "She fell . . . from the roof. Jumped one of the bastards, but he dodged—" He shook his head, shaggy hair falling to cover his eyes. "Gone. All gone. Tried for revenge. But too many."

"Too many." I stood, the water cascading down me. "Tell me again how many. Tell me again how many is too goddamn many." The bottle I hurled at the wall exploded into purple-coated shrapnel. It wasn't as sharp as the rage whirling inside of me. The Auphe weren't the only ones that didn't like to get their way. "Because you know what? I'm thinking that number is only one."

The werewolf's lips peeled back to reveal clotted black blood and a still impressive set of choppers. Then the bravado shriveled and his head hung low. "My girl. My beautiful girl." The back of his hand made a pass at his nose. "Two. There were two. Human. Other. They took my sweet girl from me."

Two. Niko was one. Goodfellow would be the other. That son of a bitch was starting to annoy me. Why that stupid rabbit wouldn't run, I had no idea. It was enough to make me lose my temper, and I liked to think of myself as an easygoing guy. I took a step and felt a sliver of pain stab through my instep. Hissing, I reached down and pulled a shard of bloody glass free. Flimsy body. It was a side effect I didn't find too pleasant. One more annoyance, but it wasn't as bad as the one echoing in my ears. Wolfgang was howling now. It was a mourning song for his lost love, plaintive and haunting as the stars' last cry before the universe winked out. Wistful. Lost.

And loud as shit.

A broken bottle in the trachea cured that quickly enough. I dropped the remnants of the bottle neck on the floor. It landed in the rapidly spreading pool of blood and broke as thoroughly as Wolfie's heart had. Then there was silence, blessed silence. Stepping over the still body, I went to get dressed. I was going to have to leave the maid one helluva tip over this mess. Just went to show . . . you never send a dog to do a Darkling's work.

Luckily enough, I had my plan to take care of Niko, and now Goodfellow, already in place. As for George, she'd have to be moved to the back burner. Either she hadn't talked or it was too late to worry about it now. I was going with my gut instinct that she hadn't. In the soda shop when one and one had been but a half I'd seen her tears. Fatalism had surrounded her like a nimbus of blue light. What will be, will be and not in that happy *"que sera, sera"* way either. There's a theory that destiny cannot be changed, cannot be maneuvered, cannot even be tweaked. If you ascribe to that philosophy, then delivering bad news is rather pointless . . . unless you enjoy the look on someone's face when you tell him a piano will fall on his head next Wednesday and there's not a damn thing he can do about it. While that'd be reason enough for me, sweet little Georgie Porgie probably wouldn't go for it.

What was my philosophy? you might wonder. Simple. Live in the moment. Yeah, yeah. Sounds pretty familiar, I'm sure. Every self-help guru, every pseudoenlightened nut job, everyone who thought they were deeper than a parking-lot puddle, they all spouted it. No doubt about it, it was cheesy. But it was also true. Let the Auphe worry about the glorious past and the inhospitable future. The past was lousy with great memories, the future rife with possible ones, but so what? Nothing mattered but the here and now. Oceans of blood from the good old days weren't worth that one scarlet drop silky between your fingertips in the blessed here and now. Live in your past accomplishments and it's hard to keep up with, much less enjoy, your current disembowelments.

But that was my outlook on life and as happy as I was with it, my bosses weren't likely to agree. Or to even give a shit for that matter. Tucking the distracting thoughts out of the way, I left the hotel room. Sooner or later someone would be looking for me, what with the dead werewolf on the bathroom floor. The policy at the desk *had* distinctly stated No Pets.

17

Outside I walked, rode the subway for a bit, and then walked some more. When I reached a certain corner on a particular block, I made another call on my cell phone. This time I got Niko, and damn, was my brother pissed. A curt "Yes?" echoed in my ear. The word could've been carved from dry ice, cold and searing all at once. So much unadulterated fury buried infinitely deep beneath the arctic tundra, damned if it didn't gave me a warm, fuzzy feeling. Playing with Niko was like playing with fire, and any pyromaniac could tell you that's more fun than a barrelful of rabid monkeys.

"Hey, Nik, how's it hanging?" I waved at the doorman across the busy street. He squinted, then gave me a two-finger salute from his cap, remembering me from the day before. "Guess who?"

"You." Succinct, my brother. You had to give him that.

"Is that any way to be?" I offered mournfully. "Why can't you call me Cal, big brother? I'm still family, right?"

"Cal is my family, not you. I know your name, Darkling. I know what you are, and you are not my brother.

Do not for one moment think you can play some foolish game with me."

"Why not? You've played enough games with me over the years. Thrown me here, tossed me there. All in the name of being a good brother, of course, teaching me to protect myself. Aren't you curious to see how much I've learned?" I smiled wolfishly. Maybe he couldn't see it on my face, but I knew he could hear it in my voice. "I know I am."

"I wouldn't exactly call it curious," he responded flatly. "But if that's what it takes to get us face-to-face, then I'm more than willing."

"More than willing" being quite the understatement, even for the habitually understated Niko. He would do anything to see his brother. It was too bad for him that he never would again, not even when he stood and stared into the depths of my eyes. I wondered if he would live long enough to realize that. Here was hoping.

"Face-to-face," I mused with a flickering of memory. "And through a glass darkly. Soon, Cyrano. I'm not quite ready, not yet, but soon." With that lie still sweet on my tongue, I added, "Was Promise naked under that silk robe? Was she nothing but smooth skin and creamy pearls? You know what? Maybe I'll just have to see for myself." Without waiting for a response, I flipped the phone shut. Now, Niko . . . now we see just how good you are.

It wasn't long before they showed up, Niko and his motormouthed sidekick. Thankfully the utility belts and tights were left at home for the date crowd. Goodfellow drove his expensive sports car carelessly up on the curb and bailed out hastily to follow Nik towards the doors of Promise's building. Ignoring the outraged arm-waving of the doorman, they were almost inside when I drew them up short with another call.

"You beat me to her, big brother," I said with mock wistfulness as I heard his phone click on. "Or did you?" I knew he had called her to warn her, but a sliver of anxiety, no matter how illogical, can still give a knot to the stomach and the burn of sweet acid to the throat. And I was nothing if not about the giving. "Vampires don't turn to dust, did you know that? More of a puddle of goo really. Sticky too. The maid might want to bring an extra mop."

"You—"

I didn't wait for the happy descriptions of my personable self that were bound to follow. Instead I motioned to the kid standing ten feet away. Chomping his gum like Bessie's socially challenged cousin, he shoved the twenty I'd given him into his pocket and then slammed an elbow into the Mercedes at the curb. As I cursed convincingly, the sound of the car alarm traveled simultaneously to the cell phone and across the street. Looking over at Niko and Robin, I saw the simultaneous turn, and the realization in their eyes. Standing frozen for a second, I dropped the phone, turned, and ran.

Cal had been quick, lithe with a natural runner's grace. I was quicker. The combination was enough that I had to force myself to lag, to maintain a strictly human speed. I struggled through crowds on the sidewalk, let a car clip me on the hip with a grazing blow. I took the fall with a grunt and endured the asphalt-scraped palms all in the name of a good performance. Method acting, it was the key to believability. As I lunged to my feet, the car door swung open and a pale oval hung in the gloom. Impenetrably tinted windows, rich leather interior, caveman-browed driver . . . I should've recognized the car even before it hit me.

"Lady of the pearls." The smile that cut my face was blacker than her windows and as curdled as rancid blood. "I thought you'd be waiting for me upstairs to give me the ride you gave my brother."

Her face remained calm and untroubled. There were no pearls this time, only a hand held out to me. The darkest violet silk glove protecting it, her hand moved into the sun toward me. "Come with me, Cal. I'll take you home."

Why did they keep trying? Why the hell couldn't they see it?

"You've got it wrong, vampire," I spit. "I'm bringing home to you. To this whole goddamn world." With her hand hanging in the air behind me, I turned my back on Promise and kept running, this time flat out to regain the distance I'd lost in the fall.

The park was not that far and looking over my shoulder, I caught glimpses of Niko in the distance—Niko and that piece-of-shit Goodfellow. I was truly going to enjoy teaching the randy goat that he should've stuck with screwing as his avocation, because the noble-hero crap was getting on my nerves. The worthless son of a bitch wasn't anything more than a horny tomcat who inexplicably thought he was a tiger. He *knew* who I was, knew the things I was capable of. If he thought he was a match for me, he'd better lay off the juice. It was giving him delusions.

There were people in the park, although not as many as usual. No one gawked as I ran through. Could be I was a jogger. Could be I was a mugger chasing a victim. Hell, a mugger could be chasing me. Didn't matter. That was Central Park. They went on with their business and I went on with mine. Before long I was in the trees and moving toward a wilder area. Not like the old days wild, but as wild as it got in this time and place. Once I settled into position in a thick clump of underbrush, I took several huge breaths to hyperoxygenate my lungs.

It was a trick Niko himself had taught me. When he and Robin came into view I stopped breathing. Unless you could hear my heart beat, I was a silent presence. Niko's ears were good, but no human's were that good. And while Goodfellow had his talents, listening had never been one of them.

I watched as they paused. Niko knelt and ran a hand lightly through the yellowing grass. Standing, he exchanged a wordless glance with Robin. They knew I'd been through there. It was obvious enough if you knew how to read the signs . . . the bend of a blade of grass, the crumpling of a leaf. Obvious, and I hadn't made any effort to conceal it. But what lay beneath that grass, below that leaf, wasn't quite so apparent. Buried in dirt not nearly liquid enough to suit him, Boggle waited with all the patience of a trapdoor spider. And he came up out of the ground with the same arachnid speed. It was a thing of beauty.

They'd taken a step, intent on pursuing me. Niko was dressed in his traditional black coat long enough to conceal at least twenty lethal blades. Goodfellow was in a dark green sweater, artfully faded jeans, and a brown leather duster similar in length to my brother's. Jesus. Nik was dressed to fight. Peter Pan, on the other hand, was dressed for a photo shoot—fall wear for the monster killer on the go. Did I enjoy it when Boggle ripped that expensive ensemble to shreds?

You bet your ass I did.

On their second step, Boggle got them. He catapulted through the covering earth like a heat-seeking missile. One swat of his massive hand had Goodfellow flying through the air as weightless as a child. Green yarn hung snagged on the long black claws as they swiped at Nik in turn. The blow missed. I wasn't surprised. Bog had never been a match for my brother, not alone. Fortunately, he wasn't alone now. As Niko twisted with liquid grace out of Boggle's reach, I stepped out of the brush, aimed, and fired all in one motion. It would've been a great time to say something sharp, something witty, some catchphrase that made box office gold. Damn satisfying, but it could've slowed me down. I was a kick-ass monster, but my brother could kick some serious ass in his own right. One on one, I could take him. Since the days of apple-peddling snakes there hadn't been anyone or anything I couldn't put down. Cyrano wouldn't be any exception, but . . . he could hurt me. He was almost as deadly as I was and he could do some damage. The Auphe wouldn't be too appreciative of any delay because I happened to get my ride banged up. They wouldn't be appreciative of any of this if they found out.

So . . . no warning. No smart-ass comments. No wisecracks. Nothing but silence and a bullet to the chest. The impact knocked Niko backward several feet before he hit the ground hard. He lay sprawled motionless on his back with legs and arms spread. His face was blank and his eyes even blanker. They stared up at the sky, not surprised or shocked, not swimming with pain or fear, not full of the glory of heaven or the horror of hell. No, there was none of that. There was only emptiness.

It was disappointing, I didn't mind admitting. A complete lack of drama. With the sharp smell of cordite perfuming the air, I gave Boggle a pat on his crusty shoulder in passing. "Good job, Bog. Now go rip a leg off the other one, would you? I want to pay him some personal attention in a minute, and I don't want him scampering off." Goodfellow had his chance to run and he'd wasted it. Now I had a chance to take his ass to school, and that I was not wasting. Shoving the gun, another of Boggle's souvenirs, into my waistband, I savored the heat of the muzzle against my skin. It warmed me against the chill in more ways than one. Kneeling on the ground beside Niko's still form, I took a handful of the blond braid and gave it an affectionate tug. "Strike one, big brother. I'll bet you never guessed the bigger man would turn out to be a monster." I laid the tight twist of hair on his chest and straightened the collar of his coat. "I always told you I was one, didn't I? But you never listened." It was as the hand suddenly looped around my wrist that I noticed . . . no blood. On his chest, there was no blood, only charred cloth.

The eyes blinked, the emptiness transmuting into something far more dangerous. "You are a monster." The voice was hoarse, roughened with pain. "But my brother isn't."

Bulletproof vest . . . the bastard was wearing a bulletproof vest. Abruptly, I realized that as well as I knew Niko, he knew half of me equally as well. He knew Cal's heart wasn't in the way of the sword, but rather in the way of the gun. When push came to shove, Cal could use any weapon, but personal preference was always going to tell. All that familial intimacy had come back to bite me in the ass. The grip squeezing my wristbones until they ground painfully together wasn't too pleasant either. Sticking around didn't seem like the best idea at the moment and I flashed my other hand toward the gun at my waist. My hand was on the rubber grip when I felt a sharp pain over my breastbone. Half an inch of Niko's favorite dagger was sticking into my shirt—not to mention my flesh. A quarter-sized stain of blood blossomed around the metal as I released the gun.

"Ouch," I said mildly, touching a finger to the edge of the blade. "You play rough, big brother."

The gray eyes, a memory of what mine had been, narrowed, but Nik remained silent as he let go of my wrist, retrieved my gun, and tossed it far into the bushes. He had sat up confidently without the gingerly motion I would expect from a cracked rib or two. Stoic, hiding his pain, both the physical and the mental. The knife didn't shift in position as he moved, not even a millimeter.

"What would Mom say about all this?" I clucked my tongue in rebuke. "Oh, I know. That she should've drowned me at birth. And you know what? She'd have been right." Leaning forward purposely, I felt the blade press harder against my chest. Slowly, I took off my sunglasses and dropped them to the grass. Pewter eyes met silver. "You know something else, Nik?" Placing a hand over his, I playfully pulled at the dagger until it buried itself just a shade deeper in me. "You don't have the balls."

"Maybe he doesn't, you misbegotten nightmare, but I do." Goodfellow's voice came behind me, sharply furious. A hand buried itself in my hair and yanked me backward. On the ground in a position that echoed the one Niko had just occupied, I looked up to see Robin, the worse for wear. His coat was shredded as well as his sweater. Bloody gashes crossed his chest and his eyes were dilated black with rage. It was the same rage that had his sword swinging toward my throat so fast I could all but hear the air hiss in its wake. It occurred to me that I might have made a slight miscalculation. Niko would hesitate to kill me outright, for Cal's sake. Goodfellow didn't have any such problem. He might have liked Cal, sure, but I was pretty certain he liked himself a whole lot more. With him, sympathy was going to take a backseat to self-preservation every time. It was the son of a bitch's one good quality. It was too bad the one thing I admired about him was the one that could get me killed.

Could, but not necessarily *would.*

Niko came through, protecting me just as he'd always done. Deflecting Robin's blade at the last second with his own, he said quietly, "No."

Panting with exertion and frustration, Robin turned and looked over at Niko, who now stood with an arm held unconsciously close to his side in a protective gesture. He could try to hide it all he wanted, but I had hurt him, even if only a little. Hopefully, I'd be able to hurt him a lot more . . . hurt him unto death.

Goodfellow kept the point of his sword hovering above my neck. "Nik, you have to see. You have to realize." Calming slightly, his breath slowing, he continued almost unwillingly. "Your brother, he wouldn't want to live like this. Everything I've seen of him, everything you've told me . . . he would hate it. He would despise it with all his soul."

I relaxed against the grass, putting my hands behind my head and raising my eyebrows. " 'Nik'? 'Everything you've told me'?" I repeated with cynical incredulity. "You two have gotten awfully cozy since I've been gone. You haven't dumped Promise already, have you, big brother? Please, God, at least tell me it wasn't some sort of clichéd affirmation-of-life thing. I'll save you the trouble of shish-kebabing me and just die of embarrassment instead."

"I'd advise you to leave Promise out of this, much in the way you did *not* leave Georgina out of it." Niko regarded me impassively. "What we did to your friends we could easily do to you. I don't believe Cal would hold a thorough beating against us, considering the situation."

"My furry flunkies." I mimed wiping away a tear. "My walking throw rugs are no more. Ah, well, I couldn't afford their dental anyway. At least tell me they managed to gnaw on Georgie some. Give me that. Did they chomp on a nose? An ear? Hell, a pinkie? I'll take that."

That didn't settle well with either of them. The only giveaway as to what Niko felt was his face becoming more and more set, until it resembled a carved stone statue. Goodfellow was somewhat more demonstrative, his hand tightening on his sword and his jaw white with tension. "She's but a girl, Darkling," the puck said with acid disgust. "A child."

"A human child," I replied with a curl of my lip. "And the best part about them is they're so much easier to kill." Turning my head, I scanned the area for Boggle. There was no sign of him. If that cowardly shit had run off, he was going to be one sorry son of a bitch. Looking back at Robin, I held up my hands thumb to thumb and framed him. The blood, the torn flesh, the destroyed clothing, all courtesy of my MIA mud pie. "Who's your tailor, Goodfellow? I'm loving your new look. Damned spiffy."

That was nearly the straw that broke the camel's back. Niko had to use more force this time to keep Robin from sheathing his sword in my neck. "I said no," he rapped firmly. "I'm not abandoning my brother so quickly. He's in there and he's fighting. He's fought to survive all his life; he wouldn't give up now. It's not in him."

"No?" Robin commented softly. "Well, I do know one thing that's in him, and I don't think it has any intention of coming out. The sooner you come to grips with that, Niko, the better off you'll be." He went on, unrelenting. "And the better off Cal will be."

It was fascinating watching him push Niko to the edge, and a very dangerous edge at that. He was the ultimate pragmatist, my brother, but there was one thing he could not look at directly. Not now. Cal was a blind spot, the only chink in Niko's armor. Goodfellow could talk until he was blue in the face, and it wouldn't do him a damn bit of good. There was only one person who could convince Nik at this point that I wasn't salvageable. That person was Cal; that person was me. One in the same, even if no one realized it yet. One in the same, now and always.

"Any decisions about my brother will be made by me, Goodfellow." The warning wrapped Niko's words in razor wire and broken glass. "No one else."

Robin bowed his head slightly, brow creased. Exhaling harshly, he twisted his lips in resignation. "No matter how good the intentions, I take it."

"No matter." The message was unbending, but the ice behind it had thawed somewhat. Niko knew that Robin was trying to help, could see that he was on his side. It was a big step for someone who'd been nursed on suspicion all his life. Quite the bonding moment for the two of them. How sweet. I was all puppies and kittens from the top of my head to the bottom of my feet, the same feet I jackknifed into Goodfellow's knees.

Strike two.

The blow knocked him on his ass and that, I thought with righteous condescension, was what happened to those who got soft. The puck had obviously forgotten, but there were humans and then there was us. You forget what side you're on, you try to cross that line, and there was a price to pay. And it wasn't going to be paid in Monopoly money either.

I'd hoped that Robin careening into him would stagger Niko, at least for a second. No such luck. As he fell, Goodfellow had the presence of mind to twist away, taking down no one but himself. That left my brother still open for business and that was less than a desirable outcome, to say the least. Consequently, when Boggle breached the ground like a killer whale through the

waves, I promptly decided he was my new best friend.
Apparently, I'd overestimated his cowardice and underestimated his hatred of Niko. Shedding dirt like water,
he snatched up my brother by his coat, lifted him high in
the air, and shook him violently. The blond head snapped
back with visibly painful force as Boggle gave a gut-
turally triumphant bellow. It was a beautiful sight to see,
right up until the moment when Niko sliced off Boggle's
right hand.

His reaction was as spectacular as you'd expect it to
be. Black blood, viscous and foul, poured lava-thick
from the stump. For a short moment, barely a second,
Boggle stared stupefied at the pumping blood. It was
only a second, but it was much longer than Niko needed
to embed his sword in one round pumpkin orange eye.
Boggle's scream shattered the air as Niko fell from his
remaining hand. It was looking bleak for the home
team, but once again I didn't give Bog enough credit.
Still howling, he swung an arm, slamming it into Niko
and throwing him nearly fifteen feet. Trusting that the
two of them would keep busy, I turned my attention to
Goodfellow.

The proverbial thorn in my side was pushing his
way back up to a sitting position, his face grim and
etched with pain. I might not have dislocated his
kneecaps, but I'd definitely given him something to
think about . . . for the short time he had left to him.
He'd barely gotten halfway up when I hit him hard, my
knee hitting him viciously in the gut. The sword that
had fallen from his hand I scooped up and applied with
surgical precision to his throat. Blood welled sluggishly over the bright metal as I gave him an even
brighter smile. "Having second thoughts about your
new friends, Goodfellow?"

The green eyes of a treed fox blinked as dark eyebrows quirked upward with studied boredom. "Having second thoughts about being such a homicidal dick, Darkling?"

"Goodfellow." I shook my head and used my free hand to comb taming fingers through his wild brown curls before patting his cheek with a stinging blow. "Robin. How did you come to this? Look at you. Bloody, dirty. Your expensive clothes are ruined, and all for the sake of humans. It's a sad state of affairs and I feel for you, I do. It almost makes me want to kill you painlessly." I put more pressure on the blade. "Almost." I wished I had time to make it slow as well as painful, but Boggle wouldn't be able to hold Niko forever. I'd have to limit myself to one quick slash and let Goodfellow drown in his own blood. Then I would take care of my brother.

Unfortunately for me, my brother took care of me first. My arm was tensing for the coup de grâce when a sharp pain hit me in the back of my upper thigh. Snatching a look over my shoulder, I saw a tufted dart protruding from my jeans. Niko stood ten feet away by the motionless and muddy form of Boggle. He held a blunt-nosed pistol in his hand. A gun, the son of a bitch was aiming a gun at me. In his entire life the man had never used a gun, had never even *held* a gun. And now he had used one on me. In its way I think that made me nearly as disconnected as the drug I could feel racing through my system. He had surprised me and outthought me, not once, but twice since we'd entered the park. Outmaneuvered *me*.

That, boys and girls, is when I lost my sense of humor.

I was also losing consciousness and losing it fast. I was going and there was nothing I could do to stop it. That didn't mean, however, that I had to go alone. My grip was already numb and clumsy. My vision had shrunk to a pinpoint of light in a field of smothering black. It didn't matter. What did was bleeding Goodfellow like a slaughterhouse pig. The blade was already at his throat. All that was needed was a little weight, a little pressure, and the puck would fall into that darkness with me. I was guessing my descent wouldn't be permanent, but if I had my way, his would be. The drug was too strong, though, too quick. My fingers went nerveless and Robin ripped the sword away, disarming me, or so he thought. He was wrong. Skinning back lips from my teeth, I hissed deep in my throat and then lunged at his. I'd been around long before the Bronze Age and man-made weapons. Teeth and claws had worked then. They'd work just as well now.

The warmth of his skin radiated against my lips and I could taste the salt of his sweat on my tongue. It was a pale shadow of the blood I'd soon be swimming in. Any second now. I felt a hand at the collar of my jacket and then I was flying through the air dreamily as time slowed to a lazy crawl. My back hit the ground, but the sensation was nothing more than a distant echo. My brother's face was a bare outline across my faded and foggy sight. "We have you, Cal. We have you, little brother." His voice was unwavering in its determination and absolute in its certainty. "And we'll get you back. I promise."

Strike three.

I was out.

18

"Best hurry, Nik. I think it's waking up."

It. Honestly, Goodfellow, was that nice? Mitotic shithead.

"I'm finished," my brother's calm voice came next. With his words I felt something jerk snugly at my wrist, and a warm grip on my forearm that squeezed lightly before disappearing. *Niko,* I gloated. *Just keep opening that door, and I won't have to destroy you. You'll do it to yourself.* I drifted back and forth on the tides of semi-consciousness, mulling over the situation. I'd been so goddamn stupid, so careless, playing with them when I could've finished them off. I'd let my ego get the better of me. But while I was down, I wasn't out. I still had a few tricks up my sleeve.

"Maybe we should've had Promise stay," Goodfellow said wearily.

"She's where she needs to be now, protecting Georgina. We can't be certain Darkling doesn't have other assassins out there."

Good thought, I mused dreamily. I wished I'd hired a few more. Hundreds more. Ripping Promise and George to the tiniest shreds of flesh. I continued to float aimlessly with that happy image, in no real hurry to completely wake. That is, until someone stuck something extremely unpleasant beneath my nose. I sneezed violently and pulled back while blinking watering eyes. Clearing my vision, I saw a stone-faced Niko capping a small vial of ammonia.

"Are you awake enough to understand me?" he asked neutrally.

I blinked again, then looked down to see I was sitting in a recliner in what I recognized as Goodfellow's office at the car lot. Padded metal cuffs were clamped down securely over my wrists and ankles. Ah, shit. The Auphe were going to kick my ass. I tugged at my restraints experimentally. There was no give despite the fact I was stronger than Cal had been before the merging. I lifted my gaze to Robin and raised a sardonic eyebrow. "Raid your toy box just for me, Goodfellow? I'm touched."

"Keep it up and you will be." Goodfellow clenched a white-knuckle fist and showed his teeth in a threatening mockery of a smile.

Niko ignored the exchange; that much at least hadn't changed. Leaning in close, he said softly, "Listen to me, Darkling, and listen carefully. I want to speak to my brother. The only words I want to hear are his. Do you understand?"

Unimpressed, I rolled my eyes and took in my surroundings. It was night. I'd lost nearly the whole day. The car lot was closed and blinds were pulled down over all the windows. Only the door in the outer display room showed a sliver of blackness beneath ill-fitting blinds. Turning my attention back to my captors, I looked them up and down. Niko stood unruffled and in control, ramrod straight with every hair ruthlessly scraped back from his face. But the military demeanor didn't hide the faint smudges under his eyes that told of sleepless nights and the lingering pain of cracked ribs. Goodfellow, on the other hand, hadn't fared quite so well. There was an ugly reddened slash across the front of his throat and I could make out the bulk of bandages under his sweater. It was new; the green one was history. He'd let his fist fall away and now stood impassively with arms folded. He might have thought his face was inscrutable as well, but both the muscle twitching spasmodically in his jaw and the fury banked in the far reaches of his eyes warmed my heart.

"Well, well," I drawled caustically. "The gang's all here. What's the occasion? Hope it's not an intervention. I'm a little short on shame and regret today."

Niko took a fistful of my shirt and shook me with harsh efficiency. The back of my head slammed against the recliner with only the padding keeping me from a vicious headache. "Perhaps I wasn't clear," he said implacably. "I want to speak to Cal, not a murderous hitchhiker." He shook me again. "Just Cal."

That annoyed me, this human, this flash in the pan five generations or so from a protozoan, delegating me to hitchhiker status. Treating me as if I were no more than a minor demon with a hard-on for the Catholic Church. It pissed me off enough that I decided to tell the truth. Hell, I wanted to anyway, had been dying to all this time. It wouldn't matter at this point; there'd be no immediate danger to me. Goodfellow would believe me instantly, but not Niko. Not my brother. His head might believe, but his heart would balk long enough for me to get the upper hand again. And I would, no doubt about it.

I tilted my head in a way that was utterly Caliban. "You just don't get it, do you, Cyrano? I'm disappointed in you. Here I am, running around, creating murder and mayhem. Doing things your pathetic, whiny brother would never have the guts to do. Shit, would never have the guts to even admit he wanted to do." I narrowed my eyes and pursed my lips. "And yet, I have every memory Cal ever made, including a few he refuses to acknowledge. It leads one to a certain conclusion."

Niko's grip tightened on my shirt. I think he suspected what was coming. For the first time since I'd changed, he let himself see the shadow sliding across the sun. "I want to speak to Cal, Darkling," he repeated, with an unyielding steel that couldn't ward off unpleasant reality. "Now."

I let my eyelids drop to half-mast and laid my head back against the chair, as lazy as a cat on a summer afternoon. "That's just it, big brother. There is no Caliban. There is no Darkling. We are one. One new creature. One new soul." My lips relaxed into a blithe curve. "One. And there's not a damn thing you can do about it." His expression didn't change at my words, didn't even flicker.

"You lost him, Nik," I continued remorselessly, watching his face . . . waiting for it. "Caliban died days ago. He died on your apartment floor. He died while you watched and you never even knew it."

And there it was. Niko had never been one to wear his heart on his sleeve, but I could read him. I'd always been able to. The reserve, that imperturbable spirit that was as much a part of him as his genetic code, had faded away. Now in its place was a void, an emptiness so profound that it colored the very air around him. It was a vacuum swallowing everything that made Nik who he was . . . stubborn hope, unshakable faith, boundless determination. It was gone. All gone. And, for the most part, so was Nik.

Suck on that, you bastard, I thought with a feral satisfaction.

Goodfellow, for once, said exactly the right thing.
Nothing. He simply put a hand on Niko's shoulder and
steered him away toward the office door. As I watched
through the glass, he closed the door behind them
and left to return minutes later to hand my brother a
mug of coffee. If I knew Robin, there was probably
something extra in it besides Juan Valdez, but Niko
drank it without hesitation. I listened with interest as
Goodfellow finally spoke. "I'm sorry, Nik, but I think it's
telling the truth." The words were muffled but audible,
the glass conducting the sound readily.

"You said that male banshees had never possessed
people, only objects," Niko stated dispassionately, his
fingers blanched white on the ceramic mug. "You've not
seen this before, then. How can you know for sure?"

Ah, Cyrano, he knows in the same way you know, I
mused with a certain black affection. I tested the cuffs
again. There was still no give in the metal, but it did result in a thought.

"I guess there is no way I can be absolutely positive."
Robin ran a weary hand across his face. "But I have
seen possessions in my day, Niko, though they're much
more rare than television would have you believe. What
I have seen doesn't match up to this. And Darkling is
powerful. Malevolent and petty as a child, but very powerful. What that would do to someone, having that inside, I don't know. It very well could be irreversible."
His eyes slanted through the glass to take me in. "He
enjoyed telling us, telling *you*. He enjoyed it so much I
think that it had to be the truth."

Niko bowed his head and stared silently into the contents of his mug. He was intent enough that it could
have been a Magic 8 Ball with the solution to all his
woes. Kill my brother or don't kill my brother? Yes, no,
or try back next time? Hard choice, but then again life is

all about choices. And it was just like Nik to disregard
the one in front of him and sidetrack to an entirely different one. The big picture, it was precisely what I didn't
want them to see.

"True or not, there's something else." Unlike Goodfellow, Nik didn't look at me. I don't believe that right
then I was anything he particularly wanted to see. "Why
did this thing take Cal? The Auphe are behind it; that
much is clear. But why? All our lives have been spent
running from this moment. I owe it to . . . I need to
know the reason why." Now his eyes met mine. Bleak,
hard, and unforgiving. "And that monstrosity knows the
answer."

That was a cue the party was over if ever I'd heard it.
I didn't know how far Niko would go . . . how far he
could stomach to go, but where he left off, Goodfellow
would be all too willing to take over. That, naturally,
made me less than eager to stick around. So I decided to
leave. It was just that simple. The decision was, anyway.
The execution, however, was trickier. The cuffs were unbreakable, even with my strength, but the chair itself
was a different story. I ripped away one armrest and
then the other with a massive jerk. With my wrists seep-
ing blood and still encased in the cuffs, I freed my ankles. I was stronger, but that didn't mean this body was
any more durable than it had been. But this wasn't the
time to bitch about the deficiencies of it. This was the
time to take advantage of what it *could* do. As in run—
run like hell. Those who fight and run away live to
butcher another day, right?

Niko and Robin were surging through the door as I
picked up Goodfellow's desk and tossed it through the
plate glass of the office wall. Somersaulting over the sill
after it, I hit the ground running. I could hear the sound
of glass crunching beneath their shoes behind me as I

threw myself into one of the display models. It was a cherry red Porsche with the keys considerately dangling from the ignition for a test rev, but I was interested in more than just hearing the engine purr. I was taking that baby for a drive. As I rammed it into gear, somebody hit the back of the car hard enough to jar it. I didn't bother to look to see who it was. Either Goodfellow or Nik—bad news or worse news, it didn't much matter which. Reflecting on the joys of all the plate glass so cherished by car dealerships, I slammed my foot on the gas and rocketed toward the street. The wall-sized window disintegrated before the car like brittle ice and we hit the pavement with a screech of tires—not to mention the satisfying thump of a body falling away. I took one last look in the rearview mirror to see a figure on all fours in the street. Its blond hair was a pale glow under the streetlights, and I put an arm out of the window to give my brother one last wave. One final, happy *adiós*. Then it was time to get back to business.

No more goddamn games.

19

There was a time in every monster's life to take stock. You had to decide where you were, how you got there, and how to get back on track. I knew where I was and I knew how to get back. That was the easy part. The more difficult task was admitting just how I'd managed to get my ass in that sling to begin with. Ego. My big fat ego. I'd played when I should've been deadly serious. I'd overestimated my allies and, worse, underestimated my opponents. In retrospect I should've handled it all myself. I should've separated them and taken them out one by one. No warning, no taunts. It would've been quick and efficient.

But not nearly as much fun.

Ah, well, every experience is a learning one. I was still the baddest son of a bitch around. I didn't see any reason that had to change. I also didn't see any reason to share the recent debacle with the Auphe. After the warning they'd given me, they would not be amused, and when the Auphe weren't amused, no one was. I dumped my appropriated car several blocks away and walked the rest of the way to the Auphe's warehouse. It was considerably changed from the last time I'd seen it. All the debris had been pushed and stacked against the walls to clear the floor, which now virtually bubbled with a choking red rage. You could see the shimmer of it in the air like heat rising from a blacktop road. I stood for an exhilarating moment and basked in the spine-shivering pleasure of it. Good stuff.

Reluctantly pulling myself away from the maelstrom of dark emotions, I went over to check out the situation against the far wall. A human was raising his voice to an Auphe. Interesting. If entrails were going to be flying, I wanted to be in on it. The human turned his head toward me as I walked up and I saw a face I recognized. Imagine that—it was my buddy from the bar. Samuel. I'd thought he'd seemed more good-natured than your average New Yorker. Apparently I wasn't the only hired help on the scene. Clever Auphe. No one did sneaky better than they.

"Sammy." I grinned happily. "Well, color me surprised. You have some serious acting chops, pal. Oscar quality, truly."

His skin bleached slightly, turning an ashy gray, as he took me in. "Your eyes . . . Jesus."

Oh, fine. He could look at an Auphe without flinching, but my sparkling silver eyes did him in? That hurt my feelings, it honestly did. Samuel looked away from me quickly and I decided that maybe it was less aversion and more guilt that was etched on his face. "So, I'm curious," I drawled, and draped an arm over his shoulders. "The bosses here hired you to keep tabs on Cal in his last days. That's pretty obvious." Not that they had told yours truly about it, closemouthed bastards. "My question is, what did you get out of it? What'd you get in trade for the big chunk of your soul, huh? Something bright and shiny?"

I could feel his flesh crawl under my arm as he shook me off. Steadfastly ignoring me, he addressed the bored Auphe that crouched before him. I could see by the dull glaze over its scarlet eyes that it was more than half asleep and not energetic enough for any mutilation. Disappointing. "You said you'd heal my brother. I did what you wanted. It's time for you to keep your half of the bargain, before it's too late."

Damn, he was nothing but a big teddy bear. A sick brother. Did it get more heartwarming than that? I ask you. Yeah, Samuel was a real philanthropist. Too bad that was coupled with the brainpower of a rock. The Auphe heal? Not likely. Hell, if peckish enough, they would eat their own wounded. They had no inclination and no talent in the healing field, but they did have an affinity for lies: little white ones, big black ones, and all shades in between.

This particular Auphe had a gleeful glint behind his sleepiness that demonstrated how much he'd enjoyed dangling Samuel on a string. However, dangling time had to be nearly over. They would have no further need of the guitar player now—but I might. As I was thinking that over, the Auphe yawned, its plush velour tongue flexing behind several rows of metallic teeth. It was the last straw for Samuel. Dark hands seized the Auphe by the narrow shoulders and shook hard. "You bastard, you promised. You swore."

Have you ever noticed how people, humans, tend to revert to children in times of great stress? It's not necessarily that they want someone to take responsibility or to take care of them. And it's not that they lose the capacity to understand what's going on. What they do lose is the knowledge that life isn't fair. As their life is falling apart around them, they absolutely refuse to believe it's happening, right down to the last second. They start life as a child; they end life as a child.

It's damn near poetic.

The Auphe didn't seem to appreciate the poetry of it, though. Barbed claws circled Samuel's wrists and squeezed until blood flowed freely. "Such a strong-willed sheep. So very disobedient. What shall we do with a sheep who dares to question his shepherd?" He was waking up now, red eyes flaming torpidly to life. He didn't look especially hungry, but who among us is above a snack or two out of pure boredom? It looked like my pal Sammy was about to get sheared or eaten. Neither would leave him functioning. Too bad for Sammy. If I hadn't needed him, I would've enjoyed my ringside seat.

"Boss," I said mildly. "Mind if I have him for a while? I need him to do something for me."

The narrow face sharpened in vulpine annoyance as the Auphe hissed several words that were jagged with edges that cut the air like a rusty razor. They were words that no human would understand, although simply hearing them would give him a fierce headache. I answered back in the same language, more or less, and outlined what I wanted. It was hard to wrap a human tongue around the fifteen vowels and more than a hundred consonants, but I made do. With a peeved snort through moist nostril slits, my boss turned Samuel loose and loped off, licking the blood from his long multijointed fingers as he went. Mmmm. Finger-licking good, I thought wistfully.

Turning back to Samuel, I slipped a hand into his pocket and deftly removed his wallet. There was something I wanted to check. Ignoring his snarled curse, I straight-armed him and rifled through the contents. I stopped at several family photos and gave a self-satisfied smirk to myself. That explained it. That explained quite a lot. "I thought you looked oddly familiar." I tossed the wallet back to him and smiled placidly. "Seeing you with new eyes and all." I walked over to a wooden crate and sat down, my hands casually cupping a knee. "Did you know I can sing? Well, not so much sing as . . . never mind. You'll see soon enough. Let's get down to it, Sam-I-am. I need your band's sound system and I need you to bring it here. Tomorrow night."

"What the hell makes you think I'll do anything you say?" he spit, clenching his wallet tightly in one hand.

"A sick brother, huh?" I kicked a heel against the crate. "So very, very sick. It's sad. Sad for you . . . sad for his wife. Sad for his precious red-haired little girl. Sweet Georgie Porgie, does she know what her uncle Sammy is up to? I wonder."

Of course she did, even though it was a fair assumption that he'd never told her. That's what she did; that's what she was. It went a long way toward explaining why she'd lied to Niko and Cal and why she'd cried. It had to be a confusing situation for anyone, even a petite psychic who had her finger on the pulse of the universe. It came with the job. Finding lost dogs was a good day; your father dying, your uncle crossing a line, betraying your friends . . . that was a bad day. What was the worst day? She'd find out. I hadn't met a psychic yet who'd led a long and happy life. Long and miserable, yes. Long and happy . . . never. Wasn't part of the great game of life. Still, I had the feeling she would do her best to rise above it. She would strive to not let it destroy her, strive always to serve the greater good.

How nauseating can you get?

"Georgina." Samuel said her name softly. He didn't say "Stay away from her," or "Leave her out of this," none of the usual clichés. I guess, facing me, facing the Auphe, he had to know that would be pretty pointless. Staring at me, he demanded without emotion, "Can they heal him? Can those things heal my brother?"

"Nope." I stood, rocked on my heels, and continued cheerfully, "They couldn't even if they wanted to. As far as the Auphe are concerned, if you're sick, you either get better or you die. That's the sum total of their medical knowledge." I tilted my head as his face spasmed. "But all is not lost, Samuel. You can still save someone. You can save your Chatty Cathy niece. I know where she lives, where she goes to school, her favorite ice-cream shop. It'd be interesting to see how long her Pollyanna attitude would last with me playing 'cats in the cradle' with her intestines."

Predictably enough, he lunged at me, his hands on my throat with a strength borne of pure desperation. I let him squeeze for a while until spots darted across my vision. It was good for him, gave him hope. It's more amusing to crush someone when he thinks he still has a chance. The hopeless are massively boring. They lie there and cry or curl up in a catatonic fetal ball. Where's the sport in that? He growled and tightened his choking grip on me.

Tiring of the game, I peeled back his hands, dislocating one of his fingers in the process. "Oh, hey, look at that. Here, let Mommy make it all better." Holding on to his hand despite his efforts to break free, I yanked the finger back into place with a pleasing crunch of bone. I could've been quicker about it, it's true, but his complete lack of gratitude was still uncalled for. Balling up his wounded hand, he cradled it against his chest and glared with an unparalleled fury. The guy had guts—I had to give him that. Later on I was hoping for a firsthand look at them. But right now that was neither here nor there. Right now we had business to conduct.

"Bring the equipment here tomorrow night," I reiterated gently. "And, Samuel? Don't think you can hide her. You can't. I'd find her and if I didn't, my employers would." I tapped my bottom lip and considered. "I'm not sure which would be worse. There certainly wouldn't be enough left of her to ask."

He stood motionless, jaw working. Then he gave one jerky nod, turned silently, and left. He was down in the mouth, but you had to be firm with the puppies. Spare the rod, spoil the human. At least that collection of monkey scribbles had gotten one thing right.

Sighing glumly, I settled back against the crate and steeled myself to a miserable night sleeping on a cold, hard floor with only the heat of enraged and unruly spirits to warm me. The claws that scrabbled down the wood to pierce my shoulder weren't any huge surprise. I'd been waiting for it the moment I'd walked into the warehouse. "Can I help you, boss?" I asked with false cheer.

"What have you been doing, maggot food?" the Auphe's fetid breath cooed in my ear. For one split second a shiver raced down my spine. It wasn't an Auphe, nor was it a creature I'd had a business relationship with over thousands of years. It was a Grendel. It was a horrifying creature that had snatched me from bed and all but destroyed me. I stopped that

thought in its tracks. No, I wouldn't even accept that it
was a thought. That would mean there was a consciousness that had made it. Cal was no more and neither was his consciousness, not as a separate entity. It
was just an emotion stored in the neurons of this peculiar brain.

"Nothing, boss," I answered promptly. "Just laying
low like you told me to. Just following the plan."

A cold finger traced my jawline. "Then whence came
this bruise? It's nearly as large as your rampant ego.
You wouldn't be lying to me, would you, Darkling? You
wouldn't try to deceive your betters."

My teeth clenched and I choked down the black bile
of fury. Betters? I had no betters, but if I had, Auphe
would certainly never have been on the list. "Merely a
disagreement with a mugger in the park who mistook
me for a human. I assumed you had no problem with
self-defense. I know this body is a precious commodity
to you." I raised eyes to his red ones as he crouched on
the crate above my shoulder. "Much as I am."

He considered my words carefully. Cold and calculat-
ing, but in the end he was still backed into a corner he
couldn't escape. I was precious to him, as much so as
Caliban's body. The Auphe couldn't pull this off without
the both of us, and they knew it. "A mugger." The disbelief was rich in his voice, but so was acceptance of his
position. "You're losing your touch, Darkling." With
that, he retreated back over the top of the crate and
vanished. I had the upper hand now, and he knew it.
Later, however, I'd better watch my back.

Or I'd better run for my life.

I pushed the gloomy, defeatist thoughts out of my
head. I'd come out on top. I always did. I abandoned the
crate and curled up on the floor. There was no risking

a hotel now, not on the last night. There would be no electric blanket, no champagne, no room service. What a world. It was the same world that would end tomorrow night.

Now, that was something to sleep on.

20

Sleep was something I'd always been fond of, in either halves of my whole. I loved the darkness, silent and still, wrapped around me with inexorable arms. There was a difference, though. Humans dreamed; I did not. I didn't need to. Life was all the wish fulfillment I needed, and as for subconscious fears . . . I didn't have any. *I* was the fear that ran rampant in dreams throughout history. There was no vice versa. No dreams, no nightmares.

And I refused to start now.

Memories, that's all they were. Just a swirl of memories . . . once mine, once his . . . now ours. There was a troll, huge and gloating, Auphe everywhere, and a trailer flaming to the sky. A bitter woman spit words as painful as any stab wound, and there was year after year of running. It should have been boring stuff to one as jaded as me, but it wasn't. There was terror, fury, despair, and a long-simmering anger, but boredom wasn't any part of the equation. Of course by our now-singular nature some of the memories were mine as well. The happier ones. Deshelling a smelly knight without damaging his armor. That had been tricky and, in the end, damn messy. But it'd still been fun as hell. Sinking a canoe of natives into piranha-infested waters. The fish at least had been grateful for that one. It was one of the good things about my vocation in life; it led to my avocation walking directly into my greedy hands. They all came looking for the treasure I was possessing at the time. It was like pizza delivery, only better because it was free.

Yeah, good memories.

The trouble was that now my memories were all mixed up with those others. I was the one wearing the armor as a thousand troll tentacles slithered into every crack and began to pull flesh from my bones. The Auphe were lifting me high and tossing me into turgid, muddy water to be devoured by shredding teeth. A deadly beautiful woman sang curses at me as she methodically ripped off my arms and legs, then ears, and finally my tongue.

But they weren't dreams and they certainly weren't nightmares. No. Mixed-up memories, that's all. Nothing but mental debris. It was all I would allow them to be.

Consequently, when I woke up covered in sweat with my heart racing, I was annoyed . . . extremely annoyed. My mood didn't improve when I saw one of the Auphe was back, crouching over me. He was balanced on a stack of boxes and gazing at me with an assessing glint in his eyes. It was the same look I hadn't been happy with the night before. "What are you looking at?" I snapped as I sat up and stretched stiff muscles. I was cranky and cold and in no mood to "boss" and bow and scrape. Not now. Not today.

"Don't test your luck, little lizard." Quiet words that nonetheless had a presence all their own. "You have a task to do. Stay in control and do it." He flipped and disappeared between the crates and the wall as fast as a silverfish into a crack. There were no more threats or attempts at intimidation. The Auphe had to have guessed what I'd been up to. Once the gate was opened, they would have other things on their minds and they just might forget how I'd displeased them. And I was all too aware of what the Auphe were capable of when displeased. I didn't need a picture painted for me. Not that the insinuation that I wasn't in the driver's seat didn't piss me off. Because it did; it pissed me off quite a bit. I was in total control. Total. We were one and I was in control.

Damn straight.

Standing, I rubbed a hand over my face and absently checked my watch. I'd slept the night through, past the morning, and well into late afternoon. It wasn't that long a sleep, not for me. There were times I'd slept months if left to my own devices. Years even. Not today, though, not on the last day. Time . . . a fluid word. Soon there would be all the time in the world and yet none at all. Soon it would be time to open the gate. Now? Now it was time for school.

The gate had a power that couldn't be denied. It was a black-winged harbinger, a shivering omen of things to come. But when I actually opened one myself, all that melodramatic mumbo jumbo faded next to the reality of it. It wasn't opening a doorway. It wasn't gathering every iota of inner force and ripping the fabric of space and time itself. It wasn't an act of will overcoming the physical universe. It wasn't any of those, yet it was all of them. But more than that, it was an orgasm. Light and darkness. Up and down. Life and death. Oh, and one other thing . . .

It kicked *ass*.

Just practice for the show of shows, but still a blast. Still, class was class and the Auphe were somewhat harsher with lessons than your average ruler-wielding nun. They'd never been long on the social niceties.

Going to school under them only proved that point. Luckily, most of the lesson was only review. They had taught Cal enough about opening gates in the two years that they'd had him, and he'd been an apt pupil. Torture is nothing if not a strong incentive. The half-breed had learned all right and learned well. After all, it was how he had escaped from Tumulus—that and killing an Auphe with his bare hands. I had to give him credit. Insert applause here for the little shit. He'd never known, though; he'd never been able to retrieve the memories of what he'd done and what had been done to him. He'd never been able to open a gate again. The memory was too buried and bound up in chains of utter denial. But though it was beyond Caliban from then on, it was not beyond me.

"Concentrate. Hold it." A sharp talon to my biceps punctuated the words in a way Miss Manners would have strongly disapproved of, but it did bring my attention back to the lesson at hand. "Ahhhh, beauuutiful. Now let it go."

Opening a gate had been difficult, even with the past and present coaching and the genetic tendencies. Wrapping my mind around the twisty cogitation necessary for walking that path was rigorous. And if opening it was a bitch, closing it was that much worse. It was almost impossibly hard to let it die. In the midst of the metaphysical whirlpool, past the physical pangs, there was an exhilaration that was addictive. Plum, gold, and burgundy lights danced behind my eyes as electricity raced through every cell. Sucking in a breath laced with ice and fire, I held on to the gate for another intoxicating second before finally releasing it.

The quivering oval of light shrank to a pinpoint, and then popped out of sight. Dropping hands that tingled with residual energy, I blew on my fingernails and raised my eyebrows at the Auphe at my elbow. "Good enough for government work?"

He didn't answer, but instead turned to a blood clot of several of his brothers nearby. All of them practically vibrated with excitement. Joining together, they laughed as joyfully as hellish children and swirled round and round each other like sharks in a feeding pattern. Their time had come again and they knew it.

I left them to it. Retreating to a far corner of the building, I did my best to suppress appetite pangs. I was starving. If there'd been time, I would have run out for a burger or Chinese, but there wasn't. The clock was ticking. Ignoring the grumblings of my stomach, I wiped the sweat from my face with my sleeve and pushed my hair behind my ears. Thanks to Niko and Robin, I didn't have a change of clothing or the chance to take a hot shower. They'd rushed me, messed up my time schedule, and left me rather cranky. I wasn't the clotheshorse Goodfellow was. For that matter, neither was Beau Brummell, and I'd seen that dude in diamond-encrusted tights. The puck had no equal in the fashion department, but that didn't mean I didn't like the finer things in life. All the world's a stage, they say, and here I was doing my solo in a pair of grass-stained jeans topped off with a ripped navy blue silk sweater. It wasn't what I'd planned and not the showmanship I liked to think I was known for.

I inserted a finger into a tear at the shoulder seam and sighed. All those years of safeguarding treasures had turned me into something of a magpie, and I coveted the bright and the beautiful. Jewels, fabrics . . . souls. I had a bit of the collector in me and I'd never even realized it until now. Pulling the shirt off, I discarded it on the ground as my bare skin prickled in the cool air.

"I brought the equipment." Samuel's voice came from behind me. It rang dully with hostility and I smiled to myself. It seemed I wasn't the only cranky one here tonight. Misery does love company.

"You're a good puppy, Sammy. Keep this up and you'll get a nice treat." I turned and gave him a sunny grin. I'd heard him come in, heard his breathing, heard every measured tread. There hadn't actually been any doubt in my mind that he would do as I said, but I still had to admit it was gratifying. Made for a smoother schedule, and I'd had enough aggravation lately. "You bring Genghis with you?" I brushed disparagingly at my jeans. "I could use a pair of leather pants." Another hunger pang prompted a wistful addition. "And a snack." Genghis wasn't a cheeseburger, but beggars couldn't be choosers.

"Where do you want it?" he asked, disregarding my comment. He was all business, grim and humorless as a Baptist in a whorehouse.

Hours had passed while I was relearning the ins and outs of gates. It was coming down to the wire. "In front of the far wall, about twenty feet back." I tossed a casual hand toward the one wall not covered with boxes and crates. "Keep them to the side and leave a path. And jack the amps all the way up, Sam-I-am. I'm going to make some serious noise."

Nodding curtly, he spun on his heel and moved off. I called genially after him, "Need any help, buddy? It'll be just like old times. You won't even have to pay me this time."

"No, thanks." He brushed me off without turning. "I didn't bring my long spoon."

Literate bastard, I thought with amused tolerance as I watched him go. I could have told him there was no devil. The rest of us wouldn't have stood for the competition. I let him alone while he set up the speakers; they were an impressive set for a rinky-dink bar band. Samuel had to bring them in on a dolly and it was still a struggle—they were that massive. It was good luck for me. I had Caliban's breeding, I had the supernatural battery beneath the floor, and I had the Auphe's guidance. But more than that, I had myself. I had talents of my own and that would be the deciding factor. Millions of years was a huge chasm to bridge. It wouldn't hurt to get a boost. And if the humans' own technology led to their downfall, hell, that was just a bonus. Any ambivalence I had about losing this world's luxury disappeared under the sheer ego boost of what I was about to do . . . what only I could achieve. In the entire realm of existence only I could make this happen. Only I held the power.

"Where do you want the microphone stand?" came another question, detached and toneless. Samuel was becoming less and less entertaining as the seconds passed. His face set and remote, his eyes stony, he looked just past me as he waited for my answer.

I took a step sideways, planting myself firmly in his line of sight. I wasn't going to let him hide from what was happening. What ticked me off, though, what gnawed at me with sharp rat teeth, was that I didn't know if it was the Darkling part of me or the portion that had once been Caliban.

I thought the Auphe were damn cunning in regard to Samuel. They had finally located Cal and his brother, had shadowed them from a safe distance for nearly a month, and hadn't been found out. They had known about the friendship with Georgina. They'd known about her dying father. They'd even discovered an in with her devoted uncle Samuel, and they'd used it ruthlessly. He could do what the Auphe couldn't and watch the brothers from a front-row seat, keep tabs on them during the time his masters searched for a suitable location for the gate. He could get up close and personal with the brothers in a way that wasn't possible for the Auphe. He was the one that sniffed out that they were going to run, too. Good nose on him . . . for a human. You had to hand it to the bosses; they had tied everything in a neat and inescapable knot. Admirable.

Of course Cal would've had a slightly different opinion. His would've been more in the realm of betrayal and rage, with a generous helping of homicidal fury. I wanted to kill our good buddy Samuel—don't get me wrong. But whereas I wanted to kill him for fun, Cal would've wanted to do it out of a sense of vengeance. He would've wanted payback. He would've wanted justice.

I didn't give a shit about what he would've wanted. Caliban was gone. There was only me and when I tormented Samuel it was for kicks only. That was the end of that particular story. "No stand," I answered. "I saw your singer use a headset. That's what I want." I'd need my hands free to open the gate. Clamping on to his arm with a tight grip, I stopped him as he started to move away. "Another thing, Samuel. Since you've been such a good guy, been such a pal." I bared my teeth in a travesty of a grin that predated my human form. "I'd like you to stick around and see the show. Admission is free." More or less.

He didn't avoid my gaze this time, but simply met it with eyes as empty as what was left of his soul. "All right." He knew what was coming, knew it and wasn't going to avoid it. The curse of a conscience wasn't a problem I was familiar with, but I had heard rumors. "I'll be back with the headset." I released him and he made his way through the gathering Auphe. Frowning, I watched him go. Maybe it wasn't such a bad thing that I wasn't going to have the opportunity to kill Samuel. He was making it entirely too easy; it took all the fun out of it. Either way, it didn't matter. Once the Auphe went through the gate there wouldn't be a Samuel to kill. There wouldn't be a Georgina either, and if Samuel had known that, I don't think he would've have been quite so resigned.

"It is time."

The whisper of the Auphe was repeated a hundred times over, rising in an atonal concerto that swelled high to the rafters. The words then melted into an inarticulate, *needful* moan that twisted the air in the same way a knife twisted guts into shredded flesh and spilled bile. It was the sound of a multitude of monsters calling for home. They stood shoulder to shoulder and watched me with the intensity of an exploding sun. Hundreds of bloody eyes were locked unswervingly in my direction. I could feel the heat of it on my face. Their icy, fetid breath panted in short, excited bursts as long fingers clenched and unclenched into spidery knots. Mouths gaped, lips skimming over adamantine teeth, as they mewled uncontrollably. They were the right hand of death itself, pale and pitiless.

Anyone with less intestinal fortitude, inhuman or not, would've been curled up on the floor sucking his thumb. I basked in the attention and took it as my due. I'd always known I was a star. Without me, the Auphe were nothing. I was the key, and the gate was a lock only I could open. At this moment I was, as I'd always suspected, God. Spreading my arms, I let my head fall back and closed my eyes, my streaming hair a silk touch on my shoulder blades. "Suffer the little children to come unto me." Opening my eyes, I smiled gently at the Auphe.

A shaken breath broke beside me. "Jesus. Sweet Jesus."

I tilted my head toward Samuel. "Oh, my sights are set higher than that." His face was as gray as that of a dying man and a cold sweat sheened on his skin. He ripped his eyes from the milling Auphe to me.

"What are they going to do?" Samuel's voice was hushed and strained to the breaking point, but his apathy had disappeared. It would be hard for even the most suicidal man to be complacent at the sight before him now.

I took the headset from his frozen hand. "I think it's a little late to be worrying about that now." I slipped on the headset, my eyes following him as he backed away slowly, step by step. "You might as well stick around, Samuel. There's nowhere you can go to hide from this. Nowhere in the world." He kept moving and I let him go, dismissing him from my mind. I had but one thought now. One aim. One goal. One desire. I turned my back to the Auphe to face the empty wall and held my hands out, fists clenched. Behind me they stood . . . a concert crowd waiting for the headliner to come onto the stage. They nearly filled the warehouse now that all were gathered together in fatal anticipation. The panting grew heavier behind me and then faded completely to a deadly and waiting silence. Before me one cleared wall flanked by speakers stood blank, a canvas waiting for the artist's hand. Beneath me the undying fury of restless souls howled for release.

I gave it to them.

Their energy rocketed into me with the force of a freight train and I reveled in it. Every inner part of me was clasped with greedy, ravaging fingers as the souls continued to rush up through me. Mindless, gibbering fury and need, it kept coming and coming until I thought I would explode into a thousand shards of rage and death. And it was for me, all for me. I felt my muscles spasm into rock-hard knots, felt my eyes open wide and stare at nothing. The sizzle of ions raced over my skin like lightning and the blood seemed to boil in my veins as I rose into the air. Feet inches off the floor, I was a fly in amber. And still it went on, an ocean pouring into a teacup. I found myself straining, stretching, swelling, until every cell shrieked out in protest.

Then it stopped. Finally, the influx halted and I hung, burning from the inside out. I still couldn't see, but I didn't have to. Opening my hands to frame the gate, I channeled all of that frenzy, all of that savagery, into one amplified, earth-shattering note. Singing was the one thing I had in common with my banshee sisters. For different reasons, yes, but we all sang. Some called it wailing or screaming or even shrieking, but it was none of those things. It was beautiful, passionate, life-destroying song. And that song fed every iota of the stored energy within me into a dark creation, channeled it into a wholly unnatural birth.

The gate opened.

It was as simple as that. A little song, a little dance, a little open sesame, and here we were. Good-bye to electric blankets, good-bye to hot showers, good-bye to fast food, designer clothes, fast cars. And so long and farewell to the human race. In the end, I guess it all balanced out. In the end, it *was* the end.

My vision returned and I saw the gate swirling sluggishly on the wall, eighteen feet tall by nearly the same number wide. Through tears in the rippling and foaming gray light, I could see glimpses of a velvety purple sky dotted with stars nearly as big as your fist. Air wafted through, warm and redolent with sulfur, bitter musk, and sweetgrass. I remembered the smell. It was the scent of lava rivers, massive animals that moved as majestically as ships, and grass a shade of green no longer found in nature. It was . . .

"Home." The Auphe said it for me. In their rasping, sand-scraping tongue they said the word with more reverence than I'd known they had in them. "Home."

With the energy gone from me and now bound into the gate, I was dropped back onto the floor. My arms were still extended and I was shaking with the effort to hold the rip in time and space. "No time like the present, boss," I gritted between clenched teeth. "This baby isn't going to stay open much longer."

Behind me came a snake's hissing sigh from a hundred mouths that yet managed to sound as one. A culmination of centuries of want and work had arrived and the Auphe were joined as one in the moment. And together they took that first step in perfect synchronicity. I heard it: a ponderous thud that echoed like thunder. The lightning came a split second later in the form of a sword stroke when Niko and Robin came out of the left speaker. It was like a magician's trick: Now you see them, now you don't—only in reverse. Niko's blade had split the speaker cover from the inside with one quicksilver slash. Stepping through the opening, my brother paused as his eyes took in the Auphe army and then locked on me. His hair was gone. The waist-length, dark blond hair had been sheared close to the skull. It meant something, that. I wasn't sure what, but it tickled in the back of my mind like an itch I couldn't scratch. Robin appeared behind him and freed my attention.

The speaker, damn, that was ingenious. I'd noticed the imbalance when I had sung. I'd assumed a mechanical malfunction. I'd been wrong. As I'd ordered, Samuel had provided me with speakers . . . one for me and one for betrayal. It was one frigging inopportune time for the son of a bitch to develop scruples. He must have gone to his niece to track down Niko and then collaborated to bring him and Goodfellow here. When his conscience reactivated it'd done so with a vengeance. I should've eaten him when I had the chance.

Sweat prickled the back of my neck as the gate continued to swirl, and I could feel its pull growing stronger. Within minutes it would exhaust the power within it and begin to siphon my own life force. If that happened, it would instantly turn me inside out. While a nifty special effect, it wasn't exactly in my best interest. I was willing to work for the Auphe; I was not willing to die for them. I doubted it would come to that, however. As deadly as Niko and Goodfellow could be, the Auphe had the numbers in this situation. The numbers, the rage, and the desperation. Even Nik would have to fall before that.

"Nik." I gave my brother a wolfish grin. "You didn't say it. How disappointing. How's it go again?" I hummed a tune from an ancient cartoon. *"Here I come to save the day."*

Robin was studying the gate with a peculiar mixture of horror and longing on his triangular face. His hand moved to Niko's shoulder and squeezed until his fingers blanched white. "No. It cannot . . . *ektos mas.* Niko, it is the past. It's a time before humans. If the Auphe go through there . . ." He didn't have to finish. I could see Nik grasped the implications immediately.

"Close it." He moved until he stood between the gate and me. The point of his blade rested in the hollow of my throat. "Now."

The resulting trickle of blood coursed down my chest until it bisected the flesh over my black heart. Out of my sight I could hear the Auphe rushing forward. There were almost on us; I could feel their murderous outrage like a heat at my back. Then the sawed-off shotgun dispersed that heat with some of its own. I watched in disbelief as Robin, joined by Samuel, pulled them from beneath their coats, moved to flank me, and fired. What the hell? Had they mugged Rambo on the way over or what? Still tied to the gate, I turned my head to see Auphe flying through the air, some of them in pieces. "Ah, shit." I staggered and whipped my focus back to the gate. It was destabilizing. Setting my feet, I held on to it and did some more cursing. This time it was in my own language, one that was all but made for foul words.

Niko's eyes hadn't shifted even minutely. "Close the gate, Darkling. Close it or I'll open you."

"Do we really want to have this conversation again?" I snarled, my patience fast eroding. Past him I could see that the gate had solidified somewhat, a good sign. "You can't do it, big brother. We've already seen that."

Goodfellow and Samuel let loose with the other barrels and discarded the guns before reaching back inside their coats for more. These were more along the lines of automatic weapons, and I had to wonder with irritation where the flamethrowers were. Just goes to show that you can find anything in the Big Apple if you know the right people to ask. As they began to fire again, I risked another glance over my shoulder. Guns or not, I couldn't fathom the Auphe retreating now . . . not when they'd come so far. Apparently, they couldn't fathom it either.

They were still coming, leaping over the dead and the shattered, the wounded and the bloody. Covered with blood and ragged flesh, they kept coming. Lead-borne death was not going to stop them. As far as I could tell, it wasn't even going to slow them down. They were going to pass through the gate. Whether they went over the three in their way or through them, it didn't matter. It was going to happen. At this late stage in the game there was no way to stop it.

My brother refused to accept it. The bastard had always been stubborn. From the time I could walk he'd been bossing me around. For that matter, he'd done his best to boss all of creation around. But he'd never been able to make the world do what he'd wanted it to do—he had never succeeded in making it leave us alone. Now he stood in front of me, giving it one last shot, although I think he knew it was futile. Refusing to give in because that's who he was. From beginning to end, that's who he was. "Shut it down." The sword was unwavering at my throat. "I won't tell you again."

"You wasted my time telling me at all." I couldn't use my arms or hands in my defense, but Nik had taught me better than that. My own predatory talents didn't hurt either. I aimed a flashing kick at his knee that he avoided easily. It was a feint and I didn't expect it to work. What he didn't anticipate was the poison that I spit in his face. Even distracted by the blow directed at his leg, he still managed to dodge far enough to the side that the venom missed his eyes. He reeled backward as the skin on his left jaw and chin began to redden and swell. It wouldn't kill him; chances were it wouldn't even make him sick. This new body, merged though it was, was slower to produce toxins. It had taken me this long to make any at all and it was nowhere near full strength. If I'd hit Niko's eyes, however, I would've blinded him. As it was now, he'd have only an agonizingly painful allergic reaction.

Meanwhile, I could simply kick him to death. Perhaps it wasn't as festive as blindness, convulsions, and the vomiting up of internal organs, but it would have to do. With his free hand clawing at his face, Nik staggered and went down to one knee. I lashed out and slammed a blow to his thigh that took him all the way to the ground. The next one landed in his ribs. My headset tumbling off from the exertion, I was poised for another kick when I caught a flicker out of the corner of my eye. It was the first long slide into home base.

The bullets were still flying, but one Auphe passed through the curtain of them as if it were a gentle summer rain. He bolted past me and leaped toward the gate in a motion as liquid as flowing mercury. He almost made it. He was three feet from the gate and still in midair when Niko's sword cut him in two. One moment Nik had been on his side with my foot in his ribs; the next he'd flown to his feet, spun, and taken out the Auphe with one stroke. The newly sleek blond head whipped around and he snapped at Goodfellow and Samuel, "Keep them back!"

"Oh, was that the plan?" Robin countered acidly. "Perhaps I should've written it down." Swinging his gun, he slammed the stock into the face of an Auphe who'd made it too close. Ichor and mucus sprayed into the air in a peculiarly artistic fan pattern.

Samuel kept firing. He had less to say, but it was considerably more to the point. "Hurry, damn it!"

And then the blond head turned my way. There would be no more warnings, I saw. No more chances. That's when I remembered about the hair. The knowledge scurried out of the depths of my brain, and I heard the distant blue velvet chuckle of Mommy dearest. It was something she'd once told the two of us when I was young enough to think her booze-soaked ramblings were bedtime stories. This one had been about her Gypsy roots. I suppose they were partly ours too, although she never made any effort to include us. Sophia came from Greek Gypsy stock. The customs of both groups had been intertwined and one particular old Greek tradition had been adopted by the Rom of that region.

You cut your hair for those who have died. You cut your hair and you mourn.

"Cyrano." I met eyes that in different times had been the same color as mine and said ruefully, "Really?"

I could've stopped him. I would've lost the gate, but I could've stopped him. The picture of how it would go was clear in my mind. I would drop the gate, swivel in one motion to wrap my arm around Samuel's neck. When I turned back, I would have his gun and I would have him between glittering death and me. As the blade pierced my hostage's heart, I would unleash enough bullets to turn Niko into a distant memory. Easy, simple, and I could've done it. I could have.

But I didn't.

Instead of Samuel's heart the sword slid into my abdomen like it was coming home. My hands fell to close tightly around my brother's. His fingers were cold and they shook minutely beneath mine. We both held on to the hilt like it was a lifeline. Odd. It wasn't anything near that . . . for either of us. "Well." I barely could hear myself, my words that were softly carried on failing breath. Niko heard me, though—I could see that in his face, in his eyes . . . in the depths that swallowed all light, all hope, all faith. "Look at that." Falling to my knees, I felt the relinquishing kiss of metal inside me as I slid free of the blade. I smiled up at him, the faint curve of my lips almost genuine. "My mistake. I guess you have the balls after all. Good for you, big brother." It felt final, those words. I let go of Niko to cup my hands over my stomach and watch with detached fascination as my life simply flowed away.

And as I went, so did the gate. It fell at the same time Niko's sword did, one just an echo of the other. Where once had hung a passageway to a time long ago, now stood only a blank wall. I dropped my eyes from the nonexistent gate to the fallen blade and then looked back up at my brother. "What? No souvenir?"

Nik didn't react to the comment or to my next one about the sky falling. In fact what he was responding to was anyone's guess. He didn't seem to notice when the sound of gunfire sputtered to a halt as Goodfellow and Samuel ran out of ammunition. That this happened in almost the same instant that the building began to collapse didn't seem to catch his attention either. Every iota of his considerable concentration seemed to be focused on me. I couldn't say how long it lasted. Maybe it was only seconds, but it seemed longer, much longer. What he saw, I didn't know. Silver eyes, transparent skin, fading consciousness, and a growing pool of blood—that was a given. But what did he see beyond that? I just didn't know. For the first time I couldn't read him. I'd seen his despair, his anguish, and then I'd seen it drain away to be replaced by . . . nothing. Nothing that I could identify, in any case.

Coming to some enigmatic decision, he blinked empty eyes and I was pulled over his shoulder before I could put up a fight. Not that it would have been much of one. Then he was running. As he went my vision began to darken and I allowed a decision of my own to be postponed. I never had been one to throw in the towel, not in either of my incarnations.

Behind us came the Auphe. I couldn't see Robin or Samuel; they must have been ahead. I could see my former employers, though. There were only slices of them as I sank further into cloying blackness, but it was more than enough to let me know my ass had been canned. If they caught us, separating my remains from the others would be a matter of DNA analysis. I'd failed them, but even worse than that, I had ruined their guinea pig. This body had what was a potentially fatal wound. It was now useless to them, and without it, so was I. The rage in their faces and their fiery eyes was for me as much as for Niko, Goodfellow, and Samuel. No two weeks' notice, and severance pay certainly wasn't looking like an option. I let the thought swirl down the drain to be replaced by another. It was a repeat of an earlier one. I could've stopped Nik. I could've stopped it all. So why didn't I?

That was pretty much the last truly coherent thought I was capable of. After that, there were only flashes . . . of light, sound, and a waning comprehension. We were inside under raining debris and only steps ahead of a maniacal horde. Abruptly a chunk of time disappeared and we were outside. I was still dangling upside down and staring at a part of Niko I really had no interest in. "Not your best side, Nik," I slurred more to myself than anyone else.

I didn't get a response or if I did, I was too far gone to recognize it. Suddenly everything spun, from asphalt to starless sky, and I found myself placed into the backseat of a car. Robin's voice came from the front as he turned over the engine. "Are we sure about this, Nik? You know they'll kill him. He doesn't stand a chance."

"We don't have a choice. Now drive." Niko's answer vibrated against me and I realized I was in a reclining position with my back against his chest. He had an arm wrapped hard around me with his hand holding a wadded cloth over the slash in my stomach with an unyielding pressure. It hurt, more than anything should. Despite that or maybe because of it, my attention drifted away to the back window of the car. I could see Samuel, just barely. Although the streetlights were working, my eyes weren't as cooperative. Still I could make him out. He was at the door of the warehouse, standing just inside it. His gun and ammunition but a memory, he was swinging Niko's sword with inexpert but lethal force. He was barring the way. He was all that stood between the Auphe and freedom. A part of me was impressed, stunned. A very small part of me. The larger part sneered an internal, "Sucker." Then we turned a corner and he was gone. An instant later the glass of the car windows shook as the roar of a collapsing building was heard. Choices. It all came down to choices.

Samuel had just made his.

21

I was flying.

Passing through the silky night air, I soared and dipped in perfect silence. Flying on and on, I savored the freedom. I couldn't see, but I didn't need to. There was no up or down, no land or sky. No stars or moon. There was only endless space and endless darkness. And there were endless memories as well.

I was five and running barefoot down a dirt alley in a faraway town. I'd long since forgotten the name or maybe I'd never even known it. There was a warm weight against my chest and a tongue lapping enthusiastically at my chin. The milk breath of a puppy was sweet to my nose and I was laughing. Nik had given the pup to me. He'd borrowed it for five bucks from one of our neighbors. Even at that age, I knew we couldn't keep it. I knew better than to even ask. Sophia would've sold it in a heartbeat. It was mine only for the day, Niko had cautioned, only one day. It was one of the best days I'd ever had.

I was older than any human civilization and crouched languidly on a gold-and-lapis-lazuli sarcophagus. I didn't know the name of the Pharaoh who'd died a hundred days previously, and I didn't care to know. On the floor of the tomb was a scatter of limbs and crimson-soaked sand. I'd been ensconced in the burial chamber for barely two weeks and I'd already had several tomb robbers creep in. The priest had promised me frequent visitors and he'd kept his word. A wealthy ruler was to keep his treasure clasped tightly in his withered fingers, and I was using a freshly decapitated head as a pillow. It was a good day. Maybe it wasn't the very best I'd ever had, but it was nothing to sneeze at either.

I was almost as old as time itself and yet younger than a mayfly. I was waking up and wishing desperately that I had enough breath to curse at the burning pain. Struggling out of unconsciousness, I pried my eyelids open a sliver but saw only darkness. Was I blind? No. A blur of headlights flashed by and I realized I was still in the back of the car. The surface supporting me from behind was no longer cloth against my bare skin. It was now skin to skin, warm to my clammy cold. I realized why as Niko's voice came quietly. "Robin, I need your shirt. Mine's soaked through."

Soaked through with blood. I could still feel it, hot and wet against my stomach. As much as Nik was trying to hold it in, my blood just kept rushing out. It had a mind of its own, just like I did, I thought hazily, riding the waves from ache to agony and back again. I could see Robin's maneuvering in the front from the corner of my eye. Keeping one hand on the wheel, he used the other to pass his shirt back to Niko. "How's he doing?"

A saturated ball of cloth was discarded on the floorboards and replaced with a pad carefully folded from Goodfellow's shirt. Silence was the answer to Robin's question, and a neatly eloquent answer it was. "We're not far," Nik observed, the troubled note buried so deeply under his still reserve it was barely detectable. "Just keep driving."

And just where were we going? I wondered. Not the hospital. That wasn't an option on any level. They wouldn't want to expose my big bad self to civilians. And let us not forget that in a hospital setting, silver eyes wouldn't be considered just a fashion statement. They would attract attention, the wrong kind of attention to say the least. Then the X-rays, the CAT scans, the surgeon's nimble hands, would all see and notice things that couldn't be ignored. It was amazing what a human mind could circumvent given enough leeway, but with enough evidence society-at-large would no longer be able to bury their heads in the sand. No, there would be no hospital. Still, Niko was doing his best to keep me from bleeding to death for a reason. Now, where—

I didn't have a chance to finish the thought as Goodfellow shattered my tenuous concentration with another comment. "Darkling is stubborn, Nik. He won't give up any more than you will." He hesitated and went on with apology. "He's found a perch he likes. Short of killing Cal, I honestly don't see a way of shaking him loose."

"Take the Verrazano." As far as Niko seemed to be concerned, the puck may as well not have spoken. The bridge . . . that meant we were headed to Staten Island. It meant something, but what exactly couldn't find purchase in my hazy thoughts.

Robin's forceful exhalation was followed by a grim chuckle. "You are one exasperating son of a bitch, I will give you that. I should've given you every car on the lot and counted myself lucky to see your backs."

"It probably would have been the wiser thing to do." Niko bowed his head against mine as he said soberly. "Don't think I don't know what you've done for us, Goodfellow. Without your help Cal and I would be dead now." The "if we were lucky" hung in the air, implied if not spoken.

"Don't forget the part where I helped save the world," Robin pointed out, recovering his cockiness in a heartbeat. "Robin Goodfellow, hero. It has a nice ring to it, doesn't it?"

I almost snorted in unison with Nik at the flagrant preening. My eyelids had drifted shut some time ago and I'd not noticed. The darkness of that wasn't so different from the darkness of our rushing through the night. And that in itself wasn't so different from flying. I was slipping slowly and surely back into the swaddling arms of a state much deeper than sleep. As I went, I heard my brother's whisper in my ear. "Stay with me, Cal. We're almost there. Stay with me."

He'd known that I was awake. He'd known all along, just as he now knew I was sliding away. Gravity had seemingly doubled, pressing down with the weight of a cave-in. The air was becoming thicker, moving in and out of my lungs like sludge. Each breath took more effort, each one farther away than the last. Cal might not know what it felt like to die, but I did. Vicariously speaking. I'd inflicted enough death in my day to recognize in intimate detail every shuddering breath, every failing heartbeat. This body, this joined life, was hovering, and it wasn't long before it stopped hovering and started falling. I was hoping I made the right decision, and I was banking on Niko to save my ass. Banking hard.

I don't remember much of anything after that. Pain. The heavy touch of suffocation. And then finally there was the suggestion of motion. As I was carried along, I made one final effort, one last push to a glittering surface far above my head. I was swimming upward with everything I had in me, but I was dragging chains and concrete weights behind me. As I struggled through a still black water, a voice impacted on my ears. It was a moment before I could actually process the sounds, turn

them into the gruff demand that they were. "Quick. Lay
him down on the bed. What the hell happened, Niko?"

The voice, it was familiar. I felt a hand laid urgently
on my abdomen. It was warm. No, it was hot . . . almost
painfully hot. That brought the memory out. There was
the mental impression of shaggy auburn hair, impatient
amber eyes, and a quirked eyebrow bisected with a fine-
lined scar. It was the healer. It was Jeftichew. Rafferty
Jeftichew. Staten Island . . . bingo.

"He was stabbed. Nearly a half hour ago." That
would be Niko, succinct as always and on this occasion
perhaps even evasive. "He's lost quite a bit of blood. I
couldn't stop it."

" 'Quite a bit' being every damn drop in his body.'
Rafferty didn't sound too hopeful. What kind of gloomy
bullshit bedside manner was that? I ask you. Then again
Rafferty had never been one to sugarcoat bad news, and
he hadn't the time or the inclination for the niceties. He
and Nik, they were two peas in a pessimistic pod. The
heat of his hand passed through my skin and traveled
deeper. "You. Curly. Grab two IV bags from the top
shelf of the refrigerator for me."

That made me wish I had enough strength left to
open my eyes. I would've loved to seen the sour look
I was sure decorated Goodfellow's perpetually smug
face. Curly. I'll bet that chafed the vainglorious shit to
no end. It gave me a glow even warmer than the scald-
ing hand that was trying so desperately to knit back my
insides. There was the slosh of liquid and the squeak of
plastic as Curly apparently hopped to it. "What is this?"
Goodfellow asked quietly.

"Fresh frozen plasma," Rafferty answered absently
"Now shut up and let me work, would you?" He might
not have finished med school, but he had the attitude
and sharp-edged tongue down pat. There was a hush

after that. Deep, velvety, and peaceful, enough that I kept trying to drift away. I was attempting to set foot on that sinuous path that led nowhere yet everywhere all at once, but every time I did, there was an insistent force pulling me back. Hand over hand, the grip continued to reel me in with ruthless obstinacy.

Ruthless, obstinate, and with a devotion to healing that left Hippocrates himself in the dust—it was a short but accurate description of Rafferty. That and he did not suffer fools gladly. In fact, he did not suffer fools at all. Niko and I had crossed his path two years ago. I'd smelled the talent on him instantly. He in turn had known there was something different about me, although I'd never given him the chance to touch me and find out for sure. The laying on of hands would've resulted in his knowing something we didn't want him to know. Chances were it was something *he* didn't particularly want to know either. And if seeing Cal for what he truly was would've been a shock, seeing what I was now was bound to knock his socks off.

"How is he?"

Rafferty's sharp, frustrated exhalation followed on the heels of Niko's question. "Two phrases come to mind. 'Crashing and burning' and 'train wreck.' Take your pick." The heat of his palm intensified. "The son of a bitch sliced him up good. Who the hell did it?"

There was silence, and then Nik's unflinching answer. "I did."

"Ah." The healer was either absorbing the information or letting it flow over him, water off a duck's back. "I'm guessing that's why you skipped the hospital."

"No." There was the sound of skin on skin, a hand being rubbed wearily over a face. "That's not the reason. Be careful in there, Rafferty. Cal isn't precisely alone."

"Fine time to tell me," came the annoyed grunt. "I'm already in. I'm committed now."

Which would be exactly what Niko had planned all along. The reptilian part of me admired the insidious nature of the move and roundly despised the softer emotion behind it. The rest of me simply recognized it as Niko, through and through, and something I would've done in a heartbeat myself. At one time. Needless to say, if I survived, those days were long gone.

"Then the sooner you heal him, the sooner you can get out," Nik pointed out brusquely.

I didn't catch Rafferty's reply, but it was guaranteed to be scathing. It dawned on me slowly that I *was* healing. It was a snail-like process due to the severity of the wound, but it was happening. The sounds around me were growing sharper and even though I was still fading in and out, I was becoming more aware. Feeling stronger. In fact I felt strong enough to lever up my eyelids for a bleary glance around me. Light russet eyes took me in. "Damn, Cal," Rafferty said grimly. There was a tightening around the corners of his wide mouth, a spasm of distaste at what he was sensing as he healed me. "You look as creepy as you feel."

Thank you, Marcus Welby. Beside him Niko stood, his short hair still startling to my eyes. I saw the sick despair that lay under the tranquil surface of his smooth face, the sluggish movement of black water under ice. And I saw it fade slightly as he watched me open my eyes. His face loosened a slight amount and for one second he closed his eyes and let his shoulders sag. Then he pulled in a deep breath, straightened his shoulders to a ramrod stiffness, and snapped open his eyes. "Put him to sleep," he ordered without emotion.

Rafferty slid him a disbelieving look. "What? I'm still

healing him. He's a long way from out of the woods. Sleep is the least of my concerns here."

"Put him to sleep, Rafferty. Do it now," Niko repeated harshly.

Goodfellow stepped up to add his two cents. Nosy bastard. "You might have trouble healing after Darkling here has bitten off your hand at the wrist. At the moment it's best to let sleeping monsters lie."

I could see that Rafferty wasn't used to being told what to do, and it was clear he didn't care for it one bit. But he ignored his bruised ego for the moment and laid his other hand on my forehead. His lips shaped one word. "Sleep." It wasn't audible to my ears, but I heard it ring in a series of echoes through my mind. Sleep. Over and over again until it was a never-ending litany. Sleep. Sleep.

And I did.

22

It was an unnatural sleep. There were no dreams, no sense of time passing. It was less like sleep and more like nonexistence. When I woke, I expected that somehow Niko, Goodfellow, and Rafferty would still be standing in the same positions. They weren't. I was alone. A rustle at the doorway had me amending that. Mostly alone. A wolf stood there, its round yellow eyes fixed unblinkingly on me. The upper lip was raised enough to show a hint of pearly white teeth. Reddish brown fur bristled along its neck and the ears were flat to its skull. It was huge, male, and pissed off.

"What a big furry dick you have, Grandma," I sneered with a voice rusty from disuse. Opening massive jaws, it gave me a silent snarl, turned, and disappeared from my line of sight. With Red Rover gone, I turned my attention to the room and scanned it curiously. It was Rafferty's surgery. Mopping blood from the floor would be easy enough; it was cheap green linoleum chosen for that very reason. There were shelves upon shelves of medical supplies, a squat and ancient refrigerator that chugged on reliably, and no windows. The house was backed up to a nature preserve if I remembered correctly, but better to play it safe. What went on in this room wasn't for the eyes of your average Joe. There were three beds and I was lying in the one closest to the open door. They were all strictly yard sale quality, scarred, stained, and with the occasional kid's name carved into the headboards. "John." "Timmy." "Bobby loves Katie." I was dressed in faded blue scrubs with a threadbare sheet and blanket pulled up to my waist. None of it was in the style to which I'd become accustomed, not by any stretch of the imagination.

I sighed and focused on the ceiling. A crack ran from corner to corner and I followed it idly with my eyes. I'd fucked up. There was no way around that. I'd let two humans and a mutated goat get the best of me. I'd failed the Auphe, who very probably were now no more. Maybe one or two had escaped the destruction of the warehouse, but I wasn't holding my breath on it. No, I was most likely the sole survivor—on our side of the fence anyway. I was the last of the great and grand plan, which to be truthful I'd never much given a shit about. It was only the paycheck that had ever concerned me. But although I'd never cared one way or the other about the Auphe's success, I did care about myself. First, foremost, and always. I wanted freedom and I wanted revenge and it didn't matter in which order they came.

There was no time like the present. I used my hands to push up to a sitting position. Swinging my legs over the edge of the bed, I balanced for a moment and then stood. At least that's the way it ran in my mind. In reality, nothing happened. My arms remained still at my sides, my legs unmoving beneath the covers. The only movement I seemed to have was from the neck up. I could turn my head in either direction, tilt it back, or rest my chin on my chest, and that was the sum total of it. I might have woken up, but that goddamn son of a bitch Rafferty had made sure I wasn't going anywhere. He had paralyzed me, turned me into a temporary quadriplegic. Until he returned and lifted the hoodoo, letting my nerves talk to one another again, I was pretty much screwed. And didn't that seem to be the story of my life lately?

Now I had to wait. Eventually they would have to reverse what had been done. They had already made the decision; they hadn't let me die. It was what I'd been betting on. Niko had missed his window of opportunity. He had the chance and, from what I could tell, the absolute intention of ending my life. But he hadn't. At the last possible moment he'd shifted the angle of the blade to leave me alive, if only just barely. Since he hadn't killed me then, I didn't believe he'd let me rot now. And while Rafferty might have healed me, he wasn't about to become my caretaker, spoon-feeding me Jell-O for the rest of this body's life. At some point he would have to set me free. And then he better run like a cheetah because what I was going to do to him would make this paralysis look like a tropical vacation.

Even the fantasies of a sliced and diced Rafferty weren't enough to keep me from contemplating exactly why I'd let Niko take his next-to-best shot to begin with. However, if the fantasies weren't enough to distract me, the approaching voices were. I was peculiarly grateful. It was a subject I wasn't sure I wanted to study, even from the far corner of my eye. Tilting my head toward the door, I could see into the kitchen across the hall. The three of them came through the back door, bringing in the smells of falling leaves, frost-singed grass, and an icy wind. Niko and Robin sat at the table as Rafferty moved over to the refrigerator. Removing three frozen dinners, he shoved them all into the small microwave on the counter. Goodfellow watched, wincing, as the dinners were stacked on top of one another and the timer was jauntily spun with a twist of the wrist.

"This does not bode well," Robin said glumly, running a hand through wind-tousled curls. "I've yet to see culinary delights belched out by one of those devices."

"O ye of little faith," Rafferty rumbled. He slid a look at me across the distance. "Well, well, the baby's awake. Want me to put him back down?" he asked Niko.

Niko shook his head. "Leave it. There's nothing it can do."

Okay, now, that just hurt. My lips peeled back in a manner reminiscent of my earlier visitor. They ignored the snarl and they ignored me. That was worse. I think it was safe to say in my entire long life I'd never been ignored. Reviled, cursed, feared, but never . . . *never* ignored. Turning away from me, they continued with what passed for conversation among the sheep. Baa baa baa.

"How're the ribs doing?" Rafferty didn't wait for Niko's reply. Reaching over, he laid a hand on my brother's arm and let his eyelids fall in concentration. A second later he opened his eyes and grunted, "They're knitting. Hurting some, though, huh? How 'bout some Tylenol?"

Amusement a pale watercolor wash across his face, Niko said, "And here I thought you would simply slap the whammy on me."

"Trust me, I save the whammy for bigger and better things." The microwave dinged and he stood, calling over his shoulder, "Catcher, bring us the Tylenol!"

Minutes later, there was the clatter of nails on the worn wood floor and the wolf trotted into the kitchen holding a large red-and-white plastic bottle in his mouth. Robin raised his eyebrows. "That is one smart dog."

I saw Rafferty's shoulders tense and thanks to Cal's memories I knew why. Pretending as if he hadn't heard the comment, he went on to drop the dinners along with silverware on the table before taking the bottle and wiping the outside with a kitchen towel. Shaking out two, he dumped them in Niko's palm. "Dig in. Grub's on."

Peeling back the plastic film, Robin poked at the steaming dinner with a fork and made a face. "A grub or two wouldn't be much of a surprise. Neither would a rodent part or the occasional human thumb."

"You bitched at breakfast, bitched at lunch, and here we go again. You could always cook, Goodfellow. Nothing's stopping you." Rafferty began shoveling food into his mouth with relish.

"Nothing but the lack of even the most rudimentary of the basic food groups." Robin discarded his fork and pushed the uneaten dinner away. "Your pantry is empty and the refrigerator is developing new life and new civilizations as we speak. Perhaps your friend could share his doggy chow with us."

Niko tapped a finger on the back of Robin's hand warningly. "Not a good subject, Robin. Let's move on for the moment."

Goodfellow looked puzzled and his confusion was understandable. Nonhumans, whether monsters or human wannabes like the puck, could sense their own. Some could smell the difference, some could see it in a rainbow-chased aura, and still some sensed it in a way they couldn't even explain. Either way, you knew. . . . You always knew. But there was nothing around Catcher that hinted of anything but the canine-slash-lupine . . . not to the paranormal senses.

There was silence after that. Apparently no new subject had enough appeal to pop into anyone's mind. Robin sat with chin in hand gazing absently into space.

Rafferty had confiscated the spurned microwave dinner and was making his way steadily through it. Niko had given his to Catcher, placing it carefully on the floor. The wolf stared at it dubiously, then fastened his teeth delicately around the edge, lifted it, and promptly dumped it in the garbage can by the back door.

"Not exactly a ringing endorsement, is it?" Robin drawled.

"Shut the hell up." Rafferty glared at Goodfellow and then turned his scowl back to me. "And you . . . go to sleep, damn it." If I'd ever needed a sign as to just how powerful the healer was, I received it. Like a light switch had been flicked, I tumbled from light to darkness. He hadn't even needed to touch me. From nearly twenty feet away he'd been able to put me down. It would've been humbling to anyone with less recognition of his own superiority. As I fell, I heard him shift from annoyed to defensive. "Sorry. But he was spooking me with those silver eyes. Jesus, they're freaky as hell."

I wondered dreamily what he would think of his own eyes when I plucked them from his sockets and fed them to him. Then, once again, I was gone.

The next time I awoke, the house was dark. The only illumination was a dull yellow light that spilled dimly down the hallway. It probably came from the den. Rafferty was much too practical to have a living room. He would be harder on the furniture than Catcher.

My position had changed; I was now on my side with a pillow behind my back supporting me. They might hate me, but they couldn't seem to bring themselves to hate what they still thought of as Cal's body. They were taking awfully good care of it. I immediately went to work trying to break the paralysis that held me. It was most likely pointless, but you never knew what the power of sheer rage could accomplish. And I was as coldly furious now as I had ever been. Locked like a falcon in the cage of my own body—it had long since passed irritating and was now just this side of unbearable. I wanted to rend; I wanted to shred; I wanted to kill. I bared my teeth and shook my head violently. But the most I accomplished was one absolute bitch of a headache. I tried to curve my hands into claws, tried to kick free of the covers. Nothing. I was as petrified as a centuries-old piece of wood. Dead and gone.

Yeah, they *wished*.

Soaked with futile sweat and panting with impotent rage, I heard it. Far down the hall, in the land of the light, came the explosion. It was Rafferty. "No! I won't. Goddamn it, Niko, I *can't*."

Niko's voice was low, audible only in part. "I know . . ." and ". . . sorry . . ." were all I could catch.

"No, you don't know. If you knew, you would never ask. I'm a *healer*. I can't kill. I won't kill."

Robin joined in then. "We've tried everything. There is nothing left to us. This would be painless. Cal deserves that. You would be saving him from further suffering. Can't the healer in you see that?"

"So you had me give him life only to turn around and take it?" Rafferty said bitterly. "Why did you bring him here then? Why didn't you just let nature take its course?"

"It was a mistake." Niko spoke louder this time, more firmly, but with as weary a tone as I'd ever heard from him. "My mistake. I thought I saw . . ." He let the words trail away. "It doesn't matter. It's the only way, Rafferty. If you don't do it, I will. My brother's blood is already on my hands. I'll finish what I started."

"Jesus," Rafferty said in a voice as weary as Nik's. "Sweet Jesus."

All right, this had better be a joke. One big, frigging

mother of all jokes. Kill Cal? Kill this body? After all they'd gone through to avoid just that? Couldn't they make up their goddamn minds?

Apparently they could. After nearly twenty minutes of silence, the sound of footsteps reverberated down the hall. Any vestige of worthless humanity melted from me instantly. My lips remained locked in a snarl, and my eyes narrowed with a wrath that verged on madness. Humans. Sheep. Coming to take what was mine. *Mine*. Bastards. They had no idea what they were dealing with, even Goodfellow. Did they think they could make an end of me so easily? They were wrong. Fatally wrong.

"Cal?"

Niko stood in the door. The dark smudges circling his eyes gave mute testimony that it had been days, if not longer, since he'd slept. The lines scoring his face deepened as he stared at me. There was pain in his eyes, endless pain, but there was peace too. It was the same emotion you saw in the terminally ill. Acceptance. Letting go. Love.

Shit. They were serious about this.

He stepped into the room. "I let you down, Cal. I'm sorry." His lips curved sadly. "But you know that, don't you?" Standing by the edge of the bed, he bowed his head and rubbed knuckles over the surface of the blanket. "Kid brothers, they're a pain in the ass or so everyone says." The next words were softer, but I heard them nonetheless. "Everyone is wrong." Pulling up the covers higher on my chest, he smoothed the folds. "Good-bye, little brother."

Rafferty and Goodfellow had followed him quietly into the room. Robin moved shoulder to shoulder with Niko, a silent support. Rafferty moved to the other side of the bed and pulled the pillow out from behind me, dropping me to my back. He didn't look at me, *couldn't* look at me, if his clamped jaw and greenish white skin were any indication. "You two going to stay and watch me commit murder? Sure you don't want to make some popcorn first?" he spit with a near brutal antagonism.

Goodfellow's face solidified to ice. "If you cannot do it, then step aside." There was a knife in his hand, small but deadly. "If you won't help Caliban, then we will."

The anger melted away from his face, leaving only desperation and a numb despair. "No." Rafferty scrubbed his face hard with both hands. "No. You're right. I can set him free and I can do it without pain." Reluctantly, his eyes finally came to rest on mine.

"Touch me and it will be the last thing you do in your miserable life." Involuntarily venom began to pool and leak from the corners of my mouth. "And there'll be plenty of pain for you. Never-ending, soul-destroying pain." A thickly folded towel covered my mouth and kept me from dissolving the healer's face to a blood pudding. Niko. Always prepared. Always goddamn prepared.

Eyes still on me, Rafferty placed his hand on my chest and said soberly, "Cal . . . if you're in there . . . it'll be quick, I promise. I'll stop your heart. You won't feel a thing." Another hand, Niko's this time, was laid on my forehead in a wordless farewell.

I hated to lose. But if I had to lose, I was going to make these bleating sheep hate it every bit as much.

And just like that, it happened. I felt a coldness corkscrew through my flesh, icy fingers squeezing with a ruthlessly intangible grip. My heart staggered, skipped a beat, and shuddered to a halt. For a split second I was frozen, trapped between light and dark, life and death.

Then I split in two. Half of me ripped away, leaving a gaping, raw wound inside that felt large enough to swallow me whole. Darkling was in the air above me, looking down at me with round silver eyes. It was like double vision. I was me and I was him. I was half of a whole and God, oh, God, it felt like dying. I convulsed once and did. . . . I *died*. I died and was sucked down an infinite whirlpool of blackness shot with radiant light. There was no air, but I didn't need any. There was no sound, yet it was all around. *I* was sound, a single note resonating throughout eternity. I was in a place utterly strange to me, yet I was home.

And then I was back. I shivered in waves, though I dimly sensed my heart was beating again. I screwed my eyes shut and tried to breathe. It was harder than it sounded. Every breath was thick and unwilling and my chest ached with an inner frostbite. But I was alive. And if I was alive, then I wasn't dead.

I wasn't dead?

I wasn't dead. Way to bluff, Niko. Too bad we never set up shop in Vegas. Nice acting, Rafferty, Goodfellow. You two get an Oscar. I slitted my eyes to see Rafferty's face close to mine with ill-concealed worry written all over it. "Cal?"

"Raff," I started before coughing weakly. "My 'magination . . . or . . . did you just . . . kill me?"

"Just for a second, I swear." His grin wobbled but was sincere.

I started to grin back instinctively, but the smile wilted away as my memory caught up with the rest of me. I remembered it all in one blinding flash . . . everything I'd said, everything I'd done. Darkling had been right. I'd finally learned what it meant to be a monster. And it was a knowledge I wasn't sure I could live with.

Off to the side, I heard Robin curse and Darkling cackle with maniacal pleasure. Fighting down the acrid bile that scorched my throat, I rolled over on my side. Avoiding Rafferty's hands, I tumbled off the bed and landed hard on the floor. The jolt cleared my head slightly and I focused on the scene only half a room away. Darkling was toying with them. He crouched on the ceiling, his head twisted at an unnatural angle. "Jump, doggies," he sneered. "Jump higher." Taunting them like a school yard bully, he could've left at any time. There weren't any mirrors in the room, but he didn't need any. Mirrors were much faster for traveling, but he could still swim through the atoms of the wall as if it were a river. But no, he was choosing to stay solid. Dissipate? Leave? Where would be the fun in that? He'd wanted them to pay before . . . prior to his rushing through the trapdoor in my mind. Now? Now that he knew how they had fooled him, tricked him? "Pay" wasn't even the word.

They'd figured it out, the three of them. They'd known Darkling wouldn't die with me, no matter how fond he was of our shared body. I grabbed a handful of covers and tried to pull myself up to a sitting position. My gaze went up to Rafferty, who was leaning over the bed to assist me. "How'd you . . . ?" I swallowed and shook my head.

"Know that he'd leave himself an out?" The healer's lips twisted ruefully. "We didn't. We didn't know anything for sure. We only hoped."

With his help I'd managed to get my feet under me in a half-assed squatting position that was shaky at best. "Give me a weapon," I ordered grimly, keeping my eyes on the fight before me.

"Not in this lifetime, buddy." Rafferty's hand was like iron on my shoulder. "If I may remind you, yours is now barely a minute old."

"Weapon. *Now.*" Niko would've left me something, on the off chance their crazy plan worked. He wouldn't leave me unarmed. Not with the eater of my soul roaming free.

Rafferty sighed and muttered, "Damn stubborn son of a . . . under the bed."

Without looking, I slid a hand under the bed behind me. As my fingers touched cold metal, I watched Darkling drop from the ceiling. His back claws buried themselves in Goodfellow's shoulders as the silver eyes sought mine. "Déjà vu all over again, yes?" he purred. "Do you miss me, Cal? Because I miss you." The serpent tongue tasted the air between us. "But I won't for long." It was a promise that I knew he meant to keep.

Never. I didn't say it to him and I didn't say it to myself. I didn't have to. It was as unspoken but true as the rising and setting sun. The sword in my hand was for my own personal monster. But if worse came to worst . . . I'd been dead once today. It wasn't so bad.

Bending his head, Darkling's curved fangs snapped at Robin's neck. Niko seized the black throat and pulled him off Goodfellow. A few scattered drops of blood dribbled from the jet claws as he tore free of Niko's grip and somersaulted through the air. Hitting the wall feetfirst, he raced along the length of the room with the speed and grace of a greyhound. Robin whirled, led his target, and tossed his knife. It spun with deceptive laziness and slammed point first into the plaster, missing Darkling by scant millimeters.

"Don't quit your day job," Rafferty grunted over my shoulder.

Annoyed, Robin flashed him a frozen glare that thawed instantly as he caught sight of me. "Caliban?" The moment of distraction cost him. Darkling hit him with enough force to lift him bodily several feet off the floor and slam him into the far wall. Hissing in pain,

Goodfellow managed to get his knee up and push him off a few inches. It wasn't much, but it was just enough for Robin to pull another knife seemingly out of nowhere. He jammed it toward the scaled stomach. Sinuous as a snake, Darkling twisted and avoided the blow. Almost. The point of the blade caught the webbing of arm and side. With a gaping grin, Darkling yanked the weapon from Robin's grasp and touched the metal to his tongue, tasting his own blood. It was almost white, the blood, with a peculiarly thin and foamy consistency. It reminded me of the leaking fluid of a caterpillar accidentally crushed by my Keds fifteen or more years ago.

Pale eyes glittered as even paler liquid was licked from a lipless mouth. "Like a fine wine. Here . . . have some." Spinning, he punched the blade into Niko's shoulder like an ice pick through wet cardboard. Nik had been drifting up silently behind him, sword readied for a decapitating blow. There wasn't any way Darkling could've heard him, preternatural hearing or not. Nik was genetically human, but there were aspects to him, skills he possessed, that were beyond human. How did Darkling know, then? How was he aware of Niko's flanking motion?

Because of me.

He'd shared my mind for long enough to know Nik as I knew him. What I could predict in my brother, Darkling would see just as clearly.

Niko reeled backward with the knife still firmly embedded in his shoulder. He didn't make a sound, simply steadied himself and transferred his sword to the other hand. With a face as set as that of a stone statue, he moved back into the fray. He didn't spare a moment for the pain and he didn't spare a glance for me. He didn't have to. He was as aware of me as he was of Darkling. And right now he was focused on saving me.

Trouble was . . . I was tired of being saved. I was tired of my ass being in a sling because Mom had needed extra cash and had diddled the boogeyman. I was tired of running and I was damn tired of getting caught. One way or the other, this was the end of it. One way or the other, the monster was no more. Was I referring to Darkling or myself?

I didn't know.

My fingers felt clumsy on the hilt of my borrowed sword, and my legs felt like someone else's as my squat became the distant, inbred cousin to a crouch. Rafferty's hand was still clamped on my shoulder, but his attention was fixed on the battle. Robin had dropped to the floor and rolled out from under Darkling, reaching for another dagger tucked against the small of his back as he went. Darkling himself had done a backward flip away from the wall into the center of the room. The venom he spat at Niko was a glittering mist in the air. Nik ducked to one knee, dodging it, then lunged up again. The toll of the metal penetrating his flesh was beginning to tell. The upper part of his shirt was soaked in blood and shock sweat was beginning to dampen his hair. It wouldn't stop him, though, I knew. Nothing short of death would.

"You're quick," Darkling commended, clapping his dark hands lightly. "For a sheep. But it didn't help you before, *Cyrano,* and it won't help you now." He cocked his head sideways. "I own him, you know. Little brother belongs to me. I've been in every part of him . . . every cell of his body, every fiber of his being. He's mine to use as I want. Mine. And there's nothing . . . *nothing* you can do." His voice was a thousand times more deadly than his poison. Soft, conspiratorial, and utterly soulless. "I'll take him just as before. You can't stop me. You can never stop me."

"But I can."

The sword that I plunged through his back came out his chest spraying foamy blood like milk. My voice was rusty as I repeated, "I can, you son of a bitch. *I* can."

The reptilian head swiveled, the silver eyes disbelieving. *Didn't expect that, did you?* I thought savagely. Didn't expect this half-dead sheep to do anything but lie down for you. I yanked the blade back out of him, the action half turning him. It was just enough for me to bury the sword in his stomach this time. I felt it catch and grind on his spinal column. "And you're not quick." The smile I felt split my face felt as unnatural as the white fluid cascading to the floor. "Not even for a sheep." I leaned sideways and jammed a foot under the point of entry, pushing him off the weapon. Out of the corner of my eye I saw Nik restrain Robin from coming to my aid.

Darkling tumbled to the floor, clawed hands trying in vain to stop the outpouring of blood. "No. NO." And surreally enough one hand lifted toward me . . . as if I would take it. As if I would save him. "We are one . . . you and I. One."

The next blow hit his throat. I swung the sword high and chopped at his neck with every ounce of strength left in me. The scales were some protection, and the head stayed attached by bands of muscle and flesh . . . just barely. Blood geysered from his mouth, bubbling horribly as he tried to suck air through a bisected trachea. The wound in his abdomen was leaking other fluids now, greenish ones that smoked and sizzled as they hit the tile. He was a mess, my former monster. One helluva mess.

And that's when I really got started.

Time passed. I didn't know how much, but suddenly Niko was there, prying the hilt from my hand. Robin

had a sheet and was covering the ruined pile of muti-
lated flesh, splintered bone, and pulverized organs that
mounded on the floor. It would've been a mystery
what the creature had once been if you hadn't known. It
would've been hard to recognize what had lived in you,
controlled you, and then finally consumed you.

He'd eaten me alive, Darkling. Devoured me whole.
Yet I was still here. I studied the slowly staining sheet
blankly. How could that be? I dropped to my knees. I'd
killed and been killed. I'd been the pale shadow of a
monster and then a vibrantly gleeful, self-aware one. I
had been swallowed and my soul dissolved. But I was
still here. And I realized . . .

I wasn't at all sure I wanted to be.

The strength I'd had before melted away. I couldn't
walk. I couldn't even stand. But I could crawl, and I did.
I moved reluctant hands, pushed with my knees, and
did anything I could to put distance between the others
and myself. Now that it was over, I didn't trust myself to
even be in the same room with them. I put my head
down and ignored the sound of voices calling my name.
I ignored it and tried to move faster.

"Cal." Niko's voice, calm and soothing, tried to seep
through the cotton wool that wrapped my brain. I
wouldn't let it. I pushed one hand, one knee, farther. I'd
get away. I had to. The hand on my shoulder had me
jerking to one side, trying to escape its touch.

"Stay away," I said with numb desperation. "Get
away from me."

Goodfellow's sharp intake of breath passed by me,
leaving me untouched. He didn't understand, not really,
but Niko did. He always knew, always saw through me
as if I were a pane of glass. But I should've known he
wouldn't listen. Blocking my path, he dropped urgently
on the floor in front of me and wrapped his arms around

me. Hard enough to be painful. Hard enough that I couldn't doubt or ignore the fact that he was there. And, not coincidentally, hard enough to restrain me. One hand cupping the back of my neck, he said without a shred of doubt, "You won't hurt us, little brother. You don't have to run." Relentlessly, he held on. "We won't let you run. Not when we've just gotten you back."

I shook my head. How could he believe that? How could he believe I might not hurt them, might not try to kill them again? How could he believe that when I couldn't? The words had been only in my head, but Niko heard them nonetheless. "It wasn't you," he said vehemently. "It was not you. It was never you. The bastard is gone, Cal. The thing that did this to you is gone. Let him go."

He was gone. Yeah, I bought that. The trouble was I thought he might have taken the best parts of me with him. I pushed against Niko, trying futilely to break his grip. Finally I gave up; he was stronger than I was at the moment. There was no escape. I didn't say anything; the words simply weren't there. Hell, I don't even think there were words for what I was feeling. But there were words for one thing . . . one thing that I had to know. "My eyes." I swallowed. "My eyes . . . gray?"

Niko faltered for a second, then strengthened his hold. "Yes, Cal, your eyes are gray." He tightened his lips, then turned to Rafferty and demanded, "Do it." The healer had already moved to our side. Eyes troubled, he let his hand hover over my head as he hesitated. Niko apparently wasn't in a patient mood. His voice harshened instantly. "He can't remember. He *cannot*. Now do it, goddamn it."

The healing hand settled on my hair and I heard a soft voice beside my ear. "I can't make you forget, Cal. The memories are horrible, I know, but they're your memories. And you may need them someday. I can't make them disappear." Then more firmly, "But I can make them fade." The words shifted from my ear to a dark and still spot inside my head and became but one word. It was silent yet heard nonetheless. "Fade."

We both faded, the memories and myself. Faded like an ancient sepia portrait. And then just like Darkling, we faded until we were no more.

23

I didn't want to wake up.

Yeah, I know. That's not exactly a news flash when it comes to yours truly. But this was different. It wasn't rolling over and burrowing under the blankets because it was too cold to put your nose outside the covers. And it wasn't the entire-body hangover that kept you mattress bound because you worked too many late shifts. Last, but certainly not least, it wasn't the abject laziness that came from the love, the sheer adoration, of sleep. As much as I wished it were, it wasn't any of those things. The reason I had now wasn't nearly as easy to admit to.

I didn't want to wake up because then it would be true. Concrete and inescapable. I would have to come face-to-face with the fact it hadn't been a dream. I would have to accept that the past days hadn't been a nightmare, that they had been real life. And that good old real life had made *me* the nightmare.

Who the hell would want to wake up to that?

As in most things lately, I had no choice. The distinctive odor of dog breath puffing into my face dragged me to a place I didn't want to go: consciousness. Giving in to the inevitable, I gagged and waved a hand weakly in front of my nose. "I know you can lick your own balls, Catch. You don't have to prove it to me."

A wide grin of immaculate ivory teeth paired with a happily lolling pink tongue greeted my bleary vision. A healthy bushel of air was blown out light brown nostrils, spraying icy cold droplets directly in my face. "Gah." I rolled over and moved to a sitting position on the bed. "I'm up. I'm up. Jesus, cut it out, would ya?" A huge paw nearly the size of a small soup bowl plopped on my leg, the claws scoring my skin lightly even through the cloth of the scrub pants. "All right. All right. You win." I stood hastily and Catcher promptly took my place, curling nose to tail. Smug yellow eyes laughed at me before closing for a nice nap.

With one hand on the waistband holding my pants up and the other combing through what felt like the nest of the last dodo, I took a look around. No wonder the wolf was so insistent. This was his room. I recognized it from a long-ago visit. Apparently I'd graduated from the surgery, or maybe they just thought I might not want to wake up there. They were right. No amount of bleaching and scrubbing would clean the floor or my mind of what had lain there.

"Sleeping Beauty awakes. Did your furry prince there give you a kiss? No tongue, I hope."

Goodfellow stood in the doorway, looking disgruntled yet pleased at the same time. The reason for his annoyance was immediately clear. Dressed in some very old castoffs, he was wearing worn jeans and a sweatshirt that had once been a bright, bright blue. Now it was a bright bleach-spotted blue. It had the logo of a long-gone amusement park on it complete with roller coaster and happy, waving cartoon figures that had made me cringe even in my younger days.

"Looking good, Papa Smurf." I gave a not entirely genuine yawn, almost desperately relieved at the distraction.

"Aren't you the humorous one?" He scowled. He couldn't hold the grimace long, though. It transmuted to a smile not often seen on Robin's lips, I was sure. There was no mockery, no sly superiority, no "Hey, sailor, you in town long?" There was only deep pleasure and an honest relief. "You look well yourself, Cal. You *seem* well."

"Yeah?" I looked down at my feet, toes a bit blue themselves against the cold wood floor. Seemed well. It was a big step . . . a huge step . . . from seeming well to actually being well. But even seeming well was a step in itself, and any step forward at this point could only be a good thing.

I remembered it all. From the point of Darkling's merging with me up to Rafferty's making fresh, raw, and unbearable memories seem like old ones. Everything I had done, everything I had attempted to do, it was all still there . . . only slightly removed. That had kept me in my right mind and kept me alive. I might not be well, but I was sane, and damn . . . as far as I was concerned that was a full-fledged miracle. "I think I *am* okay." My lips twitched lightly before I amended, "More or less." For now anyway. "Where's Nik?"

"Still asleep." He leered and I saw the Robin I'd come to know come rocketing back. "Maybe I can be *his* prince."

As hilarious as it would be to see Niko chasing Robin through the house with a sword and vengeance on his mind, I didn't believe Rafferty was ready for any more disruption in his life. "I think Nik already has his sights set on a nice lady vampire," I pointed out with a true sympathy. My brother . . . he did leave a trail of broken hearts. All my girlfriends in school, Promise, Meredith. Ah, Jesus, Merry . . .

"I know," he said breezily, cat eyes teasing. "I just like to play."

I didn't have to depend on any latent Grendel blood to smell that lie. I had wondered why Robin had helped us these past weeks. What I'd seen in his eyes . . . that god-awful, devouring loneliness had hit a very real and true note, but now I knew there was something else. That it had been unrequited and an impossibility considering Nik's sexual orientation didn't change the way Goodfellow had felt. That the puck was probably thousands of years old and had known better didn't either. Thousands of years old or only a short sixteen of them, your heart will always have one up on your head. We stood there for a moment, each trapped in our own thoughts of what could've been and thoughts of what actually was. Robin broke the silence. "About Niko." Dropping his eyes to my stomach, he shook his head in unconscious denial. He couldn't see where Niko's blade had punctured me, not through the scrub top, but I imagined he could picture it in exacting detail. "He never would have. If there had been any other way . . . anything else he could've done. You have to realize . . . ," he said thickly before stopping.

"Robin—" I started before he cut me off firmly.

"If you could've seen what the week was like for him," he stated with an earnestness that contrasted sharply with his normal flippancy. "If he slept, I never saw it. We scoured the city looking for you. Nik shook down anyone who was even remotely part of the family. If their great-grandma had ever given her neighbor the evil eye or a case of the warts, that was enough for him. He had them up against the wall. He even went to that little psychic and begged her to—" Abruptly he thought better of that subject, remembering what I had sent the werewolves to do. The silence was probably for the best.

The attempted murder of a teenage girl is always touchy conversation. Go figure. "Sorry," he offered quietly.

I shrugged and nodded, my face so studiously blank that it hurt.

He didn't seem to feel much better about it, but he did continue. "He blamed himself, you know. For losing you to Darkling and for getting you back only to lose you again. He never said a word about it, but he didn't have to. . . . It was so clear. And then there was the gate. You and that thrice-damned gate." The long-fingered hand swooped with agitation through the brown curls. "What else could he do?"

Nothing. There was nothing he could've done except kill me. Which he should have . . . would have, in fact, except for what he'd seen at the very end. In Darkling's hesitation, he'd seen my hand reaching out for his. He'd seen me, when I hadn't even seen myself.

But if things had been different, if he'd been forced to free me in the only way left to him, then Niko wouldn't have walked away from that warehouse. He wouldn't have walked away from me. I knew that as well as I knew anything in this world. We'd always been together in this life. We'd always be together elsewhere as well.

"It's okay." I smiled reassuringly at Goodfellow. "He did what he had to do." I never had any doubts about that; I never would. Sharp green eyes studied me, then, reassured, took me at my word.

A sleepy grumble from Catcher brought us around. "Sorry," I apologized to the wolf. "We'll get out of your room."

"His room?" Robin exhaled, palpably relieved to be focusing on something else. He looked around, his gaze caught by the tumbleweeds of reddish hair peeking from beneath the bed. It then focused on the world's

largest rawhide bone against one baseboard, and a bowl
of water sitting on a folded towel. "Ah. Quite a few of
these things are his, aren't they?"

I took a look around myself. There was a beat-up
acoustic guitar propped in one corner, a pair of skis in
another. An open closet door showed hanging clothes
with sneakers and a battered basketball on the floor.
The bureau had a coating of dust, along with a handful
of change, a wallet, and, at the far end, a framed picture.
In comparison, the glass and frame were spotless, not a
speck of dust on them anywhere. Two men stood on
a ski slope, their arms slung casually over each other's
shoulders. One was Rafferty, his head topped with a knit
hat pulled down to his ears, and his nose red as fire from
the cold. The other man, unless you looked with ex-
treme care, looked enough like him to be his twin and
not the cousin he was. The auburn hair was half a shade
darker and the amber eyes a full shade lighter . . . yellow, in fact.

Turning my attention to identical yellow eyes, I
sensed an agreement, an implied permission, in them
before they shut once more. "They're all his things," I
said quietly to Robin. "Every last one of them." Usher-
ing Goodfellow out of the room, I left Catcher alone
with the remnants of his old life and the harsh realities
of his present one.

Robin looked understandably mystified. He peered
over my shoulder back into the room. "But . . ." At my
frown he lowered his voice, not that it would make
much difference. Catcher would still hear. "He's not a
werewolf. He doesn't have the slightest hint of other-
worldliness about him at all. How can that be?"

"It's not my story to tell." I continued to urge him
down the hall. "You'll have to ask Rafferty. I guess it'd
be a toss-up as to whether he'd tell you or just punch

you in the nose." Rafferty wasn't much on "sharing" or airing his family's laundry, dirty or otherwise, to anyone. Still . . . Robin had done a lot for Nik and me. He'd risked his life many times over for us, virtual strangers, when the smartest thing to do would've been to run for the hills. I owed him more than I could repay. Relenting, I murmured, "Catcher's sick. And it's not the kind of sick Rafferty can heal." There was more to the story than that, I sensed, much more, but that was all I knew.

Stopping at the bathroom door, I changed the subject. "I'm going to grab a shower." The fastidious wrinkle of Goodfellow's nose commented that might not be such a bad idea. I snorted, half annoyed, half amused. "You're something else, Goodfellow. It's almost enough to make me forget you saved my ass."

"Not just your ass," he reminded me with a haughty rise of his eyebrows. "It was the asses of all mankind. In fact, savior of the world wouldn't be an exaggeration. Hmmm, I wonder if I could get that on a plaque for my office wall. A nice gold finish. Polished rosewood. My face staring nobly into the distance."

The sad thing was that he probably would. The puck did love to provoke. Irritating, vain, self-absorbed, complacent as hell, and with a sexual appetite that would've had Mae West running for her mother, that was Robin Goodfellow all over. But in addition to that, he was loyal, intelligent, courageous in the heat of battle, and defiant in the face of death. Without him we wouldn't have survived. I'd still be lost inside a monster and Niko would be dead . . . or worse yet, *unmade.* It was a debt I would never forget. "Robin . . ."

The self-satisfied expression on Goodfellow's mobile face shifted to something more rueful and true. "Don't. Let's not ruin my reputation. What would my fans think?"

"Probably the same thing I do. That you're one hel-luva guy," I said with the utmost sincerity. "I owe you, Goodfellow. I won't forget that." Putting a hand on his shoulder, I squeezed it and then gave him a light push. Smiling, I added, "After all, you said it yourself on the way up here, right? You're a hero. And, Robin? You re-ally are. Doubt anything else you want to, but never doubt that."

He eyed me with an uncertainty I hadn't known he was capable of. "A hero," he echoed, bemused, as if the meaning escaped him. Although I believed it wholeheartedly, it might be a while before Robin could bring himself to.

"Doesn't mean you're not still a pain in the ass, though," I pointed out with a grin before walking into the bathroom and shutting the door behind me. I doubted he noticed I was gone. Through the door I heard him repeat "hero" again. The word had a wholly different inflection to it now from the self-mocking ver-sion he'd labeled himself with in the car. Maybe if he said it often enough, he'd finally take it to heart. I hoped so. He deserved to.

I undressed and examined the wound on my stom-ach. Rafferty did nice work. It was completely healed, leaving only a fading purple ridge of scar tissue. Touch-ing a finger to it, I thought of what it must have cost Niko to do what he'd done. What it was still costing him even now. As dark and worrisome as that thought was, something pulled my attention from it. Like diamonds it glittered in the corner of my eye.

The mirror.

Funny how something so innocuous and common-place could turn so quickly into the scuttle of a scor-pion, the slither of a snake, the hand breaking through the grave. So why wasn't I laughing? Grimly, I turned the shower on full blast. The hard-running water provided covering sound as I wrapped a towel around my fist and shattered the mirror over the sink. Only then could I turn my back on it and climb into the shower. Only then did I feel safe.

The shower was actually an old iron claw-foot bathtub. It'd seen better days, like most of us. The shower curtain looped around it on a metal pole bent into a U. There was rust on the tub's outer belly, orange stains on the pregnant curve of a waddling hippo. But on the inside it was sparkling clean and smelled strongly of soap. I picked up a bar and sudsed it absently in my hands as the steaming water flattened my hair and ran in rivulets down my body. It wasn't long before the soap squirted from my grip and landed with a clunk on the tub bottom. I looked at it blankly. At that particular moment picking it up seemed . . . pointless. And not merely mundanely so, but senseless on a cosmic scale. Like it was fate that the soap should be lying there, melting in the falling water. Since I'd gone toe-to-toe with destiny and fate fairly recently, I decided I'd do something else this time. Sitting down in the bathtub, I rested my head in my hands. And then?

I cried like a baby.

24

It was a testimony to what Niko had suffered that he was still asleep when I dragged my butt out of the shower. The hot water had long since run out and I emerged from the bathroom shivering, with parts of me wrinkled as a prune. With a towel slung around my hips, I returned to Catcher's room and borrowed some of his sweats. After I dressed, I moved on to the surgery, counting that as my best bet for finding my brother. Opening the door a crack, I saw him in one of the beds. Not my old one. I couldn't exactly blame him there. He lay on his side, face tranquil in repose against the pillow. The short hair managed to give his nose an even more Roman presence. I smiled despite myself. It might be a long time before I could tease Niko about that. It was difficult to even imagine giving him a hard time now . . . after all he'd done for me. But the day would come again; it was inevitable between brothers. Until then I tucked the image away for future ammunition.

I moved my gaze to his shoulder, the one I . . . the one Darkling had driven a knife through. A pinkish dimple was the only evidence it had ever happened.

Safe to say we'd given Rafferty a workout he wouldn't soon forget. For nearly a full minute, I watched Niko sleep on. He'd always slept the bare minimum, my brother. Too much sleep was bad for the body, he said, and made the soul lazy. I was definitely living proof of the second half of that statement. Niko, though, he was always up, always doing. Sharpening the mind, sharpening the body, and trying in vain to accomplish both with me. The contrast now was unsettling.

Closing the door silently between us, I leaned against the wall beside it. What else could I expect? Rafferty could knit the flesh, but there were things he could not do. He couldn't replace lost sleep, the same as he couldn't replace lost blood. He could speed up the production of red blood cells, yes, but not manufacture them out of thin air. Healing wasn't magic. Healing allowed your body to do what was natural, only at a much accelerated rate. Healing didn't erase all Niko had put himself through. Only time and Niko himself could do that. And if he proved stubborn about it, tying him to the bed for his own good wasn't out of the question. The four most terrifying words in the English language, aren't they? "For your own good."

Pushing away from the wall, I headed for the kitchen. I wasn't the slightest bit hungry, but my stomach had a different opinion on the subject. The kitchen was empty. Where Robin had gotten to was a mystery, but I could see Rafferty in the back working on the fence. I helped myself to whatever I could find in the refrigerator, which wasn't much, before hitting the cabinets. In the end I had to settle for canned soup and three peanut butter sandwiches. Luckily I'd never been especially picky about my food. Chasing it down with a carton of milk dangerously close to its expiration date, I wiped my upper lip with my sleeve as I watched Rafferty through the window.

Rafferty was an acquaintance at best. Maybe if we'd known him and Catcher longer, we might have counted them as friends. Although considering our levels of paranoia, it wasn't all that likely. Of course calling them merely friends now would be doing them a severe injustice. Move over, Gandhi; these guys had helped save our lives. Our lives and in my case maybe a whole lot more. Dumping the carton in the garbage, I walked to the back door and out into the yard.

He heard me coming. Glancing over his shoulder, he looked me up and down before nodding. "You're looking good. Did you eat?"

"Everything left in the house," I confirmed, settling down in the fall yellow grass and resting my arms on my knees. "Need any help?" The fence looked fine to me, sturdy as hell. Chain link, which sat oddly in the pastoral setting, and now he was stringing wire along the top. I didn't know much about that sort of thing, but he looked to be in the process of turning the fence into an electric one. A very large electric one, and I had a good idea who it was for. Catcher had . . . spells. An old-fashioned word, but an apt one. I'd seen only one of them and I had no desire for a repeat performance. It would be unpleasant, *damn* unpleasant, if he ran off in the midst of one of them.

"No. I'm almost done." The reply was a curt and clear "Keep away" sign.

I respected the unspoken request. In his position it wasn't something I would've cared to chat about either. "No problem," I said easily. "Manual labor's never been a hobby of mine anyway. Just ask Nik."

That stopped him in his tracks. Setting aside his tools, he turned, head tilted down toward me. "He's fine, you know. Healthy as a horse. I patched him up, but he probably could've done without me. Forget flesh and blood. Your brother's made of piano wire and pure grit."

"Yeah, he is." Tough and gruff Rafferty trying to reassure me, it was one for the record books. Darkling hadn't been far off on that one. The man didn't waste much time on bedside manner; he was more concerned with keeping patients alive. In the dire straits he was often called into, there wasn't always time for both. Running a piece of grass through my fingers, I ducked my head, then sucked it up and met his eyes. "Sorry for all the shit we brought to your door." Even through the haze he'd used to soften the edges of my memories, I still recalled the expression on his face as I'd watched him with silver eyes. Sheer revulsion, the kind saved for something wholly unnatural. "Not to mention what I brought inside me."

He snorted. "Don't get stuck on yourself, Cal. I've seen worse than that piece of shit. Hell, I've *wiped* my ass with worse."

Utter bullshit, every word of it, but I still appreciated the effort. "Gee, I had no idea you were such a badass," I remarked blandly. His choice in bathroom hygiene I thought better left undiscussed.

"But I always knew you were a smart one," he growled, getting back to his work with a snort. "Go wake your brother up. It's time he ate something too. After that, send him back to bed. And if he has a problem with that"—I caught only a glimpse of the smile, but it was enough to make me glad I wasn't Nik—"you come tell me."

I could handle Niko myself, but that didn't mean I wouldn't enjoy watching him at the mercy of someone else for a change. "Will do." Standing, I hesitated before saying softly, "Thanks, Raff. For saving my life, keeping me sane. I don't know how to—"

He didn't let me go on, waving a hand at me impatiently. "Get out of here, would ya? I'll never finish if you keep drooling all over me."

Thanks offered and received.

I went ahead and fixed Nik's lunch. I was willing to bet that there wasn't anything remotely acceptable to his palate in a twenty-mile radius. Once again peanut butter sandwiches were the name of the game. I made four and piled them on a plate. I'd finished off the milk and ended up carrying in a bottle of orange juice that hadn't even entered the fermentation state quite yet. A real find. In the surgery I passed through the door and made a wide circle around the area of the floor where Darkling had died. Or if I wanted to be more honest with myself . . . the area of the floor where I had turned him into a macerated mound of bleeding flesh. Honesty . . . who the hell needed it?

Putting the food on the small table beside the bed, I leaned over and laid a hand on Nik's shoulder. I could count the times on one hand I'd woken up my brother instead of vice versa. Giving him a light shake, I cajoled, "Up and at 'em, Cyrano." Dark blond lashes parted instantly to show a gleam of irritable gray. Following that, they just as promptly lowered, uninterested. "Okay, be that way," I drawled. "I can always call Robin in. He was saying something about sleeping beauties and princes. I didn't catch it all, but I'm sure he'd be willing to explain it. Maybe even demonstrate it." So much for my resolution to lay off the teasing for a while. But desperate situations called for desperate measures.

Besides, it worked.

The bloodshot glare was proof of that. But the

glower disappeared almost instantly as Nik's brain caught up with the rest of him. Speaking of whammies, Rafferty must've laid a big one on him to get him to sleep so soundly. Gripping a handful of my sweatshirt, Niko levered himself up and wrapped an arm around me. The embrace was quick and hard, his short hair rough against my jaw. I hugged him back just as fiercely. For the first time in what seemed like an eternity, we were both ourselves. Not a brother bent on an impossible rescue. Not a monster with nothing but murder and mayhem on his twisted mind. And not a traumatized leftover, crawling on the floor in panic and self-loathing. We were just family, separated for what seemed like an eternity but now together again.

"Cal," he said hoarsely against my ear. Clearing his throat, he released me and sat up. "You're better." He didn't say the next logical thing, that I was myself again. Niko had never been one to lie, even to make things easier. He was a big believer in the theory that when things are easier in the beginning, they're always worse in the end. Straightening my rumpled sweatshirt with a motherly gesture I'd kidded him about in the past a thousand times, he said pointedly, "I know those are not for me."

Sitting on the edge of the bed, I reached over and handed him the object of his ire. "Don't be a snob. If it was good enough for the King, it's good enough for you."

Dubiously, he accepted the peanut butter sandwich and peeled back the top layer of bread. "No bananas?"

"Give me a break. It's a wasteland in there. They don't even have the stuff to make a chili dog."

"A travesty," he commented gravely before taking a bite and chewing it with a distinct lack of enthusiasm. "The mystery meat consortia must be up in arms."

I watched patiently as he finished the first sandwich
and began on the second before I asked diffidently,
"Want to fill me in? Goodfellow told me some and
we . . . Darkling figured some of it out on his own."

He caught the misstep, but let it go and launched
into a succinct summary of what had transpired while
I'd been otherwise occupied. "Otherwise occupied," it
was a nice euphemism for what I'd really been doing—
laying waste to all around me. Niko regained my attention with a sharp rap to my knee. As Robin had said,
they'd searched high and low for me without any luck.
George still refused to help. If she saw anything, she
wasn't saying, even when Niko and Robin fought off a
pair of werewolves at her door. Knowing what we did
now, how could we have expected anything different?
No matter what she'd said, she would be betraying
someone. It was a god-awful position for anyone to be
in, but it was a special hell for someone like George.

"What about Samuel?" I asked soberly. It had been
Samuel who had saved the day; Darkling had been right
about that. In the end the guitarist had seen the Grendels for what they were. He'd made a decision no one
should have to make and he'd made it with a remarkable nobility. He'd turned to his niece and taken the
weight from her shoulders. She'd given him our address
and he'd gone to Niko with the location of the warehouse. The plan to smuggle my brother and Goodfellow
in had been concocted and Samuel had cooperated
every step of the way. He'd gotten them in and fought at
their side. The last glimpse I'd had of him, the warehouse had been coming down around him as he held the
Grendels back. Samson at the temple.

"He atoned." Nik wasn't a religious man by most
standards, but he had a moral code that would have
had Mother Teresa's staunch approval. Samuel had

committed a grievous act, but in my brother's eyes he had more than redeemed himself.

"Do you think he made it out?"

Niko took the third sandwich and handed me the last one. "Anything's possible," he answered with care. "If nothing else over the years, we've seen that."

We'd also seen how few fairy-tale endings actually materialized, how many happily-ever-afters survived reality. Not too damn many. My fingers pressed deep into the soft bread before I exhaled and took a bite. "He was a good guy," I murmured around the mouthful. "Deep down, where it counted, he was a good man."

"Perhaps, I think, even a great man." Nik discarded his sandwich unfinished. Studying me with an unwavering attention, he watched as I slowly worked on mine. Several minutes of this scrutiny passed before he spoke. It might have been unnerving to someone else, but I was used to it. Niko had something to say. When he was ready he would say it and not a moment sooner. When the words finally came, they were fairly innocuous—on the surface. "How are you, Cal?"

How was I? A simple question, right? Straightforward. Direct. And as loaded as a dealer's Glock. "Didn't we cover this already?" I blinked and sucked peanut butter off of my thumb. "Fine and dandy. Right as rain. Want I should go on?" I'd known that I wasn't going to get off so easily. I just hadn't known it would come so soon.

"Only if you want to tell me what's really going on." His finger poked me in the chest and then flicked my head. "In here and here."

I'd always been a pathetic liar where Niko was involved. You would think Mom's swindler genes had skipped a generation altogether. Not that trying to lie to my brother came up that often. Now, though, in post-Darkling times, I felt more reticent with Nik than I had with the others. It wasn't difficult to understand why. I had tried to kill Goodfellow and I would've made the same attempt on Rafferty if I'd been given the opportunity. But while betrayal is betrayal, history is also history. What I'd done to Nik, who had spent his entire life trying to protect me . . . it was in a realm all its own. I knew my brother like no one else did, and I knew exactly what to do to hurt him the most. In an odd way I regretted the things I'd said to him almost more than the attempts to take his life.

"Cal?" Nik prodded, not without empathy. At my continued silence, he locked fingers around my wrist and squeezed lightly. "You know this isn't idle curiosity on my part. I want to know what it was like for you. I want to understand."

So he could help me. So at least one person would know exactly how it had been for me. Yeah, I knew that. And I also knew he would suffer for the hearing of it, but that wasn't going to stop him. I had the most bizarre urge to cover my eyes like a child. If you can't see it, it's not there. Unfortunately, every time I closed my eyes I *could* see it. No trick could change that. "I remember everything, Cyrano," I said slowly. "Every single goddamn thing, every emotion, every sound, every sensation, like they were my own." I looked down and took a deep breath. "I tried to burn a man to death, beat another one to within an inch of his life. I tried to kill George." Shaking my head, I swallowed and pushed on, "And when I shot you . . . stabbed you . . ."

I stopped, rubbed my hand harshly over my face, and started to get up before Niko's hand on my arm held me back. Fight or flight, it was a sensation I'd spent a lifetime becoming familiar with. I sat back down and continued flatly, "When I did those things . . . I can still feel the emotions. Glee. Satisfaction. I have that in me now. I have every damned memory and it makes me sick." And it did. It made me physically ill, but it was more than that. Much more. "It makes me sick that I spilled your blood. That I hurt you. *You,* Nik. But you know what's worse? You know what really kicks me in the gut? It was the most goddamn fun I've ever had." That time I jerked away from him and paced the room. "It wasn't me. I know it wasn't. But Jesus, I remember it just like it was."

He slid out of bed and followed, stopping me with a hand on my shoulder. "Cal, listen to me. You're right. It wasn't you. Maybe that doesn't make a difference to you now, but it will. In time, I promise, it will. Those memories, those feelings, will fade." Thanks to Rafferty, they already had to a certain extent. If they hadn't, I couldn't imagine the shape I would be in. "It will get better. You just have to give it time."

"Not sure I can wait that long." I gave him a wobbly smile that disappeared as quickly as it had come. I wasn't the only one who had memories or who would have sleepless nights. And I wasn't the only one who would dread closing his eyes. Nik had some horrifying memories of his own . . . in many ways equal to mine. Maybe worse. He'd done things he would regret until the day he died, no matter how necessary they were. "I'm sorry, Nik. I am so damn sorry."

"I think we will both be living in a universe full of sorry for a long, long time." He gave me a look so colored with melancholy humor and undiminished affection that I felt like a child again, in awe of a brother worlds away wiser than I.

Steering me back to the bed, he waved me imperiously to a sitting position. "You didn't do any of those things. It was Darkling, not you. I do not want you apologizing for something that wasn't your fault. Are we clear?" I opened my mouth to protest, but it was futile. Niko repeated with steely authority before I had a chance, "Are we clear?"

I surrendered, conditionally. "If you admit there was nothing you could've done to stop Darkling from taking me. You didn't *lose* me, Nik. I'm not a pair of keys or a jacket. You didn't lose me. You never could. You admit that and we're clear."

He stared at me for a moment, still standing. Finally, the tension beside his mouth loosened slightly and he sat beside me. "I'll try." The corner of his mouth curled. "You try and I'll try and we'll see who gets there first."

"Only Darkling could steal the Grendels' thunder, and they were trying to destroy the world," I rasped wryly, resting my head in my hands.

"Only," he agreed ruefully, resting a warm hand on the back of my neck.

I straightened and took a closer look at his hair. It was more chopped than sheared. I suppose that happened when you cut your own hair. I reached over and tugged an uneven strand at the crown. "You might want to get that evened up, Kojak."

"A new nickname, the joy of it all," came the icy retort. But I could see he was pleased at the effort, no matter how lame it was.

I'd have to be careful in the next few nights to come or I might wake up with a head as smooth as a baby's bottom. If it happened . . . hell . . . I'd laugh. I can't imagine there was much that could happen now that I wouldn't laugh at. Life . . . it was all about perspective. Considering what we'd lived through, what we'd survived, it had to be all downhill from here on out. We had our nightmares to work through, it was true. And there was guilt we would have to banish before it chewed us hollow. It would be hard work—I wasn't fooling myself about that—but not impossible. We were fighters, after all. Weary but standing. Bowed but not beaten.

Never beaten.

25

It was sunset before we were all joined together. The backyard was buried in russet leaves that had been torn from the trees by a howling afternoon wind. I was stamping through them, enjoying the crackle and the smell that bloomed red and gold in my nose. Retrieving the Frisbee, I tossed it to Catcher, who bounded nearly six feet off the ground in an impossible U shape to snatch it out of the air. At my elbow Robin was shivering in a borrowed denim jacket.

"I'd give anything for a coat like his right now," he grumbled, his breath pluming in the air like scattered white feathers as he watched the wolf's acrobatics. "But not his breath. He could kill a troll at fifty feet with that. Maybe I'll send some mints in the mail when I get back to the city."

"You're a philanthropist without parallel." Nik was doing kata in the grass, slow movements that cut the air with deceptive grace.

"What about you two?" Goodfellow accepted the toy from Catcher and tossed it higher in the air than I could ever have managed with just a flick of his wrist.

"Will you go back?" The question had a weight that belied its casual phrasing. In many ways, Robin was as lost as Niko and I had always striven to be. How he'd become like that was bound to be a tale. The puck was simply too social a creature to have ended up in such a solitary fashion without a reason. Maybe someday he'd tell us.

"I think so," I answered, blithely ignoring Niko's narrowed gaze. It was risky; there was no denying that. The Grendels had left the bar a war zone, slaughtered my boss, killed Merry. Under the influence, so to speak, I'd burned a pawnshop to the ground and left a dead werewolf in my hotel room. Some of that had to come to police attention. But on the flip side, New York was a world all its own. If I changed my looks, dyed or cut my hair, avoided any usual haunts, I'd be invisible. Any ID they found at the bar was bogus. Niko and I had always lived as ghosts. If we were to become real now, who would honestly notice? And there was another consideration. Promise. How often did two people truly connect in our twilight world? Here was a woman Niko wouldn't have to lie to, a woman he wouldn't have to hide things from, a woman who would understand the life he'd led. It was a rare opportunity and I wasn't about to take that from him. And then there was George. . . .

"Good." Robin folded his arms with a barely believable nonchalance and cleared his throat. "But you'd better start browsing the want ads. You two owe me twenty grand for that car parked out front."

Niko and I exchanged identical sidelong glances, wondering just what the hell we'd gotten ourselves into. It was a good feeling, so normal and warm that I had to grin. "I don't see anyone fighting to pay my bill," Rafferty said dourly from behind us.

Once again, Catcher brought the Frisbee back and I tossed it. Carefree as the wind, he raced after it, legs churning until they were a blur. "We're paying you back right now," I said simply.

Moving up beside me, Rafferty watched as his cousin ran. "He's happy." He sounded surprised as he said it, but a wistfulness was there as well.

"Take it from me, Raff." I bumped my shoulder against his. "You can't choose who you are. No matter how you struggle, some things will never change. And maybe they shouldn't." They were difficult words and it'd taken me a long, long time to truly understand them. "You might be able to return Catcher to who he was—I don't know. But for now? Enjoy him for who he is." *And allow him to enjoy it as well,* I finished silently.

Catcher chose that moment to return, and this time the Frisbee was offered solemnly to Rafferty. As the air hung still, gold eyes met amber. Something passed between them, something private and as mysterious as the moon. I couldn't say what it was, but Rafferty reached out hesitantly and took the toy. He ran his hand along the rim, fingers brushing the plastic, and then, finally, he threw it. In an instant Catcher spun and was gone after it. Rafferty smiled. It was laced with sorrow, but it was a smile that had managed to slip a chain or two. Sometimes that's the best you can hope for.

I watched Catcher cavort under a scarlet sky and marveled at the beauty of him. He might not be a human, but neither was he a monster. The lack of one didn't necessarily equal the other. There was something so simple about that, yet it had taken me until now to figure it out. Catcher was no monster.

And neither was I.

ABOUT THE AUTHOR

Rob Thurman lives in Indiana. *Nightlife* is Rob's first novel. Visit the author on the Web at www.robthurman.net.

NEW YORK TIMES BESTSELLING AUTHOR
SIMON R. GREEN

PATHS NOT TAKEN

A NEW NOVEL OF THE NIGHTSIDE

JOHN TAYLOR WAS BORN IN THE NIGHTSIDE,
A MYSTICAL SQUARE MILE HIDDEN IN THE CENTER OF
LONDON. HE MAKES A LIVING FINDING THINGS,
AND NOW HE'S JUST FOUND THE MOST DANGEROUS
THING OF ALL: HIS LONG-LOST MOTHER.
TURNS OUT SHE CREATED THE NIGHTSIDE AND
NOW IS BENT ON DESTROYING IT.
TO STOP HER, JOHN MUST TRAVEL THROUGH TIME,
TO A VERY DISTANT—AND PROBABLY DEADLY—PAST.

"A MACABRE AND THOROUGHLY ENTERTAINING WORLD."
—JIM BUTCHER, AUTHOR OF *DEAD BEAT*

0-441-01319-8

PENGUIN.COM

A189

DON'T MISS THE OTHER *NIGHTSIDE* NOVELS
BY
SIMON R. GREEN

SOMETHING FROM THE NIGHTSIDE
0-441-01065-2
The adventure begins in the first novel of the Nightside.

AGENTS OF LIGHT AND DARKNESS
0-441-01113-6
A quest for the Unholy Grail—the goblet from which Judas
drank at the Last Supper—takes John Taylor deep into
Nightside—the secret, magical heart of London.

NIGHTINGALE'S LAMENT
0-441-01163-2
Detective John Taylor sets out to find an elusive singer called
The Nightingale—whose silken voice has inexplicably lured
many a fan to suicide.

HEX AND THE CITY
0-441-01261-2
Lady Luck has hired John Taylor to investigate the
origins of the Nightside, threatening the magical realm—and the
rest of the world, as well.

Available wherever books are sold or at penguin.com

B188

Roc Science Fiction & Fantasy
NOW AVAILABLE

DEATHSTALKER CODA by Simon R. Green
0-451-46024-3
As prophesied, Owen Deathstalker has returned to
save the Empire from the mysterious entity known
as the Terror—leaving his descendant Lewis
with the task of leading an army against the legions
of the madman who has usurped the throne.

SHADOWRUN #3: FALLEN ANGELS
by Stephen Kenson
0-451-46076-6
Welcome to the Earth of 2063—a world of
magical creatures and cypernetic-weapon duels
to the death. Kellan Colt is drawn into the paranoic
elven homeland of Tir Taingire, where she must
unravel the most difficult riddle of all:
who can she really trust in the shadows?

Available wherever books are sold or at
penguin.com